I0602395

Praise for The Path to Misery
Book I in the Hallowed Treasures Saga

"A sheltered princess's desire to travel before her arranged marriage places her at the center of a legendary quest in this YA novel....A page-turning fantasy set in a richly textured world, made all the more delightful by a thoughtful yet spirited heroine and her wonderfully oddball companions."

-Kirkus Review

Praise for In Lonely Exile
Book II in the Hallowed Treasures Saga

"The series continues to stand out for its foregrounding of friendship, diplomacy, and exploration over gory sword fights. A delightful reunion with old friends, sure to leave fans of strong female heroines craving the final installment."

-Kirkus Review

GATE OF DREAMS

A Thirteen Kingdoms Book

GATE OF DREAMS

A Thirteen Kingdoms Book

VICTORIA STEELE LOGUE

RAVENLORE

Gate of Dreams
Copyright ©2024 by Victoria Steele Logue

Victorialogue.com

Published in the United States by Ravenlore,
an imprint of Low Country Press

ISBN 978-0-9992500-8-2
eBook ISBN 979-8-3306099-3-2

Cover art copyright created using AI
and is in the public domain
Cover design, map, and heraldic crests by David Hayworth

Printed in the United States of America

10 9 8 7 6 5 4 3 2 1

Dedication

To all of our furry creatures: Olive and Rue our indoor calico girl cats; Mesquite, Sago, and Cempasúchil, our outdoor boy cats; Lyra and Cleo, our granddogs; and Aleister, Yōkai, and Maddie, our grandcats.

WESTERN KINGDOMS

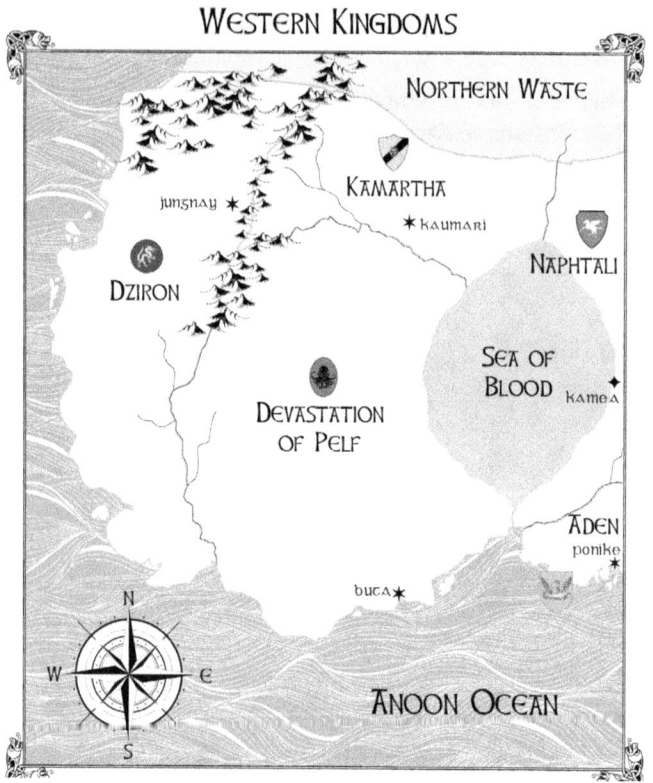

NORTHERN WASTE

KAMARTHA

★ kaumari

jungnay ★

NAPHTALI

DZIRON

SEA OF
BLOOD

kamea ▲

DEVASTATION
OF PELF

ADEN

ponike

buca ★

N
W   E
S

ANOON OCEAN

Eastern Kingdoms

Northern Waste

muezi-barafu

sigwald

Simoon

soshen

Sheba

Naphtali

Zion

jazeel

prythew

kamea

Annewven

arberth

stonehelm

Aden

seemu

Favonia

ponike

Adamah

Dyfed

portuma

Tarshish

cartessos

Author's Note

The events in this book take place about twelve years after the end of the Hallowed Treasures Saga. It features quite a few characters from those books as well as some new characters. There are also a number of references to the Quest for the Thirteen Treasures, which happened during the trilogy, which I hope are adequately explained.

For more information about the Thirteen Kingdoms after the Alliance as well as some of characters in Gate of Dreams, see the pages at the end of the book.

GATE OF DREAMS
A Thirteen Kingdoms Book

"Home interprets heaven. Home is heaven for beginners."
-Charles Henry Parkhurst

"The ache for home lives in all of us.
The safe place where we can go as we are
and not be questioned."
-Maya Angelou, *All God's Children Need Traveling Shoes*

"Never make your home in a place.
Make a home for yourself inside your own head.
You'll find what you need to furnish it -
memory, friends you can trust,
love of learning, and other such things.
That way it will go with you wherever you journey."
-Tad Williams

Midsummer

"The summer solstice, or Midsummer Day,
is the great turning point in the sun's career, when,
after climbing higher and higher day by day in the sky,
the luminary stops and thenceforth retraces
his steps down the heavenly road."

-Sir James Frazer

Parisa & Chokhmah

In the early morning light, Chokhmah could see someone kneeling near the front of the small chapel. She would recognize that bowed head anywhere. What was her daughter doing here?

"Darling?" she said, sliding into the pew to sit beside her daughter.

Parisa turned a tear-stained face toward her mother, eyes swollen and puffy, even her lips were swollen. "Mama, I dreamed that I could see you through a window sitting on a throne. You had a beautiful crown on your head. It was gold and had pearls and diamonds and . . ." Parisa trailed off.

"And?"

Parisa blew her nose into her handkerchief, cleared her throat, and continued, "And on the front of the crown, in the center, was a black-enameled kraken carved into an enormous ruby."

Until that moment, Chokhmah had not realized she was holding her breath. She released it, shakily.

"Does this mean we're going to Pelf, Mama?"

"I do not know, my darling," Chokhmah admitted. "I do not see how that is possible."

Parisa

FOUR DAYS EARLIER . . .

Perched atop the stone wall that encircled the family's farm, Parisa searched the horizon for any sign indicating the approach of their weekend guests. But, other than birdsong, the hum of the bees in the wildflowers, and the gentle whisper of the breeze rustling the leaves of the oak that towered above her, she heard nothing out of the ordinary.

She glanced at the oak that towered over the wall, seriously considering climbing it to obtain a better vantage point. Parisa studied a low hanging branch, then sighed. No, her mother would be angry if she ripped or dirtied the silk skirt she wore. Chokhmah had worked hard on it, piecing together patches of copper and sapphire blue silk—the copper to match her eyes, the blue because it was her favorite color.

Usually, she'd be dressed in leather breeches with a sweater or shirt, depending on the time of year, because it made it easier to do her chores. It was the imminent arrival of the King and Queen of Aden with their children, and whichever cousins and children who chose to accompany them from Castle Abbert in Portuma, that had demanded she dress up a bit.

It promised to be an amazing weekend. Not only was her cousin, Conall, getting married, but one of her favorite holidays of the year—Gulivan— was just a few days away. Parisa loved all the ceremony connected to the holiday from the bonfires and the procession with torches to gathering the mistletoe.

She and her father had already gathered the nine different types of wood they needed for the bonfire from the various trees on their horse farm. Most of the farm at Bogaine consisted of rolling, grassy hills, but there were still small patches of woods dotting the property. They had gathered the oak first, of course, as it was the most important, but also ash, birch, rowan, hawthorn, hazel, holly, willow, and apple. They stacked the collected wood neatly inside one of the white-washed stone out-buildings where they kept the logs they would use to heat Rose Cottage during the winter.

Parisa jumped down from the wall and walked up the road towards the first curve. The designated lookout while her Uncle Olcan and Aunt Beibhinn prepared for the wedding with the help of their daughter, Fianna, Parisa vowed she'd remain alert for signs of their guests' arrival. Her mother watched Fianna's baby boy, Dylan, while her father, Faolan, and Fianna's husband, Gruffydd, took care of the daily chores. Conall, and his bride-to-be, Bledwen, would arrive with her family that afternoon but her parents' friends, Eluned and Uriel, were supposed to get to Bogaine before lunch.

Chokhmah and Faolan had met the couple during their quest for the Thirteen Hallowed Treasures. The Quest had taken them and four others the length and breadth of the Thirteen Kingdoms as they searched for the treasures that would bring peace to their world.

Well into her twelfth year, Parisa loved to hear the tales of their adventures. Her father was always glad to regale her with stories, particularly during the winter months when they spent much of their time inside Rose Cottage. But, while her mother had been a part of the Quest longer than her father, she preferred living in the present moment and would only talk about the Quest on the rare occasions she was feeling nostalgic.

Already tall for her age, Parisa brushed some lichen from her skirt, which hid her long and lanky legs. The vibrant colors of the outfit accented her amber eyes and made her olive skin glow. Other than her long-fingered hands, she looked nothing like her father. She even had her mother's dark brown hair with its coppery highlights. Most days, her father braided her thick mane into a long ponytail that hung neatly down her back. Today, though, she had decided to wear it loose and was already regretting that decision as the warm summer sun caused the sweat to soak the hair at the back of her neck.

Pulling her hair to the side, she loosely braided it so that it would hang in front. Later, she'd do something else but at the moment she was without ribbons or pins.

Rounding the curve, she saw dust rising in the distance. It had to be them, she thought. Parisa hightailed it back to the farm to warn her parents that Eluned and Uriel, who her mother and father still called Gwrhyr, would arrive soon.

BY THE TIME THE PARTY FROM PORTUMA ARRIVED, Faolan had braided his daughter's hair so that she would be free to gallivant with Eluned's children and their first cousins once removed. Parisa's cousin Fianna's wedding had been a smaller affair as preparations had been well underway for the Year X meeting in Kaumari and Eluned and Uriel had been unable to attend. Besides, Parisa had been sick that weekend and had spent most of it in bed with a fever. She had watched some of the events from the windows, but she had not been allowed around the few other children that were there in case she was contagious.

This year, though, the King and Queen arrived at Bogaine with both of Eluned's cousins, Gittan and Bryan, who had each brought their children, except for Gittan's oldest son, who felt it was beneath him to fraternize with the younger children. Their spouses chose to remain behind at Castle Abbert in order to give Eluned more time with her cousins.

Other than the baby, Dylan, Parisa had not met any of these children. She had met Eluned and Uriel when she was five. It was the year they had traveled to Zion for the Year V meeting of the Thirteen Kingdoms. Eluned had just given birth to their first child, Fuchsia, who she named for her great grandmother. So, Parisa couldn't really claim to know her as Fuchsia had been an infant, and she hadn't seen any of them since. They hadn't attended the Year X meeting in Kaumari because by that time her mother's grandniece, Leleua, was ruling the Kingdom of Pelf with her husband, Raynor of Simoon, and they had attended the meeting to represent Pelf in Chokhmah's place.

She remembered her father being angry about that because he'd been looking forward to both traveling to the Kingdom of Kamartha as well as seeing his fellow Questers again. Chokhmah had been firm, though, insisting their presence would undermine what Leleua and Raynor were doing in Pelf. Parisa shook that thought away. It seemed like her mother and father argued all the time now. Although arguing for them meant her father getting red-faced and bellowing at her mother, and her mother getting quieter and quieter before withdrawing mentally, then physically by leaving the house to work in her herb garden or to go pray in the chapel.

Now, Eluned and Uriel arrived at the gate on horseback with another adult on a horse and two mules pulling a wagon behind them. The wagon was full of kids and one adult. Parisa counted six children, all about her age or younger. She knew two of them belonged to Eluned and Uriel, who, she needed to remember, should be addressed as Queen and King. And what about their children? Should she call them Princess Fuchsia and Prince Gavreel?

Parisa had grown up knowing that her mother was actually a queen, Queen Parisa, in fact, but had given up that life for Faolan and her daughter as Chokhmah noted to Faolan constantly.

"I am here because this is the life that appeals to me and in it, I find contentment," being her constant refrain. These days, it sounded more like a mantra than the truth.

And certainly Queen Eluned's cousins, Gittan and Bryan, must be addressed as prince and princess, as well, she thought, as they were the children of the Queen and King of Dyfed. Did that mean all the children she saw in the back of the wagon were princesses and princes? She didn't see how it couldn't. She supposed that she could actually be called Princess Parisa. Or was that only true if one was the child of a ruling king or queen? Parisa sighed. It was all so exhausting. She would have to wait and see how they were introduced although it would certainly be tiresome to be constantly saying Prince and Princess before someone's name.

As the adults dismounted, the children were scrambling out of the wagon. Parisa couldn't tell which child went with which parent. She knew that Eluned's son, Gavreel, was the youngest of the lot at four. He was now clinging to his mother's legs, his jade green eyes wide as he surveyed the hustle and bustle around him.

Eluned's face split open in a grin as her eyes alighted on Parisa. "By Omni, I'd know you anywhere," she approached the girl, arms open for a hug. "You're the spitting image of your mother."

Parisa accepted the hug, but demurely. "Thank you, Queen Eluned," she said, eyes lowered. She had heard this more than once growing up, but now that she was heading toward thirteen, it was a lot more common. Her uncle, aunt, and cousins had known her mother since nearly the beginning of the Quest for the Hallowed Treasures and before time and the stress of that adventure had begun to age her, so she didn't doubt they were telling the truth.

Chokhmah joined them, Dylan planted firmly against her hip. "Gavreel, if I am not mistaken?" she nodded at the little boy whose head was buried in Eluned's skirt, the only thing visible being the black curls he shared with his mother.

"Gavreel," Eluned commanded. "Say hello to your aunt Chokhmah."

Parisa allowed herself to relax a bit. So, they were to be family. The boy muttered something unintelligible.

"And this is your cousin, Parisa," Eluned said. "I've told you about her." Gavreel's head turned a fraction of an inch and one green eye appeared.

"It's an honor to meet you, Prince Gavreel," Parisa bowed slightly and smiled at the boy. He hid his face in his mother's skirt again but not before Parisa saw the smile and dimple at the corner of his mouth.

Uriel joined their small group, dragging Fuchsia along with him. She was now seven and while she had his dark brown hair, her eyes were the deep azure of an autumn sky.

"She has got the eyes of her grandmother," Chokhmah exclaimed. "It is so good to meet you again, Princess Fuchsia. I have not seen you since you were a babe in arms."

Fuchsia curtsied. "A pleasure to make your acquaintance, Queen Parisa," she said albeit a little stiltedly.

Chokhmah laughed. "Please call me Aunt Chokhmah, my dear. We do not stand on formality at Bogaine, right, Gwrhyr?" she said, winking at the king.

"One hundred percent," Uriel agreed. "It's one of the reasons we like to come here although we haven't been able to make it as often as we would have liked."

"Gwrhyr?" Fuchsia queried.

"It's what he called himself when we first started the Quest," Faolan said, joining their group. "Shall we introduce the rest of the bunch?" He turned, and waved Gittan, Bryan, and their children over.

"So many new people," Parisa murmured, tugging on her braid, a nervous habit of which her mother despaired of breaking her, but she hadn't found a suitable replacement. Chewing her nails had been quickly dispatched with the help of hot pepper juice on her fingertips. Her mother had suggested deep breaths, which she claimed worked for both her and Eluned, but she always ended up hyperventilating.

"Why don't we do this systematically?" Uriel suggested as Eluned's cousins approached. "We'll start with you, Gittan, if you don't mind? We'll drop all formality while here, which should make it easier on all of us."

"I agree," Gittan said, "We're all aware that we're all royal." She was about Chokhmah's height and looked a lot like her mother, Queen Chelli, with her auburn hair and green eyes.

"Not all of us," Faolan said under his breath but Gittan heard him.

"I'm sorry, Faolan, that's not what I meant. Besides, I understand that you're a shapeshifter. I think that's much more exciting than being a princess."

"What's a shapeshiffer, mommy?" Gavreel asked.

"It's someone who can take on the shape of an animal," Fuchsia explained to her brother, but her voice held a note of condescension.

All the children's eyes turned to Faolan, who colored and tried to brush it off, "It's a blessing and a curse."

But Gavreel, whose eyes were once again wide with dismay, squeaked, "What kind of animal?"

Uriel hefted Gavreel in his arms. "It's nothing to worry about. Faolan can turn into a wolf but he won't do it while we're around."

"That's right, darling," Eluned said, ruffling his curls. "Shapeshifters can control when they shift."

"But I want to see him turn into a wolf," shouted Cian, his voice cracking on the last word. Gittan's 13-year-old son also had the curly black hair that was so predominant in the family. "That would be really amazing," he continued in a lower tone.

"I'll think about it," Faolan stalled. "You know, my brother, Olcan, and his children can also shift into wolves."

"As can Bledwen, Conall's bride-to-be," added Chokhmah.

"That's a whole pack of wolves," Cian exclaimed, his voice cracking once again though he didn't appear to notice this time. "Are you sure it's safe here, mother?"

Gittan laughed, pulling her daughter, Arianell, closer. "I'm absolutely positive. There have been shapeshifters in Dyfed for centuries. Some of them become seals, others, deer. If they were dangerous, I'm sure they would have been exterminated, as horrible as it is to think that."

"I have no doubt that you're right," Olcan, who had been standing quietly behind his brother, said. "We would never kill a human or even someone's livestock while in wolf form."

"I'm glad to hear that," Arianell, who was a year younger than Parisa and had her mother's auburn hair, said. "Will we have a wolf protecting us tonight?" she giggled, referring to the large tent where all the children would be bedding down while visiting Bogaine.

"I don't know, Aria," said her uncle Bryan, Gittan's younger brother, who was nearly as tall as Uriel and had the signature black curls. "Will there be someone there besides me and Gittan?"

"Yes," said Olcan, "we intend to have Bledwen's brother, Bryn, in the tent, as well. He's also a shapeshifter. But his daughters are too young to stay in the tent, so they'll stay in our home with their mother."

"Where is he?" asked Bryan's youngest son, Rhodri,

scanning the small crowd. Except for his stockiness, he would be a miniature version of his father.

"Why? Are you afraid?" his older brother, Madoc, taunted him.

"No!" Rhodri said, punching his brother in the arm. "I'm not afraid, Madoc. I think you're afraid."

"Take that back, or you'll be eating dirt," Madoc threatened.

"Boys, boys, that's enough," Bryan's voice was firm, and both boys quieted and looked at the ground.

Cian rolled his eyes at Parisa, who was looking his way, as if to comment on their immaturity, but she didn't see him as she was a thousand miles away. All the talk of royalty and shapeshifting had caused her thoughts to drift.

She'd never really thought about it hard before, but she was both—a princess and a shapeshifter. Or would be, anyway, she had yet to reach the point where she would be able to shift but she was beginning to feel the changes in her body. Her parents had told her that once she started menstruating, she would also be able to shift into a wolf. It all kind of scared her—both being the last of the royal line of Pelf and a shapeshifter.

Sometimes it made her sad that her mother had turned away from that life. Not that she cared about all the trappings of royalty, but that that long-ago prince, Alborz, had worked so hard to maintain the purity of the Pelfans. And her mother had destroyed that by marrying not only someone who was neither royal nor from Pelf but was also a shapeshifter. Parisa had already determined that she would not marry a shapeshifter. Then, at least, that 'curse' would die with her in this particular branch of the family. Her cousin, Fianna, had also chosen to marry a man who wasn't a shapeshifter so that was something Dylan, and any other children they might have, wouldn't have to worry about.

"Parisa, Parisa," her mother gently tugged on her braid.

"What?" she said, abruptly, before realizing where she was, and blushing when she saw that everyone was looking at her. "I'm sorry," she apologized, cheeks coloring again. "I was thinking."

"Thinking about what?" her father, never one to mince words, asked.

"I, uh," she stuttered, cheeks turning an even deeper shade of crimson, "shapeshifting."

The children regarded her with interest.

"Are you a shapeshifter?" Cian asked.

"I will be," she admitted, hugging herself, and glancing guiltily at her mother when she realized her left hand had been repeatedly tugging at her braid.

"Interesting," Bryan said, "so one isn't born a shapeshifter?"

"No," Olcan said, "you can't shift until after you've reached puberty."

Bryan and Gittan, and even Cian, nodded in understanding but Rhodri piped up, "What's puberty?"

Cian snickered, Parisa blushed yet again, and Bryan told his son he'd explain it to him later.

"I believe it is heading toward time for lunch," Chokhmah changed the subject. "Picnic tables have been set up by the stable," she pointed toward the large building to the left, "if you would all like to go and find a seat, I will see how Beibhinn and Fianna are doing with lunch preparations. Would you mind taking Dylan, Olcan?"

"Of course," his grandfather said, taking the baby from Chokhmah.

"I'll help you, Mama," Parisa said, looking for any excuse to remove herself from the curious crowd.

"I am sorry about that," her mother said when they far enough away.

"I guess someday I'll get used to it," Parisa said, "but it's embarrassing talking about puberty to children, especially the boys because it's so different for them."

"And at the moment, you all seem to be outnumbered. Fortunately, when Bryn and Gwen arrive tonight, they will be bringing their two daughters."

"What about Dylan? Won't that just even us up?"

Chokhmah laughed. "You are right. Fortunately, he is just a babe. Perhaps, though, you should give Cian a chance."

"A chance at what?"

"Understanding what you are about to go through. He is also about that age. I imagine his body is changing as well."

Parisa remembered his voice going suddenly higher when he had become excited earlier. "Like his voice?"

"Yes, that is one example," her mother agreed. "It is not an easy time for anyone."

"I guess I might as well," Parisa said. It wasn't like they were leaving the next day. She knew they were staying, at the very least, through the Gulivan celebrations, which means they'd probably be there for nearly a week.

A FEW MINUTES LATER, Parisa found herself carrying two baskets filled with half a dozen loaves of soda bread out to the picnic tables. Beibhinn and Fianna followed behind her carrying two large crocks containing a soup made with summer vegetables in a light broth, and behind them, her mother with another crock filled with freshly made butter.

"It's a light lunch for a change," Beibhinn called out as she approached the picnic tables. They usually had their biggest meal midday, but they were planning a festive meal tonight, which would include the bride's family, to celebrate the marriage on the morrow.

Parisa noticed that the picnic tables were nearly full and

the four of them had yet to sit down. By the time she settled a basket of bread on each table, she decided she'd much rather grab a bowl of soup and some bread and sit on the bench under the eaves of the stable than squeeze herself into one of the overflowing picnic tables. She knew that today was an exception, and meals would be much less formal in the following days.

Besides, she smiled to herself as she walked over to the bench, she preferred to be alone. She settled herself on the bench, placing her bowl of soup next to her to give it a minute to cool down. She closed her eyes for a moment, listening to the happy chatter at the picnic tables.

"Care if I join you?"

Parisa startled. Once again, she had been lost in her thoughts. Fortunately, she had just taken a bite of bread when Cian walked up so all she had to do was brush away a few crumbs and not mop up any soup. She nodded to the bench beside her while finishing her mouthful. "Sorry," she told him, pointing to her mouth after she swallowed.

He laughed. "I have a knack, unfortunately." He paused. "You didn't want to join us at the table?"

Parisa found herself blushing again. He made it sound as if she'd rejected him, personally. "It just seemed so crowded. I didn't want to add to it."

Cian studied the table. "Fair enough," he finally nodded. "They do seem elbow to elbow, don't they? I was on the end, so I didn't notice as much."

They ate in silence for a while, Parisa going out of her way not to slurp her soup. She felt as if she'd already embarrassed herself enough as it was.

Cian set down his bowl and stared at the bread in his hand for a moment. "I don't mean to make you feel bad or anything," he finally spoke, "but can I ask you a personal question?"

Parisa unconsciously tugged on her braid. "I guess so," she

said, then added quickly, "as long as I don't have to answer it if I don't want to."

Cian nodded. "Um," he started as if he wasn't sure how to phrase the question, "I was just wondering if you have any friends that will be coming to the wedding or Gulivan?"

"Friends?"

"You don't have any friends?"

"I have my family."

"I mean," Cian tried to explain, "I have my brother and sister and cousins, of course, but there are some other boys my age that I take lessons with, and . . ."

"No girls?" Parisa interrupted.

"The girls have lessons with other girls."

Parisa nodded.

"But I also do other things with some of those guys like sports, horseback riding, weapons practice, that type of thing," Cian added. "Then, of course, there's worship. Don't you go to church?"

"Yes, of course," Parisa said. "Olcan was trained as a priest because it was his cover when he was spying, back before we were born. My father used to be a spy too, but," Parisa paused, remembering that his days as a spy were now a bone of contention between him and her mother because he missed the excitement of those times.

"But?" Cian prodded.

"But that changed when he joined the Quest and met Mama. Anyway, we have a small chapel. It's in the woods near the oak tree where we'll get the mistletoe next week. Olcan leads the service there, but it's small so only family go there. It's even too small for the wedding tomorrow, so we're going to have it outside." The chapel, she didn't add, was often where her mother could be found after she and her father had had a particularly bad argument, and the weather was too bad for her to escape to her herb garden. No need to tread in that pile of manure.

Cian was silent for a minute, once again studying the table. "So, what you're saying is that all your time is spent here at Bogaine and you never really spend any time with anyone other than your family? Do you go to school?"

"My mother and father teach me, and sometimes Uncle Olcan or Aunt Beibhinn, depending on what they want me to learn."

"But the only child I see is a baby," Cian said.

"Dylan," Parisa said. "Yes, but he doesn't live here. Fianna and her husband live in Thírnagall. Gruffydd is a sailor. But, when he's at sea, Fianna usually stays here or with Gruffydd's mother. She doesn't like to be alone, particularly now that she has Dylan."

Cian regarded Parisa for a moment, brow furrowed and brown eyes squinting a bit, as if he were troubled by what she just said. He shook his head and said, "Don't you get lonely?"

Parisa laughed, "Why would I get lonely? I always stay so busy with chores and lessons and that type of thing that I actually look forward to the times I can get away and be by myself."

"Wow," Cian said. "What do you do when you're alone?"

Parisa blushed. Usually she pretended she was a princess or that she was on her own Quest or some other adventure. "Uh, usually I grab a book and head to one of my favorite spots to read it or I just walk around the farm or in the woods." It wasn't an untruth; it just wasn't the complete truth.

"What are your favorite spots?" Cian was asking as Chokhmah walked up to them.

"Could you two do me a big favor?" Chokhmah asked.

Parisa sighed and stood. "Is it that time?"

"Yes," her mother confirmed.

"What time?" Cian asked, standing as well.

"It's time to go to the south pasture where we've set up some games for us kids to play," Parisa explained. "Is Gavreel going to come?"

"No," Chokhmah said. "I believe Eluned wants him to nap so that tonight he is not too cranky."

"Okay, then I'll get Fuchsia," Parisa said, "if you'll get your sister and cousins, Cian."

"They may wish to relieve themselves beforehand," Chokhmah advised.

"Good point," Parisa agreed. "I'll take Fuchsia and Arianell to our outhouse, and Cian and his cousins can use the bathhouse at Uncle Olcan's?"

Chokhmah nodded as Cian blanched. "You don't have indoor plumbing?"

Parisa laughed, spreading her hands as if to say, 'look around you'.

"Do not worry young man," Chokhmah said. "The outbuildings are well appointed. They are piped to a sewage field, but we maintain separate buildings because . . . well, I suppose it is because we have not taken the time to build bathrooms into our homes."

"Plus, we still have to handpump our water," Parisa added.

Chokhmah nodded. "It is true that we are still a bit rustic here at Bogaine."

"The bathhouse is just behind the house, and there is even a corridor leading from them into both houses so that no one has to brave the weather," Parisa said. "But Uncle's bathroom has two toilets and ours only has one."

"We do not usually have this many people here," Chokhmah said, "but we will all be learning a little patience this week."

"Besides, if you really have to go, you can always duck into the woods," Parisa added.

"Parisa," Chokhmah exclaimed.

Parisa shrugged. "Well, you can."

Cian laughed. "Okay, where should I meet you?"

Parisa pointed to a green gate in a stone fence. "We can meet up there."

"Your mother wasn't joking," Cian said as they herded the younger children to the south pasture. "Except for having to toss a bucket of water into the toilet each time, the bathrooms were just as nice, if not nicer, than anything we have at Castle Abbert."

"That's good to hear," Parisa replied. "I stayed at Castle Mykerinos, but I was only five, and I just don't remember the bathrooms there at all. All I remember is spending most of the day in some room where someone read me stories when I wasn't playing with the toys that were there."

"So," Cian began as they climbed the hill along a well-worn path, "I know you said you had some games set up . . ."

"Sack toss, battledore, and ground billiards."

"I thought it would be something like that," he said. "but what if I taught you a game that we play at home?"

"Can we all play it?"

"Yes," Cian said. "The more people the better, even."

"How do you play?"

"It's kind of like tag but I think it's more fun."

"What's 'tag'?" Parisa asked.

Arianell was walking in front of them and looked at Parisa over her shoulder, mouth agape. "You've never played tag?"

"Keep marching, sis," Cian pointed at her.

She stuck out her tongue at him. "Mother says you're not allowed to order me around."

Cian rolled his eyes at Parisa and explained the game of tag to her.

"And what is more fun than tag?"

"He probably wants to play 'statues', Arianell said over her shoulder.

"Not only is it more fun," Cian said, "but then we don't risk staining our clothes. I don't know about your mother but ours gets really angry if we tear our clothes or get them dirty." He glanced down at his spotless trousers before flicking something unseen off his shirt.

"I wish he were joking," Arianell said, dropping back to walk beside Parisa, "but it's only when we're in our good clothes. She doesn't care as much if we're in play clothes."

"Play clothes," Parisa repeated. "That's also new to me, but I guess it must be like the leather breeches I wear to do my chores."

"Your mother lets you wear pants?" Arianell nearly shouted. "That's not fair!"

Fuchsia, who had been walking ahead of her with Rhodri, said, "My mother allows me to wear pants. It sure makes horseback riding easier."

"Mama says that all the women started wearing pants while on the Quest," Parisa said. "She said it made traveling and camping much less difficult."

"Mommy said that she was the first one to think of it," Fuchsia said. "She said that after crossing the Mountains of Misericord during a blizzard while wearing a skirt changed her mind about it forever."

Parisa shivered at the thought of it. "I imagine that would be pretty miserable."

"Well, I'm going to ask Mother if I can wear pants some time," Arianell said.

"You should," Parisa and Fuchsia said together.

"Curses!" Cian shouted as Parisa and Fuchsia flashed the sign to ward off the evil eye, before laughing about having done so.

They started descending the hill and a few seconds later, Madoc called out, "I see it."

Parisa looked at Cian and raised an eyebrow. "What a surprise," she muttered.

Cian chuckled. "Anyway, the game. Statues is tag but when

you're tagged you must stand in whatever position you were in when you got tagged."

Arianell giggled. "Except most people try to stand in really silly ways."

"That sounds like it could be fun," Parisa said. "Does everyone want to play 'statues'?" she shouted.

"Yes!"

Clearly, they had all played before. For the first time, Parisa realized just how isolated she had been all her life. She had assumed that life at Bogaine was the way people lived everywhere, the time spent in Zion for the Year V meeting a rare exception for everyone, not just her.

"What?" she said, when she realized Cian had been speaking to her.

"I was saying that I'll be the tagger first since I suggested the game," he said.

"Sure," she attempted a smile though her heart felt like one of Bogaine's horses had stomped on it. She knew she ought to enjoy having other kids to be with for a change, but at the moment all she could think about was the fact they would all be gone in a week and she would have to return to life all too aware of what she had been missing.

CHOKHMAH

Sitting in the darkness of the chapel, Chokhmah watched the flickering candles on the altar, taking deep breaths of the air, which smelled faintly of incense. She had been trying for hours to silence her mind, calm her soul before the onslaught of guests arrived later that morning. But one minute she would find herself wallowing in utter despair and the next she would have pulled herself together sufficiently enough that she seemed on the verge of making a decision that would change the course of her life forever.

And that was the real problem—she was more than willing to do whatever she had to do to find contentment in her life. She had always known that the ardor, the passion, of being in love again could not last forever. Those first, heady months with Faolan had been exhilarating, and she suspected that the fact they were simultaneously engaged in a dangerous quest for the Hallowed Treasures had added more than a dash of spice to her relationship with him. And, barely a year after meeting him, she had discovered she was pregnant with the first child for both of them.

After returning to Bogaine, they had decided they wanted to commit to each other and Olcan had married them here in this chapel dedicated to Saint Colmán, the patron of horses. Chokhmah could not help but smile at the remembrance. They had been so happy and so full of hope 13 years ago. Unconsciously, she pressed her hand against her now flat stomach. For her wedding gown, she had borrowed an old maternity dress from Beibhinn as nothing she owned would fit across her swelling belly.

And those first years had been so wonderful—building their lives around the horse farm and Chokhmah's herb garden, which brought the occasional patient from the surrounding area, and watching their daughter grow up. The trip to Castle Mykerinos for the Year V meeting had also been a highpoint because they had a chance to visit with another two of their fellow Questers, Queen Njima and Yona, again as well as Eluned and Uriel, and their recently-born daughter, Fuchsia.

It was after their return to Bogaine that Faolan began to chomp on the bit, so to speak. That was because that was when the Kingdoms of Dziron, Kamartha, Naphtali, and Aden started putting together a plan to take an army to Pelf and reclaim it, making it part of the Thirteen Kingdoms again. Despite his wounded leg, which meant he would never walk without a limp again, and the fact he was in his mid-40s at the time, Faolan still really wanted to be a part of that mission.

Had his desire to be involved in the planning and execution of an attack on Pelf been for an admirable or beneficent reason, perhaps because his wife was actually that Kingdom's queen, Chokhmah might have felt more sympathy for him. Unfortunately for Faolan, it did not take long for Chokhmah to discern that her husband was really just looking for a reason to be away from Bogaine and participating in something exciting again.

And two years later, when the campaign had been successful, they had argued over whether or not she should return to Pelf as their queen. There were numerous reasons she had not wanted to live into that at the time. The most important reason was her daughter. Having been raised by the Roma meant that Chokhmah had spent her entire life moving from one camp to the next. It was her life and she had accepted it at the time. She had even enjoyed being part of the Quest for the Hallowed Treasures, as difficult as that had been.

At that time, they had been settled in Bogaine for eight years, far longer than she had ever lived in any one place. Her herb garden was flourishing as was her daughter. She was content in her life even if Faolan was not completely content in his. It was difficult enough to keep a household running. She could not imagine what it would mean to rule a kingdom. She had demurred, suggesting Leleua and Raynor reign in her stead. Faolan had been angry but he had also understood her reluctance.

Things had really started unraveling in Year X, the year that she decided that their presence at the meeting in Kaumari would be a hindrance as the Quest was long past and two perfectly capable rulers had the Kingdom of Pelf well in hand. Even Eluned had elected not to go to that meeting. She had written Chokhmah that Uriel would be attending but that she felt that it wasn't fair to travel that distance with Gavreel, who was not yet quite three years old at the time.

By Year X, all Thirteen Kingdoms had settled or were settling into the peace time routine—strengthening their infrastructures and reveling in a freedom that had not been felt in centuries. Chokhmah suspected that like herself, everyone knew that it would not and could not last. Peace never does. But, while they had it, they would enjoy it.

It was a time when spies were not yet needed again. Rather, ambassadors traveled freely, and the people of the Thirteen Kingdoms were enjoying getting to know more about each other. Chokhmah supposed that Faolan would prefer to become an ambassador for Dyfed rather than be confined to

Bogaine for the remainder of his life. Unfortunately, Olcan had settled happily into this new existence. He knew better than anyone what it was like to leave a spouse and children for six months at a time; just how much he had missed by not being around for large segments of his children's lives.

In the past year, Faolan's dissatisfaction with his life, and Chokhmah had to give him credit, not her or Parisa, person-ally, had led to more and more frequent arguments and his becoming more and more aggressive towards her. She supposed he had no other way to relieve his frustration, but it was beginning to scare her. She supposed that with Eluned's help she could secure him a post as an ambassador or some other job in which he could travel more frequently. And yet.

And yet, she did not want to be the woman sitting around waiting for her husband to return, wondering what he was do-ing at that moment while she raised their child alone. Perhaps if their life together had started out that way, if she had entered into the marriage knowing that he had a second job that would keep him away from Bogaine part of the year, she could have been content with that situation.

It was the fact that he had actually been fine for years, had seemed perfectly happy being with her and Parisa, helping Olcan build a bigger and more productive operation. Their horses were now sold to buyers from all over the Thirteen Kingdoms. Perhaps if they had created a business model that had them taking the horses to the other kingdoms rather than having the buyers come to them, Faolan would have found a way to satisfy his wanderlust.

He always ended up making her feel so guilty. Technically, it was her fault that he could not do as he pleased. But she was trying to look out for what was in the best interest of all of them, not just Faolan. It is what the arguments always boiled down to—him accusing her of being controlling, her pleading with him to think of what was best for Parisa, and even herself.

Last night had been the final straw—he had accused her of ruining his life. That had left her speechless. They had been together nearly 14 years. They had a 12-year-old daughter who was intelligent, beautiful, kind, caring. They could not have asked for a better child. And he felt she had ruined his life? Yes, the words had been spoken in anger, and maybe he had had one drink too many, but he would not have spoken them if there had not been at least a kernel of truth in them.

The light at the windows was now a murky grey, which meant that dawn was fast approaching. She needed to pull herself together. The week ahead would not be an easy one. Eluned and Gwrhyr would be arriving with their children and whomever chose to accompany them from Castle Abbert. And she was taking care of Dylan today! She had forgotten. As if she wasn't exhausted enough already. And then Bledwen's family would arrive this afternoon. There would be so many people around, including an extra three in Rose Cottage, and she would have to act like everything was normal when inside it felt like she was fracturing into a million pieces.

What she wanted more than anything in the world was to sit with Eluned and, for a change, be the one to pour her heart out to the younger woman. She was thankful she had been the one that Eluned had often confided in during the Quest. That is, she frowned, until Faolan had disrupted that. While she was so wrapped up in their romance, Eluned had turned to Yona as her confidante. And then that position had been taken on by Gwrhyr, just as it should have, as their romance blossomed and Yona and Njima were getting to know one another better.

But, since the Quest had ended and Thirteen Kingdoms had aligned once again, she paused in her thought. Of course, that alignment had come at a great cost, which she must never forget. The deaths of Jabberwock and Bonpo had been the most heartbreaking, but Faolan would never walk right again and Eluned would always be marked by the scar that ran from her ear down across her cheek. Fortunately, things had shifted a bit once they had all gone on with their lives. Eluned turned to Chokhmah again, writing her frequently, discussing the memoir of the Quest that she was writing up, as well as the quotidian, and even sending the occasional pigeon when she needed advice more quickly.

Chokhmah groaned and stood up. She needed to get back to the cottage before Parisa woke up. Her daughter did not need to know that she had spent the night in the chapel. Still, she approached the altar slowly, savoring the last moments of silence and the peace of being alone, before blowing out the candles.

SILENCE DESCENDED UPON ROSE COTTAGE after the thud of the front door being closed signaled that Faolan and Uriel had left for the stable. Gavreel was still sleeping peacefully so Chokhmah and Eluned took their mugs into the living area and settled onto the couch for their morning chat.

"Tell me honestly, Chokhmah," Eluned said, placing her cup of tea on the side table, "is everything all right between you and Faolan?"

Chokhmah glanced at Eluned, startled out of her reverie. Her friend's face, not so much marred as made more interesting by the thin line of white scar tissue that traveled across her face from her left ear and downward across her cheekbone to her mouth, was filled with concern. "Is it that obvious?"

"I've been here three nights now," Eluned unconsciously fingered the scar that Chokhmah's eyes had lingered on for a moment, a constant reminder of the tolls the Quest for the Hallowed Treasures had exacted. "And I feel like you two have barely spoken to each other."

Chokhmah's eyes filled with tears and the next thing she knew she was sobbing uncontrollably.

Gently removing the mug from Chokhmah's shaking hands and placing it on the table, Eluned took her friend into her arms, and waited for the sobs and tears to cease. Chokhmah finally pulled away and dabbed at her eyes and nose with a handkerchief.

Eluned waited until Chokhmah had regained her composure before saying, "Would you like to talk about it?"

"Oh Eluned," Chokhmah said, voice breaking, "last night I had a dream."

PARISA

A nightmare catapulted Parisa from a troubled sleep. She listened intently for a minute, praying she hadn't cried out. It was still dark inside the tent, which either meant it was the middle of the night or that the sun had not yet risen enough to illuminate the interior.

No. Everyone seemed to be sleeping, even the adults. A few cots away, Bryan continued to snore; Rhodri mumbled something in his sleep and turned over; other than that, the quiet inhalations, and exhalations of breath.

Just a few more days and she could be back in her own room. She missed her bed, and she missed her journal, which she'd had to hide or risk Eluned or Uriel finding it. She also missed her wolf doll, Echo, that she still cuddled as she drifted off to sleep at night. She hadn't had the guts to bring Echo with her to the tent afraid the other kids might think it was too babyish.

What she didn't miss was her parents' nightly arguments. She sighed, remembering her nightmare, which had involved two wolves, one black, one white, tearing at each other's throats. She had been watching them fight and was terrified they would kill each other. Had she been a wolf or herself? The details were slipping away.

Parisa carefully edged herself out of bed and padded to the doorway, which was just some fabric hanging across the entrance. She pulled it aside to see the pearlescent grey light of impending dawn. It was warmer than she'd anticipated with a light mist floating above the pasture beside the stable, but still chilly enough to make her shiver.

She hurried back to her cot and gathered the clothes and toiletries that were stowed beneath it. Slipping out of the tent, Parisa made her way to the bathhouse. If she were lucky, she would have enough time to bathe and get dressed for the day before anyone else was stirring. She smiled to herself. Did they all sleep so late because this was a holiday for them or was it because they were royalty. Bryn didn't have that excuse, but this was definitely a holiday for him, and his last chance to sleep in as they were heading back to Thírnagall the following morning.

That reminded her that today was Gulivan, and that after breakfast they would be collecting the mistletoe. She couldn't wait. Cian and the others had never participated in knocking down the golden bough as it had always been done for them. Humming quietly to herself, she skipped the rest of the way to the bathhouse.

After her bath, Parisa tucked her things into a cabinet to retrieve later, and then went to find her father, pulling a cotton sweater over her blouse to help ward off the morning chill. While they had gathered the wood for the bonfire prior to the wedding, she'd completely forgotten about collecting the stones needed to knock down the mistletoe. And, before she wasted time accumulating a bucketful, she needed to make sure it hadn't already been done.

Her father was usually in the stable about this time so Parisa made her way there first, pausing to watch a hawk circling high above the pasture hunting for its breakfast. Too bad she wouldn't be able to shift into a bird. She would love to be able to fly. It looked so peaceful up there with nothing but the wind to accompany it.

She had just stepped into the barn when she heard her father say, "I don't know how much longer I can take it, Gwrhyr."

"What about your daughter?" The king's voice sounded almost accusing, and Parisa froze in her tracks.

"I don't know, I don't know," Faolan said. "I only know that our marriage is falling apart, and I need some time to myself. Being stuck in one place for all these years is killing me."

"Is there not enough here to keep you busy?"

"I can always find ways to keep myself busy, but it would also be easy enough work for Olcan and Conall if I were gone part of each year."

"Like when you were a spy?" Uriel asked.

"Something like that," Faolan agreed. "Obviously, we don't need spies anymore but surely there is something I could do."

"Oh, I'm sure we could find you something," Uriel said, "but I ask, again, what about your daughter? How does Chokhmah feel about it?"

Parisa stopped listening. She knew exactly how her mother felt about it and happened to agree with her. She didn't want her father being away for half a year or more. What if he wasn't around the first time she shifted? Yes, there'd be Olcan, and even Conall, to guide her but it wasn't the same thing as having her father beside her when the time came. She was scared enough about shifting as it was.

She turned and slipped quietly out the back before they noticed her. She needed to talk to her mother. Parisa entered through the bathhouse, grabbing her things on the way so she could leave her dirty clothes in the hamper. They'd spent the previous day exploring the woods, riding horses, and playing games in the south pasture after a late morning worship service in front of Chapel Saint Colmán (there were too many of them to fit in the pews) led by Olcan, and followed by a midday meal. The adults had been moving slowly as more than one glass of wine had been raised to celebrate the union of Conall and Bledwen the previous night, but the children were full of energy. She might have gotten a little dirtier than normal, she realized looking at the grass- and dirt-stains on the clothing she carried.

Parisa hurried down the hallway, confident that her mother would assure her that she would never allow her father to disappear for months on end. But her mother's words brought her to a standstill.

"Oh Eluned," her mother was saying, and Parisa heard her voice break, "last night I had a dream."

"A prophetic dream?" Eluned asked, voice full of dread. Chokhmah's prophetic dreams were rare, but Parisa knew they were always fulfilled, like the time she dreamed the Knife of Llawfrodded was in New Buta on the coast of the Kingdom of Sheba and not in Pelf where two of the Questers, Jabberwock and Bonpo, were traveling to find it.

Parisa's heart was hammering so hard in her chest that she could barely hear her mother's next words.

"Yes, I believe so."

"You're scaring me, Chokhmah," Eluned said, taking the woman's hands into her own. "What did you dream?"

Parisa held her breath.

"I dreamed I was sitting on the throne of Pelf enjoying the view out the window opposite me where a white wolf with wings of polished copper cavorted in the sky with a large raven."

Stepping into the room, Parisa confronted her mother. "I don't understand."

"Parisa," Chokhmah gasped, jumping up and hurrying

over to where her daughter was standing. Cupping Parisa's face in her hands, she was quick to reassure her. "It was just a dream, darling. Perhaps it means nothing."

"But you said you thought it was prophetic," Parisa accused her. "Does that mean you are going to be Queen of Pelf? And what about the wolf? I've never heard about a wolf with wings."

"Well," Eluned offered, "there was Rua. Remember him? He was a fairy fox."

Chokhmah nodded, "True. I am not sure what the wolf and raven meant in the dream, but the throne, the view all seemed very real. And yet maybe I am making more of the dream than I should. It is just that . . ."

"Things have gotten so bad with Papa?"

Chokhmah's eyes filled with tears again, and Parisa noticed for the first time that they were already red and puffy. She must have been crying before she arrived. "Yes," Chokhmah whispered.

"He was just telling Uriel that he can't take it here much longer," Parisa said, tearing up herself. "Papa wants Uriel to find him something to do that can let him be away from here for part of the year."

Eluned stood up. "No. That's not going to happen. I will not allow him do that."

"But what if he leaves anyway?" Parisa said. "What if he no longer cares what we want?"

"Mommy?" They turned to see Gavreel standing in the hallway, lip quivering. "What's wrong, Mommy?"

"Oh, sweetheart," Eluned rushed to her son, grunting as she picked him up. She wouldn't be able to do that much longer, Parisa realized. "It's nothing for you to worry about, I promise. Are you ready for breakfast?" She carried Gavreel into the kitchen.

Parisa and Chokhmah regarded each other for a moment. "Now is not the time for us to worry about this either,"

Chokhmah said. "We have guests and the Gulivan to celebrate, and," she paused as Eluned appeared back in the doorway.

"Do you know that it has been 15 years to the day since I was nearly sacrificed to the Sacred Three?" Eluned reminded her.

The color drained from Chokhmah's face. "I will always regret that we did not believe you. Not even Jabberwock believed King Arawn would kill the daughter of another king. We thought he intended to make you his bride."

"Thank Omni for Uriel," Eluned laughed, relieving some of their tension. "And then I was idiot enough to fall for Irirangi." She shook her head, remembering. "Anyway, I'm saying this because no matter what the dream means, we know that we are always in Omni's hand and that things always work out for those of us who trust in It."

"This is true," Chokhmah agreed. "No matter the hardship along the way, the path will always lead us in the right direction."

Eluned returned to the kitchen with Gavreel, and Chokhmah turned to her daughter.

"We do not have to make a decision today," she told Parisa. "Let us worry about this later. Why do you not go and see if the others have awakened yet?"

PARISA TRUDGED OVER TO THE TENT, feet dragging. How had her favorite holiday suddenly become the worst day in her life? The most discomfiting thing about having overheard her father, and then her mother, was the fact that she felt divided loyalties. She was furious at her father, but he was her father and she loved him.

And yet it was her mother's love for her and for her father that made Chokhmah insist that Faolan be around while she was growing up. This was all her fault, she cringed, inwardly. If her mother had never gotten pregnant, perhaps they would never have been married, and her father could have lived his life the way he wanted to live.

And what about her mother? She had spent the past thirteen years in Dyfed, far from her family, just so she could make a stable home for her daughter. She had yet to see her nephew Daniel's children, and Parisa knew she was also worried that she wouldn't have a chance to see her brother, Moshe, again before he died.

Not to mention the dream. What was that all about? A flying wolf, her mother a queen. Despite enjoying her time with Cian, Arianell, Fuchsia, and the other children this weekend, she was also looking forward to returning to her normal life. Or was she? Parisa wondered, remembering the nearly constant fights she had to endure lately, her normal life had not felt normal for quite some time now.

If her father was really that unhappy, shouldn't her mother compromise? But then again, why should they have to be without him for half the year just because he was too selfish to stay? It was all so complicated.

"Hey!"

Parisa, who been walking head down, jumped, startled into awareness. She looked up to see Cian watching her in amusement.

"I don't think I've ever met anyone who can disappear into their heads like you can," he laughed.

"I was thinking," Parisa mumbled.

"I know," Cian watched her. "Are you all right?"

"I didn't sleep well last night." It wasn't completely a lie. After all, she was clearly awake and dressed for the day unlike him. "Is everyone waking up?"

"Yeah, but I think Bryn is still asleep."

Parisa surprised herself by laughing. "Wow, he really is

taking advantage of every second of his holiday, isn't he?"

"You don't think he does that all the time?"

"I doubt it," Parisa said. "His family runs an inn in Thírnagall, The Lion and The Unicorn. I imagine he works really hard every day. I think he's the inn's cook."

"Oh." Cian looked embarrassed.

"Kind of amazing how different it is living a life of privilege compared to those who don't, isn't it?" Parisa pointed to her father, who was wheeling a barrow of horse manure out of the stable.

"I'll say," Cian said. "I hope I didn't offend you. I just never really thought about it."

Parisa shook her head, "Nah, but it wouldn't be a bad idea to always keep that in mind, that the people who are working for you and serving you at Castle Abbert have lives too." And problems that they don't necessarily want to talk about, she thought, but needed to deal with, nonetheless.

"Good point," Cian said.

"Well, I'd better go tell Mama and Aunt Beibhinn that it's time to get out the breakfast for today," she said, turning on her heel and heading toward her aunt's house. "See you in a minute." Personally, she wasn't sure she could stomach any food that morning.

But as she was laying out a platter of toasted bread and jams on the picnic table, her mother insisted she eat a little something even if she didn't feel hungry.

"I know you are upset, my dear," her mother said quietly, placing a pitcher of goat's milk and a pitcher of apple juice on the table, "but people will notice if you are not eating, and will wonder why a healthy 12-year-old is turning down food."

Parisa sighed, heavily. "All right, Mama." But she would wait until everyone else had started eating first because then they might not notice how little she was eating.

Fortunately, other than Gittan and Bryan, no other adults

joined them at the picnic tables. Everyone else, apparently, had already breakfasted. Parisa buttered a piece of toast and nibbled on it while sipping on the tea her mother had brought to her. "It will improve your appetite," she had whispered to her as she set it down next to her plate.

It hadn't. Yet. But she was managing the toast, so that was something.

"Is everything set up for getting the mistletoe?" Cian, who was sitting across from her, interrupted her thoughts.

Parisa grimaced, inwardly. She had never got around to asking her father, and honestly, at this point, she didn't want to have to look him in the eye. So, she lied. "Oh no, I forgot to get the stones. Do you want to help me do that?"

"Sure," Cian said. "What do we need to do?"

"I want to help, too," Arianell, who was sitting next to Parisa, interjected.

"Help with what?" Madoc asked around a mouthful of scrambled eggs.

"Getting the stones to knock down the mistletoe," his younger brother said, happy to know something Madoc didn't.

"Does everyone want to help?" Parisa had to force herself not to roll her eyes.

When that was affirmed, she stood. "I'm going to get a bucket. Can you all be ready in ten minutes?" They would have to be finished with breakfast by the time she got back, she decided, especially if she walked slowly. It was clear that Cian would have liked to have helped her, but if she let him, she'd have to let anyone who wanted to do so tag along. "I'll be right back," she said. She knew there was a bucket she could use in the building that the tack was stored in. That way, she hoped, she could avoid running into her father.

Unfortunately, that was not to be. When she arrived, the door was standing open, and her father was in the midst of cleaning a bridle.

"Hey kid," he smiled when he saw her standing awkwardly at the door. "What do you need?"

Her cheeks colored despite herself. "I, um, was looking for a bucket?"

"For?"

"We were going to get some stones for the mistletoe," she said.

"I believe there is a bucketful in the stable," he said, frowning. "You didn't think I had forgotten, had you?"

"I guess I just assumed you had been too busy," she lied, "um, you know, with Uriel and Eluned here and all."

"I'd never be busy enough to forget your favorite day of the year," Faolan said.

"Oh." Parisa blushed again and tugged on her braid. "I'm sorry. I guess I'd better go tell everyone that we don't need to do that," she said, as she started backing away.

Faolan frowned again. "Are you okay, Parisa?"

"Yeah, I'm just tired. I didn't sleep well last night." She forced a smile onto her face. "I may take a nap after lunch, so I won't be too tired for the bonfire tonight."

Faolan nodded. "Sounds like a good idea. You definitely seem out of sorts. I guess it isn't any fun sleeping in a tent full of people you don't know well."

Parisa nodded. "I'm not used to all the snoring."

"Well, if you're heading back that way," her father said, "why don't you ask everyone to be ready for the mistletoe gathering, in, say, an hour? We can gather at the picnic tables."

"Sounds good," she forced another smile. "See you then," she said as enthusiastically as she could manage, before hurrying back the way she came. She had known that the first time she encountered her father after hearing him that morning was going to be awkward, but she hadn't realized how very angry she was about it. The toast now felt like a stone in her belly, a very hot stone that was making her stomach boil.

She barely made it to the bathhouse before losing her toast and tea to the toilet. She tossed two buckets of water into the bowl before thoroughly rinsing her mouth with water. She couldn't risk anyone finding out that she had thrown up. It would destroy her mother to know how much all this was tearing her apart. And if anyone else found out, they would think she had a stomach bug and keep her away from everyone else. She wanted to weep but she couldn't risk that either. Then everyone would wonder why she had been crying.

No, she'd have to keep her pain to herself until she could be alone again. The next few days would seem like an eternity. Meanwhile, she would have to pretend that she was enjoying Gulivan as much, if not more, than she usually did.

Pasting a not very convincing smile on her face, she hurried back to the picnic tables to inform the rest of the kids that they wouldn't need to round up any stones and that they should meet back at the picnic tables within the hour to go gather the mistletoe.

CHOKHMAH

Gathered under the ancient oak that towered over the Saint Colmán's chapel, all but a few of the adults chose one of the rounded stones Faolan had gathered. The weather was perfect for the first day of summer. The sky was a forget-me-not blue unmarred by a single cloud. A light breeze provided just the right amount of movement to keep the sun from making the day too uncomfortable.

Chokhmah settled herself next to a willow tree that hung over the burbling creek that she called, to herself, Shamay, because that is what her mother had called heaven. Its actual name was much more mundane—Coldwater Creek. It bisected the farm, flowing past the house and then the chapel and continued on eastward joining other streams that eventually emptied into the Comnan River, which formed Dyfed's eastern border with the Kingdom of Adamah. She took a deep breath to calm herself and then watched the annual event from afar. Fortunately, she did this every year, and it would not be remarked upon as unusual.

Starting with the youngest child capable of throwing a stone and the lowest clump of mistletoe, the process of knocking the mostly parasitic plant from the boughs of the oak tree soon began.

At three, Eiriol was the youngest, and she insisted on taking a turn. Fortunately, no one emitted as much as a snicker when her stone bounced off the trunk of the tree a good twenty feet beneath the mistletoe. Parisa, whose sweater was now wrapped around her waist, even insisted that she be given a second chance, and no one argued with her.

Enfys and Gavreel also missed but were told they were too old to get a second chance. Parisa could tell they wanted to protest but neither did they want to belie the fact everyone considered them old enough to be treated like the older kids and adults.

Parisa, who had years of practice as well as the fact she worked on her rock throwing skills throughout the year, was the first to knock down the cluster of mistletoe. In previous years, it had often taken her a lot more tries, which she had been allowed because she was by far the youngest person present.

This year, she smiled rather than crowed about her accomplishment, and stepped back so Cian could take a turn. Unfortunately for him, though, the next bunch was even higher, and he missed. Then it was time for the adults to show off, which in this case mostly meant Faolan and Olcan, as they had a long-standing rivalry. But maybe because the energy was higher this year, most of the other adults joined in the game. The only ones to stand back and enjoy the game from afar were Chokhmah and Beibhinn and Bledwen's parents, Cai and Olwen.

"Too bad Njima and Yona aren't here," Eluned said to Chokhmah, referring to the queen of Naphtali and her partner. She had taken her turn and missed and was walking toward her friend, "I'd bet that they would be really good at this."

Chokhmah smiled, nodding. "Certainly, Njima would

succeed. Her aim was always true," she said, remembering the Queen killing the blind cobras with her throwing axe when they had sheltered in the ruins of Shamash Palace in Kamea. "And oh, how I miss the exuberance of Yona. She could brighten any day."

Her meaning was not lost on Eluned. It would be so much easier to pretend things were going well between Chokhmah and Faolan if Yona were here. Instead, both women had to force themselves to seem engaged in the activities.

"How is Parisa?" Eluned whispered. Chokhmah's daughter was flanked by Cian and Arianell, the latter of whom was chattering away. Cian was clearly absorbed in the competition but Parisa, as usual, seemed lost in her thoughts, pulling absent-mindedly on her braid.

Chokhmah wished she had Jabberwock's ability to telecommunicate with her child so that she could raise her from her reverie without attracting Faolan's attention. It had not passed her notice that her husband kept glancing at his daughter, brow furrowed. It was true that this was far from normal behavior for their child on this her favorite holiday.

"Could you do me a favor, Eluned?" Chokhmah asked, quietly.

"Sure, what do you need?"

"Could you rouse Parisa from her wool gathering before her father makes a scene?"

Eluned glanced Faolan's way just as he turned to send another frowning look his daughter's way.

"I understand," Eluned grimaced. "That could be bad for all of us. Parisa!" she called, waving the girl over, and breathing a sigh of relief as the girl startled and looked in her direction. Eluned started making her way toward her, and Parisa met her halfway. Putting her arm around Parisa's shoulder, Eluned led her back toward her mother.

"Darling," Chokhmah said once they arrived, "you must

pull yourself together. Not only has your father noticed your behavior, but soon your Uncle will as well."

Parisa swallowed, audibly. "I'm sorry, Mama. It's just so hard."

"I understand, darling, but it is neither the time nor the place to sort this out. I prefer to keep our family matters as private as possible."

"Eluned knows, and so does Uriel," Parisa argued.

"That's true," Eluned said, "but you have to understand that Uriel and I have known your mother for 15 years. She pretty much started the Quest with us, and she will always be my closest friend."

"But," her mother continued, "there is no reason that Eluned's cousins or Bledwen's family should have their holiday ruined by our troubles."

Parisa sighed.

"Please, my darling," Chokhmah said, using the voice that had soothed and coaxed more than one soul over the years, "please go and join your new friends and show them why this has always been your favorite holiday."

"Okay," Parisa said, removing the sweater from around her waist, "but you have to promise me two things: one, that you won't put any mistletoe under your pillow tonight, and two, that you'll hold my sweater for me."

Chokhmah laughed. It was said that placing the mistletoe under one's pillow would bring dreams of omens both good and bad. It had once been Parisa's favorite part of the ceremony, the anticipation of possible dreams that foretold the future. But today, Chokhmah understood her daughter's reluctance for her mother to do so. "You have my word, my dear," she said, holding out a hand for the sweater. It was an easy enough promise. Chokhmah did not need mistletoe in order to have prophetic dreams.

Parisa

Once enough mistletoe had been gathered, Parisa volunteered to make sure that everyone that had remained at the chapel (Fianna had returned to the house to change Dylan's diaper) received a sprig of the plant to put under their pillow that night. She even gave one to her mother, who winked at her before tucking it away in the pocket of her skirt.

Parisa decided that if she could avoid her father as much as possible for the next few days, she might be able to survive. So, in order to not be caught alone again, her plan was to make sure that someone was always with her whether it was Cian or Arianell or one of the other children and even one of the adults, if necessary, including, of course, her mother.

Cian offered to help her carry the remaining mistletoe to Chokhmah's garden where they could place it on a drying rack. The largest branch of mistletoe would be used to replace the bunch currently hanging over the door of the stable, protecting Bogaine's horses for another year. The remainder would become decorations for the Yuclog Celebration, which helped mark the beginning of the new year.

"So, what's next?" he asked as they walked in that direction.

"Actually, this is the part that is always the worst for me

because we can't do anything else until dark," Parisa said. "My father and Uncle Olcan will get the bonfire ready, and Mama and Aunt Beibhinn will make sure the cartwheel is decorated. I usually help with making the torches but with so many adults here this year, they'll probably want us to go to the south pasture again and entertain ourselves until dinner time."

"We'll have lunch first though?"

Parisa giggled. Cian was always hungry. "I think I'm going to start calling you 'Bottomless Pit.'"

"I'm not that bad, am I?"

"Nearly!" she guffawed, and realized it felt good. It was the first time her heart had lightened since morning. She decided her plan was a good one. She would let the others keep her distracted until all their guests had left Bogaine. "But you're right," she said, "we will have lunch first. They are probably on their way to help fix it now." She nodded at Gittan's and Eluned's backs, ten yards or so in front of them.

Beibhinn and Chokhmah had already left to join Fianna in the kitchen at the big house, and Gittan and Eluned had followed behind to offer their help as well.

By the time they'd finished hanging up the mistletoe on the drying rack, lunch was being served on the picnic tables. Eating had become more casual over the past couple of days, and Parisa and Cian cobbled together some sandwiches for themselves, grabbed some apples, and headed over to what had become their regular spot—the bench under the eaves of the stable.

"I wish we could come up with a new game to play," Parisa said after swallowing the first bite of her sandwich. Suddenly she was ravenous.

"Why?"

"I'm getting so tired of the games we've been playing," she said, taking another bite.

"Me too," Cian agreed. "It's just that coming up with something that a seven-year-old can play just as well as a 13-year-old is difficult."

"Hmmm," Parisa mused while chewing. Fuchsia was small like her mother so it had to be something that wouldn't be too difficult or dangerous. Not to mention the fact that other than herself, all these kids were royalty and their parents probably wouldn't take kindly to them injuring themselves. You couldn't grow up on a farm and not get hurt once in a while. Parisa had learned to ignore minor cuts and bruises. Besides, her mother made some really good balms that soothed her injuries quickly.

She watched as her uncle guided a wheelbarrow full of wood along the path that led up the hill that overlooked the south pasture. It was the highest point on the farm and where they always built their bonfires. Taking another bite of her sandwich, she stared unseeingly at her uncle's back as it disappeared around a curve in the trail up the hill.

"What if . . ." she said, thinking.

"What if what?" Cian asked.

"There's six of us, right?"

"Yes."

"What if the three oldest, you, me, and Arianell, held the legs of the youngest, and they used their arms to race. You know, like we were pushing wheelbarrows and they were the wheelbarrows we are pushing?"

Cian looked confused, and Parisa knelt down on the ground in front of the bench. She looked over her shoulder. "Now hold my ankles."

Cian stood up and reluctantly bent over and grabbed Parisa by the ankles.

"Now stand up, still keeping hold of my ankles."

He did as he was told, leaving Parisa balanced on her arms.

"Now walk forward and I'll walk forward using my hands."

They had moved forward several steps before realizing the conversation had stopped at the picnic table.

"What are you doing?" Gittan was hurrying toward them. Cian let go of Parisa's ankles and she quickly folded her legs so that she was kneeling again. She stood up, brushing off her hands, then the knees of her breeches which had dust clinging to them.

"We were playing wheelbarrows," Parisa told his mother. "It worked," Cian was laughing. "It really worked."

"You just have to be careful with whomever you're wheeling," Parisa said. "You wouldn't want to push them faster than they could go because they could hurt themselves."

"Well, we'd definitely need to practice before we had races," Cian said.

"You'll do no such thing," Gittan said.

"Why?" Cian asked

"Someone will get hurt," she said.

"You've obviously never seen Arianell play Battledore," Cian said.

"Or Madoc playing sack toss," Parisa added.

"Or Rhodri playing ground billiards," chimed in Arianell, who had now joined them.

"Or you, playing statues," Parisa laughed, slapping Cian on the back gently. He went out of his way to come up with difficult stances and had overbalanced himself on more than one occasion.

"Besides, Mother," Cian reasoned, "you all trust us enough to send us out to the south pasture every day, alone, to … what does Uncle Bryan always say? Expend our reserves of energy? For all you know, we could be torturing each other down there."

Gittan regarded her son for a moment, then shrugged. "Fine," she said, "but don't come crying to us if you hurt yourselves."

Cian rolled his eyes and bit into his apple, clearly dismissing his mother.

"Teenagers," Gittan said, shaking her head, and sending a meaningful glance to Chokhmah who stood nearby watching with interest, as if to say, 'see what you have to look forward to.'

THE SUN WAS FINALLY SETTING, and adults and children alike were gathered at the stable following their traditional Gulivan meal: salmon with vegetables straight from their garden, grilled over hot coals. There was also fruit from the Bogaine orchard and honey cakes. Even the children had been allowed a thimbleful of the honeyed mead the adults were enjoying.

Next, they lined up by family with their torches. The youngest children, Gavreel, Enfys, and Eiriol, were holding candles with bobeches because the torches had seemed too dangerous to entrust them with.

Because Olcan was the oldest, he and his family were first in the procession, followed by his children and their families, and then, because they were guests, Eluned and Uriel, Gittan, Bryan and their families. Faolan, Chokhmah, and Parisa brought up the rear, much to Parisa's chagrin. She'd rather be walking with Cian and Arianell. But if she had to be last, she pouted, she intended to be the very last.

She slowed her pace gradually and soon was a good twenty feet behind her parents. Chokhmah had also slowed as Faolan was busy chatting with Uriel and Bryan who were just ahead of him. Only the moon could see that two very troubled females trailed behind the procession.

Chokhmah stopped and waited for her daughter to catch up. "How are you doing?" she asked once Parisa arrived.

"It'll be easier once we get to the bonfire," Parisa said. "I just don't even know what to say to Papa anymore."

"Hmmm," her mother said, wrapping an arm around Parisa's shoulders, "that would be true for both of us."

"What are we going to do, Mama?" Parisa asked, glancing ahead to make sure her father was still occupied.

"I do not yet know, my love," Chokhmah sighed, "but believe me, it has consumed my every waking thought."

Parisa slipped her left arm around her mother's waist, and they walked in silence the rest of the way up the hill. The flickering of the torchlight cast shadows across their faces, hiding, then revealing, the despair etched there.

Once atop the hill and gathered around the pile of wood that would become that year's bonfire, Olcan explained what would happen. First, they would light the fire using a couple of charred logs from the previous year as well as nine different kinds of wood from around Bogaine. As soon as the fire was burning brightly, they would light the cartwheel, which was swathed in straw.

Then Olcan picked up his pipe from the instruments that had been placed there earlier, Faolan retrieved his drum, and Beibhinn her tympanon. Heart in her throat, Parisa took her mother's hand, and they stepped forward with Fianna and Conall to sing the traditional song of summer solstice in the ancient tongue of Dyfed.

The fire was now blazing, flames reaching hungrily for the heavens. Olcan took his torch, while Faolan held the wheel. The next step had to be done quickly to prevent Faolan from burning his hands, but he had a lot of practice and the wheel lit quickly and was soon rolling down the south side of the hill toward the pasture where the children had played earlier that day.

All the games had been moved aside so they would not interfere with the cartwheel's progress. Everyone watched, holding their breath, as the cartwheel, still burning, made it to the center of the pasture before losing momentum and falling over. The thick, damp, grass there prevented the fire from spreading, and soon the flames flickered out.

A collective sigh of appreciation escaped the crowd as they turned back to the bonfire. According to the tradition, they could expect a good harvest that year.

Instruments were once again picked up, and the group sang and danced to the music, quenching their thirst with more mead and ale, well into the night. There was watered down ale and lemonade for the children and they sang and danced and played alongside the adults. One by one the youngest children curled up into the waiting blankets and drifted off to sleep. About midnight, the families made their way back to their waiting beds and cots.

Before Parisa pulled her woolen blanket up, she slid a hand under her pillow. Despite what she had asked of her mother, she just couldn't risk falling asleep without knowing that the mistletoe she had stashed under her pillow was still there. She felt the little sprig just where she left it and breathed a sigh of relief. Before she drifted off to sleep, she said a quick prayer to Omni, asking that she dream of good omens that night— omens of hope and reconciliation.

CHOKHMAH

Chokhmah sat up in bed, listening. The house was completely silent. Eluned, Uriel, and Gavreel must still be sleeping. Faolan had never made it back to the cottage as he, Bryan, and Bryn had remained behind with the fire to make sure it was thoroughly extinguished before returning. She was pretty sure that was "man speak" masking the fact that they wanted to continue drinking without the 'worrisome women' around.

Omni only knew what Faolan would say about them when he was fully in his cups, she thought, shaking her head in annoyance. Fortunately, Bryn was leaving today and Bryan in a couple more. She was sure Eluned would set him straight if need be. She got out of bed and quickly pulled on a linen dress of forest green and her leather boots. If she hurried, she could go say her morning prayers in the chapel before the others were awake.

She had always been the earliest riser in this household with the rare exception of her daughter, although if Parisa woke up early, she usually stayed in her room reading or writing in her journal until she heard her parents moving around.

On the way out, Chokhmah grabbed a woolen shawl the color of autumn leaves from a hook by the door and wrapped it around her shoulders. It was still a little chilly in the mornings, and the chapel would probably be cold as well.

She stepped out into the morning stillness, enjoying the silence of the world. The air was almost eerily quiet as if even the birds had decided to sleep in. She could still smell the smoke of the previous night's bonfire, the odor trapped by the low-lying clouds. They would probably have rain later.

Chokhmah pulled the shawl more closely around her and hurried down the path to the chapel, wondering where her husband had ended up. Was he still up on the hill, passed out in the grass? Or had he made it the stable and curled up in the straw there. To give him some credit, he might have done that very thing in order to not risk waking her up. Either way, she was not sure she wanted to know.

She had just shut the door to the chapel, quietly so as not to disturb the stillness, and was beginning to walk towards her regular pew when she realized she was not the only person there.

In the early morning light, she could see someone kneeling near the front of the small chapel. She would recognize that bowed head anywhere. What was Parisa doing here?

"Darling?" she said, sliding into the pew to sit beside her daughter.

Parisa turned a tear-stained face toward her mother, eyes swollen and puffy, even her lips were swollen.

Chokhmah gasped and pulled her daughter into her arms. "Oh, my love! What has happened?"

"Did you dream last night, Mama?"

Her mother paused, thinking, then shook her head. "No, I do not remember a single dream." She had fallen into an exhausted sleep as soon as her head hit the pillow and slept soundly until morning.

"I did," Parisa's voice hitched as she held back a sob, and she tugged hard on her braid as if it might help her regain some control over her emotions.

"And your dream upset you?"

"Mama, I dreamed that I could see you through a window sitting on a throne. You had a beautiful crown on your head. It was gold and had pearls and diamonds and . . ." Parisa trailed off.

"And?"

Parisa blew her nose into her handkerchief, cleared her throat, and continued, "And on the front of the crown, in the center, was a black-enameled kraken carved into an enormous ruby."

"The sigil of Pelf," Chokhmah shivered, gooseflesh raising along her arms.

"But what was weird," Parisa continued, "is that the sigil changed while I was watching. It morphed from a black kraken on a ruby into two dolphins, kind of entwined. One was black and one was white, and the jewel became a sapphire."

"That's interesting," Chokhmah mused. What could that mean?

"There's more," Parisa choked. "I was flying. And there was a raven flying with me. That means . . ."

"You are the white wolf," Chokhmah whispered. And you have inherited my gift for prophetic dreams, she thought, but did not say. "I did not see my crown. What did the window look like?"

"You were in a tower room with rounded walls, but it was a square window."

Chokhmah nodded. Yes, that was what she had seen. "Did you see the throne?"

"It looked simple. Maybe not the main one? It had a high back, higher than your head, and it seemed to be covered in red velvet. Your hands were in your lap and you looked happy or content, not sad like you do most of the time now."

"Yes," Chokhmah said. "That is exactly how I dreamed it." She had told no one those details and she certainly had not described a crown she could not see. She paused to think. "What was I wearing?" she asked.

"It was a gold brocade dress with long sleeves, and your hair was in two braids that were braided with gold ribbons."

"Well, there is no denying the fact that we dreamed of the same place," Chokhmah said. "Were we in a castle?"

"Yes! Wow!" Parisa could not help but enthuse. "It was beautiful! And huge. And it was on a cliff above the ocean."

Exactly what Jabberwock had told her about Zhaleh Palace. Parisa fell silent again, and another tear slid down her face. "Mama, does this mean we're going to Pelf? Do we have to leave Bogaine?"

"I do not know, my darling," Chokhmah admitted. "I do not see how that is possible. But I have never before dreamed like this nor has anyone ever shared a dream of mine. We will not make any rash decisions, though, that I can promise you."

"Thank you, Mama," Parisa sniffed.

"Shall you join me in prayers? I believe we are desperately in need of them." Parisa held out her hand and her mother handed her a prayer book.

AFTER THEIR MORNING PRAYERS, Parisa and her mother returned to Rose Cottage where Chokhmah brewed them a restorative cup of tea.

"It's so quiet," Parisa whispered as they sipped together in silence.

"It is nice, is it not?"

"Yes," Parisa agreed. Normally, mornings were filled with sound, Chokhmah reflected. She would be preparing breakfast, and Faolan would be telling Parisa what chores he expected her to do, and then together they would arrange whatever school lessons Parisa would have during the day.

And, of course, her daughter would be chattering away at them about whatever was currently on her mind, from what she had dreamed the previous night to talking about whatever book she was reading at the time.

Things were always more normal in the morning, Chokhmah thought. It was after dinner that her husband would get angry. She had come to learn that the more he had had to drink on a particular night directly affected just how easily irritated he would get.

It had not taken Parisa long to learn to retreat to her room on the nights he was drinking heavily, and that deeply saddened her. Chokhmah had explained to Parisa early on that her father drank at night because by the end of the day his leg often pained him. Unfortunately, over the years, it began to take more and more alcohol to relieve the pain.

She had offered to brew him some teas that would help him control the pain, and when Parisa was younger, he was more open to it. It was only in the past few years that he had begun turning more and more frequently to alcohol, and she had long since lost any say over how much he drank. She had even found bottles hidden in places she suspected Faolan did not know she was aware of.

It was nice right now, the quiet, and sitting here sipping tea with her child. And that caused her great sorrow, as well. What she would not do to go back to those early years when she had no expectation that things could get so bad that her husband, Parisa's father, no longer enjoyed being part of their lives.

A hearty "good morning!" startled Chokhmah from her reverie.

She turned to see Uriel in the doorway, Gavreel by his side. "I am sorry," she stood up, "I did not hear you get up."

"No problem," Uriel said, pulling out a chair, "Gavreel was awake and I wanted to give Eluned a little more time to sleep, so we went for a walk."

"Did you see my father?" Parisa asked.

"No, is he not here?"

"He did not make it back last night," Chokhmah said. "Perhaps, he is still up on the hill. Were Bryn and Bryan in the tent when you left this morning, Parisa?"

Parisa's brow furrowed as she thought back. "No, now that I think of it, I don't think either of them were there."

"Well, I won't be disturbing their slumber," Uriel laughed. "If they're still on the hill, they're going to need as much sleep as possible."

"If who is on the hill?" Eluned asked from the doorway.

"Fy Drysor," Uriel said using his pet name for his wife, which meant 'my treasure'. "Did you get enough sleep?"

"Yes, I did." She kissed the top of his head and Gavreel's cheek. "Thank you so much."

"My father, and Bryan and Bryn spent the night on the hill," Parisa explained once Eluned was seated. "Mama, is there something I can do?"

"Yes, my dear, can you run over and check the tent? Make sure no one has awakened?"

Parisa looked put out but did her mother's bidding. When they heard the door shut behind her, Uriel asked, "Does Faolan often drink as much as he's been drinking while we've been here?"

Chokhmah's hand shook as she poured tea into their mugs, and she set the pot down and wiped up what she had spilled to give herself some time to control her emotions before turning to speak.

"I am afraid it has become all too common for him to drink himself senseless every night."

Uriel grimaced and Eluned looked stricken.

"Oh, Chokhmah," Eluned said, "I knew things were bad, but I didn't know they were that bad!"

"I am really at a loss as to what to do," she said, setting their mugs down in front of them. A jar of honey and a pitcher of cream were already on the table and she handed them spoons before turning back toward the stove to prepare breakfast. She started some bacon frying and began to crack eggs into a bowl. "Faolan seems unwilling to compromise," she added. "He wants to be gone six months out of the year. Period. I told him that every other month could work or even up to three months. It is just that this is a crucial time in Parisa's life. If he could only wait until she has experienced shifting. I am positive it will happen within the year."

"He has been harassing me daily about finding him a job," Uriel said. "I keep trying to stall him, but he is persistent, and I don't feel like I can flat out say no to him. We've been friends too long."

"So, he is determined, then," Chokhmah frowned. "Parisa will not be happy. Of course, already she is not happy. She . . ."

The front door slammed shut and they all jumped, looking at each other as if they had just committed some crime.

Parisa appeared in the doorway with Fuchsia. "Fuchsia was the only one awake, so I figured it was okay to bring her back here."

"Of course!" Eluned said, relief apparent on her face. "Come here, sweetheart." She held out her arms to her daughter.

Chokhmah breathed a sigh of relief and her heart returned to its normal rate, "Could you bring me a few more eggs, Parisa?" She asked, turning back to the bowl and adding some herbs to it. Things must be bad, she reflected, if just the thought of Faolan entering unannounced set their hearts to racing.

ONCE AGAIN SITTING IN THE QUIET OF THE CHAPEL, the light quickly disappearing as the sun dropped below the horizon, Chokhmah weighed her options. The easiest thing to do would be to just give up. Let Faolan find the dream job that would take him away from his family for half a year and leave her and Parisa to carry on at Bogaine. She would have Olcan and Beibhinn and even Conall and Bledwen to help her when needed. Conall had been building a cottage about a quarter of a mile from his father's house alongside Coldwater Creek and expected to finish it that summer. Meanwhile, he and his bride would live with his parents.

She did not understand why she was so resistant to a solution that involved dependency on Olcan and his family. Chokhmah sighed. If she were being completely honest with herself, she would just admit that despite the fact they had always treated her like she was one of the family, she had always felt they only did so for Faolan's sake.

Growing up Roma had accustomed her to that feeling of separateness. And that feeling always made it more difficult for her to fully participate in any of their traditional celebrations. She feared that if left alone here for months on end, that feeling would grow. It was not in her to be needy, and if Faolan were gone, would she and Parisa become a burden to the family? It was different before they were married. When Faolan was gone, there were no extra mouths to feed. Now there were two. She could return to her gypsy family. She had no doubt they would take her in but knowing that she was, by birth, pure Pelfan, and Roma only by name, weighed heavily on her. And, once again, she would be giving them two more mouths to feed.

And then there was the dream that she and Parisa shared. But she could not return to Pelf and rule that kingdom. First, and most importantly, she knew nothing about managing a kingdom. All the rulers in the Thirteen Kingdoms had been born into royalty and taught from birth what they needed to know, even the children who might never reign over a kingdom. Secondly, she would feel really guilty about removing Leleua and Raynor. They had been on the throne for four years now. They had children, twin daughters and a son, who were being raised in Zhaleh Palace. It was such a dilemma.

Chokhmah shook her head and picked up her prayer book. She should hurry. Tomorrow was the last full day Eluned and her family would be here, and she needed to spend the remaining time with them. She felt sure that Faolan, who had finally shown up about lunchtime, was currently badgering poor Gwrhyr about a position that would have him traveling for the Kingdom of Aden. What he did not know was that Gwrhyr had admitted to her that he had nothing that he felt Faolan had the competence to do, and Eluned had grudgingly agreed to talk to Gittan about something with Dyfed.

Chokhmah had just opened her prayer book and was kneeling to pray when the chapel door opened. She cringed, worried that it might be Faolan, but when she turned to look it was Eluned walking up the short aisle.

"I've been talking to Uriel," her friend said, sitting down next to her.

"Yes?"

"And he agrees with me."

Chokhmah chuckled. "He often agrees with you."

Eluned laughed. "That's true. Anyway, we both agree that no matter what your end decision is, you and Parisa need to get away from Faolan for a while. It is hard to think clearly when things around you are falling apart."

"Yes," Chokhmah nodded, "it makes a certain sense."

"And so, we want you two to return to Ponike with us. We have plenty of room at Castle Bennu and you can stay as long as you need to."

"I accept," Chokhmah said, as it seemed like the perfect solution for the current situation. "Now comes the difficult part."

"Telling Parisa?"

"No, I think she will feel a sense of relief as it will forestall a permanent decision," Chokhmah said. "No. I think the difficulty will be in explaining to Faolan why this is necessary."

"Perhaps," Eluned said, "But Gittan says she has an ambassador in Sigwald who is pregnant, and she and her husband would like to come home and have the baby here in Dyfed. She is willing to ask her father if Faolan can take on that post temporarily, up to six months, and see how he does. We could send a pigeon tonight."

Chokhmah nodded, considering. She doubted he would say no as he was familiar with the language. It had been quite ironic that they had been commissioned to steal the treasure in Simoon and he had spent most of his time there as a wolf, unable to speak.

"If they both agree," Eluned continued, "he could travel with us to Portuma, be briefed by my uncle on what would be required of him and sail on from there to Arberth."

"Before traveling north to Simoon," Chokhmah added, thinking aloud. She and Eluned had spent nearly three months at Castle Emrys in Arberth. Yona, and Jabberwock, and even Bonpo had been there until they managed to help the latter escape. They had saved his life that time. "Well, he will get to see Castle Emrys, even if from afar. I have told him so much about our time there."

"I wonder if Queen Morrighan is there now," Eluned mused. "I imagine Annewven is a huge change for Prince Huang. Dziron is so much different!"

It brought them both a certain happiness that Morrighan, King Arawn's illegitimate daughter, had been allowed to marry Princess Xiang's brother. Eluned had spent much time with Xiang before the chess tournament in Tartessos and the redistribution of the Hallowed Treasures. She had shared those adventures with Chokhmah, and they both agreed that it must have been a love match as alliances were no longer quite as necessary as they once had been when the Kingdoms were threatened by war.

Morrighan, despite the fact her evil father was still imprisoned in the dungeons at Iqbal Palace in Tartessos, had outgrown her teenage immaturity to become quite the young aristocrat. Eluned had told Chokhmah that she had been pleased to spend more time with her during the Year V meeting in Zion. She'd been so impressed that she had been the one to recommend that Morrighan and her husband take over the rule of Annewven in Year X so that Prince Aahil and his family could return to Tarshish.

"But if Faolan accepts, then it will not be necessary for us to go to Ponike," Chokhmah said, feeling disappointed.

"I don't know about that," Eluned said. "Wouldn't staying here just remind you of Faolan? Besides, I'm being selfish. I want you to come spend some time at Castle Bennu. You've never been there, and I've always wanted you to see it. Now seems as good a time as any, right?"

Chokhmah sat in silence a moment, thinking. Eluned was right. At this point, getting away from Bogaine seemed just as important for her and Parisa's mental health as Faolan claimed it was for his.

"Well," Chokhmah stood, after replacing the prayer book, "I suppose we should go and send your uncle a pigeon so that we can discuss this with Faolan and Parisa first thing in the morning." She had no doubt that Faolan would jump at the chance, but how would Parisa react knowing her father was happy to head off without them. Perhaps knowing Faolan would not be at Rose Cottage would make her daughter more amenable to traveling to the Kingdom of Aden. But would getting his way really solve all of Faolan's discontent? What was really at the root of his need to get away from them?

After breakfast the next morning, while Eluned, Uriel, and Gittan took Faolan aside in the kitchen of Rose Cottage to discuss the possible ambassador role, which King Cian had agreed to, Chokhmah took Parisa to the chapel.

"Well, there's no way he's going to turn that down," Parisa rolled her eyes when her mother told her about the offer that was being made to her father. "But hopefully he'll feel at least a little bit guilty about it." Her tone made it clear how very much she doubted that. "So, we will be staying here until he gets back, I guess."

"We do not have to do so," Chokhmah said.

Parisa looked alarmed. "Wuh, um, we're not going to Pelf, are we?"

"No, of course not," Chokhmah assured her. "But Eluned has graciously invited us to travel back to Ponike with them. She says we can stay with them at Castle Bennu for as long as we like."

"Will we be there the whole six months?"

"We do not have to be," her mother said. "We can return home whenever we feel ready to do so. I thought it might be nice to be away from here in the beginning, anyway, in light of the fact it might make your father being gone seem not quite as, I do not know, obvious?"

Parisa nodded. "I guess it would feel kind of weird to be at   Rose Cottage without Papa there. Even being here at Bogaine would seem kind of strange, wouldn't it? Besides if he is going to be gone either way, I would love to have the chance to visit another kingdom and stay in a castle."

Chokhmah stood. "Then I suggest we start packing. We leave tomorrow."

Parisa

He didn't have to seem so damn jubilant about it, Parisa glowered at her father's back. She was riding in the wagon with the rest of the kids and her mother, who had offered to do so in order that Gittan might have a chance to discuss the ambassador's job with Faolan. She glanced at her mother, who seemed to be wiping away a tear. She noticed Parisa looking at her and managed a sad smile.

Parisa shook her head, frowning, and then turned to answer a question Cian had just asked her. He and Arianell had been beyond delighted to find out that Parisa would travel with them back to Castle Abbert and stay there a few days before they left for Ponike.

Her father would sail in the opposite direction on his way to the Kingdom of Simoon. Parisa hoped he would leave before they did so she could conveniently disappear and avoid the goodbyes. The depth of her anger at her father sometimes caught her off guard but she couldn't seem to tamp it down. She pulled hard on her braid a couple of times to clear her head. She needed to concentrate on Cian and the others and let them keep her thoughts from drifting.

Cian was asking about her favorite weapon, and she had to admit that other than throwing rocks, she'd never really had the chance to try anything else. In addition to reading, spelling, and writing, her mother had focused her learning on herbs and other plants and what they could be used for. Horses and history and some science had been her father's forte. Olcan had taught her arithmetic, and Beibhinn basic domestic skills. And both her father and Olcan had taught her about horses and other farm-related things. But weapons? They hadn't really needed them as it was easy enough for Faolan and Olcan, and Conall when he was older, to shift and hunt as a wolf, if they had a taste for venison. Any other animals they slaughtered for meat usually just had their throats slit because pretty much all the parts of the animals were used.

The truth was she had created her own weapon, a sling, and had practiced with it whenever she was practicing throwing rocks. She'd become quite adept and so far, hadn't been caught with it. It was tucked away in her travel bag along with Echo. There was no way she could leave her beloved doll behind despite the fact it had become rather worn and raggedy.

"Girls aren't supposed to use weapons," Arianell said.

"What?" Parisa and Fuchsia exclaimed simultaneously.

"Curses," shouted Cian and the two girls quickly flashed the sign to ward off evil.

"Why should not girls use weapons?" Chokmah asked.

"Yes," said Eluned who had reined in her horse, a beautiful gelding whose hair was as black as hers, to wait for the wagon to catch up to her so she could check on her children. "Why can't girls use weapons?"

"Because," Arianell said, her fair cheeks coloring, "it's a boy thing?"

"Gittan," Eluned shouted, "have you taught your daughter that girls shouldn't use weapons?"

Gittan stopped her horse and looked over her shoulder. "Have I what?"

"Told your daughter that females shouldn't use weapons?"

Gittan snorted and her green eyes sparkled. "Me? No. Sounds like I need to have a talk with Cadfael." She nudged her horse and started moving forward again.

Cian laughed out loud, "Uh oh, father is in trouble."

Gittan eyed her brother. "Unless it was you?"

"No. Absolutely not," Bryan shook his head. "I would never say something like that to your children. Right, Aria?"

"It was Grandfather," Arianell said, defensively.

Gittan and Bryan guffawed, and Eluned chuckled. "Of course it was," she said. "Don't listen to him, Aria. Women are perfectly capable of not only using weapons but becoming quite proficient at it. My friend, Yona, actually made her living for a while as an archer."

"And," Uriel said, who was following behind the wagon. "Eluned is quite the swords, uh, person."

"And Parisa is pretty good at throwing rocks," Cian said.

"Pretty good?" Parisa punched him in the arm. "I'm amazing."

"Yes, you are my love," Chokhmah smiled at her daughter, glancing at Faolan's back. Parisa followed her mother's eyes. Her father was riding at the front of the group now. It hadn't escaped her notice that not only had her father not participated in that conversation, he hadn't even slowed down to listen to it.

Parisa shook her head again, this time in disbelief, and turned back to Cian, "Anyway, why do you ask?"

"Just curious, I guess."

"What about you?"

"I've been learning to use the crossbow. I really like it," he said.

"Maybe you can show me while we're there," Parisa said.

"I'd be happy to," Cian smiled.

"My mother is teaching me how to defend myself with a sword," Fuchsia bragged.

"A real sword?" Cian seemed impressed.

"Not yet," Fuchsia admitted, "real swords are heavy. My Daddy had one made for me that I could hold."

"Well, I'll definitely have to see that," Parisa said. "I have no idea how to handle a sword."

Fuchsia clapped her hands together. "I'm so glad you're coming home with us, Parisa."

Parisa smiled back at the little girl. It felt nice to be wanted.

ABOUT HALF AN HOUR BEFORE NOON, they stopped for an early lunch at The Hound and Hare in the small town of Cellabega.

"This is where we stayed on the way to Bogaine," Cian told Parisa. "I doubt we'll stay long, though, because my mother said they want to make it as far as Errigal tonight so we can get home before lunch tomorrow. But, fortunately, their food is excellent."

Parisa had been to Cellabega a few times, although they usually went to Thírnagall if they needed to go to a town. She had never eaten at the Inn, though. It cost a little more than they could afford.

Of course, now she was traveling with royalty and they probably didn't worry about the cost of their food.

A private dining room had been prepared for their party of thirteen. As soon as they were seated, plates were placed in front of them. Parisa was still overwhelmed by the large oaken dining table and upholstered chairs they were seated in. She picked up a silver fork and looked at it wonderingly. Most of their utensils had been carved from wood.

No wonder her mother had made her clothe herself in one of her better dresses this morning. The herringbone-woven linen was the color of moss and was very soft. She liked the dress a lot, but it suddenly seemed very old fashioned. They had only packed her nicest clothes for this trip. And her leather breeches, as she knew that she would be allowed to wear them at Castle Bennu.

Parisa looked down at her plate where a fileted and sautéed river trout sat on a bed of lettuce alongside some green beans and mashed potatoes topped with a pat of butter.

Her stomach rumbled, and next to her, Cian snickered. "I'm hungry," she whispered.

"Shall I give thanks?" Chokhmah asked.

"Yes, thank you," Eluned said.

"Omni be with you," she said.

"And also with you," everyone responded before bowing their heads.

"Thank You, Omni, for this food. For rest and home and all things good. For wind and rain and sun above. But most of all for those we love. Amen."

"Amen."

For the next ten minutes or so, only the sound of implements scraping plates and the murmur of quiet conversation broke the silence.

"This is really good trout," Parisa said to Cian.

"It is, isn't it." he agreed.

Less than half an hour later, they were climbing back into the wagon to begin the trek to Errigal, a village on the Abbert River. The village had only one hotel, the Riverview Inn, and Cian didn't know anything about it.

"Honestly," he told Parisa, "I barely remember traveling through that village."

Parisa didn't think that sounded very promising but she kept her opinion to herself. It wasn't long before most of the children had nodded off, the summer sun and their full bellies, despite the bumpy ride, induced somnolence. Even Chokhmah dozed off and on, startling awake when they hit a particularly bad bump in the dirt track.

They arrived in Errigal in the late afternoon and pulled into the courtyard of the Riverview Inn. Like the village it was small.

While Uriel and Bryan went in to check on their rooms, the kids and adults stretched their legs in the courtyard, which was dusty and bare. Fortunately, the men weren't gone long.

"They don't have many rooms," Uriel informed them, "so we will be sleeping in family units. Also, each room has only two single beds in it, so they are putting an extra cot in each room. Well, two in ours."

"Someday I'll get to sleep in a real bed again," Parisa groused to Cian.

"Tomorrow, I promise," he said. "We have good beds at Castle Abbert."

Parisa smiled. Yet another thing to which she could look forward. The list kept growing.

Once settled in their rooms, the road weary travelers washed some of the grime of the day away before meeting back downstairs for an early dinner. The plan was to settle down for the night on the early side so it would be easier to get up and get going in the morning.

While her mother washed up, she asked her father about his job, begrudgingly, but he didn't seem to notice. Actually, he seemed pleased that she had asked.

"Basically, I'll be Dyfed's representative in Simoon. I'll be there to help any visitors or tradesmen from Dyfed that run into problems while in that Kingdom. It will be that sort of thing. I'll learn more what King Cian wants when I talk to him tomorrow."

Parisa nodded her head as if interested, but honestly, it sounded quite dull to her. That was the reason he was leaving them for at least six months?

She wondered how many more nights she would have with her father around. She wasn't sure that this was a good time for the three of them to be stuck in one room together, considering how angry and hurt she and her mother felt, but she would do her best not to antagonize him.

"Well, at least we'll have a chance to visit another kingdom while you're gone," Parisa said. "Hopefully, that will make it easier not having you around."

"You know, if I end up doing this again next year, you and your mother could go visit Njima and Yona in Naphtali. Your mother actually has connections all over the Thirteen Kingdoms—in Sheba, Favonia, and wherever her family happens to be."

"That's not a bad idea," she said, inwardly aghast that his plan involved shuttling them off to whomever would take them during the times he was away. Did that mean they weren't really wanted at Bogaine? The thought they might be seen as unwelcome guests horrified her.

The door to the bathroom opened and Parisa jumped up from her cot. "My turn," she called hurrying into the room as her mother was vacating it. She wasn't sure how much longer she could hold it together.

The cold water she splashed on her face and neck was soothing, and as her heart rate slowed, she took her mother's advice and tried breathing slowly and deeply. "Omni within, Omni without" she whispered as she inhaled and exhaled. It only took a few breaths to regain her control. A final deep breath, and she turned the knob on the door, and stepped back into the room.

Her mother was removing their bedclothes from their bags while her father told her what he and Gittan had talked about while traveling that day—mostly the arrangements for returning the two Bogaine horses that she and Faolan were riding.

"I hope the food isn't as bad as these beds," Parisa joked, sitting down on her cot, as her father took his turn in the bathroom. It might be more comfortable to sleep on the floor, she mused.

Chokhmah chuckled. "Certainly things do not bode well for that, do they?"

"Well, at least we had a really good lunch," Parisa said.

"Yes, it was excellent, wasn't it?"

"But I guess you've had the chance to eat in places like that lots of times, huh?"

"Yes, I have," Chokhmah agreed. "Thanks to Eluned and the time it took to gather the Thirteen Hallowed Treasures, I have experienced a lot more than I might have otherwise. I would not even have you if it had not been for the Quest."

"That's a scary thought," Parisa shuddered. Life might be difficult right now because of her father, but she didn't like the idea of never having had the chance to exist at all.

"Yes, it is," her mother said. "I cannot imagine my life without you."

The door to the bathroom opened and Faolan stepped into the room. "Ready for dinner?"

Parisa needn't have worried about that evening's meal. The beef stew with potatoes, carrots, and parsnips was both good and satisfying. And the hot brown bread was perfect for soaking up the rich broth of the stew. Parisa was also happy to see that her father confined himself to one mug of ale. There would be no shouting tonight, thank Omni.

IT WAS A VERY GROUCHY GROUP that set out shortly after sunrise the following day. Not a one of them had slept well. Whether a bed had been too hard, or a faucet had dripped all night, they all had a complaint. But Parisa thanked Omni that they hadn't stayed in the room with Bryan, Madoc, and Rhodri because she would take a hard bed over bed bugs any day.

They looked miserable, scratching at their red and swollen bites, and as soon as they arrived at the Castle, they were rushed off to make sure their clothes weren't contaminated—everything they had taken with them into the room, including themselves, had to be scoured clean. Parisa didn't see them again until the following day.

Parisa was given a room of her own with a connecting door to her parents' room. It was probably intended for people with younger children, but she didn't care. She was happy to have a room to herself and the knowledge that she would sleep in a decent bed that night did wonders for her mood.

There were two single beds in the room, and she tried them both before choosing the one on the right side of the window and furthest away from her parents' room. She lay atop the royal blue duvet for a moment, closing her eyes and enjoying the silence before getting up to see what the view from her window looked like.

Parisa realized why Gittan and Bryan had been so focused on the time of their arrival in Portuma as soon as they entered the port town. Located on a tidal island a half mile distant from the town in the Harbor of Lunatane, Castle Abbert clearly spent a good portion of the day separated from the town by water. During low tide, the castle could be reached by a graveled road. Otherwise, they would have had to load themselves, the horses, mules, and cart onto a ferry.

Parisa's room faced the Anoon Ocean and from her window she looked down on the some of the larger homes belonging to Dyfed's lords. It was all quite breathtaking—the sun glinting off the water, waves crashing against the rocky shore, the seagulls wheeling around the island, searching for scraps. She couldn't help but smile.

As her mother had directed her, Parisa removed her nicest dress from her bag. It was made of the same copper silk her mother had used to make her patchwork skirt, and had three-quarter length sleeves, a rounded neckline, and a fitted bodice that buttoned down the front. A band of pewter lace encircled the waist, and the full skirt fell to her ankles.

She smoothed it out the best she could as it was wrinkled from travel, but her mother told her they needed to get their travel begrimed clothing to the launderer that day so that her father could sail off with clean clothes.

There was a bathroom in her room, as Cian had promised, and she started a bath running while she undressed. Running water, she sighed. What a luxury. She was thankful that she didn't have to pump it herself like she had to do at Rose Cottage and at the Riverview Inn, which had not had a view of the river. And the water at Castle Abbert was hot.

She tossed her dirty clothes outside the door to the bathroom, shut the door, and stepped into the tub, settling into the water slowly as she got accustomed to its heat. There was a lavender scented shampoo on a table next to the tub, and she ducked her head beneath the water to get her hair wet before pouring a liberal amount into her palm and sudsing up her hair. Parisa sighed again, happy in the moment. In her humble opinion, this was heaven.

CHOKHMAH

Lunch in the dining room was a serve yourself buffet. Parisa chose a pasty filled with chicken and root vegetables, and Chokhmah nodded approvingly, and pointed to the fruit.

"What are these, Mama?" Parisa asked, holding up a couple of tangerines. "They look like baby oranges."

"Those are tangerines, my dear," Chokhmah said. "They are similar to oranges, but maybe a little sweeter. Try them. I am sure you will like them."

Chokhmah served herself some salad and added a small bunch of grapes to her plate.

They were the only ones in the dining room when they arrived but as they were sitting down, Eluned and her family joined them.

"Are your rooms to your liking?" Eluned asked, once seated.

"I love it," Parisa exclaimed. "The bed is perfect, the view is great, and the bath was wonderful." She pulled her braid to her nose and sniffed.

Chokhmah raised her eyebrows and Parisa laughed. "It still smells like lavender," she explained.

Chokhmah chuckled. "It is nice to no longer have to fight her about taking a bath.

Parisa blushed. "Mama, I haven't minded for years."

Chokhmah held up one finger. "Singular. Year."

"Well," she looked at Fuchsia, "it was a lot of trouble. I had to pump the water and heat it in the winter."

Fuchsia wrinkled her nose.

"My spoiled little girl," Eluned pinched Fuchsia's cheek. "We need to take her camping, Uriel."

Faolan laughed. "True. Camping can really help you learn to appreciate the finer things. Wait until you've been stuck in a wet tent for days."

"Or tried to start a fire when it's so cold you can barely move your fingers," Eluned added.

"Or having to relieve yourself when there is not a tree in sight and you're in the company of two women," Uriel said.

"Or having to cut your own trail and being so tired and sore you can barely hold your machete," Chokhmah said. "Or getting blisters on your hands and working until they bleed," Chokhmah looked pointedly at Eluned.

Eluned put her face in her hands. "I was so young and foolish," she groaned.

"Well, camping sounds perfectly horrible to me," Fuchsia said, picking up her chocolate chip cookie.

"She's got a point," Parisa said, laughing, "but there are times when it can be perfectly wonderful. Why don't we go camping when we get to Ponike? You've got to try it at least once, Fuchsia."

"Well, if you're going, maybe," she said, washing her cookie down with some milk.

Gittan arrived with her family and introduced Chokhmah, Faolan, and Parisa to her husband, Cadfael, and oldest son, Cadoc. As they left to serve their plates, Gittan told Faolan that as soon as he was done eating, her father wanted to speak with him.

"I'm finished," Faolan said, standing. Clearly, he had been nervous, Chokhmah thought, as he had only managed to eat a little soup. Was this post really that important to him?

He squeezed Chokhmah's right shoulder, and Parisa's left, simultaneously. "See you two later," he said, following Gittan out of the room.

"I'm sorry," Eluned said as soon as the door shut.

Chokhmah sighed. "I am so glad that we decided to travel on with you." The idea of being at Bogaine, and even more so, Rose Cottage, with all its memories, was more than she could bear.

"Why doesn't Papa want to be around us anymore, Mama?" Chokhmah, who was tucking Parisa into bed, looked at her, startled. Her father was still sequestered with the King and would set sail for Arberth early the next morning. They had eaten without him in the big dining room that night where they had met Queen Chelli and Bryan's wife, Gwendolyn. The two men had taken their meal in the room where they were meeting.

"Why do you say that?"

"Because when you were in the bathroom at the Riverview Inn, he was talking about you and me traveling to Naphtali and Favonia and other places while he is gone each year."

That was news to her. He was already thinking about continuing before he had even given the job a trial run. That was not promising.

"I do not think it has anything to do with us," Chokhmah said. "At least, that is my hope." His need to leave had to be something internal to him. She had thought they had a fine marriage, and they objectively had a wonderful child.

Parisa stared into space for a moment. "The only other reason I can think of is that he's completely written us off."

"I cannot believe that is true," her mother said. Six months away from his family would make him realize just how much he treasured them, right? But what if it did not change anything? What then?

"Will he come say goodbye to us?"

Her mother shook her head. "I cannot answer that. He has barely spoken to me since we departed for Portuma." There had been that shoulder squeeze at lunch, though. Perhaps he was feeling guilty?

It must be guilt, Chokhmah thought. "He must be feeling some guilt," she told her daughter. "Your father has gotten his way and now he feels bad for leaving us."

But where would he be six months from now? Would he miss them and decide to stay at Bogaine, or would this be everything he dreamed of and they would have to put up with his grouchiness for half a year until he left again?

There was a knock at the door and Chokhmah's heart leapt to her throat, whether with fear or hope, she could not tell.

"Come in," Chokhmah called out but there was a tremor in her voice.

The door opened and Eluned entered. "I just wanted to see if you two needed anything before we head to bed, ourselves." Chokhmah shook her head. "No, we are fine, thank you."

"Well, then," Eluned smiled, "sleep as late as you like. They'll serve you breakfast in the dining room whatever time you arrive."

"Even if it's lunchtime?" Parisa couldn't resist asking.

Eluned laughed. "Even if it's dinner time."

"Papa!"

Eluned turned to see Faolan standing behind her. "Well, I'll say my goodbyes to you now," she said. "I understand that you set sail at dawn. How about a hug?"

Faolan hugged her, then she ducked out the door, waving over her shoulder. "Goodnight. See you in the morning, you two."

Faolan stepped into the room. "I came to say goodbye, Parisa. I imagine you'll still be asleep when I leave in the morning."

Chokhmah stood and moved over to the adjoining door and opened it, but she didn't leave the room because she could see in Parisa's eyes that she didn't want to be left alone with her father.

Faolan sat down on the edge of his daughter's bed and pulled her into his arms.

"Will you miss me, Papa?" she asked.

"Of course I'll miss you," he said. "How could I not miss you?"

Parisa shot her mother a glance over his shoulder that made it clear what she thought of his saying that. If he would miss them then why leave? What she said was, "I'll miss you, too, Papa." Parisa pulled back and Faolan kissed her forehead before standing up.

"I love you darling," he said as he backed toward Chokhmah. "Please don't forget that."

"I love you, too, Papa," she said as her parents stepped through the door and closed it.

Chokhmah walked over to their bed and sat down on it and Faolan sat down next to her.

"I'm so sorry I'm doing this to you," he said, taking her hand in his. She lifted her other hand and put a finger to his lips.

"Let us not talk about it," she whispered. "It is done." She removed her hand and kissed the lips she had kissed so many times in the past fifteen years. She felt him respond to their pressure, and she pulled him against her as she lay back on the bed. Something told her that this would be her last time in his arms.

IT WAS STILL DARK when Faolan crawled out of bed and stumbled toward the bathroom in the dark to get ready for his trip. Chokhmah sat up in bed and reached for the nightgown that she had tucked under her pillow earlier. After pulling on her night clothes, she lit the candle on the nightstand. Then she walked over to Faolan's side of the bed and lit the candle there, too, before lighting the oil lamp on the dresser. Then she sat down in the armchair in front of the fireplace and waited. She had already packed his bag. When he came out of the bathroom, she stood up.

Faolan tucked a few things into his bag and then placed it before the door to the outer hallway, before returning to where Chokhmah stood waiting. He took her in his arms and leaned his forehead against hers.

How did she tell him? She still had not decided what to say. Before he left for Sigwald, he needed to understand that he had a decision to make in the next six months. Despite what he wanted, she did not want to depend on the kindness of loved ones and family for six months out of every year. Nor did she want him to absent himself from his daughter's life that long. She knew that he would argue that Olcan had done so successfully. But she was not Beibhinn and Parisa was not Fianna. They had both had the advantage of having family nearby, among other things. And yet, neither did she want to give him an ultimatum. That rarely turned out well for the one making the ultimatum. She sighed, inwardly, and kissed him one last time.

"Please keep in touch," he said.

"Let me know where you are lodging once you get there, and I will." She had a suspicion, though, that it would be quite a while before she heard from him again.

A tap at the door meant it was time to leave. Someone had arrived to take him to the ship.

Faolan rushed to the door and grabbed his bag. "I love

you," he said while opening it and stepping out into the hall-way, but he had shut the door before she had a chance to echo his sentiment.

It is just as well, she thought, as she blew out the lamp and snuffed out the candle on his bedside table, because I am no longer sure that what he feels for me, for us, is love. She got back in bed, pulled the duvet up, and blew out her candle, but she did not sleep again that morning. She, too, had a decision to make. How did she want their relationship to continue once the six months had passed?

Parisa

The days following her father's departure seemed to fly by for Parisa. She and Fuchsia sat with Arianell and her tutor, Mistress Chani, while the boys were at their lessons. Because Parisa was older than the other two girls and was ahead of them as far as history and arithmetic were concerned, she was happy to spend her time with the tutor working on literature as she had access to many more books at Castle Abbert than she had had at Bogaine.

Mistress Chani set her to work reading *Great Expectations*, an ancient book that Parisa found herself getting caught up in immediately. Because her time there was so short, she received permission to take the book to her room so she could finish it before she left. But, Mistress Chani said that she could only do that on the condition she wrote a book report on the tome.

Parisa had to admit that she had never done a book report.

"What if I don't finish it in time?" she asked after she'd been told.

"I prefer that you finish it," Mistress Chani said. "On your last day here, if you have or even if you haven't finished the book, you can write about Pip's expectations and whether or not you find them reasonable, and why."

Parisa nodded. That seemed fair. She had already read enough that morning to begin thinking about that question.

After lunch each day, she would meet Cian and they would practice with the crossbow together. Then, while he went and played team sports with his friends, she curled up in the library and read *Great Expectations* as she was determined to finish it before they left for Ponike.

In the late afternoon, she would go horseback riding with Cian and Arianell, who wanted to show her around their little island. On their second day out, they rounded up some swimming clothes and took her to a well-protected little cove with a sandy beach where they played in the water and built sandcastles, something else she had never experienced.

By the evening of their final day, Parisa got ready to leave Castle Abbert with not a little regret. She had really grown to like Cian, and after their farewell party that evening, they promised each other they would keep in touch. And they did so for a while, but the letters became more and more infrequent and within a few months, stopped altogether.

Parisa did finish *Great Expectations*, but never could decide whether or not Pip's expectations had been unrealistic. Yes, he wanted a lot for an orphaned boy of his station in life, but she could also understand why he did. Comparing her life at Bogaine to her several days at Castle Abbert had made her realize just how much the world had to offer.

Had she remained at Bogaine, Parisa might never have been the wiser. She probably would have settled down with someone who didn't mind her being a shapeshifter when she reached an appropriate age or, perhaps, she would have decided that she didn't mind being with another shapeshifter after all. Hard to know when she had yet to shift. Had Pip remained in Kent and never been introduced to Miss Havisham and Estella would his expectations have been different?

At any rate, she was looking forward to the library at Castle Bennu because Eluned had told her that they had a couple of books by the same author there—a book called Bleak House, which sounded intriguing by title alone, and another called Oliver Twist, which Eluned had told her was about another orphan. She wondered if there were a lot of orphans long ago or if it was just because Charles Dickens liked writing about them.

She was surprised the morning of their departure to find Cian dressed and ready to accompany them to the dock. They were leaving in near darkness, and she rode with him in the back of the luggage cart so that he wouldn't have to squeeze into the carriage, which was tight for four people, let alone six.

"I don't usually like being around girls," he admitted, "but there's something about you that makes it easy to talk to you."

"Thank you," Parisa said nonplussed. "I've never really had a chance to be around other kids, especially other kids around my age. I have to admit that I've had a lot more fun than I realized was possible. I'm going to miss you guys a lot, especially you and Arianell."

Cian took her hand in his, and they rode the remainder of the way in silence. Parisa thanked Omni that it was dark because she was sure her cheeks were flaming. She hadn't realized Cian liked her in that way. She thought she was just a buddy to him.

When they arrived at the dock, he kissed her cheek and said, "Don't forget to write." He was still standing there when she reached the top of the gangplank, and she waved.

"Goodbye," she called. "Don't forget to write me, either."

She turned to find her mother watching her. "It feels good, does it not?"

Parisa blushed. "What?"

"Being liked."

"Yeah," Parisa smiled back. "It kind of does."

PARISA HAD NO IDEA that sailing would feel so good. It was what flying probably felt like, she thought, or maybe flying in the rain because she could feel the ocean's spray in her face as well as the wind.

It didn't hurt that it was a beautiful day for sailing. Standing on the deck of the forecastle, the sun warmed her enough that the breeze didn't bother her. Her mother and Eluned lounged on the deck below her, in the shadow of the forecastle, so that they could keep Gavreel and Fuchsia out of harm's way.

They were sailing on King Uriel's personal brigantine, The Phoenix, which the couple and their children had used to sail from Ponike to Portuma. It only needed a small crew, but space was still limited. Although they would only have to spend one night on the ship, Parisa and her mother would have to share a bunk.

It was worth it though, she thought. She would have gladly slept on the deck if that had been allowed, but her mother thought it too dangerous. She'd even been allowed to wear her leather breeches today so that she could explore without worrying about messing up her clothes. It was definitely easier to descend and ascend ladders while in pants, she had thought that morning as she climbed the ladder to the forecastle.

Tomorrow, she would have to dress up a bit as they would be arriving at Castle Bennu, and all eyes would be on them as they made their way from the port in Ponike along the road that would take them up to the castle that sat on the plateau that towered more than a thousand feet above the harbor town.

Parisa was really excited about arriving at the castle as Eluned had promised her friend's daughter her own room and had told her that she could outfit it anyway she pleased.

"As long as you're going to be with us," Eluned had said, "you ought to make the room your own. I think it will help you settle in more quickly. You, too, Chokhmah. Your room at Rose Cottage seemed to have more of Faolan's touch than yours."

"It is true," her mother had said. "I moved in with him, but he was reluctant to change it much."

"Well, there's a certain irony to that, isn't there? I mean, considering that he's been straining at the leash for so long."

"You have a point," a shadow seemed to cross Chokhmah's face. "Perhaps, that was an alarm bell that I did not hear."

"Anyway," Eluned had changed the subject back to Castle Bennu. "You two should definitely decorate your rooms in whatever way that makes you feel most comfortable. Take advantage of being the guests of King Uriel."

Parisa's mind had been churning ever since. Back at Rose Cottage, her room had both grown with her and in some respects, had stayed the same. The plastered white walls had never been painted and she still had the same down comforter tucked into a faded pink duvet that she'd had as long as she could remember.

The things on her walls had changed from childhood drawings to a wreath she constructed out of vines, pinecones, found feathers, and favorite poems and quotes she had copied down using her best handwriting. She had drawn flowers and animals to decorate the borders of the paper. Although a painting that her mother had done before she was born—butterflies and dragonflies wheeling over a field of golden poppies—still held a place of honor in her room, she had not brought it with her because her mother said what they could carry with them had to be limited.

It would be there when she got back, she thought, assuming they ever went back to Bogaine. She was beginning to think that that choice would be left to her father. Parisa would have liked to know more about what was on her mother's mind, but when she had tried to broach the subject after her father had departed, all her mother would say is, "I am not prepared to speak about it right now."

Parisa wondered if their last night together had been really bad, but she had fallen asleep, exhausted from her lack of sleep the previous night and the final leg of their journey to Castle Abbert, not to mention the stress created by her father's leaving them. All she knew is that she had not been awakened by her father yelling at her mother.

Her mother calling her to lunch brought Parisa back to the present, and she hurried down the ladder to where a picnic lunch had been spread on the lower deck.

THE NEXT MORNING as The Phoenix sailed into the Gulf of Eudaemon toward the bay that sheltered Ponike, Uriel stood by Parisa on the deck of the forecastle.

"You seem to really enjoy sailing," he said.

"I love it," she enthused.

"It's not always fair weather, you know. Even the hardiest sailor can get a little green around the gills when a storm hits."

"No one ever gets used to it?"

"I think some people are better adapted to sea travel than others," he said. "You may be one of those people."

"I'd certainly love to learn more about sailing," she said.

"That can probably be arranged," Uriel said. "See that island," he pointed.

Parisa nodded.

"That's Khamsa Island. Look closely when we pass, and you might see some seals."

Parisa was looking so hard for seals that Uriel had to tap her on the shoulder to get her attention. He pointed again, and Parisa mirrored Eluned's reaction when she first saw Castle Bennu. Perched high above Ponike, the polished grey and white granite edifice sparkled in the morning light.

"That's where we're going?"

Uriel grinned. "That's Castle Bennu."

Golden banners bearing the Crimson Phoenix that was the sigil of the Kingdom hung from each tower and trembled in the slight breeze.

Parisa was speechless. That was going to be her home for the next six months? She'd thought Castle Abbert had been amazing, but Uriel's castle literally glittered. It was breathtaking. And he had said she could learn to sail. Living here would be like a dream come true. Too bad she wouldn't be able to tell her father about it. Maybe she could keep a special journal just for him that he could read when she saw him next. Certainly, she thought, they would all be back at Bogaine in time for Yuclog.

Once they arrived at the dock, they waited for their luggage to be loaded into a wagon before they disembarked and climbed into a waiting carriage. She sat down on a bench with her mother and Fuchsia, and watched with awe as they made their way along a road that was crowded with the citizens of Ponike who were eager for a chance to see their King and Queen. She tugged on her braid, anxiously, until her mother placed her hand on hers, and shook her head.

Everything had been so casual at Bogaine, and the trip to Castle Abbert had been low key as well, perhaps because Bryan and Gittan didn't want to draw attention to themselves. But, having just spent more than a week with royalty from princes and princesses to kings and queens, Parisa knew that they were just as human as the people lining the streets.

And yet. And yet, what King Uriel and Queen Eluned represented to the people of Ponike was obviously very important. It seemed as if they were the focus for the Kingdom of Aden's national identity, their unity and their pride; that these two people and their children gave the kingdom a sense of stability and continuity because they were so clearly beloved.

It was something she'd never really thought about while at Bogaine.

King Cian and Queen Chelli just were. Parisa hadn't really thought of them one way or the other caught up as she was in her own little world. How much could change in such a short amount of time. Is this what it would be like for them if her mother were Queen of Pelf? She glanced at her mother who was watching her reaction.

"It is almost overwhelming is it not?" Chokhmah said.

Parisa nodded. And she had thought there had been a lot of people at Bogaine.

"Is it always like this?" she asked Fuchsia.

"Yes, pretty much," Fuchsia said, and continued waving.

"You know," Eluned leaned forward to be heard over the noise of the crowd hailing the royal family as the carriage passed, "you two can wave as well. Technically, you are both royal."

Parisa grinned and looked at her mother. "Can I, Mama?"

Chokhmah smiled back. "Yes, my dear, why not?"

Parisa flung her braid over her shoulder, sat up straighter, and mimicking Eluned, began to wave. They don't know I'm a princess, she thought, smiling, but would they assume that she was? For the first time in her twelve years, Parisa thought she might actually like to be a princess.

Once at the castle, a lady's maid led them to their new quarters. Eluned had sent a pigeon from Castle Abbert, directing the staff to prepare the two rooms she thought would suit her friends the best.

The Queen had selected two rooms that had an adjoining door so that Chokhmah could be as near to her daughter as possible while still allowing her some privacy.

The rooms, Eluned told them, were very basic, but they were larger than Parisa could have imagined. They were also far from basic—a queen-sized four-poster bed with a nightstand, an armoire for her hanging clothes, a small dresser, a desk and chair, and a small settee in front of a fireplace, made them very well-appointed, in Parisa's opinion. She had a smaller bed, no fireplace, and a smaller armoire back at Bogaine. And she only had her desk chair, not a whole sofa.

Currently, the walls were a pale blue. They weren't offensive, Parisa thought, but she would definitely want to repaint them. The duvet and curtains on her bed were a light shade of yellow. And the settee, a dark blue. All colors she could live with until she decided how she'd make the room hers.

At the far side of the room, arched doors with heavy leaded glass opened up onto a small balcony, which Parisa stepped out onto. The wind was stronger up here, but chest-high walls protected the occupant and Parisa walked over to them and peered out before looking down. The Gulf of Eudaemon twinkled in the sunlight below her. Boats and ships were scattered across the bay, seagulls wheeling above them or settled at the docks in the harbor. She could see the northern end of Khamsa Island as well as the sandy beach along the coast of the long and narrow island, Athame. She was in a room on the third floor and below her she could see the castle wall, and beyond that the plateau fell to the sea, she knew from her approach to Ponike, but the wall blocked her view of it.

"Is it not breathtaking?" her mother called from her adjacent balcony.

"In my wildest dreams, I would never have imagined this," Parisa said, turning toward her mother. Tucked against the wall at the back of the balcony was a granite bench. Parisa walked over to it and sat, stroking the polished stone that had soaked up the warmth of the summer sun. Now out of the wind, she felt very protected. It would be a great place to curl up and read, she thought, lying down and stretching out. There was not a balcony directly above her so her view of the sky and the granite of the castle walls rising another story or two above her was unimpeded.

She watched as the fluffy clouds above her slowly changed shape as they moved westward. The croak of a raven propelled her to a sitting position. It was standing on top of the balcony wall, head cocking first one way and then the other as it surveyed her.

A raven, she thought, remembering her dream, why had a raven landed on her balcony?

"Hi," she said, tentatively.

The bird croaked again, and then took off, westward, following the clouds. She stood up and went back inside, knocking on the adjoining door.

"Yes, my dear?" Chokhmah asked, opening the door. She had her green linen dress in one hand and a wooden hanger in the other.

Parisa glanced guiltily at her bags, still sitting next to the door where the porter had put them. "A raven just landed on my balcony," she told her mother.

"A raven," her mother said. "What did it do?"

"It just looked at me and cawed and then flew away."

"Hmmm," Chokhmah said. "Perhaps it is just a coincidence. If it returns, then it may have more meaning." Her mother looked over her shoulder at the bags sitting by the door.

"I know," Parisa sighed. "I need to unpack. What do I do with my dirty things?"

"There is a basket for them in the bathroom," Chokhmah said, a glint in her eye. "Get to work, my dear. We will have to go down for lunch soon."

Parisa removed her dresses and hung them in the armoire and then took the clothes she had dirtied while aboard The Phoenix into the bathroom. Three long arched windows allowed enough light into the room so that the room was bathed in sunlight. They were open and a breeze stirred the pale blue curtain that blocked the toilet from the tub and sink.

She dumped her clothes into the basket and took her time examining the rest of the room. The tub had been carved from granite and polished until it shone. The walls and floor were also of polished granite except for the wall behind the tub, which had been left in its unfinished state. When she had seen that Castle Bennu was constructed of granite, she had had no idea that the stone, which Uriel had told her had been quarried in the eastern corner of the kingdom, would be so much a part of the interior of the castle, as well.

Pale blue towels and cloths were stacked inside a small cabinet that sat next to the tub and was level with it. Shampoo and soap were tucked into a niche in the corner of the tub.

A sink carved from quartz was set into a granite table and another blue curtain hid the pipes that ran downward through the floor. There was also a small shelf under the sink for any personal items Parisa might want to tuck there. Two oval rugs, both dark blue, sat in front of the sink and the tub.

To Parisa's eyes, her room was the height of luxury and she couldn't wait to make it her own. The only problem about that was what exactly did that mean?

She walked back into her room to finish unpacking. She wanted to put her journal in the drawer of her desk. She had kept it hidden at Rose Cottage because once she'd caught her father reading it. But she was pretty sure that was something her mother would never do.

Parisa removed her toiletry case from her travel bag and was turning toward the bathroom when there was a tap at the adjoining door.

"Yes?"

Her mother entered and glanced around the room. "Interesting. All the guestrooms must have their own color schemes."

"Why? What color is your room?"

"It is in different shades of grey."

"Are you going to keep it the same?"

"No," her mother said, walking toward Parisa's door. "It is time to go downstairs." As they walked toward the stairs that would take them to the main floor, she added, "I am thinking, perhaps, shades of purple might be nice. Before I met Eluned, I lived in a vardo that was painted lavender and Yitzak and I painted all kinds of things on it."

Her mother rarely spoke of her first husband who had left her both a widow and childless. He had died nearly 18 months before she'd met her father. She assumed it was because her father didn't like hearing about him, but she had never asked.

"You never talk about him much," Parisa said.

"Who? Yitzak?"

"Yes," Parisa said. "Did you love him?"

"I loved him very much," Chokhmah smiled, remembering. "He was a little older than me, and I had such a crush on him when I was about your age. I did not think he even knew I existed. I mean, I knew he was aware of who I was, but I was just Moshe's younger sister. I assumed he would get married before I came of age, but he waited for me. I did not know that at the time, of course, but as soon as I was 18, he gave me his scarf."

"I don't understand."

"It is our tradition that if a man is interested in a woman, he gives her his neck scarf. If she is interested in being his wife, she wears it on her head."

Parisa laughed. "That's interesting! Did you put it on right away?"

"I wanted to," she said, "but I knew that would seem too needy. But, when I left our wagon the next morning, I was wearing it."

"Did you get married right away?"

"A few months later," her mother said. "We wanted all the traditional parties. Yitzak loved to dance."

"Wow," Parisa paused on a step and looked back at her

mother. "You must have been with him a long time." She was aware that her mother and father met when her mother was 44 and that she had been born almost three years later a few months before her mother turned 47.

"Nearly 25 years," she said. "Unfortunately, his disease started presenting itself when we had been married about ten years. And it kept getting worse and worse and by the end he could no longer walk or even remember who I was. I was sad about being childless at first, but then I was thankful that our children never had to see their father degenerate like that."

"I'm so sorry, Mama," Parisa said, looking stricken.

"Thank you, my love," Chokhmah joined her daughter on her step, and hugged her. "But now I have you and I cannot imagine having lived my life any other way."

They descended the final staircase, and Parisa grabbed her mother's hand and pulled her to a stop.

"Mama?"

"What is it, my love?"

"Will you still feel the same way even if things don't work out with Papa?"

Chokhmah did not pause, "Absolutely. There is nothing that could happen that would change how much I love you. As for your father, as the Calé say, 'chuquel sos pirela, coca terela.'"

"I don't understand."

"It means that the dog who roams will find a bone."

"I still don't understand," Parisa said.

"My darling, you do not have to understand," Chokhmah said, "The only thing that matters is that I love you."

"I love you too, Mama."

Summer

"One swallow does not make a summer,
neither does one fine day;
similarly, one day or brief time of happiness
does not make a person entirely happy.
                    -Aristotle, *The Nicomachean Ethics*

CHOKHMAH

It was only their second day in the Kingdom of Aden, but Chokhmah was excited to get started on her room. So, while a crew from the castle was painting her room—three walls lavender and the wall behind her bed, a royal purple—she and Parisa had been taken into Ponike so that they could do some shopping.

Chokhmah was looking for a duvet cover and bed curtains that were made from cloth of gold or some other golden fabric, and she also wanted to find some pewter-toned sheets, and maybe a couple of throw pillows for the bed, that would match the color of the settee in front of the fireplace.

"Does that mean that we have to keep the sofa that's already in our room," Parisa asked.

"Not if it does not suit you," her mother replied. "Eluned said that we may switch it with a settee from one of the other guest rooms, if we like. Or, have it reupholstered, if we prefer. I happen to like the one in my room. Why? Are you not happy with yours?"

"I haven't decided yet, really. I'm still not sure what I want to do with my room."

"You have all the time in the world, my love. There is no need to decide immediately."

Once her mother had found her bedclothes and pillows, they were ready for the next item on their list.

Eluned had also ordered them to go to her favorite fabric vendor and choose some material so that the castle's seam-stresses could make them each a couple of dresses. They were woefully short of clothes in which to dress up, and there were a lot of formal dinners to attend at Castle Bennu.

"There are so many to choose from!" Parisa exclaimed when they entered the shop—silks, brocades, linens, wools, cottons, damasks, laces, velvets, satins and more in a rainbow of colors overflowed the shelves and tables. "How am I ever going to decide?"

"I would suggest," Chokhmah said, "that we both choose lighter fabrics as it is only the beginning of summer, and the weather will continue to get warmer for a while."

Parisa tugged on her braid, still looking overwhelmed.

Chokhmah led her over to a stack of silks. "Start here. See if there are any you like."

Half an hour later they left the shop and headed back to the area where the carriage was waiting for them; Parisa holding her choices close to her chest as if she feared someone might grab the package. Chokhmah was pleased with her daughter's choices—a pearlescent white silk that shimmered with the colors of the rainbow and a glossy black satin with just a hint of midnight blue when struck by the light.

She had chosen a crimson silk with a pattern of roses woven into it, and a deep purple silk with a gold brocade woven along one edge of the fabric. Eluned had teased her that morning about her royal purple wall, and Chokhmah had laughed and told her friend that for once she wanted to know what it was like to feel regal.

"I have been running away from my heritage for so many

years now," she said, "and for once, even if it ends up only being six months, I have a chance to live into it."

Eluned had hugged her, tears in her sea green eyes. "You don't know how long I've waited to hear you say that."

"Since a certain campsite on the outskirts of Jazeel?" Chokhmah's smile was self-deprecating as she remembered that cold morning when she had discovered that one of the Treasures, a coat that would only fit royalty, had fit her like a glove.

"Yes, about then," Eluned agreed. "And definitely since Jabberwock explained why he thought you were the only remaining member of the Pelfan royal family."

Chokhmah smiled, remembering. They had had a wonderful Pelfan meal that evening, a meal that felt somehow familiar to her, then said, "Fortunately, I am no longer the only remaining member of the royal family." And, for the first time, it occurred to her that she might be doing her daughter a disservice. Parisa could be Queen of Pelf one day, but to do so, Chokhmah would have to wear the crown first.

And while she did not have to make a decision immediately, it would be something about which she would have to speak to her daughter. She had promised them both that she would not make a decision until Faolan had returned from Simoon. But there was no reason why she could not begin preparing herself for that eventuality.

Being a healer was all well and good, but it was not worth a fig when it came to ruling a country. She suspected Eluned and Gwrhyr would more than welcome a chance to teach her the ropes, so to speak.

"Mama?"

"Yes, my love?" Chokhmah asked, her daughter's voice drawing her back to her surroundings.

Parisa had stopped in front of stationary shop. "My journal is almost full. Can I pick out a new one?"

"Of course, darling." She did not want to discourage her daughter from writing. They entered the shop and Parisa walked straight to the journal that had caught her attention when she had looked in the window.

She picked up the embossed leather journal, which featured a polished oval of a black star sapphire in the center of the cover. The diary had a metal closure. "It's beautiful," she said showing it to her mother.

"It is indeed," Chokhmah agreed. "You know, I think that I would like to start keeping a journal, as well. Do you mind if I look for a minute?"

Chokhmah wandered around the shop while Parisa looked at the inks, which came in a variety of colors.

"This is perfect," Chokhmah said as she joined her daughter at the ink shelf. She showed Parisa a leatherbound journal that was closed with a wrap-around leather strap with an ornate key at the end that tucked into a leather tab. "Shall we get a quill and ink to go with them?"

Parisa's eyes lit up. "I know just the one I want!" She led her mother over to the quills and picked up one that was decorated with a raven's feather. "It looks like my fabric!"

Chokhmah picked up a quill with a couple of feathers from a snowy owl protruding from the end. "Lovely," she said. Parisa opted for black ink, and Chokhmah, perhaps not surprisingly, for purple. Arms loaded with packages, they returned to the carriage.

It was time for lunch by the time they returned to Castle Bennu and a porter took their packages upstairs to deposit in Parisa's room as Chokhmah's room was still in the process of being painted.

She would have to sleep in another guest room or with her daughter that evening. She preferred the latter if Parisa would have her.

Parisa finished her seafood salad first and asked permission to go to her room.

"I was hoping you would pick out a couple of dress designs first," Eluned said. "I have some drawings in my office."

Parisa looked less than enthused.

"Would you prefer that I choose them for you?" Chokhmah asked.

"Could you, Mama? It was hard enough picking out the fabric."

"At least you got to pick out the fabric," Fuchsia said. "I never get to."

"Well, if it's any consolation," Parisa said. "This is the first time I've been allowed to pick out my own fabric."

Fuchsia nodded her head. "Do I have to wait until I am twelve, Mommy?"

"Perhaps not that long, darling," Eluned said. "Could you eat a little more of your salad, please?"

Fuchsia wrinkled her nose and speared a shrimp on her fork. "I'd rather have some cake," she told Parisa.

Parisa, who her mother knew wasn't particularly fond of sweets, laughed, and said, "Me too." Her mother was well aware that it was the wolf making itself known. Like her father, Parisa preferred protein. Her daughter usually kept a stash of dried meat in a wooden box in her room in case she needed a snack. Definitely not the normal snack for a child.

Chokhmah could see the changes taking place in her daughter's body whether or not Parisa was yet aware of them herself. She was filling out and becoming more rounded in the areas that had once been lanky. She needed to take that into account when she picked out the patterns for the seamstress.

Uriel, who had had a meeting, had not joined them for lunch, so after Gavreel was sent off with his nanny, Faltuel, and Fuchsia with her tutor, Zimbra, and Parisa had returned to her room (Chokhmah felt sure she was anxious to use her new journal), she and Eluned headed to the latter's office to pore over dress designs.

She had not yet been to Eluned's office, and the Queen apologized for the fact it was beginning to look dated. In tones of lavender, pink, and sea green, it reminded Chokhmah of Eluned's bedroom in Castle Mykerinos, her childhood home in the Kingdom of Zion.

"I did get rid of the glitter," she told Chokhmah, and I think I am finally ready to change the furnishings. For years, it made me less homesick to be in here, and then: children. But now that Gavreel is about to turn five, there is no reason not to get back to work. I keep up with the schools I've started, but I'd like to be more hands on with them again."

Chokhmah nodded to the courtyard that was visible through the window in front of Eluned's desk. "That is lovely, though."

"That's still my favorite part of this room," Eluned laughed. The women admired the view for a moment—a weeping willow drooped next to a fountain where a bench offered a place to watch the birdfeeders and suncatchers and listen to the tinkling of the windchimes. "On a good day, you'll usually find me out there reading a book."

"It looks like the perfect place to read," Chokhmah said. "Parisa and I have been enjoying our balconies. We both sat outside and read yesterday afternoon. She is enjoying Bleak House as I am enjoying The Ghost of Loss.

"Finally," Eluned laughed. "It took you long enough. I have all Geillis Saille's books if you want to read another. They're here in my office," she pointed to a shelf.

"Thank you," said Chokhmah. She thought it was very likely that would happen more than once in the next six months. "Shall we look at the dresses? Parisa picked out some very lovely fabric. I was thinking of doing something a little more elegant for her. Most of her clothes look like they are for a child."

Eluned nodded to a sea green loveseat in front of which

was a coffee table with a sheaf of papers sitting on it. "She's definitely showing the signs, isn't she?" Eluned said. "I'm sure we can find something more appropriate. And what about you? Are you happy with what you were able to find?"

"Oh yes, I like it very much. I cannot wait to show you."

Soon they were immersed in the drawings and it was late afternoon before Chokhmah finally returned upstairs to check on her daughter.

PARISA

Parisa practically flew to her room, the three flights of stairs passing beneath her feet like air beneath the wings of a bird. She couldn't wait to start her new journal. The empty pages were calling to her, and it had been hard to stay focused on what she was eating, much less the conversation at the table when all she could think about was what she wanted to write in its pages.

She flung open the door of her room to see that all of their packages had been deposited on the floor next to the door. She guessed that the porter preferred to enter the room as little as possible because the packages were in the same location that her luggage had been left in the previous day.

She looked at her bed and frowned. She had very carefully made it herself that morning before they went down for breakfast. It looked as if a maid had come in and remade it because Echo was now sitting in a different spot. Parisa didn't like the idea of someone else touching her wolf.

Walking over to the bed, she moved Echo to her preferred position. She liked looking out the window if she couldn't be outside because why would a wolf want to be caged in a room if it could be outside running through the woods? And clearly Parisa couldn't leave her outside. Something might happen to her. Looking out the window was the next best thing.

Well, she thought, returning to the packages. If someone was going to come into her room every morning and make her bed, she wouldn't make it herself. And she would find someplace to leave Echo until she returned to her room and could place her on the bed herself.

She retrieved her journal, quill, and ink and placed them on the desk after deciding she ought to use the bathroom before going out on the balcony to write. It was a beautiful day and it seemed silly to write at her desk when the granite bench was available just outside her room.

It was clear that the maid had been in her bathroom, too. There were fresh towels and it looked as if the sink and granite counter had been wiped down. She sighed. Changing her towels daily felt wasteful to Parisa but she assumed it was part of the normal routine in a castle. They did employ a lot of people, after all. That was a good thing, right?

So many new things to get used to, Parisa thought, picking up her new journal and writing implements from her desk and taking them out to the balcony.

Thinking about the maid moving about her room had thrown her off, and she sat for several minutes staring into space as she recentered herself. She decided to lie down on the bench again and watch the clouds for a moment. What was it that she had wanted to write about?

When she picked out the journal that morning, she had been thinking it would become the special journal that she would give her father at Yuclog and she had been excited about the idea of telling him about everything that had happened so far since he had sailed away.

A cloud passing in front of the sun echoed her new mood. Parisa felt a shadow had been cast over her heart, as well. She was no longer sure she wanted to tell her father anything about their time away from him, much less everything. He was the one who had wanted to be apart from them. They hadn't made that decision.

It was too soon for him to have reached Sigwald. It was a much longer sea journey to Arberth than it was to Ponike. Then he had to ride northward. It could be nearly a month before they heard from him again, if at all. Her mother didn't seem really confident about that.

"The truth is, my love," her mother had said, "your father and I have not really been apart since we met. There were only those three months, after we left Sigwald and were separated by his broken leg and my journey to Mifugo to get the Knife. He had no way of getting in touch with me, and I did not know that he was still alive until I returned to Goshen. So, I do not know whether or not he is good at communicating. I suppose we will find out."

Unfortunately, she shared her mother's doubts. Her father never had been much of a reader nor did he like to write. It was she and her mother who shared a love of those leisurely pursuits. He might send a pigeon, though. That would be brief enough for his liking.

So, what would she use the journal for? She picked it up and let the sun, which was free from its cloud, cause the star within the sapphire to glimmer.

Parisa heard a flutter of wings and a telltale croak and sat up to see the raven had returned. She assumed it was the same one, anyway. "Hi," she called to the bird, delighted. "You're back."

The raven croaked and hopped a little closer. It seemed intrigued by the gem on the cover of her journal.

"Oh, that's right," Parisa laughed. "You guys like shiny things. Well, I'm afraid you can't have this. I only just got it." She thought for a moment. "You know, I do have something you might like." Around Echo's neck was a shiny piece of tinsel that she pretended was a collar. She headed inside, journal clenched firmly in her hand, just in case, and untied the ribbon from around her wolf's throat.

But, when she returned, the raven was gone. She returned to the bench, dispirited. Of course it was gone. It couldn't have possibly understood what she was saying.

She looked around the balcony. Where could she leave the ribbon? If the raven ever returned, she would want to get it quickly. She couldn't leave it on the wall because the wind would blow it away.

There was a hook by the door. She guessed it was there to hang a lantern on if you wanted to sit on the balcony at night. She could tie the tinsel around that. That would probably work. She used a manger knot because it would enable her to release the tinsel quickly should the raven appear again. Parisa tugged on it and it felt secure enough, so she returned to her bench, satisfied.

But she still didn't know what she wanted to write about. She picked up her quill, admiring the raven feather. There was something about that deep, glossy black that spoke to her right now. Maybe it was a symbol of the despair she felt about her father. It was him talking about them traveling to different places while he was gone that had done it.

Up until that moment she had felt some hope that things might return to normal. And although hope lifted its wings once in a while, mostly she despaired of ever having a normal family life again.

Her thoughts returned to the dream. She had written about it in her other journal, but she thought she might want to rewrite it in her new journal. Or sketch it. She wasn't quite as gifted as her mother at drawing, but she wasn't bad. What if she drew what she had seen? Parisa looked down at the quill. She would have to do it in pencil. She wasn't confident enough in her drawing skills and she'd probably have to erase and start over a lot. But, once it was to her liking, she could go over it in ink.

They might never end up in Buta, but if they did wouldn't it be amazing to see how close her dream had come to reality? What if she started having prophetic dreams like her mother? What if her mother really became the Queen of Pelf one day?

Parisa shuddered as a thought struck her. If her mother became Queen of Pelf one day, that meant that she, too, could one day be that kingdom's queen. She leaned back against the wall of the castle eyes wide but unseeing. She couldn't believe that had never occurred to her.

Life at Bogaine was life at Bogaine. She had even pretended at times to be a princess when she hadn't even needed to pretend. And while not all princesses became queens, all princesses who were the only child of their mother, who was also a queen, or could be one if she wanted to, could one day be a queen.

Parisa jumped up and hurried into her room to grab her pencil, eraser, and pencil sharpener. Suddenly it seemed very important that she sketch the details of the dream before they faded away completely. She also grabbed her other journal so she could check to make sure she hadn't forgotten anything.

When her mother came upstairs in the late afternoon, Parisa was still out on the balcony. Her mother stepped outside and said, "Have you been out here all afternoon?"

Parisa, who was nearly done with her drawing held up her hand as if to say, 'hold on a second.'

Less than a minute later, Parisa handed Chokhmah her journal.

Chokhmah studied it quietly for a while before saying, "Is this how you saw it?"

"It's the closest I can get to it. That's just the view through the window. I think it will take another drawing to show the castle."

Her mother looked at the drawing more closely. "I see that you have drawn the intertwined black and white dolphins."

"I like them better," Parisa explained. "The kraken is scary. The dolphins make me happy."

"I agree," Chokhmah said. "The kraken was probably a way of visually making the Kingdom of Pelf look threatening."

"So no one would try to fight them?"

"Exactly."

Parisa was silent a moment. "Hmm. Look how that turned out."

Chokhmah laughed. "Not so well."

"But things are better there now, aren't they?"

"Yes, by all accounts, Pelf is doing fine."

"I still like the dolphins better."

"So do I," her mother said, handing Parisa her journal. "This is an excellent idea, my love. I think that I should do the same while I still remember the details."

Parisa set to work on her next drawing while her mother went to fetch her own journal.

"Parisa?"

"Yes, Mama?" She looked up to see her mother standing at the open doors.

"What is this?" She pointed to the shiny ribbon attached to the hook.

Parisa blushed. "Oh, that's Echo's collar. I forgot to tell you that the raven came back. I thought it would like something shiny because it liked the sapphire on my journal. But by the time I got the ribbon, it had flown away."

"So, you tied it here in case it returns?"

Parisa nodded.

"That is an excellent idea," she said, and stepped into the room.

Parisa grinned and turned back to her drawing.

THAT NIGHT, AS THEY WERE GETTING READY to go to sleep, Parisa was lying in bed watching the candlelight flicker on the walls and turning over in her mind what she might do with her room.

Although the paint had dried in her mother's room, it still smelled too strongly to sleep in there, and she'd readily agreed to her mother sharing her bed.

"What are you thinking about?" Her mother asked as she lay down and pulled the duvet over herself.

"It's funny," Parisa said. "I would have thought that it would be easy to choose how I wanted my room to be but since I have so many options, I can't decide on anything. How did you decide?"

"I decided based on how I wanted the room to make me feel when I was in it," Chokhmah said.

"How does it make you feel?"

Chokhmah chuckled, "You might not like the answer, but I will try to explain why it is so. Do you still want to know?"

"Yes. Now I am even more curious."

"It makes me feel like a queen."

Parisa felt like her heart skipped a beat. "Why do you need to feel like a queen?"

"Because a queen is strong, and she is in control. She gets to make the choices and live with the choices she made knowing that she is the one who made the decision. Does that make sense?"

"Yes, if it's because Papa made a decision for us that we have to live with knowing that we had no choice in making it?"

"Yes," Chokhmah said. "Right now, I want to feel like I have the power to make my own decisions."

"I can understand that," Parisa said. She was silent for a while.

"Are you ready to blow out the candle?" Chokhmah asked. She had already snuffed the flame in the lantern.

Parisa sat up and blew out the candle on her nightstand then lay back down. "Mama?"

"Yes, my love?"

"What do you have to know to be a queen?"

"That is a very good question," her mother replied. "I would have to ask Eluned and Gwrhyr about that," she paused. "Well, I should now call him Uriel because that is his name. The Quest is long since over. Perhaps it is time I moved on from that." She chuckled to herself.

"What's so funny?"

"It is just that when I settled down at Bogaine with your father and you, I was moving on with my life. Eluned and Uriel have moved on with their lives as have Yona and Njima, and even Dev and Princess Xiang," Chokhmah said, noting the two princesses who had helped them with the Quest although Dev, the former Divya, was now a prince. "Not a one of us thought it was necessary to continue our lives as if we were still on the Quest."

"Except for Papa."

"Except for Papa," Chokhmah agreed. "He is the reason I continued to call Uriel, Gwrhyr, because that is how he thought of him. It made your father happy to be with those he shared the Quest with, and he was very angry that I insisted that we not attend the Year X meeting."

"I remember that," Parisa said, "but I think it was the right thing to do, right? I mean, we lived on a horse farm. We weren't the rulers of any of the Kingdoms."

"Exactly. I did not feel that it was our place." Chokhmah paused. "Perhaps we would not be where we are now if we had gone to that meeting."

"Do you really think so? Even Eluned didn't go," Parisa said. "Besides, it's not like he could have attended the meeting himself. He's not a king, and by then wasn't your grandniece already ruling Pelf?"

"This is true," Chokhmah reflected. "I also heard that Njima took Dev with her instead of Yona because she and Yona have made him their heir."

"So, it would only have been Uriel and Njima that had been on the Quest?"

"Yes, and if he had said he wanted to take a trip to Ponike to visit with Eluned and Uriel, alone or with us, I would have agreed to that. But he never asked to travel to either Aden or Naphtali to visit with our Quest friends."

They were silent for a while.

"Maybe we'll never really know what it is he's looking for," Parisa said.

"Only Omni knows if we will or not," her mother said. "Anyway, you were asking about what a queen needs to know and I cannot answer that. But I know what a child needs to know and you, young lady, must get back to your lessons. Fuchsia's tutor is more than willing to teach you."

Normally this would not have thrilled her, but suddenly she had a panicky feeling that she was wasting time and needed to learn as much as possible before the six months were up. Because, what if they did end up in Pelf? "When do I start?" she asked.

"Tomorrow?"

"Okay." Parisa was silent for a minute. "Mama?"

"Yes, my love?"

"I love you."

"I love you, my dear. Good night and sweet dreams."

"Goodnight, Mama." Parisa turned over on her side and hugged Echo to her chest, drifting off to sleep within minutes.

Chokhmah

Following breakfast the next morning, Parisa joined Fuchsia in the room next to the library where she met with her tutor, Zimbra. Gavreel was still working with Faltuel on basics, but he learned quickly and was just starting to read. He would join Fuchsia with her tutor in a few months.

Chokhmah finished her tea and then she and Eluned retired to Eluned's office.

"What did you want to talk about?" Eluned asked her friend.

"Parisa asked me something last night and I had to admit that I did not know, but it was something I have been wondering about myself."

"What's that?"

"What is it that a queen, or king for that matter, must know about ruling a country?"

"To be honest," Eluned said, "because my parents always knew that I was going to be marrying Uriel, I was mostly taught the basics—math, science, literature, theology, and a few languages." She thought for a moment. "And, of course, there were things like etiquette, and learning to play an instrument."

"Ah yes," Chokhmah said. "The harpsichord." She recalled

Eluned playing for her at Castle Pwyll in Annewven, and later, when they were at Castle Mykerinos for her wedding to Uriel.

"And the harp, remember?"

"Yes, I do. It was how you wiled away all those lonely hours waiting for the unicorn to appear."

Eluned nodded. "So, it's really Uriel you should ask about that. I used to be astounded at all the languages he spoke, but he took becoming a king seriously, and without his father there to guide him, he wanted to know as much as possible. It was as if he wanted to make him proud."

"I imagine King Gavreel is very proud," Chokhmah said. "Uriel seems much loved here. All of you do."

"We've tried to ensure that even the poorest of those who live in this kingdom have access to the basics of survival— food, shelter, healthcare. And I now have schools in all of the bigger cities so that anyone who wants to avail themselves can learn to read and write and perform basic arithmetic."

"How are your schools doing?"

"Quite well," Eluned said. "As soon as Gavreel starts his tutoring with Zimbra, it is my plan to travel to them all and check on them personally. It's been years since I've been able to do so." She paused. "Actually, I wanted to spend as much time as possible with my children when they were young. I know Uriel would have been happy for me to check on the schools if I had wanted to. But in another couple of months, I think Gavreel will be ready to be with Zimbra and Fuchsia."

"And Parisa," Chokhmah added. "I wonder . . ."

"What?"

"Do you think we could find someone to teach us Pelfan? Parisa has also realized that it is possible that we will not go back to Bogaine. And just in case . . ." she trailed off again.

"Just in case you decide to return the royal family to Pelf?"

"Yes," Chokhmah said. "I know it is highly unlikely. After six months away from us, there is a chance that Faolan will want to stay at Bogaine. Do you know that he suggested to Parisa that we travel while he is gone? He told her we could go visit with Njima and Yona in Jazeel, or with my family. He even mentioned Favonia."

"That's a bit premature, isn't it?" Eluned looked at her friend, aghast.

"One would think so," Chokhmah said.

"Well no wonder Parisa is having second thoughts."

"I think at this point she is bouncing back and forth between despair and hope," Chokhmah said. "Today, she is excited by the idea of being a princess and, possibly, a queen. But who knows? Tonight? Tomorrow? Next week? Next month? Someday, I think she will be asking when are we going to go back to Bogaine."

"Will you leave soon if that's what she wants?" Eluned asked.

"Not if she wants to go soon, no," Chokhmah said. "I am not comfortable going back at all, at this point, but she also does not know that her father lied to us."

"What do you mean?"

"He kept saying his post would be for six months," Chokhmah said.

"Yes?"

"What he did not tell us is that it would be for six months once he arrived there. The travel time to and from does not count. That is what Gittan told me when I was talking to her about it."

The color drained from Eluned's face. "Chokhmah, Omni have mercy! It takes nearly a month to get from Portuma to Sigwald."

"And from Sigwald back to Bogaine."

"Eight months," Eluned looked sick. "He was willing to be away from you and his child for eight months?"

"I have not had the heart to tell Parisa. He will barely make it home in time for her thirteenth birthday, much less Yuclog, and she is still looking forward to spending Yuclog at Bogaine."

"Perhaps the sooner you tell her the better," Eluned said. "Obviously, you can spend Yuclog with us, but what about her birthday? What are you going to do, Chokhmah?"

"Pray," she said, "Pray that the answer comes to me before then. Meanwhile, I must learn as much as I can about being a queen because if I am not to go back, then what else shall I do? I cannot depend on you to care for us forever."

Eluned started to protest and Chokhmah held up her hand. "Understand that I have absolutely no doubt that Uriel, and you, would have no problem with that. And I could probably even find some way to make myself useful. But I am not sure, no, I know. I know that it would destroy my soul to always feel beholden. I would prefer to meet you as an equal."

Eluned nodded. "I actually understand that. If it weren't for my schools, and my children, I don't know what I would do, but I know that I couldn't just sit around. If nothing else, the Quest taught me that."

"We need a sense of purpose?" Chokhmah suggested.

"Yes," Eluned agreed. "A sense of purpose." She stood up. "Now, why don't we go see when you can meet with Uriel and find out about getting someone to tutor you both in Pelfan?"

THAT AFTERNOON, Chokhmah found Parisa sitting out on her balcony again. She was reading *Bleak House*, and the piece of tinsel still fluttered from the hook alongside the door.

"Are you enjoying this book as much as you enjoyed *Great Expectations*?" her mother asked, sitting down next to her on the bench.

"Yes," Parisa said. "It's very good."

"I see your raven friend has not returned?" Her mother nodded at the ribbon.

"No," she said, "I haven't seen it today although I've only been up here for a little while. The tests I told you about at lunch were just the beginning. She had even more to give me this afternoon."

"But she now has a better idea where you should be, studies wise?"

"Yes. I will start actual lessons tomorrow."

Chokhmah nodded. "I was talking with Eluned today, and I was wondering . . . would you like to join me in being taught Pelfan?"

"We can learn Pelfan?" Parisa asked her mother, eyes wide with excitement.

"Yes, Uriel said that he thinks he can find us a tutor."

"Oh, Mama, that would be so amazing even if we never go there. I mean, we are Pelfan, or at least, I am half Pelfan. And I speak Dyfedian. It just seems right, somehow."

Chokhmah smiled at her daughter. "Good," she said, patting Parisa's leg and standing up. "I will let you, and Zimbra, of course, know when our tutor is ready for us."

"Thanks, Mama!"

Her daughter looked so joyful for a change that Chokhmah did not have the heart to tell her the truth about her father's job. "I am going to work on my room some more," she told her, "and then, perhaps, read and journal until dinner time. I do not want to risk scaring the raven away."

"Thank you, Mama," Parisa said, picking up her book. "Will you let me know when it is time to get ready for dinner?"

"Yes, my love," Chokhmah said. "Enjoy your book."

Chokhmah returned to her room and surveyed it. The paint had dried, and the furniture had been put back in place. But did she like where it was sitting?

The bed, yes. She had painted that wall royal purple

because she wanted it behind her bed, and she liked the fact that from her bed she could see the sky from her window. It would be particularly nice on nights when she could see the moon or when there was a thunderstorm.

The fireplace and settee were on the wall opposite her bed and were, essentially, immovable, although she might turn the sofa a bit so that its back was toward the door, and see if she could get a small table to set in front of it so that she could drink tea and read there on bad days.

It was her desk that bothered her the most. It sat against the wall adjacent to the door to Parisa's room. Chokhmah thought she would prefer it where the armoire and dresser now were. She would move the dresser to the other side of the fireplace or maybe on the wall next to the arched doors. The armoire would take the place of the desk.

She could move everything but the armoire herself and did so. Then she went to find someone to help her with the armoire.

Fortunately, it did not take long, and once everything was to her liking, she began replacing the sheets, duvet cover, and bed curtains. She placed the pewter-toned throw pillows on her bed, and the gold pillow she had purchased for the sofa, on her settee, and stepped back to inspect her work.

Perfect, she thought. She sat down on the settee and hugged the throw pillow to her chest. Yes, she could be very happy here for a while. Standing, she went to her desk to retrieve her journal, ink, and quill, picked up *The Ghost of Loss* from her bedside table and went out onto her balcony to enjoy the last hour of that early summer afternoon.

When it was time to get ready for dinner, she walked over to the wall of the balcony closest to Parisa's.

"Darling!" she called.

A second later, Parisa appeared. "Is it time to get ready for dinner?"

"Yes," she said, "but come see my room first. It is finished, at least, mostly so."

"I'll be right there."

Chokhmah met her at the adjoining door, waiting as she deposited her book and journal on her desk.

"Wow," Parisa breathed, as she entered the room and looked around. "I really like it. Are you happy with it?"

"I really am."

"Well," Parisa said, "it certainly looks queenly." She laughed.

"What is it?" her mother asked.

"Now we just have to get you a crown."

Chokhmah chuckled. "I do not think I yet feel that regal."

"Well," Parisa said, walking over to her mother and hugging her, "you'll always be a queen to me."

"Thank you, my love," Chokhmah squeezed back, "that means a lot to me."

"Do I need to change into something else for dinner?" Parisa asked. She was wearing her patchwork skirt and a blouse.

"Please do not," Chokhmah said. "I love you just the way you are."

"Very funny, Mama."

"The answer is no," her mother said. "Early dinner tonight, so it is casual. I believe tomorrow night they are expecting guests and we will be expected to dress for that. As a matter of fact, we have a dress fitting first thing in the morning. We are supposed to go see the seamstress immediately after breakfast."

Parisa's eyes lit up. "Do you know whether it's the black or the white dress?"

"I do not know for either of us," Chokhmah said. "I guess it shall be a surprise. Either way, the dresses should be lovely."

"I can't wait to see what you picked out for me."

"It is kind of exciting, is it not? It did not occur to me to specify which dress to make first, but both designs were perfect for a formal dinner party, according to Eluned."

Parisa nodded. "Well, I'll just go wash up then."

She watched her daughter's retreating back before going to wash her hands in her bathroom where she had retained the dove grey towels and pewter throw rugs. Chokhmah decided she would take Eluned aside that evening and explain to her why she intended to wait a few more days before she told her daughter about how long her father would be gone. Parisa had a new lightness to her step that she had not seen in months, perhaps longer. It was as if a burden had finally been lifted from her shoulders and Chokhmah did not want to replace it anytime soon.

Parisa

That night, lying in her bed and staring into the darkness after she blew out her candle, Parisa let her eyes slowly adjust to the light. It didn't take long for the light of the stars and the moon shining through the leaded glass of the arched doors to alleviate some of the gloom. There were no details, but she could make out the fireplace and the settee in front of it, and the deeper darkness of her desk by the adjoining door. To her right, the bulk of her armoire blocked her view of her dresser.

She liked what her mother had done to her room, but neither did she want to copy it. But she also didn't want to keep it the way it was. She didn't want it to look like all the other guest rooms. Would some of the guests that were arriving tomorrow be staying in any of the rooms on this floor? The other problem was that she couldn't start moving furniture around until her walls were painted. And that was yet another dilemma. She still wasn't sure what color she wanted to paint her walls.

Parisa sighed. Maybe she was making this a bigger issue than it actually was. How much time, awake, did she really spend in her room? Most of the time she was asleep. Otherwise, she was at lessons, meals, or out on her balcony. And, she assumed, she would be getting outdoors more as the summer wore on as it wasn't long before their summer break from lessons.

She was looking forward to horseback riding, learning how to sail, and even going camping at least once. She loved being outdoors. It made her happy.

What would be nice, she thought, would be to bring the outdoors in for the cold moths and rainy days. Could she paint the ceiling blue and paint white clouds on it? If she left the walls the same, could she paint trees on them, so it looked like she was in a forest? That way even on days with inclement weather she could feel as if she were outside. Was that too crazy?

She liked the idea. She'd ask her mother in the morning. Parisa finally drifted off to sleep anticipating the coming day.

It was taking her mother forever to finish her tea, Parisa thought. She was also talking to Eluned so she couldn't push her to finish. Fuchsia was talking to her about the weird dream she'd had the previous night so Parisa was unable to hear what her mother and Eluned were saying. She wanted to tell Fuchsia to hush for a moment but knew that would be considered rude. Instead she tugged on her braid and bit her lip to remind her to keep her mouth shut.

On the way down to breakfast, she had told her mother about her idea for her room, and Chokhmah had liked it. She was supposed to be asking Eluned if they could have permission to paint trees on the wall and clouds on the ceiling.

"Isn't that weird?" Fuchsia was saying.

"Very," Parisa agreed although she hadn't really been paying attention. She reached for another piece of bacon despite the fact she was allowed no more than three pieces each morning. Maybe that would distract her mother. Unfortunately, it didn't work, and she was too full to have another piece.

Fuchsia was asking her what she had dreamt last night.

"I don't remember, Parisa said. "I usually do, but for some reason I don't remember any of my dreams from last night."

Parisa had forgotten it was the weekend so there were no lessons that morning. Other than the dress fitting following breakfast, she was free the entire day. She had been hoping that she could go sailing, but Uriel had not yet had the time to set up anything. In addition, he would be involved with their guests all day, the ambassadors from Adamah and Naphtali, whose kingdoms bordered Aden. They and their spouses would then join them for dinner before returning to their homes in Ponike later that evening. Eluned would be entertaining the spouses while the ambassadors met with Uriel.

Parisa had learned from Fuchsia that when the adults retired to the living room, she and Fuchsia and Gavreel would probably be sent off to their rooms.

"They don't really want us around then," Fuchsia had said. "You know, grown up talk."

Parisa knew otherwise. Grown up talk was not really all that interesting. She had been deeply disappointed when she'd finally aged enough to realize that grownups rarely had deep and meaningful conversations. It seemed like all Beibhinn and Fianna did was gossip about other families in their corner of Dyfed. And her father and his brother talked business most of the time.

Gavreel's nanny appeared to take him to the nursery room upstairs and told Fuchsia she was expected to come as well. Zimbra had the weekend off.

"I can't wait until I am old enough to just go to my room," Fuchsia whispered as she pushed in her chair. "I can read there as well as I can in the nursery."

Parisa nodded in commiseration and watched as they departed. She turned back to see her mother watching her.

"Are you ready?" she asked.

Parisa stood. It was about time, she thought.

The seamstresses were in another wing of the castle, and a page had to lead them there. On the way, Parisa asked about her room.

"Eluned thought it was an excellent idea," her mother said. "I told her you would want an azure blue for the sky. I hope that is correct."

"That's perfect," Parisa said. "Just like the sky on an autumn day."

It was another ten minutes before they arrived at a large room filled with women and men, working on making clothing for the royal household and some of the lords who lived there, as well as their spouses and children. Parisa had never really thought about it but she supposed it was a fulltime job.

Once there, they were pointed to a curtained-off area where they would find their dresses.

"When you have them on, come out and someone will be there to make sure they are fitted," the woman told them.

Having only ever worn clothes made by her mother, Parisa was somewhat awed by the activity and the number of people in the room, and not a little embarrassed by the thought that she would have to strip down to her underclothes before she could put on the dress.

Parisa was handed a dress made out of the black silk, her mother the purple with gold brocade. They stepped behind the curtain and pulled on the dresses and then each helped the other button up the back before admiring their dresses in the long mirror whose wooden frame had been mounted to the wall.

The slim A-line dress Parisa wore made her already long and slender body appear even taller. The dress had cap sleeves and a fitted bodice, and the lace lined collar was rounded in front just below her collarbones and fell to a deep V between her shoulder blades. Small onyx buttons fastened the dress from her waist to the V. Just as she hoped, the fabric shimmered in the light pouring through a high window and the fabric flowed from her waist to the floor. She suspected hemming was all it would need.

Chokhmah's dress featured a square neckline and three-quarter sleeves. The pleated bodice stopped at an Empire waist which was encircled by a band of the brocade. Another band of brocade skimmed the top of her feet. And buttons covered in the brocade were used to fasten the dress in back.

"They're beautiful," Parisa whispered. She had never dreamed of having a dress this beautiful, and another was on the way.

Her mother had taken her braid and wound it into a bun at the back of her neck and turned her to look in the mirror. With her hair up, she looked much older, maybe even 16, she thought.

"You are starting to look like a woman," her mother said. Chokhmah let go of the braid, and Parisa looked twelve again. She sighed and pulled back the curtain, saying, "Can I wear my hair up tonight?"

"Of course you can, my love," Chokhmah said, "we will see if Eluned has any jeweled pins you can borrow. I am afraid mine are very plain."

Other than hemming Parisa's dress, there was no extra work needed. They'd been given their measurements and clearly were experienced enough to work with that.

As they were being led back to their wing, Parisa learned that her mother had been asked to spend the day with Eluned and the spouses of the ambassadors.

Parisa was disappointed. She had been hoping they could begin work on painting the trees on her walls.

"I am sorry, my love," her mother said, "but considering everything that Eluned is doing to make us comfortable here, I did not feel that I could decline the invitation."

Parisa couldn't argue with that, she thought, considering the beautiful gown she would be wearing tonight or the fact she'd been given permission to paint objects on her wall and ceiling. It looked like she would have lots of time to read today. She needed to find a hobby that didn't require another person to arrange for it first, like knitting or practicing an instrument. No, she thought, someone would have to teach her those things before she could take them on.

She stopped in her tracks, and her mother and the page walked several more steps before they realized she had done so. She hurried to catch up. "Sorry," she apologized once alongside her mother again. "I thought of something."

Chokhmah raised her eyebrows, and Parisa blushed, rushing on, "It's just that I was trying to think of what I could do today besides read because I don't have any extra lessons work to do yet and I don't have any hobbies and I don't know how to play an instrument and I don't have any chores, and I remembered that Cian taught me how to shoot a crossbow. I'll bet there is someplace here that I can practice that."

The look on her mother's face made her continue, "Don't worry, I don't mean today. I know there's a lot going on today. But when things aren't so busy maybe I can be shown where it is, and I can go there on my own?"

Chokhmah nodded. "Yes, that sounds like an excellent idea. There is absolutely no reason why you should not work on those skills—the crossbow and of course, the sling."

Parisa's cheeks colored and she had to clench her fist to keep from tugging on her braid. "How did you know about the sling?" she asked in a small voice.

Chokhmah chuckled. "Darling, did you think that your father and I were completely unaware of what you were doing when you went off on your own? Bogaine is safe but accidents can still happen."

Like the time she'd fallen when she was trying to climb a tree and sprained her ankle really badly. She'd barely had time to cry out before her father was rushing into the clearing. He had carried her back to Rose Cottage, and her mother had treated the swelling with a cold cloth and a poultice to reduce the swelling before binding her ankle firmly with a long bandage.

They were back in their wing and standing in front of the door to the library. Chokhmah thanked the page and turned back to her daughter as he hurried away to see what his next duty might be.

"I . . ." The truth was she had thought they were completely unaware of what she was doing when she was alone, but now that she thought about it, and despite her father's current absence, they did love her a lot. Of course they worried about her. "I guess I just didn't think about," she finally admitted.

"One day you may have a child and then you will understand," her mother said. "It is like having a piece of your own heart outside your body, and your heart is not something you want to lose track of."

Parisa hugged her mother. "Now I understand how one of you was always there shortly after I hurt myself. I can't believe it never occurred to me."

Chokhmah kissed the top of her daughter's head. "Believe me when I say that it has been a joy watching how resourceful and imaginative you are, not to mention how skilled you have become both with throwing rocks and with the sling. Your father was very proud."

"Not proud enough to at least wait to leave until I've learned to shift," Parisa groused. "It seems to me that the chances are very high that he won't be there when I finally do."

"I suppose that was a risk he was willing to take," her

mother said. "Honestly, I do not understand it any more than you do. So, how will you occupy yourself until lunchtime?" Chokhmah changed the subject.

"I guess I'll read," Parisa said. "I'll go up to my room and grab *Bleak House* and then come down here and read in the library."

"Not on your balcony?"

"I'm kind of hoping they'll be up in my room painting the ceiling," Parisa said.

"I had not thought of that," her mother said. "They do work quickly around here. So, I will see you when the lunch bells ring?"

"Yes, Mama, see you then." And Parisa turned and headed for the staircase as her mother went to meet Eluned in her office.

Upstairs, Parisa found one woman in the room, hard at work painting her ceiling. The furniture had been draped in tarps and the woman was on a ladder.

"Do you mind if I reach under that tarp and get my book?" Parisa asked her.

The woman, whose dark brown hair was mostly covered by a kerchief, stopped painting and looked down at Parisa, amusement making her hazel eyes twinkle. "Ya do know tha' you don 'ave ta ask, yeah?"

Parisa blushed. "I don't understand. It would seem rude not to."

"Ya royl-tee, ain't ya?"

"No! Well, um, technically, yes, but I don't understand what that has to do with not being polite."

"It's in tha manner of speakin', yeah? Ya say: 'I'm gettin' ma book', yeah?"

"So, you're saying that I am supposed to say what I'm going to do, not ask?" Parisa said.

"Ex-ackly."

"I don't know," Parisa said. "Still seems rude to me. You know, because I'm the one who is disturbing your work."

"Work I was ordered ta do."

"Because it's your job?"

"Yeah, it's ma job."

"Nope, still seems wrong to me," Parisa said. "I'm Parisa, by the way. And you're . . ."

"Haniel."

"That's a beautiful name," Parisa said. "I really like it."

"It's a ol' Aden name," Haniel said. "Parisa's nice ta."

"Thank you, it's an old Pelfan name."

"Ah, so ya tha one."

"What one?"

"I heard thar was Pelfan royl-tee hea, yeah?"

Parisa blushed again. "We are, but my mother decided she'd rather not be queen. I actually live on a horse farm in Dyfed."

"Well, tha explains a lot," Haniel laughed. "P'raps all royl-tee should spend thar early yeas on a fahm, yeah?"

Parisa smiled. "Thanks. And thanks for painting my ceiling."

"Ya hopin' it looks like tha sky, yeah?"

"Yes," Parisa said. "My mother and I are going to paint a few clouds on it and paint some trees on the wall."

Haniel nodded in understanding. "Bringin' tha outside in, yeah?"

Parisa laughed. "That's the idea."

"I'd like ta see tha," Haniel said.

"When it's finished, I'll let you know," Parisa said, "if you really want to see it."

"Thank ya, I really would," Haniel said. "Now grab ya book so I can get back ta work." She laughed to show she was kidding, and Parisa giggled and hurried around to her bedside table to get her book, before heading back to the door.

"It was nice to meet you, Haniel," she said before leaving her room.

"It was nice ta meet you ta, Parisa," Haniel said.

Parisa returned to the library and curled up in an armchair. By the time the lunch bells rang, she had finished *Bleak House* and was perusing the shelves to find the book she was going to read next. She wanted to take a break from the stilted language of these ancient novels and find something more contemporary.

She knew Eluned really liked Geillis Saille, but preferred to find something on her own, something not recommended by someone else. She slid out a book called *The Bone Dolphin* by Tenar Atuan because the title intrigued her. It was about a girl her age that discovers she is actually a dragon. For some reason, that made her tear up. She swiped at her eyes as she hurried out of the library, book clutched to her chest, and made her way to the dining room, musing about the tears. It must be that it reminded her of her impending shift, and the fact her father might not be around to help her through it.

Parisa took a seat next to her mother so she could tell her about meeting Haniel, but before she could speak, her mother nodded at the book she was holding, "What are you reading?" she asked.

Parisa showed her the book.

"It looks very interesting," Chokhmah said. "Have you started it?"

"Not yet," Parisa said. "I went up to my room to get *Bleak House* and someone, um, Haniel, was already painting the ceiling."

"Haniel?"

"She was really nice," Parisa said. "We talked for a minute."

Eluned, who was on the opposite side of the table, leaned forward. "Really? What did you talk about?" She was always trying to get her children to talk to the various servants that worked at Castle Bennu because she remembered being a spoiled little princess herself and how Uriel had taught her to see everyone she came in contact with as an individual.

Parisa blushed. "She told me that because I was royalty, I didn't have to ask for permission to get my book, that I could just tell her I was getting it."

"And what did you say?"

"I said that I didn't agree, and that I thought it was rude."

Eluned grinned at Chokhmah. "Just what I would expect from your child." She turned back to Parisa. "That's wonderful. Good for you."

"She was curious about what I was doing to the room, and I told her when we were finished, she could come and see what we'd done. Is that okay?"

"Of course," Eluned said. "Who did you say it was again?"

"Haniel," Parisa said.

"I don't think I know her," Eluned said. "I'll have to ask Uriel if he does. Please remind me at dinner tonight, Parisa."

"I will," she said. "Thank you."

"By the way," she turned to the man to her right who'd been watching their exchange with interest, "this is Parisa, Chokhmah's daughter."

"Ah," he said, his voice resonant and tinged with the accent of Naphtali, "I have heard much about you this morning."

Parisa blushed again.

He stuck out a hand much larger than Parisa's and she reached for it. His shake was firm but also gentle. "I am Abayo-mrunkoje."

Parisa looked at him wide-eyed.

He laughed, and said, "But you may call me Abayo. My wife, Folade, is the ambassador from Naphtali. I will introduce you to her at dinner."

"Nice to meet you," Parisa said. "I look forward to meeting your wife."

"And this," Eluned said, turning to the woman on her left,

"is Yantine. Her husband is the ambassador from Adamah."

Yantine stretched out her hand and Parisa shook it. "Nice to meet you," she said.

Yantine, who had glossy auburn hair that was cut in a shoulder length bob, looked at Chokhmah and said, "She is just as lovely as you said she was."

Parisa found herself blushing again. "I love your hair," she told Yantine. "I don't think I've ever seen hair cut like that, but I really like it."

"Thank you, my dear," Yantine said, "it is very popular in Stonehelm right now."

A plate with roasted chicken, rice with a peppery brown gravy, and crisp green beans with slivered almonds was set in front of her. Guests, Parisa thought. They usually ate relatively simple lunches—soups, salads, or sandwiches. She had no intention of complaining, though. She loved chicken and rice.

After lunch, Parisa returned to her room to see if Haniel had finished painting. She was gone, and the tarps had been removed, but the smell of paint was still strong.

She took her journal and *The Bone Dolphin* out onto the balcony. The tinsel fluttered in the slight breeze, and Parisa wondered if she would ever see the raven again.

She lay down on the bench to read, but her full belly made her feel drowsy. Parisa closed her eyes, enjoying the feel of the warmth of the sun against her closed lids.

A loud croak woke her from her doze. Her book had fallen to the floor of the balcony, and as she reached down to pick it up, she realized that she was face to face with the raven. Its head was cocked, and it was looking at the gem on her journal again, which had also fallen off the bench.

"Sorry," she said, picking them both up, "you still can't have that. But," she pointed to the ribbon as if the bird could understand what she was saying, "you can have that."

Parisa stood up on the bench and walked down to the end

before jumping off and walking the last few steps to the door. She was trying to startle the bird as little as possible. She pulled the tinsel loose and lay it on the balcony floor before stepping back away from it.

The raven hopped over, picked the ribbon up with its beak, cocked its head at her again and then flew off.

Parisa watched it fly away, thrilled to death. She couldn't wait to tell her mother about it. But, while she waited, she would write about it in her journal.

CHOKHMAH

Chokhmah was not an idiot. She knew what Eluned was doing. Clearly, the woman was doing everything in her power to convince Chokhmah that she should become the queen of the Kingdom of Pelf. And it was not that she was disinterested. But whatever she chose, the choice would have to take what her daughter wanted into account.

If she had known when Parisa was five, and re-taking Pelf was in the planning stages, that seven years later her marriage to Faolan would be falling apart, things might have happened differently. But those seven years had passed, and Parisa was rapidly heading toward womanhood and should have some say in where their lives might be leading.

Still, there was no harm in learning what might be expected of her, and it would be nice to meet some new people.

Once at Eluned's office, Chokhmah was introduced to Abayo and Yantine, and although this was the beginning of her fourth day in Castle Bennu, she was finally treated to a tour of the building. They spent the morning seeing everything from the kitchens and laundry to the guestrooms and meeting rooms.

They also talked a lot, comparing both what they knew and what they had heard about each other's kingdoms. Both Chokhmah and Eluned, because of the Quest, had traveled significantly more than Abayo and Yantine, although both, as spouses of ambassadors, had already held posts in other kingdoms—Abayo in Sheba and Yantine in Annewven.

Eluned and Chokhmah were particularly interested in life in a kingdom no longer under the specter of the Crimson King, Arawn. Yantine said that it was her understanding that with Arawn imprisoned, and all his lords either removed, or imprisoned themselves, the people of the kingdom breathed much more easily.

"Basically," Yantine said, "anyone who was directly involved in the ongoing sacrifices to the Sacred Three was imprisoned."

Eluned told them about the costume party the night before the summer solstice, and just how many people had been complicit in her near sacrifice.

"I gave Prince Aahil all the names I was aware of," Eluned said, "and he promised me retribution. Were you there while he was there or was your tenure there since Queen Morrighan arrived?"

"We were in Prythew during the crossover," Yantine said.

"So, you were able to meet both Aahil and Merieme as well as Morrighan and Huang?"

"Yes," she said, "and they all seemed extremely competent."

Eluned sighed. "Well, I guess I will just have to trust that Aahil ferreted out those people, particularly Auron and Celyn."

"Yes," Chokhmah agreed. "You did spend quite a bit of time with them, both in Prythew and Arberth, which makes their betrayal so much worse."

"I tried to get Uriel to find out what had happened to them," Eluned said, "but he insisted that we had to take Aahil's word for it or risk 'sowing seeds of dissent' I think he said. And there were two other couples, as well, Bronwen and Gwenda, I think. I can't remember their husbands' names, and they weren't part of the inner circle, but they were definitely complicit."

"I'm confident that they were all punished for their part in the, um, sacrifices," Yantine said, "as was anyone who participated in the attacks that happened before the meeting in Tartessos. But I can ask my husband if he knows."

Eluned nodded. "All I remember is that their husbands oversaw something important like vineyards or livestock or something like that. It's not that I don't believe you . . ."

"But that you have yet to let it go?" Chokmah asked, eyebrow raised.

"If it hadn't been for Uriel, I'd be dead now," Eluned protested. "I still occasionally have nightmares about it when I am stressing over something."

"I promise I will check," Yantine said. "Honestly, the peace has been a boon for those of us who were opposed to the Awen Alliance."

"And for the neutral kingdoms, as well," Abayo said. "We are proud that Queen Njima was part of the Quest and that she sided with the Triquetra Alliance. These past twelve years have been wonderful."

CHOKHMAH RETURNED TO HER ROOM midafternoon in order to rest and get ready for the dinner that evening. Their dresses had been delivered to her room, so she knocked on Parisa's adjoining door to let her know she was back.

Receiving no answer, she opened the door and stepped in. The arched doors were open. She lay Parisa's dress on her bed before stepping out onto the balcony. Her daughter was writing in her journal.

"Hello darling," she said, softly so as not to startle her.

Parisa looked up from her journal, "Hi, Mama. That's funny."

"What is funny?"

"Something happened that I wanted to tell you about, but since you weren't here, I've been writing about it in my journal."

"And what is that?" Chokhmah asked, leaning against the door jamb.

"The raven came back," Parisa said. "I had dozed off and it woke me up. It wanted the sapphire on my journal again, so I gave him," she paused, "or her, the ribbon, and he flew away with it."

"That is quite exciting," her mother agreed. "What are you going to give it next time?"

Parisa paused, thinking. "Well, I'm not giving it my sapphire, that's for sure."

"Yes, you should definitely not do that," Chokhmah said. "What about something like a marble? I would imagine that there are some marbles in the nursery."

"That could work," Parisa said. "I'll check there and keep an eye out for something else that might work."

"Anyway," Chokhmah continued, "I wanted to let you know that your dress is finished, and I have laid it out on your bed. Also, Eluned gave me a few jeweled hair pins for you to use tonight."

Parisa looked alarmed. "I have to put up my hair myself?"

"Of course not, my love," her mother said. "I will do that for you."

"Oh, good," she said. "It's not that I don't think I can do it. It's just that I don't think I can do it well."

"Someday, with practice you will do it quite well,"

Chokhmah said, "but today is not the day to start practicing."

"It's not time to get ready yet, is it?"

"No, my love," she said. "I just wanted to check on you. I am about to go lie down for a little nap, if I can fall asleep. Or, perhaps, read. I would just like to rest before this evening as it will be later than usual for us. It sounds like you have already had a nap?"

"I didn't mean to," Parisa said, "I was going to read but instead, I fell asleep."

"Then it was meant to be," her mother said. Chokhmah turned to step back into Parisa's room.

"Mama?"

"Yes, my love?"

"Can we start painting trees on my walls tomorrow morning?"

"We are going to church tomorrow morning, but perhaps in the afternoon?"

Parisa nodded. "That's fine. I just want to get started so that I can rearrange my room and get it all finished."

"I understand," her mother said. She definitely felt more comfortable now that her room was complete. "I will let you," she covered her mouth with her hand as a yawn interrupted her speech. "I apologize. I am sleepier than I realized. I will let you know when it is time to get ready."

"Thanks, Mama," Parisa opened her journal. "Have a nice nap."

THAT EVENING WHEN CHOKHMAH RETURNED to her room after the dinner, she thought her daughter had acquitted herself quite well. Parisa had met the ambassadors like a lady, had been greatly complimented on both how beautiful and grown up she looked as well as on her intelligence and composure.

And, she had not even complained when she had to sit at a separate table with Fuchsia, Gavreel, and Faltuel to eat dinner. After a meal of tender and juicy lamb, served with rice, salads, yogurt, and a spicy tomato chutney, they were all served spiced dates, nuts, and fresh fruit to finish the meal.

While Faltuel took Gavreel off to bed, Eluned and Chokhmah gave Fuchsia and Parisa permission to accompany them to the library where they were allowed to stay for another hour, playing cards quietly in the corner while the adults sipped on brandy and talked.

About half an hour after Parisa headed off to bed, Chokhmah said her goodbyes and returned to her room as she was not accustomed to staying up so late.

She realized as she changed into her bed clothes that for more than two weeks now, she had been socializing nonstop. That had not been that unusual for her during the time of the Quest, and certainly growing up with the Roma had been a very communal experience with lots of celebrations.

But during the past twelve years at Bogaine, by and large she had spent most of her time alone, whether it was in her garden tending her herbs or making poultices, creams, and other concoctions while Parisa took lessons, did chores, or played.

In addition, and with rare exceptions, her community had remained very small—just her small family and Olcan's. Her community had narrowed even further when the fights with Faolan began as she became more and more withdrawn from his family, assuming they would take his side over hers.

Chokhmah had enjoyed herself that day and that evening too. She had forgotten how stimulating it could be having lots of other people around all the time. These past couple of weeks had also caused her to remember just how much she enjoyed being in the company of Eluned and Uriel. She was glad she would have six months or so to spend with them at Castle Bennu.

She intended to take advantage of every minute of her time there and encourage her daughter to do so as well. Chokhmah stood up, and taking her candle with her, went to the adjoining door and tapped lightly. No response.

Opening the door, she stepped into the room. Parisa was curled up in her bed, Echo snug against her chest. Chokhmah could see that her daughter must have hung up the black dress as it was neither in a pile on the floor or flung over the back of her chair or even the settee. And she doubted seriously that she had dirtied it enough to throw it in the clothes basket.

Chokhmah also noticed that Parisa had pulled away from the walls any piece of furniture she had felt strong enough to move. The armoire was still against the wall, and the bed, but the desk and dresser were several feet removed from it.

Smiling, Chokhmah returned to her room. She realized she was biased, but she was very proud of her child. Parisa was going to be an extraordinary woman.

CHOKHMAH, PARISA, AND HANIEL stepped back to observe their handiwork. When the latter had brought the ladder to Parisa's room so that they could work on painting clouds on the ceiling as well as trees and plants on the walls, they had discovered that Haniel also had a gift for drawing.

After church, Chokhmah and Parisa had worked on painting trees, birds, and even a few animals. Parisa painted a wolf peeking out from behind one tree while her mother worked on a deer and a rabbit.

The following morning, Haniel joined them to complete Parisa's room. She had worked on the clouds.

"It's almost like you can see different shapes in them," Parisa said, staring up at the ceiling. "When I look at that cloud from here," she pointed to a particular cloud, "it looks like a dragon breathing fire. But, if I move over here," she said walking to the other side of the room, "it looks like two dolphins swimming in the ocean."

"That is truly amazing," Chokhmah said to Haniel. "You have quite a gift."

"Thank ya, ma'am," Haniel said. "I'm ahways glad ta paint mor'an walls when I can, yeah?"

"Well, I will certainly let the Queen know of your talent," Chokhmah said. "How are your skills with painting people?"

"Not ta bad, yeah?" Haniel said. She turned to Parisa. "Ya got some paper?"

Parisa went to her desk and ripped a sheet out of her lessons book. Haniel walked over and moved the desk chair and asked Parisa to sit in it. Then she picked up one of the pencils on the desk and glancing at Parisa occasionally, quickly drew a sketch of her.

"By Omni, that's lovely!" Chokhmah said when Haniel had finished.

"Let me see." Parisa jumped up and joined them at the desk. She smiled. "I really like it. You made me look beautiful."

"That's because ya are, yeah?" Haniel said.

Parisa blushed. "Thank you. It's hard to think of myself that way."

"Of course, ya motha raised ya right, yeah?"

Chokhmah chuckled. "Thank you, Haniel, that means a lot." Then she turned to Parisa. "Well, thanks to Haniel, it looks as if you can resume your lessons with Zimbra this afternoon."

"Oh no," Haniel said, "Should I have taken longer?"

Parisa laughed. "No, it's fine. I'm actually looking forward to getting back to my lessons although," she looked at her mother, "what I'm really looking forward to is learning Pelfan."

"As am I," said her mother. "I will check with Uriel during lunch to see if any progress has been made in finding us a tutor." Chokhmah looked around the room again, and nodded, approvingly. "We did an excellent job, did we not?"

"We did," Parisa agreed.

Haniel laughed. "Ya know, I may jus' do this ta my room, assumin' Colomba will let me."

Chokhmah assumed Colomba was a roommate. "Do you live here at Castle Bennu?"

"Naw," Haniel said, "I live in Ponike wih ma woman. She has her own fishin' boat and sells what she catches. We live above tha store."

"If she needs to see this room for you to convince her," Parisa said, "you're more than welcome to show her."

"Yes," Chokhmah agreed, "I am sure that will not be a problem."

"Well, thank ya," Haniel said, closing the ladder and picking it up, "I may take ya up on that. And thanks again fa lettin' me help ya paint."

"No," Parisa said, "thank you. It's even better than I imagined."

The bells for lunch chimed, and Parisa and Chokhmah hurried downstairs. Chokhmah hoped that Uriel would join them for a change, otherwise she was going to have to seek him out.

Fortunately, he was already in the dining room when they arrived.

"Eluned told me that you were painting trees on your walls and clouds on your ceiling," he said to Parisa as she was pulling out a chair.

"I hope that's all right?" she asked. "We were told it was okay."

"It's fine," Uriel assured her. "How did it turn out?"

"It's incredible," Parisa said. "Haniel painted the clouds and you can see different things in them depending on how you look at them."

"She is quite talented," Chokhmah said, passing him the sketch she had done of Parisa.

"This is outstanding," he said, handing the drawing to Eluned.

"By Omni," Eluned said, "why are we wasting her talent having her paint rooms? She could be doing a portrait of us."

"I want to see," Fuchsia said.

Her mother held up the drawing so that her daughter could see it.

"Me too." Gavreel chimed in.

The drawing was turned in his direction.

"It looks just like you, Parisa," Fuchsia said, and Gavreel nodded agreement.

They were interrupted by the arrival of food—sandwich makings and fresh fruit.

Uriel slapped a sandwich together and added an apple and some grapes to his plate. "I'll see you all at dinner," he said. "I'm working on a speech to give at the military ball this coming weekend, so I'll just take this back to my office."

"Before you go," Chokhmah said, "is there any word yet on someone who can teach us Pelfan?"

"I haven't heard back from Raif yet, but I'll let you know as soon as I do."

"Thank you, Uriel."

He leaned down to kiss Eluned, "See you later, Fy Drysor."

Eluned pointed to her heart and then tapped his chest over his heart.

Chokhmah chuckled, "Are you two still doing that?" Eluned laughed her tinkling of bells laugh, which was her most genuine, and Chokhmah smiled. "Actually, it makes me very happy that you are."

She and Faolan had never really done anything like that despite the fact they had had a very physical relationship for many years, she thought as she put some fruit on her plate as well as a couple of slices of cheese and some chicken. She was old enough that she had to watch her weight more carefully.

Chokhmah looked up to see that while Eluned was preparing a sandwich for Gavreel, Parisa was helping Fuchsia with hers. Once again, she thanked Omni for such a selfless daughter.

As she bit into her apricot, her thoughts returned to Faolan. For the most part, he was a very practical man. He had always made fun of Eluned and Gwrhyr for what he called their 'sappiness'. Chokhmah had always attributed it to his wolf side, but in hindsight, she wondered if that was just the way he was raised. He, nor Olcan for that matter, had never really spoken about their parents who had died of the flu the winter their sons were away on their first postings as spies.

And, if she had tried to bring his parents up, he would change subjects as quickly as possible. She got the feeling that his father had been abusive, particularly when he had been drinking. No wonder his sons had found a way to be away from Bogaine for six months out of the year. But what about their mother? Did they dismiss her because she had never stood up for them when they were the brunt of their father's anger?

Olcan and Beibhinn had a good relationship, and while Olcan would drink on occasion, he mostly chose not to drink alcohol. Perhaps, he worried he might become like his father. Is that why Faolan felt being away from Bogaine was necessary for his sanity? Was he worried that he was turning into his father?

"Chokhmah?"

She realized that Eluned had been trying to get her attention.

"I am sorry," she apologized. "Seeing you and Uriel together has brought back so many memories." She was not going to talk about Faolan in front of his daughter.

"Good ones I hope," Eluned said.

"Yes, the good ones," Chokhmah smiled. "What were you saying?"

"I was saying that the military ball speech is a tough one

for Uriel because he needs to keep the military engaged enough that they want to keep training but balance it with the fact that we hope to live in peace for a long time."

"Yes, that would be tricky," Chokhmah agreed. "I wonder how long the Thirteen Kingdoms can remain friendly before some king, or queen, decides they need more."

"More power, more money, more land," Eluned said. "Only Omni knows what the trigger will be for new tensions to begin."

"The only thing we do know for sure," Chokhmah said, "is that peace never lasts forever."

"No, sadly," Eluned paused. "On to happier thoughts . . . after our children go off with Zimbra and Faltuel, I'd like to go see what you've done with your rooms."

"I still haven't fixed my furniture," Parisa said, overhearing.

"True," her mother said, "but it will allow her to see the painting more clearly."

Parisa nodded and took a bite of her sandwich.

"So? We'll do that?" Eluned asked.

"Yes, absolutely," Chokhmah said. It would give her a chance to talk to Eluned about Faolan.

"That all makes sense, Chokhmah, but does it change anything?" Eluned asked. They were sitting on the bench on Chokhmah's balcony. Living on the Gulf of Eudaemon, Eluned had long since given up trying to maintain her ivory complexion, which had been much easier in Zion than in Aden. She had slowly allowed her skin to tan to the shade of a heavily creamed coffee and there was now a sprinkle of freckles across her nose and cheeks.

"I do not yet know," Chokhmah said. "I know that I cannot

live at Bogaine if he is gone six to eight months out of the year. That is nonnegotiable."

"But what if you were Queen of Pelf?"

"As Queen, I could make him an ambassador and send him off myself or even find another position for him that would allow him to travel."

"Would he have any problem with you having authority over him?"

"I honestly do not know," Chokhmah sighed.

"Speaking of which, I assume you haven't told Parisa about her father's arrival date yet?"

"No," Chokhmah said, "Not yet. But I intend to the first time she mentions him again. She has been so caught up in other things these past few days that I have not had the heart to say anything to her."

"I suppose that makes sense," Eluned said. "I don't mean to bug you about it but the longer you wait, the angrier at you she will be."

"At me?"

"For waiting so long to tell her," Eluned said.

"Ah yes," Chokhmah said, "she would think that I had been deliberately holding it back. All right, I promise. I will tell her within the week."

Parisa

As Castle Bennu settled into its summer routine, Parisa established one of her own. She had barely started lessons with Zimbra before their summer break occurred, the tutor always being allowed to travel back to her hometown of Himyar in the northeast portion of the Kingdom of Aden to spend a month with her parents. As that did not include travel time, it meant that Parisa and Fuchsia had a two-month break from their schooling.

And the weekend after Zimbra left for Himyar, they had celebrated Gavreel's fifth birthday with a trip to the island of Athame because he wanted to spend a day at the beach. The royal family had a beach house on the pretty little island, which was known for its sandy beaches. They had left shortly after the early service at church with the intention of spending the night and returning to Castle Bennu early the following morning.

It was the first time that Parisa had had a chance to go sailing since they arrived and Uriel and his crewman started teaching her some of the basics of sailing, including the terms that were used, from port and starboard to tacking and jibing.

Shortly before lunch time, the sloop, which Uriel had named Fy Drysor, sailed into the small cove that was reserved expressly for the royal family. Fuchsia told Parisa that they called it Dolphin Haven because sometimes the mammals could be seen cavorting in its waters. Parisa hoped that they would see some before they left the following morning.

There was a cottage on stilts at the end of the dock with three bedrooms, a living room, a kitchen, and a bath, which they used any time they wanted to spend more than just a day on the beach. Each year the family spent a week or two in the house at Dolphin Haven, but that was usually just before the children's school year began again in earnest.

When Parisa had enquired as to why the house was on stilts, Eluned had explained that during some high tides and often during storms, the waves would wash up under the house.

"And it doesn't hurt the house?" Parisa had asked.

"It shakes the house a little," Eluned said, "but the piers are buried very deeply. There's nothing to worry about."

It had been an enjoyable day up until sunset, when her mother asked her to go for a walk. When they were far enough down the beach that they were out of hearing, Parisa's mother said, "There is something I must tell you that I have put off for far too long. I hope you will forgive me."

Parisa turned toward her mother, amber eyes large with dread. "What is it?"

"Your father will not make it back to Bogaine in time for Yuclog."

"But that's more than six months after he left," Parisa exclaimed. "I don't understand."

"What your father neglected to tell us before he left for Sigwald is that he was not counting how long it would take to travel there and back."

Parisa was furious. "So, he's six months in Simoon and it takes a month to travel there," she calculated the new information. "That means that we'll be lucky if he's back at Bogaine by my thirteenth birthday."

"I am afraid that is exactly what it means," her mother said.

"That," Parisa sputtered, "that son of a bitch."

"Parisa!"

"I can't help it." She angrily swiped the tears away from her eyes. "How could he do that to us?"

"I wish I had an answer for you," Chokhmah said. "The only thing I can think of is that he knew I would put down my foot if I knew he would be gone that long."

"But he will be all alone at Yuclog. Did he even think about that?"

"Honestly," her mother had said, "I do not think he was taking anything or anyone into account, just his need to get away."

"Then I am not sure I want to go back to Bogaine," Parisa pouted.

"Fortunately, my love," Chokhmah said, "that is not a decision we have to make any time soon."

"How long have you known this?"

"Gittan told me the night before we left for Ponike," Chokhmah said.

"Why did you wait so long to tell me?"

"Because you have been so happy and . . . I really have no excuse except that I dreaded seeing that look in your eyes again."

"Again?" Parisa looked startled.

"It is the same look that I would see when your father started yelling at me, and you would slink off to your room. Do not think that I did not notice. It broke my heart every time."

A few more tears slid from Parisa's eyes.

"And again, when he was so happy about leaving for Simoon."

"You've had your own look too," Parisa said.

"Have I?" Chokhmah asked.

"Yes," Parisa said. "I don't know how to explain it. Like shock, maybe? Like you can't believe that he could disappoint you so much?"

"So much for my, what was it that Eluned called it? Poker face?"

"Poker face?" Parisa asked.

"She learned it in one of her great grandmother's books, the same great grandmother that Fuchsia was named for. Supposedly, it is a face devoid of expression because if you were playing a card game called 'poker', you could not let the other players know whether your hand was good or not."

Parisa nodded. That made sense for more things than card games. "So, you were trying to remain expressionless and failed?"

"Apparently," her mother said, then murmured, "I wonder if your father saw that, as well?"

"You know," Parisa paused, they had turned and were walking back toward the beach house, "I don't think he did. First, he was drunk and too angry and later, he was just too happy."

"You knew he was drunk?" Chokhmah asked, quietly.

"Maaamaa," she dragged the word out, "I'm not an idiot."

Chokhmah chuckled. "No, my love, you are definitely not that."

Parisa stopped again and made a show out of looking at the shells scattered above the high tide line. Picking one up, she showed it to her mother and said, "Don't think that I'm not furious with Papa. All I want to do is be in my own bed in my own room at Castle Bennu right now. But it's Gavreel's birthday and he doesn't deserve to have his birthday ruined because my father is a, um, because he's a jerk."

"That is very noble of you," her mother said.

"I'm telling you mostly because if I look like I'm not having fun, pinch me or something to remind me to cheer up."

"I will remind you," Chokhmah said, "but it probably will not be a pinch."

Parisa sighed. "Well, as long as you know what I mean."

For the next couple of hours, Parisa kept her word, but after the cake had been eaten and presents opened, she begged exhaustion and headed off to bed. Fortunately for her, it had been a long day for everyone, and the others soon followed suit.

Now, a month had passed since Gavreel's birthday, and Parisa filled her weeks with crossbow and sling practice, learning Pelfan, sailing lessons, horseback riding, drawing, journaling, and lots of reading.

Her favorite thing, and something she had yet to grow tired of, was the occasional visits from the raven she was now calling Pallas. When she had asked Eluned for ideas on shiny objects to set out for her raven friend, Eluned had offered some broken pieces of costume jewelry and the next morning at breakfast had handed her the jewelry along with a book that contained an ancient poem, called appropriately enough, "The Raven".

The poem was by someone named Edgar Allan Poe, and she had liked the poem so much that she had taken the book up to her room and copied the poem into her journal. It was while she was sketching the raven onto a bust of Pallas that she decided she would call her raven by that name.

She'd had to make up what Pallas looked like, so she gave him a vague male face, mostly hidden by the raven's claws. According to Eluned, Pallas was a Titan. Parisa hadn't known what that meant, so Eluned found a book in the library on ancient Greek mythology and she had tried to valiantly to read about it.

It was all very confusing, and Parisa found that she just couldn't summon any enthusiasm for a place that no longer even existed. She did like having a name for her raven, though. She'd briefly considered Lenore and Nevermore but had settled on Pallas as it seemed to suit the bird. Besides, that way both their names started with P-A, and Pallas sounded like palace, and she was beginning to think that she wouldn't mind living in a palace the rest of her life. Perhaps, Zhaleh Palace in Buta in the Kingdom of Pelf. She repeated it aloud, "Zhaleh Palace in Buta in the Kingdom of Pelf." Yes, she thought, that has a nice ring to it.

Pallas dropped by every few days or so, and so far, she'd always managed to find him something—costume jewelry, shiny ribbons, chipped marbles, glittery rocks. Parisa had also started speaking to it—the same short phrases over and over, "Hello, Pallas" and "I'm Parisa".

Today, while she sat on her balcony bench, conjugating some Pelfan verbs, and nibbling on a piece of dried meat, the cookie Fuchsia had sneaked out of the dining room for her sitting next to her untouched, Pallas with a flutter of feathers and a croak landed on the pavement of the balcony.

Parisa looked up in surprise, "Pallas, I wasn't expecting you today."

The raven croaked again and cocked his head at her.

"I don't have anything for you," she said, spreading her hands to show they were empty. She glanced down at the cookie, a sugar cookie, her least favorite. She picked it up and held it out to him, "Unless you want this?"

Pallas hopped over and plucked the cookie from her outstretched hand. Then, cookie clasped firmly with his beak, he flew off.

Parisa shook her head. Maybe she could keep some snacks on hand. Whatever she could grab from the dining room that was healthy. She didn't think it would be good for Pallas to eat cookies all the time. Nuts, maybe? Fruit? Eggs? It would just have to be things that he could easily clasp with his beak.

Parisa turned back to her verbs but her thoughts kept drifting. It had been a couple of weeks since a pigeon had arrived with a note saying that her father was in Sigwald, and that he'd write again once he was settled. But they had yet to receive a letter. Cian's letters were also becoming fewer and farther apart.

That wasn't too surprising, Parisa guessed. How many times could she write about her crossbow practice or horseback riding or sailing lessons? Maybe the long-promised camping trip coming up later that week would be worth writing about.

THEY LEFT CASTLE BENNU at the crack of dawn so as not to make a stir. Everyone had dressed in leather breeches and light cotton sweaters because of the early morning chill, and the females had tucked their hair into the caps they were wearing in order to give the appearance that there were six males heading out for a day of hunting. Except for Gavreel who was riding with his mother, they all rode their own horses. Parisa held the lead for Eluned's donkey, Tikvah, who was carrying the three tents and cooking gear.

Uriel had picked a camping spot about five miles or so west of Ponike alongside a small creek in a mixed hardwood forest that was a hunting ground for the kingdom's lords and other officials in the autumn. In the summer, they should have the woods to themselves barring any poachers, although Uriel's gamekeeper had assured him that he was not having a problem with poaching that summer.

They arrived at the site about nine o'clock and got to work setting tents up immediately.

"Seems like old times, doesn't it?" Eluned said to Uriel and Chokhmah.

"Not quite," Uriel said, "because I'd be sharing a tent with you and Jabberwock, and Chokhmah would be sharing one with Faolan. Instead . . ." he pointed to Fuchsia and Parisa who were relieving Tikvah of the rest of the gear she was carrying. "Where's Gav? Hey! Gavreel! Don't go down to the creek by yourself. Wait until one of us is with you."

"But I want to catch a frog."

"We'll look for frogs as soon as the tents are set up," Uriel promised. With three adults, they had decided they needed three tents, and each adult would sleep with a child.

"I have an idea," Chokhmah said. "Why do not Parisa and I each share a tent with Fuchsia and Gavreel, and you two can take a trip down Memory Lane."

"That's not necessary, Chokhmah," Eluned said.

"Of course it is not necessary," Chokhmah said, "but it might be nice. You do not mind sharing a tent with Fuchsia, do you Parisa?"

"Not at all," Parisa said. "It'll be fun."

"Can I Mommy? Please," Fuchsia said.

"And you really don't mind taking Gavreel?" Uriel asked.

Chokhmah shook her head. "Besides, you are right here if for some reason he needs one of you. Do you mind sharing a tent with me, Gavreel?"

Gavreel shook his head, "No Auntie Hawk-ma."

Parisa smiled. Gavreel had a difficult time with the fricative 'ch' at the beginning of her mother's name and was convinced the rest of them were pronouncing 'hawk' funny. Fortunately, her mother enjoyed Gavreel's pronunciation.

"It is the closest I will ever get to being another creature," she had told Parisa.

"I'd rather be a hawk than a wolf," she had told her mother, "at least then I could fly."

Once the tents were set up, and the bed rolls unfurled, they walked down to the creek so that Gavreel could catch a frog.

"What are you going to do with it once you catch it?" Fuchsia asked.

"Keep it as a pet," Gavreel said.

"No," Uriel and Eluned said together.

"Why not?" Gavreel wanted to know.

"Frogs are not pets," Eluned explained.

"Why not?"

"Because it is not fair to the frog, Gav," Parisa said. "Look at the creek."

Gavreel studied the creek for a moment then turned back to Parisa.

"Can you make a creek for your frog?"

"No, but I can give him a dish of water."

"It's hardly the same thing, is it?" Parisa said. "Some things just need to be free. You wouldn't want to spend the rest of your life in a bowl, would you?"

"Well . . . uh . . . no."

"Can I play with it while we're here and put it back in the creek before we go?" Gavreel asked his mother.

"Yes, but if it wants to get away, let it," she said.

"Yeah, frogs aren't really excited about playing," Parisa said, "but it may let you hold it for a minute."

Gavreel did find his frog, and he held onto it for maybe ten seconds before it wriggled out of his hands, and somehow, maybe accidentally on purpose, he managed to fall into the creek while trying to catch it again.

Fortunately, it was summer, and the morning was warming up so Parisa and Fuchsia retreated to their tent to change into clothes they could get wet before returning to the creek with Chokhmah. And while Eluned was hanging Gavreel's soaked clothes out to dry, Uriel helped his son change into his bathing clothes and took him back down to the water.

The children played in and around the creek until it was time to head back to the clearing for lunch. Parisa found a thin sheet of mica nearly the size of her palm on the creek bottom and set it aside to take back to Pallas.

When she got back to their campsite, she tucked the mica into her journal, changed back into dry clothes, then headed back outside to help with lunch.

Eluned was setting out crackers, cheese, and pickles, and Uriel and Chokhmah burst into laughter.

"Pickles," Gavreel shouted. "I hate pickles."

"I'm not a big fan either, Gavreel," Parisa said, "but there is only so much you can carry when you're camping."

"I think Eluned is being silly, my love," her mother said.

Uriel still laughing said, "I think she's replicating a lunch we had when we nearly ran out of food once."

"And those crackers were stale," Eluned said joining in their laughter. "Don't worry my dears," she continued, "there's more." And she pulled some hard sausage, some pears, hard boiled eggs, and nuts from the bag.

Parisa fixed herself a plate, and went to sit against an oak tree that towered over the clearing they were camped in. She had just assembled a cracker with a slice of salami and cheese on it when an object fell from the tree and into her lap.

A voice croaked, "Parisa" and she looked up to see Pallas perched on the branch above her.

She looked down at the object in her lap, and picked it up, mouth dropping open. It was a small dolphin carved out of white quartz.

"Pallas!" She jumped up, dolphin in one hand, cracker in the other. "Wait." She set the cracker down on her plate, and picked up a hardboiled egg, holding it up for the bird to see.

Pallas launched himself off the branch and landed at her feet. Before taking the proffered egg from her hand, he croaked 'Parisa' once more before taking off. She watched him until he disappeared from view, then turned to see everyone staring at her in awe.

"Well," Uriel said, from where he was sitting on a blanket with his wife and son, "that was unexpected."

"What did he give you?" Her mother asked, standing and walking over to Parisa, who put the object in her mother's outstretched palm.

As Chokhmah studied the little dolphin, the others walked over to the oak.

"That's beautiful," Eluned said. The dolphin shimmered in the sunlight.

"It's almost like the one in my dream," Parisa said.

"Extraordinary," her mother replied. "Coincidence?"

"What dream?" Uriel asked.

"Before we left Bogaine," Chokhmah answered, "Parisa had a dream similar to the one I had."

"But in my dream, I could see Mama through the window, and she was wearing a crown," Parisa continued, "and the sigil of Pelf on the crown changed from a kraken into two dolphins, one black and one white."

"Well, that sounds better than a scary kraken to me," Eluned said. "Men always have to have such threatening sigils. I'll bet you the sigil of Favonia was designed by a woman."

As Parisa shuffled through the thirteen sigils in her mind, Chokhmah chuckled. "It is true that Favonia was once matriarchal."

"What's matrichal?" Gavreel asked.

"In this case," his mother answered, "it means that the kingdom is ruled by women."

"It is true that only three of the thirteen sigils are non-threatening," Parisa said. "The Unicorn of Dyfed, the Flying Horse of Naphtali, and the Sea Turtle of Favonia. And do we really have a chance to make Pelf matriarchal?"

"That could be done," her mother agreed.

"Hmmm," Parisa mused. "What if I only give birth to sons?"

"In that case," Uriel said, "it would be your decision. Either the kingdom could switch back to being patrilineal or your son, or you for him, would have to choose a bride who would rule in his stead."

Parisa nodded, looking at her dolphin. "Or together, but with the knowledge that a daughter would rule next?"

"That could work," Eluned agreed.

It was something to think about, anyway, Parisa decided.

"I didn't know Pallas could say your name," Fuchsia said, changing the subject, an accusing glint in her eyes.

"I didn't either," Parisa said. "That's the first time he's said it." She looked up at the sky again, wondering how he had found her here in the woods so far away from the castle. She guessed, technically, as the crow flies, or in this case raven, the thought made her smile, it probably wasn't as far from the castle. But had Pallas followed her, or did he live in these woods?

"I think we should finish our lunches before the bugs do," Eluned said.

Parisa sat down again as the others returned to their seats and picked up her uneaten cracker after flicking an ant off it. Were they really destined to end up in the Kingdom of Pelf? It was beginning to seem like a foregone conclusion rather than a choice they had to make.

After they finished lunch and put away the leftovers, the group got ready to go on a hike. Parisa heard Eluned telling her mother than she didn't want to risk Gavreel getting dozy and then keeping Chokhmah awake all night.

They followed a well-worn path into the woods that Uriel told them was used by hunters and deer alike. The early afternoon sun was mostly blocked by the trees and dappled the trail they followed with light. Uriel was in the lead with Gavreel, and at one point he stopped, and held up a finger to his lips.

They quietly gathered behind him and he pointed out an owl sleeping in a hole in a cottonwood tree.

Parisa picked up on it quickly despite how well its camouflaged plumage hid it from the casual passerby. Gavreel never saw it, and they continued hiking, and Parisa suspected that Fuchsia had not seen it either, but rather than embarrass herself said that she did.

The trail ended at a cart track and they turned east and took it back the way they had come. They had crossed the track earlier that morning on their way to the campsite, and when they finally reached that trail, they turned right on it and walked the short distance into the woods where the clearing that held their tents was located.

Other than spotting the owl, nothing of note had happened on the hike, and Parisa was eager to get her journal and find a private spot in which she could write about what had happened with Pallas. It wasn't that she hadn't enjoyed the walk. She always loved being in the woods, but it had been hard to keep focused when all she could think about was what had just happened with the raven.

Uriel had brought a single rod, and he and Gavreel headed off to dig up some worms and try their hand at fishing at a quiet spot in the creek. Fuchsia and her mother set off to find some wildflowers with which to make flower crowns, and Chokhmah said she was going to take advantage of the quiet and read for a while. Parisa suspected 'read' was code for 'nap' but didn't say so.

With everyone occupied, she returned to her oak and opened her journal. When she had finished writing, Parisa headed back to her tent, tucking the journal into her bag, and retrieving her current book. She grabbed one of the picnic blankets and spread it out under her oak so she could lie down and read. Fuchsia and her mother returned about a quarter of an hour after she started reading and she readily agreed when

Fuchsia asked her if she wanted to help them make the flower crowns.

While they were chaining the flowers together, Uriel and Gavreel returned empty-handed.

"The fish weren't biting," Uriel said, "and I remembered I needed to get a fire going if we want to start cooking dinner at a normal time. Anyone want to help me collect some wood?" Parisa jumped up. She was already bored with making the crowns. "I'll be glad to help," she told him.

"I've got to finish making my crown, Daddy," Fuchsia said.

"Gavreel, can you look around the edge of the clearing and pick up any little sticks and twigs you can find and make a pile right here," he pointed to a spot he had cleared earlier. "We're going to need them to help start the fire."

"Yes, daddy," Gavreel wandered away toward the edge of the clearing just as Chokhmah emerged from her tent.

"I will keep an eye on him," she told Uriel, following behind Gavreel so that he could load her arms with sticks.

Parisa watched her for a moment before following Uriel out of the clearing.

"How's she doing?" Uriel asked her.

"She seems happier, to me, than she has been in a long time," Parisa said to him. "Papa could be really mean to her when he'd been drinking."

Uriel sighed, bending over to pick up a good-sized log, "I'm sorry to hear that. Your mother is one of the wisest and most truly good people I've had the luck to know."

"Yes, she is," Parisa said. "When we left Bogaine, I couldn't wait to get back there again. I just wanted things to be normal again. Now I know that things will never be that normal again, so I have to decide what I want my new normal to be."

"I think that's the toughest part of life to come to terms with," Uriel said. "Things change continually. Bad things happen and good things happen, but nothing ever stays the same."

Parisa glanced up at him and nodded. Looking back over her short twelve years, she had to agree. Look how just how much things had changed in the past two months.

She and Uriel scavenged for wood until their arms were full and headed back to the camp, dropped the wood, and then returned to the woods for another round.

When they returned, Uriel got to work building the fire while Parisa returned for a third round. You could never have too much wood. Even if they didn't keep the fire going all night, they would want it burning for some time after it grew dark. After a fourth trip into the woods, she decided to take a break and wait to see if Uriel wanted any more wood after he finished building the fire.

She picked up the book she'd left under the tree and returned it to her tent, and then went to look for her mother. Chokhmah was at the creek retrieving some small clay pots that held butter and sour cream that had been sitting in a small pool of water and a large package of waxed paper bound with twine and resting in a pool of very shallow water next to the creek bank.

"What's in there?" She asked her mother who was handing her the pots to carry back to camp.

"I believe that these are the steaks we are going to eat tonight," Chokhmah said.

"How do you cook steaks in a fire?"

"I believe that Uriel packed a little metal grate," she said.

"Oh, is that what that was," Parisa had removed the grill from one of Tikvah's panniers. It had been small. She guessed they would have to cook the steaks one at a time.

"A little different from our grill at Bogaine, is it not?"

Yes, it was, Parisa thought. The grill at Bogaine was large enough to cook a whole deer on and was constructed from stone into which a metal grate had been securely anchored. They built the fire on a large flat stone under the grate.

They returned to camp and deposited the food with Eluned and Chokhmah offered to forage in the woods for greens, herbs, and mushrooms so that they might have a salad.

"See it is just like old times," Eluned laughed, handing Chokhmah a basket. Parisa and Chokhmah headed into the woods that bordered the creek as her mother thought they would more likely find mushrooms there.

"Oh look, Parisa," Her mother was pointing at a vibrant orange fungus near the base of a tree. She picked it and held it up to Parisa's nose. "What does it smell like?"

"Lobster," Parisa laughed. "I didn't know a mushroom could smell like seafood."

"And that's why it's called a lobster mushroom, and they taste as good as they smell. I can sauté them in some of that butter. Let us see if we can find some more."

Parisa and her mother scrounged up half a dozen more, hurried down to the creek to wash them, and then carried their treasure back to camp.

Considering they were camping, their dinner felt like a feast with potatoes that had been baked in the coals, mushrooms sautéed in butter, and steaks grilled over the fire.

Eluned had even carried along some chocolate cake for dessert but they were all too full to eat it.

"We can have cake for breakfast," Fuchsia suggested.

"We'll see," Eluned told her, which Parisa knew was mother speak for, 'that's not going to happen'. That was fine with her. She'd rather have her leftover steak or bacon and eggs.

They ended the evening with Eluned and Uriel taking turns playing the harp. Each camper was allowed to choose a familiar song for the group to sing along to.

Gavreel was nodding off when they decided it was time to get ready for bed and crawl into their bed rolls for the night.

The following morning, after a breakfast of leftovers (Fuchsia was allowed a very small piece of cake), they packed up and returned to Castle Bennu.

"So, what did you think of camping?" Parisa asked Fuchsia after they had ridden about a mile.

"It was fun," Fuchsia said, "but not something I want to do all the time."

Parisa thought she could live outdoors pretty much all the time—in the woods, on the water, or even in the air—as long as she had someplace to curl up that was warm and dry when the weather got too bad.

Autumn

"Delicious autumn!
My very soul is wedded to it,
and if I were a bird I would fly about the earth
seeking the successive autumns."

-George Eliot

CHOKHMAH

Parisa's summer break had ended and she was once more immersed in lessons with Zimbra. Other than their Pelfan lessons, Chokhmah saw little of her daughter during the day. She finally had a chance to take advantage of all the time that stretched ahead of her and accompany Eluned on her trips to visit the schools she had started.

The school in Ponike was their first destination as they could easily make it there and back within the day. Eluned told Chokhmah that the Ponike School was her largest with half a dozen teachers and more than seventy students. At first, Eluned's schools had focused on basics like reading, writing, and arithmetic. But, after a few years, science and history had been added to the curriculum.

Chokhmah wanted to sit in on a class or two so following a tour of the facility—a one story building with a view of the ocean and lots of windows—Chokhmah joined the science class.

"Do you not think that the students will be distracted by what is going on outside?" Chokhmah asked as they headed to the cafeteria where they would join the students and teachers for lunch.

"Perhaps," Eluned said, "if this were a school in which they were forced to sit all day and take lessons they were not interested in. But the thing about my schools is that attendance is not required. I understand there was a time when all children had to go to school whether they wanted to or not, but that was when the world had too many people and everyone had to work, and many people couldn't afford to pay someone to take care of their children. Now that we are reduced to thirteen kingdoms and there are so many less people, schooling should be something one desires."

"Because if you do not want book learning, you can learn a trade?" Chokhmah asked.

"Exactly," Eluned agreed. "Not all jobs require that one read or write, but if it's something you'd like to learn, there is no reason you shouldn't be able to do so. We also encourage those who are interested to study to become teachers themselves. We had to start the schools with teachers who had been educated at home. Now, all of the schools have at least one teacher raised up by the school."

"Do the students have to pay a fee?"

"No student is required to pay in order to attend," Eluned said, "although we encourage an offering of some sort, if possible, because it somehow gives the student a little more investment in learning."

They sat down at a long table with some of the teachers and students. "Uriel has included my schools in the Kingdom's budget, but some of that money comes from donations and fundraisers, and not just taxes."

A tray with a bowl of vegetable soup, a chicken sandwich, and a pear was placed in front of them along with a glass of water.

"Also," Eluned said, picking up her spoon, "we try and feed our students a healthy meal each day because, sadly," and she lowered her voice to a whisper, "you can't guarantee they are being fed well at home."

After lunch, Chokhmah sat in on a history class, and was delighted that they were currently studying the history of the Kingdom of Aden.

"That was highly illuminating," she told Eluned afterwards. "I know much history in general, but I know very little in detail about any of the Kingdoms. Which reminds me, did not Nahid say that they had a written history of Pelf in their library at Kuna?" Chokhmah had met Nahid, the leader of the Pelfan community in the Kingdom of Naphtali, while the Questers were enroute to the former capitol of Kamea where they intended to search for the crock and dish that together made up one of the Thirteen Hallowed Treasures.

"I had completely forgotten about that," Eluned exclaimed. "So much has happened since then that it totally fled my mind, but I do remember her offering you a chance to read it."

"I wonder if there is some way in which it could be sent to me to read and return or perhaps a copy made," Chokhmah mused. The thought alone of making the trip to Kuna and back exhausted her, although this time, at least, she could travel the main road to Jazeel and not have to risk a dangerous river crossing.

"We can send a pigeon to Njima and Yona when we get home," Eluned suggested, "and see if they might be able to arrange something."

A FEW DAYS LATER, a pigeon returned with the answer: We will look into that immediately. Sending Dev to Kuna to arrange something. We miss you all so much! Much love, Njima and Yona

Chokhmah and Eluned were in the midst of planning an extensive trip to visit the Queen's other four schools. The furthest was two weeks away in Himyar.

"That's where I discovered Zimbra," Eluned told Chokhmah. "She was daughter of the town's Lord Mayor and was my first teacher there. When Fuchsia was old enough to be tutored, I asked her if she'd be willing to do that because she is excellent with children. I realize that it's selfish of me to take her away from Himyar, but the opportunity appealed to her."

"You did not want to teach Fuchsia, yourself?"

"I liked the idea of separating myself from that aspect of their growing up," Eluned explained. "I liked the idea of being their mother only. You would probably have felt the same had you been Queen of Pelf when it was time to school Parisa." Chokhmah was silent.

"Does that make sense?" Eluned hurried on. "I wasn't trying to offend you."

Chokhmah chuckled, "Do not worry about that, my dear. I was thinking about what being a queen requires, and believe me, I am already seeing just how different it is from being a Roma or a healer on a horse farm."

"I have to admit I was somewhat oblivious to what my mother was doing while I was growing up," Eluned said, "and now I have developed great respect for her. She clearly paid attention when she was growing up."

"And I am paying attention now," Chokhmah laughed. "Where do we go after Himyar?"

From Himyar in the northeast corner of the Kingdom near the source of the Caumeda River, they would travel westward to Qataba on the Sandcana River near the borders of Zion and Naphtali. That was the shortest distance they would have to travel, about three days. It was another four days or so to Yahirr on the southern banks of the great lake known as Baxcour. And, finally, another eight or nine days to the school in Awsan, a port town on the Anoon Ocean west of Ponike. From there, it was another two days back to Castle Bennu.

They would be gone nearly five weeks, but both women

felt they could leave their children in the capable hands of Uriel, Zimbra, and Faltuel for that long.

Traveling with the Queen's entourage and staying in inns and hotels made the journey a much easier one than Chokhmah had experienced while on the Quest, which had interspersed grueling days of travel with the occasional pampering at a hotel or inn, not to mention the lovely stays at Castle Indalo in Jazeel, Castle Mykerinos in Goshen, and Salama Palace in Sheba. She had even spent a couple of nights at Castle Rodolph in Sigwald although that had been fraught with anxiety because not only had she needed to find the Whetstone of Tudwal Tudglyd while there, but she needed to heal the infant son of one of the princes. Fortunately, she had accomplished both.

Chokhmah was musing on this on the last day of their trip and suddenly laughed out loud.

"What is it?" Eluned asked.

"I've just realized that I have stayed in castles in nine of the Thirteen Kingdoms, two in Annewven, actually."

Eluned was silent for a moment, counting. "You've got me beat. I can only think of eight, and I didn't actually stay at Tsering Palace in Jungnay."

"That means that somehow, between us, we have to get to Kamartha, Adamah, and Pelf." Chokhmah laughed again, pleased. She really had had quite an amazing life.

"I imagine you don't have to worry about making it to Zhaleh Palace," Eluned said. "I still have a strong feeling you're going to wind up in Pelf."

"It is looking more and more likely, is it not?"

"Yes, it is," Eluned said, voice serious. "And according to Uriel, Parisa seems to be getting more on board with it, as well."

"I believe she is harboring some deep anger towards her father right now," Chokhmah said. "After his last letter, I asked him to please write his daughter a letter that was just for her and not for the both of us. If he does not somehow explain his behavior to her in a way that she can understand, I am afraid he might lose her love for many years to come."

"I understand," Eluned said, "and it would be wrong for you to try to explain away his behavior. She needs you to stand up for her because he doesn't. It would feel like a double betrayal."

Chokhmah nodded. It would indeed. His few letters had been very spare as if he had not known what to say. At least, she now knew where he was living and that his job was keeping him very busy, or so he had said. Personally, she found it difficult to believe, but she supposed it was possible. She had not been to Sigwald in more than thirteen years. She imagined things had changed a lot in that time with King Hamartia and Queen Foehn no longer ruling the Kingdom with iron fists.

A minute later, Eluned laughed.

"What is it?"

"You have to become Queen before Year XV," she said.

"Why is that?"

"The Kingdom of Pelf is hosting the next meeting of the Thirteen Kingdoms," Eluned said, "and if you are Queen of Pelf, I will definitely be in attendance, and I will bring Fuchsia and Gavreel with us."

And Yona and Njima would probably both come if that were the case, she thought. All the Questers that were still living could be there. The only question was—would Faolan be there?

IT WAS LATE AFTERNOON before they finally reached the road that led to Castle Bennu. As they rounded a bend and the castle came into view, Chokhmah felt that usual flutter of butterfly wings in her stomach. She could be away from home, trusting all was well, until she saw her place of abode upon returning.

Then it was as if all the anxiety that she had neatly stored away while gone came rushing back, and suddenly she was dying to know that everything had gone well in her absence.

As she rushed toward the main staircase, Chokhmah was trying to calculate where her daughter would be at that time. Had she stayed in her own room? Would she be there? Or maybe, she had grown lonely and would be with Fuchsia.

She need not have worried because her daughter was rushing down the staircase and throwing herself in her mother's arms.

"Mama," Parisa was nearly sobbing, "it felt as if you were gone forever."

"Oh my love," Chokhmah said, tearing up as well, "it did feel like a very long time."

"Promise you won't leave me again."

Chokhmah lifted her daughter's chin with a finger and looked into her eyes. "Was it really that awful?"

"It wasn't awful," Parisa said, sniffing, "it's just that I missed you."

"I missed you, too, my love," her mother said. "And I promise that I will not again make a trip that long without you." The truth was that most nights she had keenly felt her daughter's absence, particularly their morning and bedtime rituals.

Uriel was now coming down the stairs with Fuchsia and Gavreel just as Eluned arrived at the bottom of the main staircase.

"Did you grow a pair of wings or something?" she laughed when she reached Chokhmah, "Because, I vow you flew out of the carriage."

"Parisa too," Uriel laughed. "She was up in her aerie, watching for the arrival of the carriage, and then she took wing and was gone."

"Aerie?" Chokhmah asked.

"When we realized you were due back soon," Uriel said, "we made a little playroom up in the southwest tower so we could be on the lookout for your arrival."

"Parisa calls it a nest," Fuchsia said, clinging to her mother's right side while Gavreel clung to her left.

"That she does," Uriel laughed.

"We were so high up," Parisa explained, "that it felt like I was in a nest."

"We did have a bird's eye view," Uriel laughed.

"And I'm the one that has the eagle eye," Parisa snickered.

"Well, you did spot them first," Uriel agreed but he was still laughing.

"And now my love," Chokhmah chuckled, "I can take you back under my wing."

"Where I'll be as happy as a lark," Parisa said and dissolved into laughter.

"To continue the bird imagery," Uriel said when they had stopped laughing, "we'll add a couple of birds to our flock tomorrow, birds of a feather, even."

"What do you mean?" Eluned asked.

"Njima and Yona sent a pigeon," Uriel began.

"Another bird," Gavreel interrupted.

Uriel laughed, "Yes, Gav, yet another bird. Anyway, they sent a pigeon saying that they would be arriving tomorrow." Chokhmah chuckled, "And if I remember correctly, Njima and Yona both mean 'dove.'"

Eluned and Uriel laughed, appreciatively, but Parisa looked somewhat stunned.

"What is wrong, my love?" Chokhmah asked

"It's just," Parisa said, "I just never thought to wonder."

"Wonder what?" Fuchsia asked.

"Wonder what my name means," she said. "I mean, I knew Parisa was a name that was always used by the royal family of Pelf, and I knew that Mama's name would have been Parisa if she hadn't been raised by the Roma, but what does Parisa mean?"

"That is a good question, my love," Chokhmah said. "And if Njima and Yona are arriving here tomorrow it must mean that they are bringing the history book with them."

"Correct," said Uriel.

"Perhaps the history of the Kingdom of Pelf will say something about that," Chokhmah said.

"I hope so," Parisa said, "because now I really want to know. I could also ask Fatemeh. She might know. Do you know what Chokhmah means?"

"It means 'wisdom,'" her mother said.

"Well, that's apt," Eluned said.

"Thank you, my dear," Chokhmah smiled.

"What does my name mean, Mommy?" Fuchsia asked.

"A fuchsia is a type of flower, a very beautiful flower, I might add," Eluned said, "but as you know, you were named for my great grandmother."

"What about me?" Gavreel said.

"Well, you were named for my father," Uriel said, "but it means 'man of Omni' and my name means 'light of Omni', and that is why we both have 'el' at the end of our name. 'El' is another name for Omni."

"What about Papa?" Parisa asked.

"I believe it means 'little wolf,'" Chokhmah said.

Parisa guffawed then apologized when everyone looked taken aback. "I'm sorry, but that's even more apt because they're both true—he's kind of little, I mean compared to you, Uncle Uriel, and he's a wolf."

"Can't argue with that," Uriel said.

"Well," Eluned said, "Chokhmah and I need to get unpacked and wash off the grime of the road before dinner."

"I'll help you, Mama," Parisa said, following her mother up the stairs.

"Care to help me?" Eluned gave Uriel a wink, "Faltuel can watch the children until we're, I mean, I'm done."

"So does Pallas still come around?" Chokhmah asked Parisa after her bath. She was sitting on her desk chair because it allowed Parisa to stand behind her while she combed out the tangles from her mother's long, mostly grey hair.

"Almost every day now," Parisa said. "He even lets me touch him now."

"Touch him," Chokhmah exclaimed. "How?"

"He likes to be scratched around his beak and head, but I have to do it carefully, in the directions of the feathers."

Chokhmah chuckled, "Ah, he does not like to have his feathers ruffled."

Parisa giggled. "So that's where that came from."

"And does he still say your name?"

"He flies in and says, 'Hello, Parisa!' and I answer him back, 'Hello, Pallas!' But that's pretty much it, so far."

"And your lessons are going well?"

"Yes, very well," Parisa bragged. "Zimbra says it won't be long before I'm teaching her."

"And you must be ahead of me in Pelfan, as well."

"Not too far," Parisa said, "Fatemeh and I decided that I would work on reading Pelfan and mostly stick with stuff I've already learned. She's also talked to me a lot about what Pelf is like."

Their Pelfan tutor had been born in Buta and ended up in Ponike with her parents when her father became Pelf's ambassador to Aden. She had been fourteen at the time, and now at 18 was glad to be of assistance to King Uriel. Fatemeh, Chokhmah had thought when they had been introduced, the

Pelfan version of Fatimah, no doubt, the young woman Faolan had been so madly in love with in Tartessos. And probably not extraordinarily different in appearance, Chokhmah had decided, as Fatemeh had the telltale Pelfan eyes and dark hair and was a beautiful young lady.

"Fatemeh says that now that the people of Pelf are aware that someone from the royal bloodline is still alive, they would be really happy if you would return and be their queen."

"Did she now?"

"That's what she said."

"She never said anything to me," Chokhmah mused aloud. "I wonder why?"

"I think she was afraid to," Parisa said.

"Afraid? Of me?"

"

"Mamaaa," Parisa rolled her eyes. "I just told you. She sees you as her queen. She doesn't want to make you angry with her."

Chokhmah thought back on the lessons she and Parisa had taken with Fatemeh and realized that the young woman had always been extremely deferential towards both of them. Chokhmah assumed it was because she was working for Uriel, but maybe it had been as Parisa said. That in the eyes of someone from Pelf, she was more their queen than a prince from Simoon and a princess from Favonia.

And, now that she thought about it, hadn't Eluned written her that Raynor and Leleua had only been allowed to reign in her stead if they did so as Prince and Princess.

"According to Uriel," Eluned had written, "Pelf is still very nationalistic. In the people's eyes. Only a Pelfan can be king or queen of Pelf."

She wondered if it was difficult for Leleua and her family to live there. Were they seen as outsiders? Would it help them for her to be the Queen or would they be resentful of her and Parisa? And would they want to remain there to help her? Because she would need their help probably. No, not probably, she admitted to herself, she would need their help. She would be 59 next spring and had been raised a Roma, married young, and was widowed before joining a three-year quest, which, while it had introduced her to royalty more than the occasional visit to see her great aunt in Favonia had done, still had not prepared her to be a queen. Neither had spending thirteen years on a horse farm in Dyfed.

Parisa was young enough that she could be trained. And Eluned was helping them both work towards knowing how to rule a kingdom. The truth, Chokhmah admitted to herself, was that she could never be much more than a figurehead. But was that so awful?

Neither Raynor nor Leleua would be anything more than a prince and princess in their kingdoms as Irirangi ruled in Favonia and Kaiser in Simoon, and both those men had sons. There was so much to think about.

"What are you thinking about?" Parisa interrupted her thoughts.

"I was thinking that life is complicated," her mother replied, and stood. "And I was thinking that it is probably time to get ready for dinner."

Because they didn't know what time Yona and Njima would arrive, the people of Castle Bennu went about their daily routine as if it were a normal day. A room had already been prepared for the women, and the kitchen staff had been warned there would be extra mouths to feed.

After breakfast, Chokhmah and Fatemeh followed Parisa up to the room she called her nest in the southwest tower.

"I think it would be fun to meet up there today," she had explained to them during breakfast, "because we can study and keep watch for Queen Njima and Yona."

Her mother could not argue with that logic.

Uriel had allowed the children to spread blankets and pillows on the floor of the tower room, and Chokhmah, Fatemeh, and Parisa soon made themselves comfortable there.

Parisa checked out the window before settling in, then asked, "Before I forget, do you know what my name means in Pelfan, Fatemeh?"

"What Parisa means?" the young woman asked.

"Yes."

"I believe eet means, 'like a fairy,'" Fatemeh said.

Parisa pondered that for a minute before smiling. "I like it," she said. "It may be the closest I ever come to having wings."

With Parisa jumping up and peering out the window every once in a while, on the lookout for the arrival of the Queen of Naphtali's carriage, Chokhmah and her daughter worked on their Pelfan for another hour before taking a much-needed break. Fatemeh, who had spent the night at Castle Bennu, returned to the home of her parents in Ponike for a couple of days, Parisa joined Fuchsia and Gavreel in the school room with Zimbra, and Chokhmah went in search of a cup of tea.

Chokhmah had picked up some of Parisa's excitement, and she carried her tea back up to the tower to keep an eye on the approach to the castle so that she could give the warning that their guests were arriving, if need be.

She pondered the thoughts that had occupied her the previous evening, and finally decided that the only way to solve the problems—that of Raynor and Leleua and that of Faolan—was to write to them and see what they thought of her taking on the Crown. She could make it clear that, at this point, she was just considering all her options and had made no absolute decision.

Chokhmah also decided that as soon as possible she would

need to seriously discuss the possibility with her daughter.

She glanced up at the sky. The sun was nearing its zenith, which meant the lunch bells would be chiming soon. Chokhmah picked up her empty mug and started working her way back downstairs.

Her timing was impeccable. As she reached the lowest step, the bells rang. She waited for Parisa and the others to emerge from the school room and then walked with them to the dining room.

They were just getting up from the table to return to their various occupations when they heard a commotion in the hallway.

Eluned squealed and embraced Chokhmah. "They're here! I'm so excited. I haven't seen them in seven years."

"Neither have I," Chokhmah reminded her, laughing.

"And I haven't seen Yona in that long," Uriel grinned. "Shall we?" he said, opening the door and allowing the others to file out ahead of him."

"Does that mean I get the rest of the day off, Your Highness?" Zimbra, who was last out, asked the King.

Uriel laughed. "Very funny, of course you do. You were being silly, right?"

Zimbra laughed. "It just seemed apropos considering who is arriving. Or are they informal too?"

"While we were on the Quest, they were very informal, but things can change, I guess."

"Well, until I hear otherwise, I will address those concerned formally," Zimbra said. "I don't want to risk seeming impertinent."

"That's a good point," Uriel said, "but I will let them know as soon as possible that Eluned and I don't stand on formality with those who share our dining table. They, of course, may choose to do otherwise, but I will let you know before you meet them this evening."

"Thank you, sir, I appreciate that," Zimbra smiled before heading off to her room.

The others were waiting for him, impatiently, but he soon caught up.

"By Omni," Yona called out as Eluned, and the others, appeared in the Great Hall and she ran to meet them. Yona embraced Eluned first, as the Queen had been her first friend on the Quest. Then she hugged Chokhmah and Uriel before stepping back to allow Njima to greet them.

"By Omni, Chokhmah, your daughter is a younger version of you," Yona said. Yona, like Eluned, was a little fuller of figure than she had been in her early twenties, but at 34 the deep auburn of her hair was still unstreaked by grey although there were the fine lines that would later become crow's feet around her dark brown eyes.

Njima was studying Parisa now. "She really is, Chokhmah. And that is a good thing," she told Parisa. "Your mother has been my role model since the Quest."

Chokhmah found herself blushing for a change. Had she really redeemed herself in their eyes following the tragic accident with the donkey, Derry? She still felt like a fool when she thought about the incident in which she and Faolan, had been so caught up in an amorous moment that they had failed to keep a look out for predators, and Eluned's beloved donkey had been killed by a wildcat.

"You blush," Njima said, "but you still, pretty much single-handedly, obtained two of the Treasures. And always with that air of composure."

"And you never complained," Eluned said, "not once that I know of. She is a born Queen."

"Yes, she is," Njima agreed.

"Where are your children?" Yona asked Eluned.

Uriel pushed them gently out from where they stood beside him. "Fuchsia and Gavreel," he introduced them, "this is Queen Njima of Naphtali and her partner, Yona."

"I haven't seen you since you were an infant," Yona said to Fuchsia, "and I've got to say that you look like your mother and your father."

"She's a beautiful blend, isn't she?" Eluned said.

Yona nodded, and stuck out her hand, "It's nice to meet you, Fuchsia."

"Thank you," Fuchsia said. "It's nice to meet you too. Mommy talks about you all the time."

Yona raised an eyebrow at Eluned who laughed.

"It's all good, I promise," she said.

"Gavreel is definitely your child," Njima smiled. "He looks just like you."

Gavreel looked up at his mother, "Do I, Mommy?"

"A male version of me, but yes, I think so," his mother said, "but you're already tall for your age, so I imagine you got your father's height."

Gavreel looked at his father, and his father gave him a thumb's up.

"Thank you, Queen Njima," he said.

"You are quite welcome," the Queen said. Still slender and clear-complexioned at 42, Njima's height, right at six feet, could be quite intimidating, but Chokhmah noted that Gavreel had matured some in the past few months. Perhaps taking lessons with Parisa and Fuchsia had instilled a little confidence in the boy. But no, she realized, it was more than that. Recalling the scared little boy at Bogaine and the boy who stood before Njima now, Chokhmah realized that the boy had been getting braver and more composed since his time at Bogaine. Very interesting, she thought. Perhaps having her and Parisa here had not been as disrupting as she had worried it might be.

"Well, I know you two have been on the road all day," Eluned said. "Lilia!" she called over a young woman who had been standing near the staircase.

"Yes, ma'am?" Lilia curtsied.

"Could you show these two women to their room? I'm sure they'd like to wash up and get out of their travel clothes."

"Yes ma'am." Lilia curtsied to the two women.

"Thanks, Eluned," Yona said. "I do feel grimy. Where shall we return to?"

Uriel pointed to the library. "We have a perfectly good sitting room but, and I am sure you won't be surprised, Eluned prefers the . . ."

"Library," Yona and Njima said together and laughed.

"Curses," Parisa shouted, and Yona laughed and flashed the sign against evil.

"By Omni, I haven't played that game in ages," Yona said.

"Some things never grow old," Eluned laughed, "and the one thing I've always encouraged my children to do is have fun when they can."

"Absolutely," Uriel said. "I try to have more fun now because I had so little as a child."

"I can sympathize with that," Njima said. "That is probably what I miss most about the Quest—the camaraderie and the fun times. Despite how difficult it could be, there are many, many good memories."

"So, yes," Eluned said. "Meet us in the library and we can take a trip down Memory Lane."

Njima and Yona, led by Lilia, started up the stairs.

"Wait," Eluned called out after they had ascended a few steps.

"What?" Yona paused and looked back.

"Let's go ahead and dress for dinner," she said. She glanced at the large clock in the hallway with its gilt pendulum slowly swinging away the time. "How about we meet back here about three o'clock?"

Yona nodded. "Sounds good. We'll see you then." They continued ascending.

Eluned turned to Chokhmah and Parisa. "That's fine with you two, right?"

"Of course," Chokhmah said. "Otherwise, we would have to find something to do until they arrived. No, I agree, it is better to be dressed and interrupted for dinner than to have to find time to return to our rooms and dress, especially if we get wrapped up in our memories."

"And, if the children get bored, they are more than welcome to play games in the corner of the room," Eluned said.

"But I can listen if I want to, right?" Parisa asked.

"Yes," Uriel said. "I do not believe we will be telling tales that a child's ear can't hear, right?"

"Absolutely," Eluned agreed. "We were paragons of virtue."

"Much to our chagrin," Uriel said.

"Not all of us," said Chokhmah, quietly.

Eluned guffawed, and seeing that Parisa looked confused, said, "There was a time when your mother and father were head over heels in love."

"They were definitely inseparable," Uriel said, dryly.

"And perhaps someday," Chokhmah sighed, "we will be again."

"You want that, Mama?" Parisa asked.

"More than anything in the world, my love," she said, "but it is going to have to be on my terms as well as his."

WHEN THEY MET DOWNSTAIRS, Chokhmah was attired, once again, in her purple silk dress accented with the gold brocade. Parisa was wearing her white silk dress, which had become her favorite since Pallas had dropped the quartz dolphin in her lap. It was a Greek Goddess-style dress with a halter top and was cinched at her waist with crisscrossing gold braid. Tonight, she carried a sapphire blue shawl that her mother had knitted her because it was beginning to get chilly at night.

Parisa and Chokhmah were the first ones to reach the library. While Parisa walked over to the window to see if there were any birds at the feeder outside, Chokhmah paced the room nervously. She was not sure why she was nervous, but she was more excited about receiving the history of Pelf than she cared to admit. Maybe it was because she hoped she would discover something about her ancestors within the book that would help to ground her in who she really was. She had felt somewhat adrift ever since Jabberwock had told her that he had reason to believe that she was the last surviving member of the royal Pelfan family.

Then when she had met Jahan and Cyrus and Nahid and the other residents of Kuna, she felt like she was looking at different versions of herself and had finally arrived home. And finally, there was the trip to New Buta and the village of Mifugo where she had seen what had been pillaged from her family, including the Knife of Llawfrodded with the sigil of Pelf embossed on its handle.

Yona entered the library, followed by Njima carrying something wrapped in fabric, and Chokhmah's heart skipped a beat. She hurried to meet them, and Njima handed her the package.

"It is why we are here," Njima said, "and in our excitement at seeing all of you again, I didn't want to forget."

Chokhmah unwrapped the fabric as Parisa joined them. There were two books.

"One of the books is the history," Yona explained. "Dev was there a week while a number of the residents worked on copying the book so that you would have your own copy."

"Ah, yes," Chokhmah remembered. "The hyper-photographic memory mutation, which allowed some members of the community to memorize anything and everything that they saw perfectly. And the other book?" It looked like a novel with the illustration on front, and the title was in Pelfan.

"I can read it," Parisa said, "It says 'Ship of', and I think that's a name, 'Theseus'. At least, there was a Theseus in that book on Greek mythology that Eluned had me read."

"Probably so, then," Njima agreed. "Dev said that Jahan wanted Chokhmah to have the book. He said that it will help you to understand Pelfans as much as the history will."

"It's by one of their most revered authors," Yona added.

"V.M. Straka," Parisa read. Her mother was still fixated on the mention of Jahan.

"He must be in his early twenties by now," she mused.

"V.M. Straka?" Parisa asked.

Chokhmah chuckled, "No, my love, Jahan. I met him when he was about eight years old while we were on our way to Kamea to search for the Crock and Dish of the Cleric. On our way back to Jazeel, he helped nurse me back to health when I was very sick. Do you know if he became a healer?" she asked Njima.

"I think Dev said something about that," she replied. "What did he say, Yona?"

At that moment, Eluned and her family entered the library.

"What's going on?" she asked as she approached them.

"They were giving us the history book and a novel," Parisa explained.

"And I was just asking about Jahan," Chokhmah said.

"By Omni, I'd forgotten about Jahan," Eluned said.

"He really took to you, I remember that," Uriel said, recalling the boy sitting on Chokhmah's lap after dinner when they were in Kuna.

"Anyway," Yona said, "Jahan did become a healer. And according to Dev, he still has very fond memories of you."

Eluned was reminiscing too. "That's where I got Tikvah.

Your mother named her that, Parisa, because it means 'hope' and she hoped that Tikvah would live. And she has," She beamed at Chokhmah.

"Why did you hope that she would live, Mama?" Parisa asked.

"Because we had already lost two donkeys on the Quest," Chokhmah began.

"Technically, Hayduke was a mule," Eluned interrupted, "but I left him at Castle Pwyll when we escaped on the Phaeton," she paused and looked questioningly at Parisa.

"Yes," Parisa said, "I know about the Phaeton and how it can travel at the speed of light or sound or something."

Eluned nodded. "Something like that, and I am certain King Arawn would have had Hayduke killed in retribution."

"Derry was a donkey, though," Chokhmah continued, "and because your father and I were not watching out for him and the horses like we were supposed to, he was attacked by a wildcat and killed."

"Oh," Parisa said. "I'm sorry, Mama."

"And what did we learn from that tragedy?" Eluned asked.

"That we all make mistakes," Chokhmah, Yona, Njima, and Uriel said together.

"Curses," Yona shouted, and they all flashed the sign to ward off the evil eye before laughing. Making their way over to a group of couches, they seated themselves and began talking about the Quest.

"I wish Jabberwock were here," Eluned said, misty-eyed at the thought of her fox-shaped mentor. "He was the one that planned the whole thing. I never got to ask him how it all came about. And he never told Uriel, either."

"That's true," Uriel said. "I figured it out pretty early on, but in the beginning, he disguised it as a way for Eluned to fall in love with me because she was so opposed to marrying me."

"Look how that turned out," Eluned laughed.

"Anyway, after I realized that we were on a quest for the treasures, I confronted him about it," Uriel continued. "Jabb said he was essentially 'killing two birds with one stone'".

"I miss him," Eluned said. "And I miss Bonpo. Sometimes, I still can't believe they're gone."

"Neither can I," Chokhmah agreed, wistfully, picturing the Yeti's deep voice and beaming face and, thinking that despite his intimidating size, he never spoke an angry word.

They were silent a moment thinking about their lost friends.

"Tell us about them again, Mommy," Fuchsia said. "Tell us the story about how Jabberwock rescued your great grandmother from a dragon."

So Eluned retold the story of how Jabberwock saved the first Fuchsia from an Aberration, that monstrous mutation of a human that had managed to cross from the Devastation of Pelf into The Wilds of Discord where it had been searching for fresh meat.

PARISA

Sitting on the bench on her balcony, waiting for Pallas, Parisa mulled over the visit from Queen Njima and Yona. Although her mother had spoken about both Jabberwock and Bonpo over the years, Parisa had never heard the story of Fuchsia being saved from an Aberration. Very few, if any Aberrations still existed as the mutant creatures had been removed from Kamea as a part of the reclamation of Pelf. There were still rumors of Aberrations along the shores of the Sea of Blood, which Fatemeh called the Djed Sea.

"My father thinks that they are dragons," Fatemeh had told her, "not Aberrations."

Parisa had marveled at that, but she had not doubted it. After all, unicorns, faeries, and gnomes, among other things, had all played a part in the Quest.

What a brave creature Jabberwock had been, Parisa mused. And how horrible for him that he had lost the love of his life to one of the Aberrations. She also felt a degree of pity for the Aberrations. They had not asked for what they had become; at some point they had been human beings.

Life was full of complicated decisions—like her mother becoming Queen of Pelf. Both Yona and Njima had encouraged Chokhmah to take on that role, and, honestly, she was no longer opposed to it, herself. The question was: would her father be? And did she care?

Like her mother, she really did want them to be a happy family again, but what that looked like had changed. The past five months had really opened her eyes to what was available to her not only just where her education was concerned but her future potential. Did she really want to go back to life on the horse farm or did she want to be Queen of Pelf someday?

It was still nearly four months before she would see her father again. His letters had been few and far between and not particularly revealing. She wasn't really surprised. He'd never really been much of one for reading or writing like she and her mother were. He preferred to be active. Maybe that was at the root of his need to be doing something more than working with horses.

Nosglangaea was fast approaching. Another favorite holiday of hers. She wasn't as enthusiastic about it as she usually was, but she had promised Fuchsia and Gavreel that she would teach them the customs surrounding it, and even Zimbra and Fatemeh were interested in taking part.

Because the castle was essentially like a small town with all its outbuildings and people running around doing their various jobs, and because there were no real hills in sight because they were already at the highest point in Ponike, they would not be able to build a bonfire outdoors. Instead, they would build a fire in the large fireplace in the library. Parisa supposed that would have to do although it wouldn't be as exciting as being outdoors.

A drawn-out croak startled her out of her thoughts. Pallas had landed on the bench next to her, and head cocked, was eyeing the piece of jerky still clutched in her right hand. She hadn't even taken a bite yet. She tore it in half and handed a piece to Pallas. The raven clutched the dried meat in his right claw and ripped a piece away from it with his beak.

Parisa held up a mug of water so he could immerse it in the water before swallowing it. She had learned that this helped the meat go down more easily.

"Good?" she asked, still chewing the bite she had taken.

"Good," Pallas agreed, then ripped loose another piece. While his vocabulary was increasing, it was still very limited. Parisa didn't mind, though. She still felt a thrill of pleasure every time the bird visited her, which had become nearly daily. She took great comfort in his visits and considered him a better friend than any human.

After they'd finished their snack, Pallas settled down on the pillow Parisa had made for him, a large square sewn from a scrap of burlap and stuffed with fabric scraps. She thought it made it more comfortable for him to remain on the granite bench if he could nest on the pillow.

While Pallas dozed in the warmth of the autumn's late afternoon sun, Parisa worked on her homework—more verbs to conjugate and learn in Pelfan, fractions in math, and learning about commerce and trade in the Thirteen Kingdoms, particularly the main exports of each kingdom. It bored her to tears, but she knew these were things she would need to know, or at the very least, be familiar with.

Her eyelids began to droop, and she set her work to the side and stood up to wake herself up. She walked over to the wall to gaze out over the Gulf of Eudaemon. Everything looked so peaceful down there—fishing boats bobbing in the waves, ships heading into and out of the harbor, birds wheeling above. Yet, she knew for a fact if she were down there, it would all seem very riotous with the shouts of sailors, the squawking of gulls, the crashing of waves.

Pallas was now perched on the wall next to her.

"It's like another world up here," she told him. "Sometimes I forget just how chaotic it is down there." Particularly on the days, Parisa thought, when her world was confined to her bedroom, the dining room, library, and school room.

The sun disappeared behind a huge bank of clouds to the west, and she shivered. *A ghul has breathed on my neck*, she thought, remembering Eluned telling her that was the preferred saying for 'a rabbit ran over my grave' in Simoon. It was definitely creepier. They said 'goose' instead of 'rabbit' in Dyfed, which was also pretty innocuous. But whether it was a ghul breathing on her neck or a rabbit hopping over her grave, she wasn't sure why the sun disappearing behind some clouds had disturbed her.

Maybe it was Nosglangaea, speaking of ghuls. Suddenly, death and being spooked didn't seem quite so much fun to her.

"Parisa," Pallas croaked, startling her from her reverie.

"Sorry, Pallas," she said. "Is it time for you to go?"

The bird rubbed his head against her shoulder, and she ran her hand down his glossy back.

"See you tomorrow?"

"Morrow," he croaked before taking off and flapping his way to the northwest.

Parisa returned to the bench and picked up her books and notebooks. It was probably time to get ready for dinner. After placing her books and things on her desk, she entered her bathroom and surveyed herself in the mirror. She was appropriately dressed as it had been a language day and not a weaponry or horse-riding day. Because of the wind on the balcony, her hair could stand to be brushed and re-plaited. Parisa slowly pulled the three strands apart, staring pensively at herself in the mirror.

Ever since the sun had disappeared behind the clouds, she had felt off kilter somehow. She needed to pull herself together. It was just a few more days until Nosglangaea and she didn't want to disappoint Fuchsia and the others.

She brushed her hair and pulled it back into a free-flowing ponytail. It was still a bit early, and she'd finished her book before she'd started her homework. She ought to go by the library before dinner so that she'd have something to read before bedtime. Parisa grabbed her book and headed downstairs.

Just outside the door to the library, she heard Eluned say, "I don't know how to say this."

Parisa took a step closer and peered in. Her mother and Eluned were sitting on the sofa in front of the fireplace, their backs to her.

"Just say it, my dear," her mother answered. "I assume it is bad news. If so, I can take it."

Eluned glanced down at the letter in her hand. "It's from Gittan. She says she's received a report about Faolan from King Kaiser's secretary."

"So, from the King, himself."

"Yes," Eluned agreed. "According to Gittan, Faolan …"

"Faolan?"

Eluned sighed. "I'm afraid he has not stopped drinking."

"And?"

"Apparently, he insulted the Ambassador from Tarshish at a formal dinner," Eluned paused. "And they got into a scuffle."

"Scuffle?"

"I think Gittan is trying to spare our feelings. I suspect she means that blows were exchanged."

Chokhmah covered her eyes with her hand and groaned. "I knew he had had a bad experience in Tartessos while he was working there as a spy, but that was years ago. He was fine when we there for the meeting."

Eluned was silent for a moment, then said gently, "But that was before he started drinking more heavily, right?"

Chokhmah sighed. "Yes, of course, but I was so sure that having something to do, away from us, would give him a sense of purpose and that the drinking would stop."

"I don't know what to say because that is what Uriel and I hoped would happen, as well."

"What is to happen then?" Chokhmah asked. "Does Gittan say?"

"She has recalled him to Dyfed," Eluned said.

Chokhmah shook her head. "Omni help us. That will to him be worse than death."

"I'll talk to Uriel tonight. Perhaps we can come up with something else he can do that doesn't involve diplomacy."

"What do I tell Parisa? I do not know how she will take this."

Parisa wasn't sure how to take it. She took a step back from door, heart pounding in her ears. First her father had gotten drunk and mean, then he had been so happy to leave them, but he was still getting drunk and still getting angry? She didn't understand. What did he want if he wasn't happy with or without them?

The dinner bells rang, and she turned automatically, library book forgotten, and headed for the dining room. She was the first one there, and she sat down in her accustomed spot, and stared, vacantly, into space.

It wasn't until Fuchsia nudged her in the ribs with her elbow that Parisa realized the girl had been saying her name repeatedly and that everyone else was staring at her. She blushed and mumbled something about being a thousand miles away.

"I'll say," Fuchsia agreed. "You must have been in the Peaks of Vulpecula you were so far away."

Parisa attempted a smile, and lied, "I was just trying to remember everything that needs to be done before Nosglangaea."

A quick glance at her mother told her that her lie had failed even though Fuchsia said with enthusiasm, "Just three more days."

As the food was set upon the table and everyone busied themselves with serving their plates, Parisa tried to distract herself by answering Fuchsia's questions while eating as hurriedly as possible. She couldn't wait to get back to her room. She needed to think.

But it was not to be. Her mother walked back upstairs with her, and followed her into her room, sitting down on the settee in front of the fireplace and patting the place next to her.

Parisa joined her.

"You heard," her mother said, nodding at the library book clenched in Parisa's hand that she had neglected to put down when they entered the room. Parisa placed it on her lap and stared into the flames of the fire that had been set to ward off the growing nightly chill. She had yet to experience a Ponike winter although this time of year at Bogaine was not quite as cold.

"What's wrong with him, Mama?"

Chokhmah sighed. "I wish I could tell you, my love. I do not understand it myself."

"All he wanted was to get away from us," Parisa said. "Why would he mess that up?"

"Clearly, he does not himself understand what it is he wants or needs."

"What if he is even angrier when he comes back? What if he makes us go back to Bogaine?"

"He cannot make us do anything," her mother assured her. "He needs help, and I will insist that he gets it. I am sure Gittan knows someone in Dyfed that can talk with him, or, if he comes here, then Eluned or Uriel can find him someone with whom he can speak."

"You mean to help him figure out why he's so unhappy that he needs to drink?"

"Yes," Chokhmah stood. "It is time he figures out what is causing this behavior and he has to do it on his own. It is beyond our control." Parisa stood up and hugged her mother. "Do you need to get another book from the library?" she asked then kissed her daughter's forehead.

"No," Parisa said. "I think I'll just write in my journal."

"That is probably not a bad idea," Chokhmah said, walking toward the adjoining door. "It is a lot to process, is it not?" Parisa nodded, grimacing, "Good night, Mama. Thank you for talking to me about it."

"Good night, my love. May Omni grant you sweet dreams tonight."

"Thank you. I'm going to need them."

CHOKHMAH

A knock on her door startled Chokhmah from her reverie. She was sitting on the low couch in front of her fireplace, but her journal lay forgotten in her lap. Who could be knocking at this hour, she thought, setting the journal aside? She walked to the door, pulling on her robe, and opened it to find Uriel standing there.

"I'm sorry to bother you at this hour," Uriel said, "but there has been more news and I wanted to make sure you heard it first from us and not via any gossip."

Chokhmah's stomach dropped as her brow wrinkled in consternation. What else had happened, she wondered, as she indicated that Uriel should enter. "Perhaps the balcony?" she said, "I assume I do not want to risk waking my daughter?"

"That would be best," he agreed.

Chokhmah was too nervous to sit and walked over to the low wall overlooking Ponike. It was mostly dark below, but lights flickered here and there from ships and from some of the buildings sitting alongside the wharves.

"Faolan?" she asked turning to face Uriel.

"I'm afraid so."

"It was more than a 'tussle'?"

"Apparently, he was intoxicated and making advances toward the Ambassador's wife," Uriel said.

Chokhmah was nonplussed. That seemed so unlike her husband. "And?" she asked, barely breathing.

"The husband was not amused and challenged him to a duel."

"A duel! I thought dueling was no longer allowed."

Uriel sighed. "As did I, but Tarshish has always been old-fashioned."

"But I thought that had changed after the Treasures had been gathered," Chokhmah said, "and Princess Huda was allowed to administer Adamah while King Hevel was doing his penance? If Tarshish would let a woman rule . . ."

"Yes, some things did change," Uriel agreed, "but then again some things never change particularly where men are concerned."

"Tell me they were not allowed to duel."

"You're correct. King Kaiser strictly forbade it."

"But?"

"Faolan was bodily removed from the dinner and put under house arrest until he was sober."

"I do not understand," Chokhmah said. "This all sounds very reasonable."

Uriel sighed and walked over to the bench where he sat down, elbows propped on knees, and head in hands.

Chokhmah hurried after Uriel and sat down beside him. "Uriel, you are scaring me. What is it? Is Faolan all right?"

"No," Uriel nearly shouted. "It's not that at all. I'm sorry I gave you that impression. It's just that I hate to be the one to inform you that the wife of the Ambassador is someone Faolan knew when he was assigned to Tartessos."

Chokhmah's heart sank. There was only one person it could be. "Fatimah."

"I'm afraid so."

Chokhmah was silent. How old would she be now if she was 16 back then? In her early 40s? By all accounts, she had clearly accomplished her goal of climbing higher up the social ladder, which probably meant that Faolan had not lied about her beauty. And she was also younger than Chokhmah had been when she met Faolan in Favonia.

"Omni have mercy," Chokhmah gasped, suddenly clutching Uriel's arm.

"What is it?"

"Fatimah knows that Faolan is a shapeshifter. It was she that caused those burns on his chest. What if she tells her husband?"

Uriel stood. "I'll go send a pigeon to Gittan. Faolan probably needs to be escorted back to Dyfed under armed guard. If I remember correctly, the Kingdom of Tarshish does not look favorably on those who are not fully human."

"It is true," Chokhmah said. "They were polite about Jabberwock being there, but they did not like it." And, of course, she thought, they had not known at the time that her husband could shift into a wolf.

After Uriel departed, Chokhmah paced the balcony, trying to calm her thoughts. She felt deeply betrayed by her husband—not just by his insistence that he leave her and his daughter to their own devices while he went off and satisfied his own needs, but that those needs seemed to include the continued need for alcohol and affirmation from his first true love. Though it had never been actual love, Chokhmah thought, because Fatimah had not shared it. It had been nothing but lust and projection on Faolan's part, ambition on Fatimah's.

She had thought that Faolan had found true love with her. They had had so many good years together. Perhaps he could never be happy, she sighed. It was true that there were people who could never be satisfied with what they had; that were always searching for the thing that would fill that hole within themselves.

Chokhmah knew that she could find contentment anywhere and had. She had been as happy as a Roma as she had been as a healer on a horse farm. Her faith in Omni, and her acceptance of herself as she was, made that possible.

She walked over to the balcony railing again and looked westward into the darkness. Stars twinkled benignly in the night sky oblivious to the machinations of man and beast below. Miles of land and sea lay between Chokhmah and Buta, but for the first time she knew beyond a shadow of a doubt that she could be just as happy in that cliffside palace as she had been in her little lavender vardo.

Before she went down for breakfast, Chokhmah asked Parisa to join her in her room.

Parisa groaned. "Is this about Papa?"

"I am afraid so, yes," her mother said. She watched her daughter walk to the sofa, shoulders hunched, head hanging. Parisa sat down and turned toward her mother, copper eyes as dull as the lowest coin of the realm trampled underfoot.

"Is it why Uriel came to see you last night?" she asked.

"I am sorry we awakened you."

"I wasn't asleep," Parisa sighed. "I only heard him knock on the door, and you saying something about talking on the balcony so you wouldn't wake me up. And then I heard him leave a little later. What did he tell you?"

"What are you going to do about it?" Parisa asked after her mother explained the complications surrounding the 'tussle' between her father and the ambassador.

"I am still praying about that," Chokhmah said. "At this point, I must admit, that I would prefer never to see him again."

"I don't blame you," Parisa said, angrily brushing away a tear. "It's bad enough that he left us because it was just so horrible for him to share his life with us but to keep on drinking and fighting and then, worst of all, spurning your marriage vows."

"And our anger at him is the reason I cannot make a final decision at this point," Chokhmah said. "Part of myself is so hurt and furious that I want to hurt him, the other asks, 'if he returns to us repentant and begging for a second chance, do I give him that chance?'"

"That's a good point," Parisa admitted. "I'm hurt too but I don't hate him."

They sat in silence for a moment.

"Well," Chokhmah said, kissing her daughter's cheek, "this is not something that must be decided immediately. After all, it will take him a month to get back to Portuma."

"Will we be going there to meet him?" Parisa asked. "What about Pelf?"

"Yet another of the many questions to be answered," her mother said. "Winter is fast approaching, but it was my hope that we would be traveling to Pelf come spring."

Parisa sighed, audibly. "Good," she said, standing up and heading toward the door to her room, "I was hoping you hadn't given up on being Queen of Pelf. Are you going down for breakfast?"

Her mother nodded.

"See you there," Parisa said before opening the door.

Parisa

On the morning of the Nosglangaea festivities, Parisa, along with Fuchsia, Gavreel, Zimbra, Fatemeh, and her mother made the trip down to the pebbly shore along the Gulf of Eudaemon on the western edge of Ponike. Here they all gathered the most perfectly rounded white stones they could find.

After pocketing one for herself, Parisa continued looking for a second. When she saw her mother's questioning look, she explained. "This is Papa's favorite holiday. The least I can do is put a stone in the fire for him."

Chokhmah nodded. "I suppose that makes sense."

For the first time Parisa wondered why her father got such enjoyment out of seeing his stone in the remains of the fire each year. True, the tradition meant that he wouldn't die in the coming year, but why was he so obsessed by it? If she'd kept her big mouth shut, she would have been more than happy to skip this particular holiday this year. She no longer had any interest in knowing what the future might hold. Living day to day was difficult enough.

She had tried to imagine what it would be like to be living in Zhaleh Palace but other than the shared vision with her mother, her imagination just couldn't seem to tackle it. She had more luck with Fatemeh's stories of Buta, but she did have enough imagination to realize that she would probably spend little time there if living at Castle Bennu was any indication.

Watching the seagulls that were wheeling above the waves, Parisa wondered if she would have a chance to see a dragon, if they really did exist. She imagined the scaly, shimmery-winged creatures turning somersaults over the Bay of Besu over which Zhaleh Palace loomed. She could dream, couldn't she?

She glanced down at her feet where a glossy black and perfectly rounded stone reflected the sunlight. Leaning over, she picked it up and contemplated it for a moment. The tradition was a white stone, but this pebble seemed perfect for her father this year. He had certainly done more than his fair share of casting a shadow of darkness over their lives.

It wasn't until Fuchsia said, "That's a black rock. I thought they were supposed to white," that Parisa realized that she was no longer alone.

"I was just thinking since my father loves Nosglangaea but can't be here with us that maybe I'd put a rock in the fire for him," Parisa explained.

"Why a black one?"

"I don't know. It just seemed right. You're supposed to write your own name on it and he's not here to do that," Parisa worked on justifying the black rock to both herself and Fuchsia as she would no doubt also have to explain her choice to the others. She had a suspicion that her mother would guess her true motive. She always just seemed to know. But the more she thought about it, the more it made sense. "So, did you find yours?"

Fuchsia held up an oval and creamy white stone. "Will this do?"

"It's perfect," Parisa agreed. "Let's go see how the others are doing. It looks like they're starting to set out our lunch."

They walked up the beach toward where the others were gathering.

"Is everyone all set?" Chokhmah asked when they arrived.

"Parisa picked out a black rock for her father," Fuchsia said. "Is that okay?"

"I do not see why not," Chokhmah said, eyebrow slightly raised.

Parisa couldn't help smirking. She had known her mother would figure it out.

"I want to find a rock for my father," Gavreel said.

"I have a couple of extras," Zimbra said. "I couldn't choose which one I wanted to use. You can have them for your parents," she assured Gavreel.

Gavreel held out his hand, and Fatemeh laughed. "Seems you must choose thees meenute."

"I have a better idea, Gav," Zimbra said. "Why don't you give me your rock and I will hold onto them until we go home? I even have a pouch to keep them in," she indicated the leather pouch hanging around her neck on a cord. "We're about to eat lunch and you don't want to risk losing it, do you?"

"No," he said, "but how will I know it is mine?"

Chokhmah held up a pencil. "Do not worry," she told him. "I will write a tiny 'g' on it that can be erased before your name is painted on it." She took the stone from his hand and marked it before handing it to Zimbra. "So. Who is hungry? It looks as if our lunch is ready."

They headed toward a table that had been set up on a grassy swathe of land further inland. Parisa sat on the side closest to the beach and at the end because she hated being trapped in the middle and was joined by Fuchsia and Gavreel. The adults took the other side of the table, her mother sitting opposite her.

She was oddly disappointed when the platter was uncovered to find they'd be eating chicken. What she'd really like is a rare steak, a very rare steak. She grimaced and looked up to find her mother watching her.

"What is it, my dear?" Chokhmah asked.

"I guess I was hoping we would have steak," was all she could think to say. It wasn't as if they'd created some secret code that would let her mother know she was experiencing symptoms of the change to come.

Her mother nodded, knowingly. "Perhaps we can get you one at dinner?"

Parisa nodded and picked up a thigh. "I'd like that." After everyone was served, she hastily grabbed a leg and another thigh. She definitely had a taste for meat today.

"You still must eat some salad," her mother, picking up the bowl of tomatoes and cucumbers in a vinegar and oil dressing and spooning some onto her daughter's plate.

Parisa groaned but obliged her, spearing a tomato on her fork and thrusting it into her mouth, nose wrinkled in feigned distaste. But then chuckled. "Now I understand how Papa feels when you make him eat his vegetables," she explained to her mother's questioning look.

"I want you to be a healthy wolf," Chokhmah smiled, picking up her chicken leg and taking a hearty bite.

Parisa laughed and ate another couple of mouthfuls of salad before turning back to her chicken.

ONCE THE SUN SET THAT EVENING, everyone gathered in the library where the fire had been lit in the massive fireplace. Parisa explained what it was that they were to do.

"Once the fire burns down enough, pretty much to embers, we toss our stones in and say our prayers, and then," she said, "this is the tricky part, we have to shout, 'Adref, adref, am y cyntaf', hwch ddr gwta a gipio'r ola.'"

All but Parisa, Chokhmah, and Uriel groaned.

"By Omni," Eluned complained, "it sounds like that book

on the Hallowed Treasures I found in the library at the inn in Mjijangwa."

Uriel laughed, "Nor is it dissimilar to Gwrhyr, I suspect."

"It is from the same ancient language," Chokhmah affirmed.

"I figured it would be a problem to memorize," Parisa said, "and to read for that matter, so I copied it out phonetically for everyone."

"Thank Omni!" Fatemeh said. "I have enough trouble weeth the Common Tongue and Adenese."

"What does it mean?" Zimbra asked.

"Something like 'Home, home at once. The tailless black sow shall snatch the last one,'" she explained. "Then we all race to our rooms, and we can't come back here until the morning, and we can't even look for our stones until we are all gathered together here again. We can't risk someone hiding someone else's stone."

"Why?" Fuchsia wondered.

"The tradition is that if anyone's stone is missing then that person will die in the coming year," Parisa explained.

"Well, that ees horreeble," Fatemeh said.

"I've been doing this for years and there has never been a stone missing," Parisa said. "I know Papa has been playing this game since he was a child. Did any stones go missing for his family in all those years?"

"No, never," Chokhmah said, "and if Faolan were here, I guarantee you that he would be the first one out of here once the chant had ended."

Parisa laughed. "He was determined that the tailless black sow would never catch him."

"Sow?" Gavreel asked.

"It's female pig," Uriel explained.

"Where does it come from?"

"There's no tailless black sow," Parisa assured the boy. "It was made up, probably to get the kids in bed sooner."

Fuchsia rolled her eyes. "Grown-ups are always coming up with ways to get rid of kids, aren't they?"

Eluned ruffled her daughter's hair. "There's a reason for that, darling. It's because children need more sleep than adults. You'll eventually be old enough to stay up later."

"Like Parisa?"

"Just like Parisa," Eluned agreed, "and someday you'll get to choose when you go to bed."

"And not long after that," her father said, "you won't even want to stay up late anymore."

Eluned and Chokhmah nodded in agreement. Zimbra and Fatemeh looked doubtful.

"Shall we have some refreshments while we wait for the fire to burn down?" Chokhmah changed the subject.

A table had been set up with miniature spice cakes, molasses cookies glazed with sugar, hot cider for the children, and hot, spiked cider for the adults who wanted it.

Parisa eyed the spiked cider. Back at Bogaine, she'd always been allowed a thimbleful of what the grownups were drinking on special occasions. Now she had to wonder if that was her father's doing. But her mother was pouring half a ladleful into a mug.

"That is all, though," her mother said as she handed it to her.

"Thank you," Parisa said, picking up a molasses cookie and returning to the sofas in front of the fireplace. Personally, she just wanted to get this evening over with.

It was half an hour later and with great relief that she withdrew the black and white stones from the pocket of the leather breeches she was still wearing from that morning's trip to the beach. The children had not had to dress for dinner as a concession to the unusual day.

She attracted her mother's attention, and Chokhmah called for everyone to gather in front of the fireplace.

"Everyone ready?" she asked, displaying her pebbles in the palm of her hand—one black and unmarked, the other with a blue 'P' painted on it. P for Parisa, Pallas, and Pelf, she thought.

She glanced around and noted that all seemed to be ready.

"Toss them in!" There were a number of dull thuds as the stones disappeared into the low flames and hit the charred firewood.

As it was their tradition, she took turns with her mother in saying the appropriate prayers. Parisa then handed out the phonetic verse that had been carefully printed on little slips of paper. "Remember that we are racing to our rooms afterwards, but be careful," she said, "because it would be silly to hurt ourselves over a game."

Her mother nodded approvingly.

"Okay, then," Parisa said, "on the count of three, we'll recite the chant. One, two, three."

Parisa, who knew the verse by heart, began edging toward the door, calling loudly, "Adref, adref . . ." as the others followed suit with varying levels of competency. She was first to the door as the chant finished and flung it open and raced up stairs. Her mother would be last, of course, as she always was. It used to horrify her that her mother seemed so complacent about being caught by the tailless black sow. But, by the time she was 10, she had realized that her mother was just making sure no one else was last and that all arrived in their homes safely.

When she reached the top of the stairs and turned down the hall toward her room, Parisa finally slowed down. Other than her mother, no one else would be coming this way.

She was in her pajamas and robe and settled on the sofa, reading by the light of the fire when her mother finally tapped on the door.

"I see you once again safely escaped the sow," her mother said after she entered.

Parisa laughed. "And you once again were caught by it?"

"Yes, but I have ways to charm the beast," her mother chuckled, "with the help of spice cake or two."

Parisa giggled again. "Are we meeting in the library before or after breakfast? I forgot to ask."

"Just before. Eluned thought that Gavreel would not be able to contain himself if he had to sit through breakfast first." Parisa sighed and stared into the flames for a second.

"Yes?"

"It's just that I'm not even sure why I used to like Nosglangaea so much," Parisa said. "It's really kind of meaningless. I mean, certainly people have never really believed that if their stone was missing, they would actually die in the coming year."

Chokhmah sat down on the sofa. "People were once more superstitious than they are now. I imagine there was a time when the festival was focused more on the harvest and the coming year, and there were probably some other traditions attached to it that have been lost to time as people learned more about how the world works."

"Like the fact that humans can't control the weather?"

"Yes. In fact, that we have very little control over anything," her mother said.

"It's hard enough to control ourselves."

"Much less, other people," Chokhmah agreed.

"Like Papa."

"Exactly like that," Chokhmah stood up. "Goodnight, my love. Please do not stay up too late."

"I'll just finish this chapter," Parisa said. "I've only got a few more pages."

Chokhmah nodded. "Sweet dreams, my dear."

"Goodnight, Mama," Parisa said, opening her book.

❧

USING A PAIR OF TONGS, Parisa carefully removed the stones from the ashes of the previous night's fire, counting as she placed each one on a platter her mother held for her. Eight stones greyed by the ashes. Where was the black stone? She sifted through the ashes again but failed to find the other stone. She stood up. "That's odd," she murmured.

"What is it?" her mother asked.

"I can't find Papa's stone. I guess I am going to have to put the ashes in a bucket and go through them a shovelful at a time." She looked at the others who were waiting somewhat impatiently for the announcement so that they could go get breakfast.

"All your stones are here," she told them. She pulled a rag from her back pocket and cleaned the ashes off each stone, handing it to the appropriate person each time she finished.

She retrieved the ash bucket and shovel from next to the fireplace and told her mother that she would join them for breakfast once she had more thoroughly gone through the ashes.

When she finally got to the dining room only her mother and Eluned were still at the table. Her mother looked at her, expectantly.

"I don't understand," Parisa said, collapsing into a chair. "I sifted through every bit of the ashes and all I could find were a few pieces of charred wood. Papa's stone wasn't there. How is that even possible?"

"Maybe it exploded from the heat and fractured into tiny pieces," Eluned suggested.

"That is certainly a possibility," Chokhmah said.

Parisa frowned, then nodded. "That has to be it. I can't think of anything else." The expressions of concern on the faces of her mother and Eluned convinced her that it was impossible that any of the adults had hidden the stone as a joke and she was pretty sure that neither Fuchsia nor Gavreel or even Zimbra or Fatemeh would have been so cruel as to have done that. As for any of the servants, who had been asked to leave the fireplace be, what reason would they have had to sift through the ashes to find the black stone? If, in fact, they knew the black stone was the odd one. It seemed highly unlikely but who was to say that the black pebble didn't have a small fissure and a drop of sea water within it that caused it to rupture from the heat?

She jumped up and headed to the sideboard to grab a quick breakfast before heading to her lessons.

CHOKHMAH

Chokhmah had just finished reading aloud a paragraph from *Ship of Theseus* in Pelfan and was attempting to translate it when Eluned and Uriel entered the library. It was two days after Nosglangaea, and the day after the King's 35th birthday. They had stayed up late the previous night celebrating and Chokhmah was regretting that final mug of mulled wine.

They all looked to the couple expectantly as it was rare for them to intrude on their Pelfan lessons, and the expressions on their faces could not have been only the result of their overindulgence the previous night.

"Fatemeh," Eluned said when she reached the table they were seated at, "would you mind taking a break. We need to speak with Chokhmah and Parisa."

"Of course, Queen Eluned," Fatemeh said, standing and quickly exiting the room.

Eluned and Uriel pulled out chairs and seated themselves, staring at the table, their hands, anything but meeting Chokhmah's eyes.

"Clearly it is bad news," Chokhmah broke the silence.

"And it must be about Faolan. Please do not spare us."

"What has he done this time?" Parisa moaned.

Uriel cleared his throat. "We just received a pigeon from Gittan who apparently received a pigeon from King Kaiser before my pigeon arrived."

Chokhmah put a hand over her mouth to stifle a sob as her eyes filled with tears. "Oh no," she managed to choke from behind her hand. "What happened?"

"The details are sparse at this point," Eluned said, "but apparently Faolan escaped house arrest by shifting and . . ."

"And he was killed as a wolf before regaining shape as a man," Uriel stated, though his voice cracked as he said it and he had to blink back tears.

"Papa is dead?" Parisa whispered, the color draining from her face.

Jumping up, Chokhmah hurried to her daughter's side. Parisa looked as if she might faint. "Can you help me get her to the sofa?"

Uriel stood and picked Parisa up and carried her over to the closest couch, Chokhmah and Eluned hurrying along behind him.

"I thought it was just a game," Parisa wailed, and, curling into a ball, she began to sob uncontrollably.

"Game?" Uriel asked, brow furrowed.

"I think she means the black stone," Chokhmah said quietly, pulling a handkerchief from her pocket and mopping the tears and snot from her daughter's face. "Darling, it is just a game and as long as it takes for pigeons to get from Kingdom to Kingdom, I would imagine that this occurred before Nosglangaea. This is not your fault. Your father made his choices."
She continued to talk soothingly to Parisa, pulling her into her arms and rocking her gently like she did when she was an infant. Eventually her sobs ceased, and she stared blindly into the space behind her mother's head, eyes red and swollen.

"I'm so, so sorry," Eluned cried.

"Never in a million years," Uriel said, swiping away a tear from the corner of his eye. "After all he's survived."

"Was that all you were told?" Chokhmah asked.

Uriel nodded. "We don't have any details."

How ironic, Chokhmah thought, to return to the place where he had once roamed freely by her side as a wolf only to be killed because he was a wolf. Oh Faolan, how did things spin so hopelessly out of your control? She looked back down at her daughter, tears still sliding slowly from her eyes and saturating her hair.

"Do you think you can walk, my love?" Chokhmah asked her. "I think we should get you up to your room."

"I can carry her if you like," Uriel offered.

"No thank you," Parisa pushed herself into a sitting position. "I can do it." She stood, swaying a little, and Chokhmah put her arm around her and guided her toward the door.

In the hallway, Chokhmah called over Lilia, who was passing by with the remains of Fuchsia's and Gavreel's snacks on a tray. "Can you have some brandy and honey sent to Parisa's room?" she asked. "She has had a bit of a shock, so the sooner the better, please."

"Yes, ma'am," Lilia said, "I'll do it right away." And she hurried off toward the kitchens.

"Let us know if you need anything," Eluned called after Chokhmah as she and Parisa began ascending the stairs.

"Thank you, Eluned," she said over her shoulder. "I will definitely do that."

While they were waiting for the honeyed brandy to arrive, Chokhmah helped Parisa into her nightgown, then settled her on the sofa wrapped in blanket while she stoked up the fire.

Chokhmah answered the tap at the door that indicated the arrival of the tray, which she accepted from the porter and carried over to the settee. She poured Parisa a hearty portion and encouraged her to take a sip.

After taking a sip, Parisa said, "I don't understand. He was always telling me how careful I would need to be once I started shifting."

Chokhmah sighed. "'Do as I say not as I do' should have been your father's motto. He could be rash when he was not thinking clearly. Had he seen Fatimah for what she was, a young and ambitious girl, he would not have suffered those burns to his chest. If he had been more cautious when trying to escape Simoon, he would not have broken his leg in that trap." And if I had not allowed myself to be caught up in his passion, Derry would not have been killed, she thought.

She glanced at her daughter who was taking another sip of brandy. Nor, she thought, would I now have a daughter. His passion was one of the things she had loved about him, even though it had caused her to make errors in judgment herself. Who knew how many other close calls that intensity had brought him?

"I guess he did like taking chances," Parisa agreed, her eyelids beginning to droop.

"Finish that up, and we'll get you into bed."

Parisa swallowed the rest of the brandy and handed the mug to her mother before going over to her bed and crawling under the duvet. Chokhmah tucked her in and kissed her on the forehead.

"Are you sad, Mama?" she asked.

"I am both sad and angry," Chokhmah said. "I am sad that the man I loved, and the father of my child is gone, and I am angry that his foolishness is what got him killed."

"Yeah," Parisa murmured, eyes closed. "That's why it hurts so much—I loved and hated him."

Chokhmah kissed her cheek, and said quietly, "Sleep well, my love, we will deal with this more tonight."

"Mmmmm," Parisa agreed, turning on to her left side.

Chokhmah retrieved the tray with the honeyed brandy and carried it into her room to finish it off. She could use a nap herself. Sleep would have to be her nepenthe. At least while sleeping, she could forget for a while.

UNFORTUNATELY, she was only allowed an hour or so of forgetfulness before being awakened from a dream in which she watched as her daughter climbed onto the low wall of a balcony high above the sea that crashed against the rocks below and jumped. Chokhmah startled awake with the vague memory of having seen wings sprouting from Parisa's back. And once awakened, the memory of why she had taken a nap returned and she felt as if she had been kicked in the gut. He was gone. There would be no repentance and joyful reunion. Nor would she have to let him know that she no longer wished to be his wife. No decisions to make except when to bury him.

And that was not really a decision, either, as it would all depend on when his ashes (had the black rock really exploded into the ashes, she wondered) arrived back in Dyfed. Winter was only a couple of months away. Could they get to Bogaine and back to Ponike before it became too cold and dangerous to travel?

WINTER

"I wonder if the snow loves the trees and fields that it kisses them so gently? And then it covers them up snug, you know, with a white quilt; and perhaps it says, 'Go to sleep, darlings, till the summer comes again.'"

-Lewis Carroll

PARISA

It was like living in a strange new world, Parisa thought, as she watched the snow falling toward the ground below. The once familiar landscape looked alien. The snow muffled sounds and scents, which, she thought, might be a good thing as she was still adjusting to her heightened senses of hearing and smelling.

Winter had come early this year. Ponike had had its first snowfall two weeks prior to the first day of winter. And now, the day before Yuclog and the first day of the new year, it was snowing again for the umpteenth time. They had not been able to travel back to Bogaine for her father's funeral, and now she wondered if they would ever return.

Some days it seemed pointless to travel that far just to see her father's grave; other days, she felt strongly that she needed to see it and Bogaine one last time.

It was less than two months until her thirteenth birthday and sometime during the upcoming year she would be navigating shapeshifting on her own. It wasn't that she was clueless, she had talked about it with her father, uncle, and cousins numerous times. And her mother also knew a lot about it having spent years with her father.

Parisa was both terrified and excited. Her father had been a beautiful wolf with thick grey and white fur tinged with tan and black. Uncle Olcan's fur was mostly black, but her cousins' fur was mostly grey and tan. The only thing that stayed the same were the eyes, which was a good thing because she could always tell her cousins apart when they shifted because Conall's eyes were a slightly brighter blue than Fianna's.

She heard her name and looked up to see Pallas gliding toward the balcony. It had occurred to her that if they had been able to travel to Dyfed, Pallas might give up on her if he didn't find her on the balcony while they were gone. And she was already worrying about the move to Buta. She would miss him dreadfully.

She reached into her pocket and extracted one of the cherry tomatoes she had saved for Pallas. Castle Bennu had green houses and so its inhabitants were treated to more than just winter produce during the cold months.

"Tank you," Pallas croaked before snatching it from her palm. He hopped down to the floor of the balcony, placed it on the granite, which was once again carpeted with a thin layer of snow, and punctured it with his beak before picking it up again and letting it slide down his gullet. She dropped another at his feet, and he repeated the process.

Parisa had a blanket on the bench and walked over to wrap herself in it before taking a seat. Pallas hopped over and settled next to her on his pillow. They sat in comfortable silence as Parisa continued to muse.

If it didn't stop snowing soon, she thought, she'd have to shovel off the balcony once again. If she didn't like spending time out there, even in the cold, she could leave it until it melted. Instead, she had to shovel it into a bucket, dump it into her tub and let it melt there. She couldn't toss it over the balcony because of the risk of it falling on someone below.

Parisa wondered if it was snowing in Buta. The coast of the Kingdom of Pelf stretched further south than that of Aden, and Fatemeh had said that it snowed there although not as often as it snowed in Ponike.

Moving to Buta was another thing that both terrified and excited Parisa. Her mother had begun corresponding with her grandniece, Leleua, during the Autumn, to let them know of their plans to travel there come spring. And should everything work out, remain there.

Leleua had then asked her son, Korbinian, to write Parisa. Korbinian, who wrote that he preferred to be called Körbl, was 10 years old, and like her, enjoyed reading, horseback riding, and sailing. He had two sisters that were identical twins, Foehn and Hauata. They were seven years old, he wrote, and seemed to him to be constantly coming up with ways in which they could torment him. Parisa had written him that she understood completely. Eluned's daughter, Fuchsia was also seven, and could also be very annoying.

They had managed to exchange a few letters before the snows closed off the mail routes, and she hadn't quite screwed up the courage to tell him she was a shapeshifter before they'd had to wait for the weather to shift so that the ships could sail again.

What would he think of her when he found out? Cian had been 13 and hadn't minded a bit. She tried to remember what his 10-year-old cousin, Madoc, had thought of her, but failed. Clearly it hadn't stood out to her. Besides, it was probably easier to be blasé about shapeshifting in a Kingdom in which it is not a secret and not something those who shifted felt they needed to be ashamed of.

The Kingdom of Pelf was a completely different story. That was the Kingdom Bonpo had been killed in because they were so afraid of strangers. Admittedly, a yeti must look intimidating because of their height and girth, but when he was accompanied by a Jabberwock the Janawar and a slow-witted teenage boy? How could they have been afraid of the dog-like creature and a child? It didn't make sense.

And yet despite the great wall they had built because of their xenophobia, they hadn't fought particularly hard when the army had arrived to reclaim Pelf as one of the Thirteen Kingdoms.

Fatemeh said that once the leaders of Pelf's military government had learned that the Thirteen Treasures had been gathered back together and that there was still a living member of the royal family who was now in possession of the Knife of the Horseman, they had surrendered quite willingly and allowed Prince Raynor of Simoon and his wife, Princess Leleua of Favonia, to take up residence in Zhaleh Palace and rule over them with the help of the already long established military government, which became a parliament of sorts.

And then there were the dragons. Were they just a rumor or had they actually been seen? Parisa wanted to find out more, but Fatemeh didn't know anything other than rumors. Even in Pelf, the population was concentrated along the coast and along the border with the Kingdom of Dziron because people were still afraid to venture into the Devastation of Pelf that bordered the Sea of Blood. It was entirely possible that the radiation levels had long since abated, but no one felt it worth the risk to find out.

That would be a good place for dragons to hide, Parisa thought. She sighed. It was all supposition at this point. When she was able to send Körbl a letter again, she would ask him what he knew.

Parisa sighed again and glanced at Pallas. "Well, Pallas," she said, "I've wasted enough time. I really need to go inside and finish Mama's painting." This time she had wisely kept her mouth shut about Yuclog, another tradition in Dyfed, and she and her mother intended to celebrate it quietly on the morrow. They would exchange gifts, just one each; light a candle although they didn't have the previous year's candle to light it with; and light the Yule log, which Parisa had picked out from some logs that had yet to be split.

Her mother had also arranged for a special Yuclog dinner to be sent to their room—rabbit stew and soda bread with shortbread and creamy whiskey-spiked coffee for dessert.

Standing up, Parisa said farewell to Pallas and returned to her room. After tossing the blanket on the sofa so she could use it later when she was reading, she walked over to her desk. She opened the lower drawer and removed the paints and the heavy paper on which she was painting her mother's gift.

Parisa was painting the entwined black and white dolphins from her dream. She wanted her mother to have it as a reminder that they could make some important changes when they returned to rule Pelf, including changing the sigil. She painted a decorative border around the dolphins in a wavelike pattern then set it aside to dry.

It was nearly time to go down to dinner. Parisa locked the adjoining door before hurrying to the bathroom to freshen up. She didn't want to risk her mother entering the room and seeing her gift. Though she always knocked first, her mother had a habit of stepping into the room immediately afterwards.

Before she went down for dinner, Parisa thought she would put the painting on top of the armoire again. It meant dragging over her desk chair to stand upon so she could reach the top, but it was the safest spot in the room because it wasn't visible. Tomorrow morning, she would cut the painting into a circle and then glue it to a board that had also been cut in a circle. By noon, it would be dry enough to wrap.

THE YULE LOG HAD BURNED DOWN to embers and Parisa added some coal so that her room wouldn't get too cold during the night. She then went to her desk and removed the gift for her mother. Her gift had been sitting on the mantle all evening and she was dying to know what her mother picked out for her.

"Open mine first," Parisa said, sitting down on the sofa and handing her mother the package.

Chokhmah carefully unwrapped it and gasped when she saw the contents. "By Omni, Parisa, this is beautiful. It looks like a sigil. I love the waves encircling the dolphins. I am going to hang this over my desk so that I see it all the time."

"I'm glad you like it, Mama."

Chokhmah placed her gift and its wrapping on the coffee table and stood up. Parisa sipped at her coffee while her mother retrieved her gift. Despite the caffeine, she was starting to get drowsy.

She put down her mug as her mother returned to the sofa and handed her a box wrapped in tissue paper. Parisa unwrapped it to find a small wooden box with a design using inlaid wood and mother of pearl on the top.

"This is so beautiful," Parisa said.

"Open it," her mother said, "the real gift is inside."

The top was hinged and Parisa pushed it back and found a blue satin bag within. She withdrew it and loosened the ribbon that snugged the end shut. Inside the bag was a deck of cards. Parisa removed them and drew in her breath when she saw what decorated the top of the cards—a white wolf with sapphire blue eyes.

"I figured it was about time you had your own tarot deck," her mother said.

"These are so extraordinary," Parisa said as she started looking through the deck. "Animals instead of humans." In the major arcana, The Fool was a puppy, The Magician, a raven, and the High Priestess, a black cat. She shuffled through the cards until she found a wolf. Strength, she smiled. That seemed appropriate.

Parisa stifled a yawn. "Sorry, Mama, I guess I am more tired that I realized. I'm going to wait until tomorrow so that I can look at each one of these more carefully." She reinserted the cards into the satin bag and returned them to the box.

"If you go through them every day, you will soon find that you have learned every detail of each one," Chokhmah said.

"Maybe when we get to Buta, I can do a reading for Körbl," Parisa said.

"Do you think he would enjoy that?"

"I think so," Parisa said. "He seems to be curious about everything."

"I am glad you enjoy corresponding with him," her mother said. "It would be nice to have a friend waiting when we arrive."

Parisa nodded in agreement. Yes, it would, she thought, picking up her mug and draining the last of the coffee. It would be very nice indeed.

CHOKHMAH

After tucking Parisa into bed, Chokhmah retrieved her gift and quietly left the room. Tuck-ins were becoming more and more rare, and she assumed it would not be long before they stopped completely. It made her sad, but the whole point of motherhood was to raise one's child to be independent.

She placed her painting on her desk, propping it against the wall until she could get it hanged, and began to get ready for bed. Like her daughter, she also had mixed feelings about missing Faolan's funeral. Sometimes it was extremely difficult to reconcile the man she had met in Favonia with the man who had left for Simoon all those months ago. Chokhmah wished that they had had a chance to work things out, but she also wondered if that would have ever been possible.

Chokhmah gazed without seeing at her reflection in the bathroom mirror as she brushed out her hair and braided it. Putting down her brush, she slowly refocused on her image. Would the Kingdom of Pelf really accept her as their queen?

She was quickly approaching 60 years of age and it was beginning to show—hair more silver than brown, fine lines around her eyes, deeper lines around her mouth, chin starting to go a little soft. Yet, she would bring a daughter with her, albeit no longer a pure-blooded Pelfan, but was that so bad? Maybe it was time for the Kingdom of Pelf to become more diverse.

Chokhmah returned to her room and crawled into bed, but despite her weariness, her mind would not let her rest.

It was less than two months until Parisa's 13th birthday, and she found herself fretting more and more about the upcoming shift. It could happen any time now as Parisa's senses seemed to be heightening and she was definitely showing a preference for meat. On the other hand, her daughter had yet to start menstruating although it was too early to worry about that aspect of puberty. Chokhmah had begun in her 12th year, but she had never thought to ask Fianna. Maybe it was different for shapeshifters.

Sighing, Chokhmah pulled the comforter up under her chin, closed, her eyes and began focusing on taking deep breaths. It was silly to worry about it. It would happen when it would happen, and they would deal with it then. Meanwhile, she needed to focus on learning the language of her people and anything else she could find out about Pelf.

As she drifted off to sleep, she recalled the dream image of the white wolf with the copper wings. What on earth did the wings symbolize? Freedom?

THIRTEEN YEARS. Had it really been 13 years since she had given birth to Parisa? It both seemed like a long time ago and just yesterday. She studied her daughter who was graciously accepting birthday wishes from Fuchsia and Gavreel. The previous month they had marked what would have been Faolan's 51st birthday with a day of quiet reflection, taking turns remembering the good things about him rather than the bad.

Somehow, it seemed to make up for the fact that they would probably never make it back to Bogaine.

When Fuchsia and Gavreel left to fill their plates, Chokhmah placed a flower in front of her daughter.

Parisa picked it up and nodded appreciatively.

"While I was walking in the gardens this morning," her mother said, "that camellia caught my eye. It is starting to brown at the edges, but does it not have the loveliest pattern? I thought you might like to paint it."

"Isn't it amazing," Parisa said, "how patterns in nature are often more astounding than those created by humans?"

"I agree," said Eluned, peering over Parisa's shoulder at the flower. "Happy Birthday, darling."

"Thank you," Parisa said.

"I'm looking forward to your birthday dinner tonight," Uriel said as he entered the dining room. "I can't wait to see what you've picked out for your meal."

"I tried getting her to tell me, but she wouldn't," Fuchsia complained as she sat down next to her.

Parisa chuckled. "It's nice to have some surprises, Fuchsia."

"It's also nice to share your secrets with someone," Fuchsia retorted, and Parisa laughed out loud.

"Not this time," she said, "but I promise I will share my next secret with you."

"Happy Birthday," Uriel said, squeezing her shoulder. "I meant to say earlier but was interrupted." He raised his eyebrows and made a face at his daughter who giggled.

"You're so silly, Daddy."

"He comes by it naturally," Eluned laughed.

"Can't argue with that," Uriel said, picking up his plate and heading to the sideboard.

Chokhmah watched as Parisa hurriedly shoveled the remainder of her steak and eggs into her mouth before pointing to the neglected strawberries on her plate. There were only three of them.

Parisa groaned but ate them and then stood up. "I'm going to run this flower to my room so I can put it in some water," she told her mother. I'll meet you in the library as soon as possible."

Chokhmah nodded. It might be Parisa's birthday, but there were still lessons and they were studying Pelfan everyday now. They were nearly finished with Ship of Theseus and Fatemeh had promised they would work on a book of Pelfan fairy tales next.

PARISA

Standing in front of her bathroom mirror, Parisa admired her new outfit. It had been a gift from Eluned and Uriel, presented to her early so that she could wear it to her birthday dinner. Because she was finally entering her teenage years, they were making a real occasion out of it.

Clearly Eluned had chosen the outfit she was wearing. She had a way with clothes, and these suited Parisa perfectly. The mock turtleneck sweater fell to her midriff and was knitted from chunky and soft white wool interspersed with sapphire blue yarn. A taffeta skirt of the same vivid blue featured a wide, form-fitting waist that fell in soft pleats from her hips to where it skimmed the top of her feet. And it even had pockets, Parisa smiled, as she tucked her linen handkerchief into one of them. She considered wearing her hair down for a moment, but it concealed too much of the sweater, so she opted for a loose bun at the nape of her neck instead.

Feeling quite lovely, she tapped on her mother's door to see if she was ready.

Parisa gasped when her mother opened the door. "Is that the dress you wore to meet Queen Njima?" Parisa had never seen it on her mother, but Chokhmah has once shown it to her.

She kept it wrapped in tissue paper in a cedar box. There had never been an occasion to wear such an extraordinary dress in Dyfed.

"It is," her mother smiled. "I had it refurbished. I did not want all the beads to drop off the first time I wore it again." The dress was quite simple—cap-sleeved with a modest V-neck—but her mother literally shimmered in the glow from the flames dancing in the fireplace as the dress was completely covered in gold beads.

"You look like a queen in everything you wear," Parisa said and hugged her.

Chokhmah's hair was pulled back and fastened with a gold barrette studded with tiny jewels of varying colors.

Her mother retrieved a small gold bag which contained her handkerchief and balm for her lips along with a wrapped box.

"Your birthday gift," she smiled.

Parisa wondered what her mother had picked out for her. She couldn't think of anything she either wanted or needed. She knew that her mother had little or no money, but fortunately, Uriel and Eluned had been very generous since they'd arrived. Perhaps her mother agreeing to take on her birthright as Queen of Pelf was worth it to them.

Despite the fact it was just the six of them plus Zimbra and Fatemeh, whom Parisa had wanted to be there, they were eating in the formal dining room.

The table was decorated with hothouse flowers, and the formal china of the Kingdom glittered on the spotless table-cloth. The chargers were gold-rimmed and the sigil of the Kingdom of Aden—a red phoenix rising from the flames—adorned the middle of the plates.

Once seated, Uriel said a blessing and once again wished Parisa the happiest of birthdays. Then they waited for the arrival of the first course, trying to guess what it might be.

It wasn't long before bowls of butternut squash soup drizzled with cream were placed before them.

"Delicious!" Parisa proclaimed after taking the first sip from her soup spoon.

Once the soup bowls had been cleared away, plates arrived with tuna steaks, mashed rutabaga, and greenhouse-grown green beans.

"Excellent choices so far," her mother said although Gavreel turned up his nose at the rutabagas. Mashed rutabagas had always been one of Parisa's favorites although these days she really preferred meat. But even though it was her birthday meal, she knew that they all would prefer, well, except maybe Fuchsia and Gavreel, to eat something healthy.

Finally, her birthday cake was carried in, and everyone joined in the traditional song before Parisa was allowed to make the first cut.

"May Omni bless you and keep you," they sang. "May the face of Omni shine on you and be gracious to you. May the face of Omni turn toward you and give you peace. And may Omni grant you many more years."

Grinning, Parisa cut into her cake and the smell of cinnamon, nutmeg, and cloves wafted across the table. She had developed quite a fondness for spice cake. She'd also requested cream cheese frosting because it wasn't quite as sweet as others.

Finally, they toasted to her continued health with champagne although Gavreel toasted with cider because he didn't like champagne; Fuchsia, on the other hand, was given a small amount with which to toast Parisa. Although the girl had long since admitted to Parisa that she didn't really like the drink, she had also confessed that she liked doing what the grownups did.

"Can she open her presents now?" Fuchsia asked once they had toasted and set their glasses down.

Uriel pushed back his chair and stood. "Why don't we go to the library? I believe the presents have been taken there, and a fire lit in the fireplace."

They followed the King to the library and made themselves comfortable on the sofas and chairs in front of the hearth. Parisa sat down on a cushion in front of a low table that contained a few gifts, then jumped up quickly.

"First," she said, "I want to thank Eluned and Uriel for this beautiful outfit again. I really, really love it."

"And you look beautiful in it, darling," Eluned said.

"Yes, she does," Uriel agreed.

"Open our gift first," Fuchsia said, picking up a large package and handing it to Parisa.

Sitting down on the cushion again, she unwrapped the gift and grinned at Fuchsia and Gavreel. "This is perfect," she exclaimed. "Thank you so much." She admired the new paintbrushes and paper and took a moment to glance through the half dozen new paints she'd been given. She'd been running low on a couple of them, and a few she didn't even own.

She opened Zimbra's gift next and smiled at her teacher. "You remembered."

"When you remarked how much you liked my hair clips, I knew just what to get you," Zimbra said. The stylized dolphins did not look exactly like the ones she had seen in her dream and then painted for her mother, but they were similar. Also, she liked the fact they had a little pearl for an eye.

"My turn," Fatemeh said, pointing to a book-shaped gift on the table.

Parisa unwrapped it, and her eyes widened as she read the title, "Legends of Pelf," she said, opening the book.

"Eet ees my hope that eet weel help you learn the language even more queekly," Fatemeh said.

Parisa nodded vigorously. She would just have to if she wanted to know about the legends of the kingdom. Fairy tales were fun, but legends were based on truth. Besides, she had recognized the word for dragon in the table of contents.

The only remaining gift was from her mother. Parisa opened the box and gasped, lifting a crown from the cushion upon which it was sitting. The burnished red gold glimmered in the firelight, and it was adorned with sapphires and pearls.

"A princess deserves a crown," her mother said.

"Where? How?" Parisa was speechless. There was no way her mother could have afforded to have this made, and it seemed overly generous even for Eluned and Uriel.

Chokhmah smiled. "Believe it or not, it has been sitting in the room containing the crown treasures at Zhaleh Palace since Queen Jazmin fled the Kingdom with her children before the Cataclysm."

"And her daughter was named Parisa," Parisa stated.

"And it probably belonged to other Pelfan Princesses before her," Chokhmah said. "I have no idea how ancient it is."

"So, the crown I saw in my dream is probably there too? How did they remain safe all these years?"

"The room is located deep beneath the palace, Leleua explained when she wrote me," her mother explained. "Those who have been leading the Kingdom since the Cataclysm have kept it safe in the hope that someday the royal family would return. They knew that Jazmin and her children,"

"Alborz, Gaspar, and Parisa," Parisa interrupted.

Her mother smiled. "Yes, they knew they had fled to Kamea, but not what happened when that city was destroyed." Parisa set the crown on her head. It wasn't heavy, but it carried the weight of centuries.

"When I told Leleua that we are planning to return to Pelf in the spring, she told me about the crowns and other jewels still there. And while I did not want my crown to leave the Kingdom as it feels safer for it to remain there, I could not think of a more wonderful birthday present for you—for you to be able to arrive in Pelf with the crown of a Pelfan Princess on your head. I thought it might make them more likely to accept the fact that you are not of pure Pelfan blood. And Fatemeh agreed with me."

Fatemeh nodded. "Yes. When they see you and see how much you look like your mother and a preencess, they cannot help but love you."

A tear escaped Parisa's eye, and she wiped it away. "This is all so much to take in," she said, voice choked. "I think it is finally sinking in that we are going to Buta to live at Zhaleh Palace and that someday I will be the Queen of Pelf."

"Which is why we need to live there as soon as possible," Chokhmah said, "so that you will have years to become accustomed to the Kingdom, its customs, and needs, before you become its queen."

"What about you?"

"I will learn from Leleua and Raynor and the other leaders," her mother said. "I have been assured that they intend to help me, both of us, acclimate to our new life."

Parisa nodded. "So, we need to be prepared to leave once the bad weather breaks?"

"Yes," Chokhmah said, "I believe so."

"That should be within the month," Uriel said.

A month, maybe less, Parisa thought. She would start packing in the morning. No, she thought, on further reflection, that was probably ridiculous. She could, though, at the very least make a plan for leaving. She still hadn't come up with a way to warn Pallas that she would no longer be around. Maybe she could introduce him to Fuchsia?

A LITTLE MORE THAN TWO WEEKS before the vernal equinox and not even a month after her birthday, Parisa and her mother boarded the xebec that would take them to Buta. There had finally been a break in the stormy weather and if the good weather held, they could be in Buta by the morning of the fifth day. A pigeon was sent to Zhaleh Palace to warn Prince Raynor and Princess Leleua of their imminent arrival. But, in order not to take any chances with the weather, Eluned had lent Chokhmah the black pearl that would help calm any storms that might arise.

Eluned had only used the pearl once since it had been given to her by Kiha, the priestess of Namaka on the island of Paliaina, when they had been waiting for the arrival of Yona in the Kingdom of Favonia.

"And that's when you met Papa," Parisa had said when her mother showed her the pearl.

"Yes," Chokhmah said. "He helped Yona escape from the Kingdom of Adamah with the Hamper of Gwyddno Long-shank." And then her mother had gotten this far away look in her eyes, and she had wisely left her alone to reminisce.

Now, she was standing in the prow of the three-masted ship waiting to see if it lived up to its name: Dolphin.

And Dolphin did not disappoint—it was both a fast and agile craft—and Parisa found herself once again exhilarated as they sliced through the ocean, wind and sea spray on her face. She had received permission to wear pants and a heavy sweater until the morning they reached the Bay of Besu, which made it easier for her to get around the ship.

The only thing that threw a damper on the trip was that she had finally started menstruating. It had happened two days prior to their departure, so she had a chance to become somewhat accustomed to her period before they boarded. Still, it was a little awkward to be adjusting to this new part of her existence while on a cramped ship. Fortunately, being royalty had allowed them some privacy and a personal, albeit tiny, cabin to themselves.

Only four days and four nights until they arrived in Buta, but her mother told her that chances were that being her first, her period would probably end before they arrived in there. That morning, she would dress in the outfit Eluned and Uriel had given her for her birthday and wear the crown.

Parisa was beyond excited. While her mother fretted about whether or not they were displacing anyone from their space at the palace, she couldn't wait to meet Körbl and the others.

"Mama, I told you it's a huge palace," Parisa had said when her mother first began to worry about it. "I saw it in my dream." "But you had your dream while we were living at Rose Cottage," her mother countered. "I imagine anything would have seemed huge compared to it."

"Besides," Parisa reasoned, "if they maintained the jewels all these years, don't you think that the rooms used by the King and his family would have been taken care of as well? I'll bet you they didn't put Leleua and Raynor and their family in those rooms. They are probably in a different wing altogether." "Let us hope you are correct," her mother had conceded, but she still looked doubtful.

Chokhmah

As predicted, the Dolphin entered the Bay of Besu on the fifth morning shortly after dawn. Chokhmah couldn't help but draw in her breath when she saw Zhaleh Palace perched high above the bay, the early morning sun setting the white stone of its walls aglow with a rosy light.

Parisa had seen truly—Zhaleh Palace was more than twice the size of the biggest castles she had visited—Castle Bennu where she'd spent the past three-quarters of a year, Iqbal Palace in Tarshish where representatives of the Thirteen Kingdoms had met together for the first time in centuries, and Castle Indalo in Naphtali where they had recruited Njima for the Quest.

The palace was too much to take in. From the spires and turrets, towers and domes, it might take her a year before she even began to become familiar with her new domicile.

As they sailed closer and closer, Chokhmah grew ever more convinced—this was her home. As part of a band of Roma, she had been constantly on the move for as long as she could remember. She had tried to settle down at Rose Cottage for the twelve or so years following the Quest but always had the feeling that she was an outsider despite how friendly Olcan, and his family, had been to her over the years.

The fact they had not communicated with her since she and Parisa had left for Ponike, not even after Faolan's death, led credence to that belief. She suspected they blamed her because it was easier than dealing with the guilt of never having confronted Faolan with his excessive drinking. Olcan probably did not even know about Fatimah as he would have considered his brother's behavior a weakness, and his career as a spy would have ended right there.

As they drew nearer to Zhaleh Palace, Chokhmah realized the movement along the shoreline was people rather than waves.

"It looks as if the whole kingdom has turned out for our arrival, doesn't it?" Parisa said, appearing at her mother's side.

Chokhmah glanced at her daughter and nodded approvingly. "You look like the Princess you are," she said. The crown's sapphires and pearls seemed to glow in the gentle rays of the morning sun.

"And you look like a queen." Chokhmah's dress was shimmery black and red brocade with golden thread sprinkled throughout. It was a farewell gift from Eluned, and Chokhmah had been required to promise her friend that she would not open the gift until the day they would arrive in Buta. It reflected the colors of the current sigil without the kraken being represented anywhere on the dress. Eluned knew her dislike of the current sigil and had been kind enough not to force the creature on her. Someday, when she was fully in control, she would insist that the sigil be changed to the intertwined dolphins, but there was plenty of time for that.

The most important thing on her arrival was to gain the respect of her people. Changes would be made, but not immediately. Returning her focus to the waterfront, she could now sense the excitement that rose from the crowds lining the shore.

It was a joyous excitement, not angry, and she simultaneously felt her stomach somersault in nervousness and her eyes well with tears as her heart registered that their joy was connected to the arrival of herself and her daughter.

The ship seemed to be skimming the waves like its namesake and it was not long before Chokhmah could begin to make out faces in the crowd and hear what they were shouting: Long Live Queen Parisa.

She glanced at her daughter, noting that she had heard it too.

Parisa chuckled. "I guess there are going to be two Parisas in the palace now, huh?"

"Hmmm," her mother replied, frowning. "Do you mind?"

"Of course not," Parisa said, "but I may want to come up with a nickname until it's my turn to take on the name of the queen."

Chokhmah nodded. When she had first learned of her royal heritage, in what seemed another lifetime now, Eluned encouraged her to take on her actual name, but she had balked. She had always been Chokhmah and at the time it had seemed important to remain Chokhmah, the Roma in love with a gaje man, what amounted to a barbarian to the Roma. She smiled, and rolled her eyes, inwardly. In hindsight, of course they had had no problem with Faolan. She was not actually Roma either. Regardless, retaining her identity as the Gypsy healer had seemed integral to both the Quest and then to her life at Bogaine.

Now, with Pelfans shouting "Queen Parisa" as the crew of Dolphin dropped her sails and prepared to pull alongside the wharf below the palace that towered above it, the name that she had used for nearly sixty years suddenly seemed irrelevant. She would never be Chokhmah to the people of Pelf. She was their long-lost queen, the last surviving member of the Royal Family. Chokhmah had the grace to glance guiltily at her daughter. Yes, she thought, I am the last 'pure-blooded' Pelfan from the Royal Family, but not the last surviving member. But had not the fact that her ancestors had tried to retain the so-called purity of their Pelfan blood when they had fled their Kingdom caused the problems that made it necessary for her to be raised by the Roma? A people who had taken her in and raised her as one of their own despite the fact she was gaje. And that begged the question: why did there have to be 'other'? Why were people so intent on naming those they did not like or approve of as 'other'? Pelf was the only one of the Thirteen Kingdoms that had insisted on retaining the blood purity of its people, so much so that they had killed Bonpo and who knows how many others that had sought sanctuary there; had even built a massive wall to keep people away.

Yet, with a daughter that was only half Pelfan, and half shapeshifter to boot, that was about to change. Must change. The other twelve Kingdoms had been intermarrying among each other for centuries. It was time for Pelf to diversify in that regard, and it would begin with her daughter, their next Queen.

Queen Parisa hooked an arm around her daughter's waist, as the crew moored the ship to the dock. "Ready?"

Princess Parisa nodded. "Yes," she nodded again and took a deep breath, "Yes, I am ready."

They walked down the gangplank to where Lelelua, Raynor, and their children awaited them along with numerous other officials. The noise from the crowd was deafening, but Queen Parisa just smiled and waved appreciatively.

"I had no idea," she whispered in Leleua's ear as she hugged her grandniece.

"I told you the people of Pelf were excited," Leleua chuckled, "and as you can see, there is plenty of room. As a matter of fact, we weren't even allowed to reside in Royal Family's wing."

"Hmmm," Chokhmah said, glancing up at Zhaleh Palace, "that is what Parisa thought would be true."

Leleua glanced over her great aunt's shoulder, "Omni have mercy," she cried, "is that Parisa? She looks just like you."

Chokhmah turned to urge her daughter forward and saw that Leleua's exclamation had attracted Parisa's attention. "Darling," she said, "I would like to introduce you to my grand-niece, Leleua."

Parisa stepped forward and was swallowed by Leleua's embrace.

PARISA

As they neared the end of the gangplank, Parisa stepped back and allowed her mother to go ahead of her. After all, the crowd was really here for the return of their queen. Not to mention the fact, Parisa thought, her mother knew Leleua. She was pretty sure that like her, Chokhmah had yet to meet the rest of the family. They hadn't been at the meeting in Kaumari where Raynor and Leleua would have been representing Pelf for the first time.

Parisa was so immersed in her thoughts that she nearly stepped on her mother's heels when she stopped to greet Leleua. She took another step backward and surveyed the people she would be spending at least some years with, that is, if her mother had anything to do with it.

Leleua was hugging her mother and whispering in her ear. She was slightly shorter than Chokhmah and a good deal more full-bodied than her. Today, anyway, Leleua wore her long, thick, and wavy brown hair loose and it reached several inches past her waist. She looked nothing like Chokhmah, but, Parisa thought, of course she didn't. Biologically, they weren't related at all. Still, biological family or not, Parisa imagined it would be very difficult not to like this woman.

She shifted her eyes to the man standing next to the effusive Favonian. Raynor of Simoon was practically Leleua's opposite—slender with dark hair, cut short, and greying at the temples. If Parisa recalled correctly, he was about six years older than his wife. The only similarity between the two was their dark brown eyes, which probably meant their children were brown eyed too.

Parisa felt the weight of eyes on her as if she was being studied by more than the crowd, and she looked past Raynor and found her gaze locked on the boy who stood just behind him.

His straight hair, glossy as a raven's wing, fell to his shoulders, and his dark brown, nearly black eyes regarded her with frank curiosity. Körbl, she realized, and couldn't help but smile. He smiled back, igniting a spark in his eyes, and she grinned even more. He was tall for his age, slender like his father, but his face seemed a combination of his parents with his nose not as hooked as his father's nor as blunt as his mother's. His skin was well-tanned, but not the deep, coppery bronze of his mother's skin.

She was about to step forward and introduce herself when she heard Leleua exclaim, "Omni have mercy, is that Parisa? She looks just like you." And the next thing she knew her face was smashed against Leleua's ample bosom, knocking her crown askew. She straightened it and then she was shaking Prince Raynor's hand and being introduced to the princesses, Hauata and Foehn. The identical twins probably looked a lot like their mother had at seven.

Finally, it was Körbl's turn. "And this is our son, Korbinian," Leleua was saying. "I believe you two have been corresponding."

"I told her to call me Körbl," he told his mother, before hugging her gently. Parisa hugged him back. It was so nice to arrive in a new place and already have a friend.

"Ready for the procession?" Raynor asked.

"Procession?" Parisa responded.

Körbl pointed to an open carriage. "We squeezed in an extra bench so we can all ride together. "I think you and your mother are supposed to sit in front."

"Oh," Parisa said. "I guess that makes sense."

"I'll be in the back with Foehn and Hauata," Körbl said.

"So, we are processing to the Palace?"

"And then we'll have to listen to some speeches before we finally get to eat," he continued. "They've been working in the kitchen all week for this."

Parisa sighed. So, it was already beginning.

Körbl laughed. "Now you'll know what it's been like for me the past ten years. Fortunately, for the first few, I was completely unaware."

"Will you sit with me? You can make sure I don't make any huge mistakes on my first day in Pelf."

"I'd be happy too," he smiled then nodded toward the wagon. "Ready?"

Parisa chuckled to herself. How many more times would she hear that before she was completely settled in?

Remembering the ride from Ponike to Castle Bennu, Parisa settled onto the front seat with her mother, held her head high, pasted a not completely false smile on her face, and began to nod and wave at the crowds on either side of the carriageway. She had been hearing how much she looked like her mother for most of her life, but for the first time, she truly appreciated it. It actually helped her to feel more Pelfan than Dyfedian.

They entered the palace through an arched gateway with corbels carved into menacing krakens. Parisa supposed that made sense if you were trying to scare off invaders, but how many attackers entered through the main gate? Wouldn't it be friendlier to have guests welcomed by frolicking dolphins?

From the main courtyard, they entered the palace proper after passing through a well-fortified barbican and through yet another arched doorway, this one decorated with tracery and carvings of seashells and flowers. Much better, Parisa thought as they disembarked from the carriage before continuing down a long hallway hung with tapestry upon tapestry, so many that she couldn't even begin to take them all in.

They entered a huge chamber hung with a multitude of banners—one for each of the Thirteen Kingdoms, those were easy to pick out, and perhaps the rest were of different provinces within the Kingdom of Pelf? Maybe some were the banners of royal families? She'd have to ask Körbl later.

The blare of a trumpet startled her to attention, and the room quieted as her mother was led forth to the front of the dais with Raynor and Leleua. An official, she would have to learn who they all were eventually, carrying a pillow with an object hidden by a red silk scarf draped over it, walked up to Prince Raynor and offered him the pillow. He removed the scarf and lifted a crown from the pillow.

Parisa's forehead creased in confusion. The crown was lovely—red gold studded with black opals and black pearls—but it wasn't the crown she had seen in her dream.

"As many of you know," Raynor lifted the crown for the room to see, "this is not the Royal Crown of the Queen of Pelf. That crown has the Kingdom's sigil on it and has not been worn in centuries. This is one of the lesser, more quotidian crowns. We will have a coronation ceremony worthy of the return of the Kingdom's Queen, but we did not want to leave her crownless on the day of her return."

Before he could continue to speak, the silence was shattered by thunderous applause and shouts of "Hail Queen Parisa".

Raynor placed the crown atop Chokhmah's head. Parisa was glad she'd talked her mother into winding her hair into a low bun as the crown now sat comfortably on her head.

People were calling for their Queen to speak and Chokhmah stepped forward and waited for the room to quiet.

"Honestly, I am speechless," she said, wiping a tear from her eye. "Your more than generous welcome has left me both honored and humbled and I will do everything in my power to make myself worthy of being your Queen."

More thunderous applause, during which Chokhmah motioned for her daughter to step forward. The room quieted again as Parisa joined her mother.

"Also know," Chokhmah continued, "that my daughter, Parisa, takes her new position as a Princess of Pelf very seriously."

Parisa blushed and nodded. "I do," she said, barely audible, then more loudly, in Pelfan, "I am proud to be a Pelfan."

More applause and cries of "Hail Princess Parisa".

Then Parisa stepped back to join Körbl again as his mother stepped forward to announce the speakers who would welcome the royal family's return to the Kingdom.

Parisa tried to remain alert during the welcoming speeches, particularly as she was standing with her mother and Körbl's family on a raised dais at the front of the room for all to see, but it was difficult. Her stomach grumbled, protesting how empty it felt. She had barely managed a slice of buttered toast that morning because she'd been both excited and anxious. She heard Körbl chuckle next to her and glanced over at him. He was nearly her height despite the fact she was two years older. He would be eleven in a couple of months, she remembered.

"I told you it would seem like forever before we got to eat," he said under his breath.

"But the food will be good, right?" she whispered back.

"If you like that kind of thing," he said with a straight face.

Parisa looked taken aback until she saw the glint in his eye. "Very funny," she nudged his arm with her elbow, and he grinned.

"There's so much food that you can always find something you like," he reassured her.

His father, who stood in front of them, turned his head

and put a finger to his lips. Körbl nodded but rolled his eyes as soon as he'd turned back around.

About ten minutes later, they were led from the huge assembly room to an even bigger banquet room that was filled with tables. Unlike the relatively dim assembly chamber, this room blazed with light. Floor to ceiling windows made up the south-facing wall, separated by only a foot of stone. The banquet room was clearly near the edge of the high cliffs upon which the palace was situated as Parisa could see nothing but the sea and the distinctive red sails of the Pelfan fishing boats that dotted the Bay of Besu.

Her mother, along with Raynor and Leleua were seated at the head table, which was on a dais. Just below the head table, on the main floor, and to the left of her mother who sat front and center, was a smaller table at which she was seated with Körbl and his siblings. The rest of the guests, apparently in order of importance, were seated at the other tables with the least important sitting at the very back of the room.

How unfair, Parisa thought. Would someone like Haniel, or even Zimbra, even have been invited to the banquet? It was also doubtful that Olcan and his family would be invited to something like this, and they were acquainted with royalty. She would talk to her mother about having a banquet for staff, only. Certainly they deserved to be treated like royalty every once in a while.

While she was musing on this, platters of food were being placed on their table. Parisa focused in on the steaming mounds of saffron rice that looked nearly caramelized. She preferred meat but the aroma of the rice was heavenly. She saw chunks of chicken in a puree that Körbl informed her was stewed pomegranate, walnuts, and onions. There was also a lamb stew with kidney beans that smelled of coriander and turmeric, along with stewed greens, roasted chicken with lemons, grilled lambchops, and a seafood stew in which she spotted shrimp, scallops, white fish, and octopus. The aroma of all the dishes made her nose twitch and set her mouth to watering and for a moment she was dizzy with hunger. She grabbed a glass of water and took a long sip hoping to quench the flare of hunger that burned in her belly.

As their dinner glasses were being filled with mint tea, a bell rang, and her mother stood.

"Omni be with you," she said in Pelfan.

"And also with you," everyone responded before bowing their heads.

"Thank You, Omni," she continued in Pelfan, "for this food. For rest and home and all things good. For wind and rain and sun above. But most of all for those we love. Amen."

"Amen."

Parisa quickly impaled a lambchop on her fork and using all her willpower placed it on her plate first rather than tearing into while it was still on her implement. Then she picked up her knife and as calmly as she could, cut a bite-sized piece and then, rather than cramming it into her mouth and chewing voraciously, she delicately picked it up with her fork and placed it in her mouth, chewing as slowly and politely as possible.

"I have to admit," Körbl said cramming another forkful of rice into his mouth, watching as Parisa swallowed her lamb and cut another bite, "you have the best manners of any kid I've ever seen. I'm as ravenous as a wolf."

Parisa couldn't help but laugh. "Seen a lot of wolves, have you?"

"A few," he said after swallowing. "There's a zoo on the outskirts of Buta that I like to visit, and they have a pack of wolves."

Parisa's eyes widened, but she swallowed again before speaking. "In cages?"

"No, they actually are fenced in and have a rather large area to live in, including a bit of forest. They spend a lot of their time in the meadow, though."

"I would really love to see that," Parisa said. "What other animals do they keep there?"

"All kinds," Körbl said, helping himself to some seafood stew, "from insects to mammals. I think they've got one of everything from the Thirteen Kingdoms."

"Dragons?" Parisa asked, scooping some greens onto her plate to mentally appease her mother.

Körbl laughed. "I'm not sure a dragon would submit to being put in a zoo."

"So, there are dragons here?"

"There's a rumor that dragons have been seen near the Sea of Blood in Central Pelf, but no one has ventured that way in a long time."

"Aberrations?" Parisa had heard the stories of the Questers being attacked by Aberrations when they were searching for the Crock and Dish in Kamea, which was located on the Sea of Blood.

"Possibly," he agreed, "not to mention the dragons themselves and any radioactive fallout that might still be around."

Parisa nodded. "So… if you were going to explore the area, you'd have to make sure you were really well prepared. Not just defensively but with protective clothing, fresh water, things like that?"

"Exactly," Körbl agreed. "It would not be a trip to be taken lightly. And, you'd probably have to go there on foot because how do you protect horses and mules?"

"Good point," she agreed. "Not to mention that it would be difficult enough to carry enough fresh water for yourself, much less for pack animals. Yeah, I guess I can see why no one has ventured that way yet."

Körbl nodded.

Parisa helped herself to a chicken thigh and cut a piece, chewing silently for a moment. "Well," she said, after she'd swallowed. "We're young. We have years to figure out a safe way to make that trip."

Laughing, Körbl raised his glass of tea, "To exploring the shores of the Sea of Blood."

Parisa clinked her glass to his, "and to discovering dragons."

"I want to go," Hauata said.

Parisa regarded the girl in surprise. She had almost forgotten the twins were sitting across from them. "It doesn't scare you?"

"I'm not scared of anything," Hauata said.

Körbl nodded. "I can vouch for that."

"What about you?" Parisa asked Foehn.

The little girl shook her head. "No thank you."

"She'd rather read a book," Hauata said.

"Yes," Foehn agreed. "I'd rather have my adventure, what's it called, vicasciously?"

"Vicariously?" Parisa asked.

"Yes, that," Foehn agreed.

"Probably wise," Parisa said. "Adventure can be dangerous."

"But that doesn't stop you, right?" Hauata said.

"My mother stops me," Parisa laughed, "but only until I am old enough to be on my own."

"And then the High Chancellor and others will stop you because they won't want to risk the life of their future queen," Körbl reminded her.

Parisa groaned. He was right, of course. "Does that mean I'll be guarded constantly? What about you all? Are you guarded?"

They nodded.

"Körbl sometimes manages to give them the slip, though," Foehn said.

"I try not to do it too much," he agreed, "because I don't want them to figure it out."

I'm going to have to figure out a way, too, Parisa thought, watching as their dinner plates were removed and a selection of desserts placed in front of them—a date and walnut pie, a pudding that smelled of saffron, honey cakes, little pieces of syrup-soaked fried dough, as well as an assortment of fruit, dates, and nuts.

She put a few dates and nuts on her plate.

"You've at least got to try one of these," Körbl said, "or you'll insult the cooks." He cut a small slice of the pie and put it on her plate and added a couple of pieces of the fried dough.

"Thanks," Parisa said, and popped a piece of dough in her mouth. It was way too sweet for her taste, but he was correct. She could let it be known later that sweets weren't her favorite. Taking a bite of the pie, her thoughts returned to the guards. 'I don't want them following me around when I am a wolf, she mused. That means that I am definitely going to have to let Körbl know that at some point, maybe soon, I'll be able to start shifting into a wolf.'

She needed an ally. Leleua had advised her mother to keep Parisa's shapeshifting quiet until the time seemed right. A future queen that could turn into a wolf could be an asset, but it might also scare the people enough that Parisa's life would be endangered. It hadn't been that long since they killed anyone who was different, or they felt was a threat to their existence.

And if Körbl knew of some tricks to slip away from his guards, she could use his knowledge.

Parisa wished she knew when it was going to happen so she could better prepare for it. All her father had been able to tell her is that she would just know, which wasn't very helpful. Her mother had compared it to childbirth, which also involved 'just knowing'. Apparently, you could have contractions without them being labor contractions.

"But, when you go into labor," her mother had said, "you know it. I suspect shifting will feel similarly."

Parisa had just groaned and rolled her eyes. Like her father, and her uncle, and her cousins, her mother's advice had been far from helpful. It had been easier for all of them. They all shifted for the first time in a familiar place with family around. She was all alone and in an unfamiliar place.

She sighed and popped a date into her mouth. Her plate was mostly empty now and she intended to leave it like that.

"Are you okay?" Körbl asked.

Parisa blinked and shook her head as if clearing it of fog. "Huh?"

"You were flying with dragons and sighing."

"Flying with dragons?"

"That's what they say here instead of 'a thousand miles away,'" he explained.

"Well, that certainly lends more credence to the rumor of dragons." Parisa smiled. She liked the idea. "Anyway, I apologize. My mind tends to wander a lot. I was just thinking that at some point I'll have to let kitchen know that when it comes to food, I prefer protein to sugar."

"Really?" Hauata said, mouth full of honey cake.

"It's unusual, I know," said Parisa, "but that's one way that I'm like my father."

"I'm sorry about his death," Körbl said. "I can't even imagine." He glanced up to the dais where his father was speaking with a servant.

"Daddy can be strict," Foehn said, "but we know he loves us, and I can't imagine not having him around anymore."

"How does he feel about the fact that my mother stole Simoon's Hallowed Treasure?" Parisa quickly changed the subject. She didn't really like talking about her father yet.

"Oh, I imagine he was angry at first," Körbl said, "but we are all in a much better world because they were gathered together. If they hadn't been, you probably wouldn't be here now."

"I hadn't thought of that," Parisa said. If they hadn't gathered the Treasures, she might not even exist. And would Leleua and Raynor be married? "You all might not be here either. Kind of boggles the mind, doesn't it?"

"Yes?" Körbl asked, looking at someone over Parisa's shoulder.

Parisa turned to see a servant standing at her right side.

"Can I help you?" she asked.

"Prince Raynor sent me to ask if you are ready to accompany your mother to your new lodgings," the young man said.

Parisa glanced up at the dais to see her mother watching her expectantly.

"Sure," she said, starting to push back her chair before stopping and looking at the twins, then Körbl. "Wait. When will I see you all again?"

"That's a good question," he frowned, pondering. "It could be for dinner tonight. They'll probably serve us something light in our private dining room. Although I guess that depends on whether or not your mother prefers for you to eat separately."

"Knowing my mother," Parisa said, "that would only happen on rare occasions. At Castle Bennu we always ate with King Uriel and his family."

"Well, I hope you eat with us," Hauata said. "It would be nice to have someone new to talk to at dinner besides Foehn and Körbl."

"Very funny," Foehn said, rolling her eyes at her sister, "but I agree."

"So do I," Körbl said, "but if you're not there tonight or tomorrow morning, you might be sharing our tutors so we would see you in the schoolroom after breakfast. Unless, of course, you want to take a break from lessons for a few days until you're settled in?"

"I'd rather just get back to it," Parisa said. "So," she stood up, "unless there's something I am unaware of, I'll see you if not tonight, definitely tomorrow. Right now, I can't imagine ever eating another bite." She patted the waist of her taffeta skirt, which because it was form-fitting, felt a little tight. "And I can't wait to change out of this skirt."

"It's beautiful," Hauata said.

"But awfully tight at the moment," Parisa groaned.

"It's difficult not to overindulge when they place so much food in front of you, isn't it?" Körbl said.

Parisa nodded, trying to hide her amusement. Körbl's formal way of speaking seemed genuine, but she wondered if his father hadn't been instrumental in that.

They said their goodbyes and she followed the servant, whose name turned out to be Mahbod. She would try to remember that. Mahbod, she told herself, skeleton thin, long fingers, thick black hair cropped to his ears.

Parisa joined her mother on the dais, and from there they were led from the banquet hall down a long hallway, intersected by numerous other hallways, finally turning left at the end of the corridor and after bypassing a few more hallways, they reached a staircase that curved upward and out of sight.

An older woman was seated in a chair to the right of the staircase and stood as they approached. Parisa guessed that she was probably around the same age as her mother because their hair was equally silver streaked with dark strands although Parisa could see very little of it as most of her hair was hidden by a colorful scarf.

"I will take them from here, Mahbod," she said. "Thank you."

Mahbod bowed and headed back the way they had come.

"I am Ghodsi," she bowed slightly as she introduced herself, "my family has been taking care of the privy chambers for as long as we can remember. We always hoped that someday they would once again be occupied."

Parisa's eyes widened. "That's centuries," she gasped.

"Indeed," Ghodsi smiled, "and I cannot tell you just how happy we are that you are here."

"Thank you," Chokhmah said. "It has been a long and tortuous road here, but I finally feel that I am home."

"And anything I can do to ensure that you continue to feel that way, your Majesty, will be my pleasure," Ghodsi said. "I will be the first lady of your bedchamber, and my daughter, Niloufar, will see to Princess Parisa's needs."

Parisa swallowed hard. Her own maidservant. That was something she was going to have to get accustomed to, she thought. "Will I meet her today?"

"Yes, she is upstairs making sure that everything is in order for your arrival," Ghodsi said. "First, though, I would like to show you around a little so that you do not get lost. Although, if you do, anyone you ask will be more than willing to help you."

"That staircase leads to your private rooms, most of which are in the western-most tower, although there are also some rooms in the main wing that have served as guest rooms, nursery rooms, school rooms, offices, and the like.

"When you have descended the stairs and find yourself here, you can take the hallway straight ahead," Ghodsi started down the curved hallway, which clearly led along the wall of another rounded tower, and Parisa and her mother followed behind her, "and to your left here, is the staircase leading to the chambers occupied by Prince Raynor and his family."

Parisa looked up the stairway wondering where Körbl's room was. She was happy to find he wasn't that far away.

The corridor straightened, and Ghodsi pointed out the rooms to their left—a library, a music room, a sitting room. Arriving at the fourth door to the left, Ghodsi stopped and opened it.

"This is the private dining room where Prince Raynor and his family take most of their meals. You may, of course, request that they use another dining room, or you can dine with them, and you may always take your meals in your private chambers if you so desire."

Chokhmah glanced at Parisa, who said, "I would prefer to eat with Prince Raynor and his family. Is that okay with you, Mama?"

"Absolutely," Chokhmah said. "If there is a reason we prefer not to have company when we dine, then we shall eat in our private quarters."

"Very well, your Majesty," Ghodsi said. "I have one final room to show you before we go back to the Kraken Tower."

"Kraken Tower?" Parisa said.

"The Sigil of the Royal Family," Ghodsi explained. "You will find the sigil in numerous places throughout your rooms."

Chokhmah nodded, but as soon as Ghodsi's back was turned Parisa looked at her mother and grimaced. Chokhmah put a finger to her lips, a sign that they would discuss it later.

Parisa inwardly rolled her eyes. She wasn't stupid enough to say something out loud about it, which is why she had grimaced and not said anything. Omni have mercy, sometimes grownups could be so annoying.

Ghodsi stopped in front of an arched doorway and ushered them into a large room with a parquet floor that featured an intricate star pattern in multi-tonal wood.

"Lovely," her mother gasped.

Ghodsi smiled. "It is beautiful, isn't it?"

The long room featured a multiple domed ceiling and dozens of chandeliers although only a few had been lit. Parisa wondered how long it would take to light all those candles.

The walls had been plastered and featured swirling designs of gold—leaves, flowers, vines, and birds glimmered from the walls. At the very front of the room, a canopy of crimson silk fell from an orb attached to the ceiling and covered two massive thrones like an open-air tent.

The biggest throne had been carved from ebony wood and made to look like a kraken with curved arms and legs representing the tentacles and the back of the chair, its head. Parisa walked closer. Were those the kraken's eyes set into the chairback? Were they mother of pearl?

"Wow," Parisa murmured, "that is a really impressive

throne." Clearly, it had been designed for a king. The smaller throne was golden and upholstered in black velvet with a golden kraken embroidered on the chairback. If she knew her mother, that is the one that Queen Parisa would use.

"Raynor suggested we hold audience together until I have had my coronation, and longer, if necessary," Chokhmah said, coming to stand next to Parisa.

"That makes sense," Parisa agreed.

"Are we ready to return to the tower?" Ghodsi asked.

Beyond ready, Parisa thought. She was beginning to feel a bit overwhelmed.

They made the long trek back down the hallway and climbed to the first level. Ghodsi opened the door to the left and Parisa and Chokhmah gasped simultaneously.

Ghodsi looked at them in alarm. "Is everything all right?"

"I dreamed about this room," Chokhmah said, walking over to the throne carved from dark wood and upholstered in red velvet and touching the plush arm in wonder.

Ghodsi's eyes widened, but she only explained that the room was available should the Queen desire private audiences. There were also some armchairs set around a coffee table, a small desk and chair, and one section of the room was walled off and had its own door.

Probably a bathroom, Parisa thought before returning her attention to the throne. It was a lot simpler than the thrones downstairs but still lovely, she bypassed it and walked over to the square window that looked out over the ocean. The window was open allowing a brisk breeze to enter the room.

"What a view," she said, voice filled with awe. Ocean for as far as she could see and the curve of the shore that enclosed the bay. Dhows dotted the bay and a set of steep steps descended to what looked to be a white sand beach.

"Is that a beach down there?" she asked Ghodsi.

Her mother and Ghodsi walked over to the window.

"Yes," Ghodsi said. "That is the royal family's private beach."

Parisa's eyes lit up. "How do you get there?"

"I will show you," Ghodsi said, and led them out of the room. Across the landing from the throne room was another door that opened on a large room that was part of the western wing. On the tiled wall to their right at the far end of the room a compartmented shelf contained towels and stood next to something Parisa had not seen before. She studied it for a moment. Light curtains were pulled back to reveal a square of tiled floor with a hole in the middle, and a spout or something protruded about six feet up the tiled wall with some sort of handle midway between the floor and the spout. There were three of these contraptions in a row.

"What is it?"

"It is a quick way to rinse the sea water and sand from your body," Ghodsi explained. "The water is necessarily room temperature as it would be too difficult to keep it heated all the time, but if you turn that handle, it releases water into the pipe, which then flows through that funnel-shaped metal plate with holes in it and disperses the water over your body. I'll show you."

Ghodsi walked over to the stall, picking up a mop along the way that was in a cubbyhole on the wall adjacent to the hallway. She used the mop handle to turn the handle on the stall's wall, and water poured forth from the funnel in separated streams.

Parisa's mouth dropped open in awe as Ghodsi used the mop to turn the handle to the off position. "Wow, that's incredibly clever." Turning to face the wall opposite the door, Parisa pointed to a row of stalls and asked about them.

"Most of those are changing rooms," Ghodsi said, "And one is a toilet."

"Ah," Parisa said, nodding, "so you can remove your wet swimming clothes and put on dry clothes?"

"Exactly," Ghodsi said, "and the wet clothes and towels are deposited in that basket there," she pointed to a large laundry basket that stood next to another door set in the western wall.

"I assume Prince Raynor and his family have been allowed to use this?" Chokhmah asked.

Ghodsi's cheeks flushed. "Yes, the council didn't think it was right to deprive them of the private beach, particularly as they were not allowed to use the royal chambers. I hope that is to your liking, your Majesty?"

Chokhmah nodded, smiling, "Yes, I am very relieved to hear that. Although I imagine that it is still some time before it will be warm enough to enjoy the beach this year?"

"Probably another couple of months or so," Ghodsi agreed.

Parisa nodded in agreement, although she would love to go down to the beach and just sit and listen to the waves. She walked over to the door next to the oversized laundry basket. Opening it, she found a set of stairs descending downwards and out of sight.

"Those stairs take you to a door in the outside wall and a fortified pathway and staircase that lead down to the beach you saw."

Ah, that's what I saw on either side of the steps, Parisa thought, walls from above.

"Shall we continue?" Ghodsi asked.

They left the room and reached the next level with doors on either side of the landing. Ghodsi knocked on the door and it was opened by a young woman who was probably in her late twenties or early thirties. She also wore a colorful scarf over her dark hair. Parisa thought that Ghodsi had probably looked a lot like that when she was Niloufar's age.

"This is my daughter Niloufar," Ghodsi said. "She will attend to your needs, Princess Parisa. Is the room ready?" she asked her daughter, who nodded.

"Pleased to meet you Princess Parisa," Niloufar took a step

backward and to the side and opened the door wider. "I hope you are happy with your room."

Parisa pasted what she hoped was her most neutral expression on her face and stepped into the room. Like the throne room below, it was a large, mostly circular room with a bathroom walled off to the left. There was a square window straight ahead like the one below although this one had a window seat. Also like the room below, there was another square window about two feet above the first one.

To the right, about 2 o'clock on the circle, was another double set of windows. Parisa suspected she would find an identical set at 11 o'clock in the bathroom.

A fireplace and loveseat filled the space to the right of the door, a desk and chair to the left. A large four-poster bed filled most of the wall to the right and just beyond that, on the opposite side of the windows, was a large armoire.

The set up was fine. For now. She also thought that she'd be able to put up with the colors—crimson, mostly, and black and gold, until her mother's coronation. She liked the exotic patterns on the rugs but hoped they could be replaced with lighter colors. It was so dark in here. Heavy velvet curtains with black krakens embroidered on them hid most of her bed. It would be like sleeping in a cave.

Niloufar had placed a vase of fresh flowers on the low table in front of the gold brocade sofa as well as a tray containing a pitcher of water and a glass along with a small basket of fruits and a dish of nuts.

"This is wonderful," she told Niloufar.

"Thank you, Princess." She said, bowing a little. "You are, of course, more than welcome to personalize as you see fit. Just let me know what you need."

"I think I am fine for now," Parisa said.

"I unpacked all your clothes," Niloufar said, "but I've left the personal items in a box on your desk because I didn't know where you would want them."

"Thanks," Parisa said. "I am more than happy to take care of that." She didn't like the fact that Niloufar had had access to her journal, but she felt sure that snooping would be frowned upon here. At least, she hoped it was.

"What do you think, Mama?"

"I think it is very beautiful," Chokhmah said. "I think we will be very comfortable here."

Parisa glanced longingly at the box containing her personal things but her curiosity about her mother's room won out. "I can come and see your room first, can't I?"

"Of course, darling," her mother said. "You have plenty of time to unpack."

"Oh, and can I take off my crown? It's starting to feel kind of heavy," Parisa asked. In fact, she had a slight headache.

"I will take that and put it away in the safe until the next time you need it," Niloufar said.

"The safe in the basement?" Parisa asked, thinking that sounded like a lot of trouble.

Ghodsi smiled, "No, Princess Parisa, we have a safe for the jewels in the royal apartments. It will be placed there."

Parisa nodded. That seemed better to her somehow.

As they left the room, Niloufar pointed to the door across the landing. "That is my room," she said. "If you desire something, Princess Parisa, just knock on the door, or, alternately, ring the bell on your bedside table."

Parisa's eyes widened again as she nodded and murmured her thanks. This was all going to take some getting used to. Niloufar disappeared into her room as Ghodsi lead them up another flight of stairs.

"This floor has another set of rooms for older children, special guests, or whatever you deem necessary," Ghodsi said, starting up the stairs to the next level. "The apartment of the King is on the next to last floor of the tower."

"What's at the top?" Parisa asked.

"It is a guardroom and lookout," Ghodsi said. "It is currently empty as no one has been using this tower, and it has not been used since Pelf rejoined the Thirteen Kingdoms."

"Ah," said Chokhmah, "it is not needed in a time of peace, I would guess."

"Exactly," Ghodsi agreed.

"What about now that we will be living here?" Parisa wondered aloud.

"It was not our intention to man the tower as yet," Ghodsi said, "as there have been no threats to the Kingdom or the Queen. We will be maintaining a guard at the bottom of the staircase at all times beginning at 6 o'clock this evening but it is just a precaution."

So, if someone wanted to hurt us, now would be the time, Parisa thought, though they had no reason to do so as her mother didn't intend to make any changes until after her coronation. "But if we felt safer with someone being up there, they would station someone there?"

"Absolutely, whatever the Queen desires," Ghodsi assured them. "Would you like that, your Majesty?"

"No, thank you," Chokhmah said. "I believe my daughter is just thinking out loud."

Parisa chuckled. "My mother knows me too well. I feel very safe here. I was just wondering." In truth, she preferred the tower to remain empty. If she could see the beach from the room with the throne, how much better could it be seen from the top of the tower. She might try to find out, but she would prefer to be able to walk on the beach without too many people looking on.

They reached the final landing with three doorways—one into the tower room, one across the landing from it, and one straight ahead. Parisa assumed the door straight ahead contained the final bit of staircase ascending to the tower and wondered if the door was locked.

Ghodsi opened the door to the tower room, and Parisa halted her musings and followed them inside. Her mother's room looked a lot like hers except the bed was bigger and there was a lot more black than gold and red.

By Omni they enjoyed their sigil and colors here. It might be a while before they could change the sigil, but if her mother didn't do it, she would when she was Queen of Pelf.

She saw her mother eyeing something over the fireplace and followed her gaze—a large crimson shield outlined in gold with a black kraken emblazoned on it held a place of honor over the mantle. The red enamel was cracked and the dark metal beneath it peeked through. The gold along the outer edge had worn away in some places, and the kraken itself looked a little faded.

"Is that shield as old as it looks?" Parisa asked.

"Yes," Ghodsi said. "It belonged to King Alborz before The Devastation. He was killed in the Cataclysm, but he had hidden away the shield, the royal jewels, and some other things in the underground safe after Queen Jazmin and their children had safely escaped so we were able to retrieve it."

That made the shield more than 700 years old, Parisa thought then wonderingly touched her head where her crown had sat. "So my crown is also that old?" Parisa asked.

Ghodsi nodded, "But it had been safely tucked underground for all these centuries, so the jewels and the shield just needed a little cleaning when we removed them from the safe."

"That means the wear on the shield was from being used before it was hidden away?"

"Yes, I believe it was King Alborz's great grandfather who had that shield made," Ghodsi said. "It was a time of many wars between the Kingdoms."

Parisa ran through the history Fatemeh had taught her before they had left for Pelf. They had probably been fighting Kamartha about then because by the time of The Devastation, they were friendly enough with Naphtali that Pelfans had fled there for refuge.

"Hmmm," Parisa said out loud before covering her mouth, and blushing.

"About to think out loud again?" her mother asked.

"Well, I was just comparing the Kingdom of Aden and Dyfed to the Kingdom of Pelf in my head, and clearly The Devastation had a much greater impact on Pelf than it did there. It's almost like they take their history for granted whereas Pelf treasures their history and takes it very seriously."

"I never really thought of it that way," Ghodsi said, "because we just assumed other Kingdoms treasured their histories, as well."

"It's kind of sad," Parisa said and thought that way too many people glossed over the history of their homeland rather than looking at it objectively. "I hope, I mean, I wonder, do Pelfans look at both the good and bad aspects of their history?"

"You are talking about our most recent history, I suspect."

"Yes, I mean the lengths the Kingdom employed to keep non-Pelfans out of Buta. For example, Mama knew Bonpo, the Yeti killed by the soldiers outside of Buta."

Ghodsi flushed again. "We really thought we were doing the right thing, but you must believe me when I say that when the army arrived to insist that we become part of the Alliance of the Thirteen Kingdoms, we saw the error of our ways. To know that we can all co-exist peacefully, each retaining the unique aspects of our Kingdoms and also sharing those aspects with all the other Kingdoms and learning from them, as well. Well, it is a very, very good feeling not to spend time worrying about things that are not going to happen."

"Like war," Parisa said.

"Or someone coming here and telling us we have to give up our ways and live the way they tell us to. Prince Raynor and Princess Leleua have been very good about working with the council and doing what is best for the Kingdom of Pelf."

"Rather than the Kingdoms of Favonia or Simoon?" Chokhmah said.

"Exactly," agreed Ghodsi.

"Well, you should have no worries along those lines from me," Chokhmah said. "I fully intend to work with the council, Prince Raynor, and Princess Leleua to help the Kingdom of Pelf be the best it can be."

Even if that means making it more diverse, Parisa thought.

"Thank you, your Majesty," Ghodsi said, "that is very good to hear."

"I am going back down to my room to put away my things," Parisa said. "It's going to feel strange having you so far away from me. I got spoiled at Castle Bennu."

"We were in adjoining rooms," her mother explained to Ghodsi.

"That will not be a problem, will it?" Ghodsi asked.

"No," Parisa quickly assured her. "I'm thirteen and a woman now."

Chokhmah smiled at her, "Yes you are, my love."

As she descended the stairs back to her room, Parisa realized that she really didn't mind the increased distance. Her current aspirations—to get down to the beach and explore it and up into the tower room and explore that—would be much more achievable without her mother in hearing distance. Of course, there was also Niloufar. She was across the landing, though, so that might help. Parisa would have to pay attention to the sound her door made when opening. Hopefully, it was silent.

The tower room was a little more problematic as she'd have to risk being seen by both her mother and Ghodsi. And, if the door was locked, that would present another set of problems.

Parisa reached her bedroom door and opened it, breathing a sigh of relief at the silence. Clearly, it had been well-oiled in preparation for her occupancy, and that was fine with her.

She closed it behind her, carefully, and was pleased with

the quiet click it made upon latching. On the other hand, she was actually less than pleased with her room. Despite the windows, it was dark and the heavy curtains on her bed increased that darkness.

The bed curtains were the first thing she would ask to change. She wanted something lighter, airier, maybe a light-colored silk or gauze.

But first the bathroom. She'd had a lot of tea at the banquet.

Not surprisingly, the bathroom was dark, too, with a heavy red shower curtain and black towels with gold krakens. She was getting mighty sick of krakens. The throw rug on the tiled floor was red, and the counter and tub were black granite. Even the toilet was black. She couldn't change that, but she could get a lighter shower curtain, towels, and throw rug. As for the windows, she intended to remove the curtains immediately. She was in a tower, for Omni's sake. Who was going to spy on her? A bird?

She dragged her desk chair into the bathroom and stood on it to remove the curtains. Much better, she thought, as late afternoon light filtered into the room. She opened the windows a crack and inhaled the slightly salty scent of the breeze. It was a little chilly but somehow it made it easier to breathe, released some of the darkness. She would close them before going to bed.

She returned to her room and repeated the process with the four windows there. She had no problem being awakened by the sun. After folding up the curtains and placing them in a pile on the floor next to the door, she pulled her bed curtains back as far as they would go. She was happy to find a gold chord attached to each bed post with which she could keep them pulled back until she could exchange them for something she liked better.

A heavy red duvet and black and gold throw pillows adorned the bed itself. Parisa grimaced and turned away. That would have to be dealt with later. Finally, she turned to the box on her desk.

She placed her pencils, paints, and brushes in one drawer and her sketchbook and notebooks in another. As for her journal, which was now nearly full, she didn't quite trust leaving it easily accessible to prying eyes. She glanced around the room wondering where the safest spot might be.

She lifted the tufted red velvet cushion on the window seat but discarded that idea immediately; it would just be too noticeable. But wait, she looked again, did the window seat open?

It did! Niloufar probably even knew it did because the cushion looked new. Also, Parisa peered a little more closely at the interior, it looked as if the inside had been cleaned out, as well. They certainly had been thorough. But, she wondered, did this compartment have yet another, secret compartment, like the one Eluned had told her about; the one she'd found in the window seat in her childhood bedroom?

Parisa pressed the wide wooden slats at the bottom of the compartment—all firmly set. She then felt along the edges. In the left corner, in the back next to the wall, she felt a tiny indentation, no bigger than the tip of her pinky finger. She tried pulling it upward to no avail.

She looked around her room, brow furrowed in thought. Her penknife. The one she used to sharpen her pencils. Maybe she could pry the corner up with it. She hurried to her desk and withdrew it from the drawer.

With the sharp end of the knife in between the indentation and the wall, the slat of wood easily lifted upwards. Parisa pulled it away and peered inside. It was even darker than the compartment. She would need a candle. A pillar candle sat in a dish on her bedside table, and she soon had it lit and was back at the window seat.

There was something down there. A book? She placed the

candle on the ledge of the window and reached down into the compartment, withdrawing the book. Except it wasn't a book. It looked like a notebook—a leather notebook with a leather strap wound about it. A pale piece of quartz carved into a dolphin dangled from the end of the cord. It looked very similar to the dolphin Pallas had dropped into her lap.

Parisa's heart sped up as she unwound the cord and carefully opened the notebook. It was more than a notebook; it was a journal. Parisa could barely hear for the sound of her heart thrumming in her ears. It wasn't just a journal; it was the journal that had belonged to Princess Parisa. The Princess Parisa who had fled Buta with her mother and brothers and who had later died in childbirth.

The Journal of Parisa Zirhaan, Princess of Pelf was inscribed on the frontispiece. Zirhaan, Parisa thought. She had two names. Why did she leave this here? Did they have to leave so suddenly that she didn't have a chance to pack it? Did she forget in the excitement of fleeing? Was she being watched? So many questions, some of which might be answered if Parisa read the journal.

But, just in case she was disturbed by her mother or Niloufar, she placed her journal in the secret compartment, returned the slat to the correct position, lowered the lid, and replaced the cushion. She then blew out the candle and replaced it on her bedside table. That finished, she eyed the window seat critically for a second to make sure she hadn't forgotten something. No, it looked just as she had found it.

Parisa carried the journal over to the sofa and was about to make herself comfortable when she realized that if someone entered her room, the journal would be plainly visible, and she would have to explain what it was and where she had found it. That was unacceptable. She wanted to be the first to read it. It was her treasure, at least for the moment.

Walking over to her desk, Parisa pulled the book Fatemeh

had given her for her birthday out of the box. That way, she could tuck the journal behind a throw pillow and pretend she was reading about Pelfan legends if someone knocked on her door.

Returning to the sofa, she once again set about making herself as comfortable as possible, at least as comfortable as she could on the scratchy gold brocade. The frontispiece was of heavier stock than the pages themselves, and they had all yellowed over the years so Parisa was unsure whether they had once been white or cream colored. She turned the page as gently as possible.

28th Bahman, 4611 was written in the top left corner. The year '4611' held absolutely no meaning for her, but because she had been studying Pelfan she knew that the Kingdom had, up until the Accord, or rather the Kingdom's entrance into the Alliance, used a 12-month calendar system unlike the Thirteen Kingdom's 13-month calendar. Since it was the 28th of Bahman, the date probably corresponded most closely to their month of Neeon, a winter month.

Parisa glanced at the first line and set the journal down carefully. Of course that long ago Parisa had written in Pelfan, she thought. And, while she had learned a lot of Pelfan, she was still far from fluent. Parisa returned to her desk to retrieve the Pelfan dictionary that had been created when the Kingdom joined the Alliance. She had used it many a time since beginning to learn the language. And while many people were familiar with the Common Tongue from royalty to traders to sailors and innkeepers, it was something Pelfans had forgotten during the many centuries they were isolated from the rest of the Kingdoms and were now having to relearn themselves.

Some words had probably changed or fallen out of usage in the past seven centuries, but Parisa hoped she'd still be able to figure out what the journal said using context, her knowledge, and the dictionary. She picked up a notebook and pencil, as well, because she couldn't bring herself to mess up the journal. She could transcribe the Pelfan into the notebook.

"*First, I should say that Mother gave me this journal for my birthday,*" the first sentence read. So, Parisa thought, was the 28th of Bahman Parisa Zirhaan's birthday? Parisa continued to read, occasionally picking up the dictionary or musing over a particular sentence:

I was not surprised that my 11th birthday was neither my best nor my worst birthday so far. Father was more distracted than usual with all the talk of a possible war that I am so sick of hearing about. I thought that maybe, maybe just for one day, he could think about other things, like me, his only daughter. But no. He did not even stay to watch me unwrap my presents.

This journal was my favorite gift this year. The leather cord that keeps it shut (I guess so I can put little keepsakes in it?) has a quartz dolphin on the end of it. Mother knows how much I hate the krakens. You cannot seem to get away from them here. Fortunately, being a girl and the middle child, I do not have to worry about them looming over me forever! Someday, I will get married and leave this palace. I wish I could see some of the other Kingdoms, but Pelf has become more and more isolated since Great Grandfather's time.

Maybe I will end up in one of the resort towns along the Djed Sea. I would love to see Yazfahan near the border with the Kingdom of Kamartha. It is supposed to be really beautiful, and it would get me far, far away from here.

Anyway, not a great birthday. Father gave me a bracelet—pearls with a sapphire pendant. I would rather have the crown that the eldest Princess of Pelf gets to wear, but I cannot wear it until I turn 13. It also has sapphires and pearls, so I guess the bracelet is supposed to be worn with it. Will I get a matching necklace next year?

Alborz gave me his old sword even though he knows I am

not fond of weapons. I will probably hide it in my armoire. Now that he is 14, he thinks that he is a man and is always bossing me around like he is the King already. I worry that he will be the one who chooses whom I marry as Father seems determined to fight if it comes to a war. And no one has said so, but I know it is possible he could die. You only have to look at Mother's face when he speaks of war to know that.

Gaspar gave me some drawing paper and colored pencils although I know that either Mother or Leily actually got them for him to give me. He has been too sick this winter to have done much of anything. Leily gave me a book on seashells because she knows I like going to the beach and collecting them. I cannot wait until it gets warm enough to go down there again, and Leily promised that we can learn about shells and other sea creatures for my biology lessons this spring.

That is Souri knocking at the door, which means Mother is on her way to say good night. I need to find a place to hide this. I would hate for Alborz or Father to find it!

ONCE SHE HAD FINISHED THE FIRST ENTRY, Parisa rubbed her eyes and blinked. Yes, her eyes were tired, but it was actually getting darker by the minute and making it more difficult to see. At this point, it was probably safest to return the diary along with the notebook to the window seat. She would have more time to look at it tomorrow. At least, she hoped so.

She had just returned her pen knife to the desk drawer and was musing on the fact that she was probably going to have to make the slat easier to pull out when there was a loud triple knock at her door.

Parisa hurried to answer it.

"Queen Parisa would like to know if you will join her in

her room for a light snack?" Niloufar said when she opened the door. "If you prefer to eat downstairs with Prince Raynor and his family, you are welcome to do so."

"But she won't be joining me," Parisa stated.

"Correct," Niloufar smiled.

"I'll eat with my mother," Parisa said. "I'm really tired and not very hungry."

"I'll let her know you will be upstairs in 10 minutes?" Niloufar asked.

"Yes," Parisa agreed. "I'll wash up now." As she headed toward the bathroom, she realized she had never changed out of the clothes she arrived in. Maybe a little too formal for a light dinner with her mother but it seemed silly to change now.

IT WAS THE NEXT AFTERNOON before Parisa had a chance to look at the journal again. The previous evening, she and her mother had decided that they would join the family for breakfast in the private dining room. As at Castle Bennu, there were a wide variety of breakfast items to choose from and Parisa had loaded up on the meats and eggs with a token piece of fruit to appease her mother.

After breakfast, she had walked with Körbl, Hauata, and Foehn to the schoolroom where she met the tutor, Roozbeh. He set the others to work then quizzed her for an hour to see what she needed to learn. She spent the final two hours before lunch studying Pelfan and learning more about the Kingdom's history.

Following lunch, she asked for permission to take it easy the remainder of the day. She told her mother that she was still tired from the festivities the day before although she had actually slept well, falling asleep almost as soon as her head hit the pillow.

While Körbl and his sisters headed off for their afternoon activities—music and weaponry—she hurried to her bedroom. She was eager to read the next entry in Parisa Zirhaan's journal; she had neglected to look but she didn't think there were that many more. Parisa also wanted to carve out the corner of the slat so that she could lift it with her little finger.

She needed to find some decoy items to place inside the window seat just in case Niloufar glanced in there. Perhaps the sketchbooks she had already filled? She didn't care if Niloufar looked at those.

After collecting her dictionary, pencil, and an extra blanket from the top shelf of her armoire as it was chillier than it had been the previous day, Parisa was finally able to settle on the sofa with the other Parisa's journal and her transcription notebook.

"2ND ESFAND, 4611," the next entry was dated. So, a few days later, Parisa thought. It continued:

Leily has kept me really busy these past few days. By the time I got back to my room each night, I was so tired that I just wanted to go to bed. It has been night after night of long boring dinners with representatives from each of the provinces and talk about nothing but war, war, war. I am actually starting to worry that a war with the Mobeds is unavoidable.

I have to admit that it is partly my fault that I have had so little time. If I ask a question about the Mobeds then Leily will rant about them for hours. At least, it feels like hours. The only bright side of that is that I get out of doing any arithmetic.

I can kind of understand that they think we are evil because we worship Omni who they think is a false god. But I really do not understand why they think dogs are pure and good and cats are dirty and evil.

My little Bibi is sitting right next to me on this window seat and purring. She bathes herself all the time and is always very sweet to me. I really do not understand. Alborz's hunting dog always smells bad, and he slobbers a lot!

Anyway, Leily claims that the Mobeds want to return to the old religion and are willing to do whatever it takes to make that happen. She says what makes them really dangerous is that these are mostly young men who are almost anxious to fight because of the award that awaits their deaths.

The problem is that when we were separated into Thirteen Kingdoms all those years ago, a pact was made that we would all worship Omni just so this type of thing would not happen. Religious wars were one of the many things that destroyed the world, Leily says. What happens if we agree to return to the old religion? Will the other Kingdoms then want to go to war with us? Have the Mobeds thought of that? Do they care?

By Omni, that was a funny sight! I am still laughing as I write this. There was a flash of lightning followed by a really loud crash of thunder almost on top of it and Bibi was so startled that she leapt straight into the air before hiding herself under my bed. I think she must have jumped at least three feet off the cushion, all her hair standing on end! She is a little thing, and she has very fine hair and not much of it, but I promise her tail looked just like a bottle brush. She will stay hidden under my bed until the storm ends.

The rain has made it colder. I am going to go tell Souri to get a fire started in here to warm up the room. Maybe I will have some tea, too.

PARISA CLOSED THE JOURNAL AND NOTEBOOK and stood up and stretched. She had glanced ahead and seen that there were just a few more entries. Her Pelfan was getting better but she was no longer as eager to finish because she knew the ending to the story. At some point and probably within the month, Parisa Zirhaan would be leaving her home to refugee in Naphtali. She knew they had fled first to Shamash Palace in Kamea, which was the Capitol of the Kingdom at the time. But it hadn't taken long before everyone in Kamea had to flee eastward as the radiation settled over the Djed Sea.

Along with the royalty of Naphtali, they had traveled northeast to the city of Jazeel and resettled there, building Castle Indalo. Parisa had grown up there, been married there, and then died there. How young had she been? Were there even any records of it? Maybe when she was finished with the journal, she would ask her mother to send a pigeon to Queen Njima so they could find out more, if possible.

She replaced the journal in its hidden compartment and wondered what to do next. It looked like it was still a few hours until dinner. Maybe she could sneak down to the beach and explore it. It was cold but she could wear a sweater. She thought she had the time before dinner to do that if she could get out the door and down the stairs without Niloufar seeing.

Luck was with her, and it didn't hurt that she used to practice silent walking when exploring the woods around Bogaine. She had managed to sneak up on many a deer, rabbit, and other small mammals before they realized she was there. It was probably some wolf instinct, but she appreciated it anyway.

It was a long way down to the beach, but Parisa reveled in the feeling of being completely alone. She didn't feel like she was being watched, and she even stopped a couple of times and looked back at the tower but didn't see what appeared to be faces at any of the windows.

When she finally reached the bottom of the stairs, she was surprised to see another person standing just above the incoming waves, staring out into the Bay.

Was that Körbl? She walked as silently as possible down

the path to the beach, but the wind was in her ears, so she imagined it was in his as well. Not to mention the crash of the waves also probably masked any sounds.

She was standing beside him before he noticed her, and his hand flew to his hip before he recognized her and relaxed. "What were you reaching for? A knife?" Parisa asked.

"Habit," he said. "I always keep a knife on me when I come here on my own. You probably should, as well. I think we're safe, but you never know."

"Really? It's just a precaution?"

Körbl heaved a sigh. "Promise not to say anything. I told my mother that I wouldn't tell you."

"I promise," Parisa said.

"When we first arrived, I was about six, someone grabbed me when my nanny, Avizen, left me alone for a minute to use the bathroom."

"Omni have mercy," Parisa was wide-eyed. "What happened? Clearly you lived."

"Avizen saw him trying to drag me out the door, I was kicking and screaming, and she started screaming too. A guard arrived just seconds later, and while he, we never learned his name, was distracted, Avizen stabbed him in the back."

Parisa gulped. "Avizen did?"

"I didn't even know she carried a weapon but I'm glad she did," Körbl said.

"And so now you do."

"Yes," he agreed, "but fortunately it has never come up again. My father said he thought the man was probably crazy. We never even got to find out if it was because I wasn't Pelfan or if it was some other reason altogether."

"You don't think it's too risky to come down here by yourself?" She eyed the shells around her feet, thinking of the other Parisa.

"I like it here," Körbl said. "It is the easiest place to get to when I can slip my guards, and it would be very difficult for someone to sneak up on me."

Parisa grinned, "Unless they come down from the castle."

Körbl laughed. "Yes, unless the sneak up from behind me."

Parisa nodded, thoughtfully. "I think that coming down here will get more difficult for me. At this point, Niloufar doesn't even know that I might want to occasionally, and fortunately, the way to the beach is before you reach the guard at the bottom of the stairs." She paused. "Hey, how did you get past him?"

Körbl chuckled. "I don't go that way. You probably didn't see it but there's a hidden entrance in the shower room. The servants use it to pick up the dirty towels and bathing suits and return them to the room."

Parisa thought back to the room. It had to be on the wall with the changing rooms and toilet, which she'd barely looked at.

"Anyway, when I was exploring the palace one day, before the man grabbed me, of course, no one really bothered me much because it was right after we moved there, and they were still adjusting to having royalty again . . . well, I found a doorway into the servant's halls from our apartments and most of the doors were locked, but the first one that opened led into the shower room."

"Did you go down to the beach then?"

"No, I was afraid to descend those stairs because I didn't know where they led and, well, my father believes in corporal punishment."

Parisa winced. Her parents had never hurt her physically though there was one year she spent her fair share of time alone in her room without dinner. It only took a few times for her to realize that she wasn't particularly keen on that punishment, and she changed her behavior.

"Fortunately, it was summer when we arrived, and it

wasn't long before we were shown the shower room and informed about the beach."

"So, you kept the escape route in the back of your mind."

"I thought it might come in handy one day."

"And it did," Parisa laughed.

"I actually spent a lot of time down here that summer," Körbl said. "Foehn and Hauata were too young to be carried down all those stairs by their governess, but mine thought it was a great way to keep me entertained."

"Was it?"

"Actually, I enjoyed it. I built sandcastles, collected shells, played in the waves, and Avizen sat on the sand and read; probably made it easier on her, and she got to do something she liked."

Parisa leaned over and picked up a scallop shell. It was pure white with burgundy striations.

"Nice," Körbl said.

"What happened to Avizen?" Parisa asked, pocketing the shell.

"I started my schooling that fall, and she was no longer needed. I think she was assigned to another child who lived in the Palace, one of the Lord's or Councilor's children."

Parisa nodded, looking around at the beach for the first time. It wasn't very large, and a rocky outcropping, cliff-like in height towered to each side of it. The only way to reach the beach was down the steps from the palace that descended down a rocky slope to the beach or from the water. It seemed well protected.

And, despite the wind and the waves, quiet, peaceful.

"It's a good place to come if you need to be alone," Körbl remarked.

Parisa laughed. "Does that mean I should leave?"

"What?" he looked taken aback. "That's not what I meant; I really meant getting away from people who are annoying you."

"Like twin sisters?"

He smiled, "Exactly."

"You are also right about needing to be alone sometimes," Parisa said, "and I am more than happy to walk to one end of the beach or the other if you need some time. Believe me, I know what it's like to want to spend some time alone. I got used to it when I lived at Bogaine."

"Bogaine?"

"That's the name of the horse farm my father and uncle owned. It was started by their great, great grandparents," Parisa paused. "There might have been another great or two in there. I forget."

"Well, we can also be alone together," he said. "We don't always have to talk. We can sit and watch the water."

"That would be fine with me," she said.

Körbl pulled a silver watch from the pocket of his pants and glanced at its face before returning it.

"Time to get ready for dinner?"

"Yes," he said, "they'll be missing us soon. And that's the most important part about sneaking off—not getting caught."

"Otherwise, they'll watch you more closely?"

When Körbl nodded, solemnly, Parisa turned and headed back toward the steps with her new friend on her heels. The last thing she wanted was less freedom, particularly as she was going to need it to shift occasionally, although when the first time that would happen, she had no idea.

Parisa made it back to her room unseen and quickly changed for dinner. She had just finished pinning her hair into a low bun when there was a tap at her door. That sounded like her mother's rap—tap, tap, light and respectful as if she hated the idea of disturbing whoever was within. Niloufar knocked on her door—rat-a-tat, rat-a-tat, rat-a-tat, demanding the occupant's attention.

"Ready?" her mother asked when she opened the door.

Parisa glanced around her room making sure all was in order, but the candles she had lit had been blown out and everything looked to be in its proper place. "Yes," she said, stepping across the threshold and closing the door behind her. "I'm curious to see how they eat on non-festive occasions."

"A lot more simply, I hope," Chokhmah said, "because if I ate like I did yesterday all the time, I would have to acquire a whole new wardrobe."

Parisa rubbed her belly at the memory. "Seriously," she groaned, "I think I am still full."

When they entered the dining room, Prince Raynor, who was already seated at the head of the table, jumped to his feet.

"Queen Parisa," he said, "we weren't sure you would be joining us. Leleua and I can sit next to the girls. You are more than welcome to sit here." He indicated the seat at the head of the table.

"Thank you, but no," Chokhmah said, taking the seat next to Hauata who sat next to her mother who was at the Prince's right hand. "I am more than happy to sit next to Hauata." She smiled at the girl and Hauata grinned back.

"I'll sit next to Foehn," Parisa said, heading around the empty end of the table to sit to the other twin's left. It would make it easier to talk to Körbl if she wanted to.

They had barely seated themselves when a servant entered the room, flushing when he spotted the Queen and her daughter.

"Your Ma, majesty," he stuttered. "I didn't know you would be dining with the Prince tonight."

"Is it a problem?" Chokhmah asked.

"N-no," he answered. "It's j-just that I would have been here to s-seat you had I known."

Chokhmah laughed, shaking her head in amusement. "Being seated is not something to which I have yet grown accustomed.

I promise I will wait to be seated next time, okay . . . what is your name?"

The servant ducked his head, blushing again. "Amir, Your Majesty."

"Amir," Chokhmah repeated. "Thank you for worrying about us."

"Amir," Leleua said, "please tell the kitchen that we are ready to be served."

"Yes, Princess," Amir bowed and scurried from the room.

"It's been a long time since they've had a queen," Leleua laughed. "They are not sure how much more formal they need to be with you than they are with us."

"Well," Chokhmah said, "I have never been a queen before, so I am as lost as they are."

"I think we both prefer as little fuss as possible," Parisa said.

"Agreed," said Chokhmah as a server entered with a tureen of soup.

Parisa eyed it with trepidation. She didn't think she could eat a heavy soup and meal tonight and was pleased when a ladleful of a light broth with little chunks of chicken, carrot, onion, and very fine noodles was poured into her bowl.

When the server had left the room, Raynor said, "I hope that you do not mind a light dinner? I prefer not to eat a heavy meal at night because I retire early, and it disturbs my sleep. But the kitchen will be happy to provide you something more substantial if you desire it."

"No, this is perfect," Chokhmah said. "I much prefer a light meal in the evening."

"Me too," Parisa agreed, but thought, 'as long as some kind of protein is served.' She would be embarrassed if she had to ask for it. But she needn't have worried. Once the bowls were whisked away, servers arrived to place grilled swordfish steaks, roasted baby potatoes, and cherry tomatoes in a light dressing on their plates. Even dessert was light—lemon sorbet topped with fresh blueberries. And the portions had been small enough that she didn't feel overly full although she supposed she could have asked for more if she'd wanted to as Leleua had asked for a second helping of potatoes.

After dinner, they left the dining room and went next door to the sitting room. While she and Körbl, Hauata, and Foehn removed themselves to the other end of the room to play a card game, the adults sat down in the armchairs in front of the fireplace and talked quietly while sipping on something that looked alcoholic to Parisa. What was it they used to drink after dinner at Castle Bennu? Brandy?

Parisa was a little too distracted to play the game well. Not only was she unfamiliar with this version of tarok, something about acquiring the right coins cards, but she really just wanted to be back in her room reading Parisa Zirhaan's next journal entry. It had been short, and she thought she'd be able to finish it before she went to bed.

She wasn't particularly surprised when she lost, but she did find it surprising that Körbl had as well.

"Foehn always wins," Hauata complained.

"Then why don't you play something else?" Parisa asked.

"Because the winner gets to choose the next game," Körbl rolled his eyes.

"Maybe you should alternate between the winner choosing and the biggest loser choosing," Parisa suggested. "That way there would be more variety."

"I could live with that," Foehn said. "That means you get to pick the next game, Parisa."

Parisa was torn. She just wanted to go back to her room. A glance at their parents revealed they were still deep in conversation. She sighed and picked up the deck. "I guess I could teach you the version of tarok I've played all my life. My mother taught me, and we played it at Castle Bennu too because she taught Queen Eluned the same game."

They picked up the rules more quickly than she had their

version, and within half an hour they were declaring Körbl the victor.

He chuckled as he shuffled the deck. "It's nice to know what it feels like to win again." He frowned and sighed, laying the deck on the table. Hauata and Foehn groaned.

"What?" Parisa asked, confused.

"Bedtime," Hauata sighed. "We never get to stay up late." She said it quietly, though.

Parisa looked around. She didn't see a clock in evidence. "How did you know?"

"Father gave me the sign," Körbl said.

"The sign?" Parisa asked.

The twins and their brother held up an index finger.

"It means we have one minute to finish what we are doing," Foehn explained.

"Ah, well, there's always tomorrow night, right?" Parisa said, standing up. "Are you going to teach us a new card game, Körbl? Or will we play tarok again?"

"Hmmm," he replied. "I'll have to think about that."

They said their goodnights before heading off to their respective bedrooms. When Parisa reached hers, she hugged her mother goodnight and entered her room.

Niloufar had clearly prepared things for her—the sheets were turned back, a small fire burned in the fireplace warming the room a bit, a candle sat in a holder on the table in front of the sofa waiting to be lit, and she could see the warm glow of an oil lamp coming from the bathroom.

She pulled her nightgown from the shelf in the armoire and headed for the bathroom, first. Once ready for bed, she studied the window seat for a moment. She found herself yawning and realized it would probably be more frustrating to try and puzzle out the journal entry that night than first thing in the morning.

It was late and the trip down to the beach and back had

tired her more than she realized. She wasn't accustomed to climbing that many stairs. She would have to get down there often enough that she would soon grow used to it.

By the dim light of the fireplace, she climbed into bed, burrowing into the covers. As she drifted off to sleep, she hoped that she would wake early enough to decipher Princess Parisa's next journal entry.

3RD ESFAND, 4611. Leily says thing are 'accelerating' quickly. I had to ask her what that meant. Speeding up. They must be. At dinner tonight, Mother told me that she had asked Souri to pack a bag for me in case we have to leave at 'a moment's notice'. She also told me that if there was something that I could not bear to leave behind that I should pack that, too.

I want to bring this journal, but I do not want to risk Souri finding it if she needs to add something to my bag. I will leave it in the secret compartment in the window seat until I know more.

When I asked Mother where we would be going if we have to leave, she said that in 'all likelihood' it would be to Shamash Palace in Kamea. That is where Aunt Banafsheh lives. That is kind of exciting because I have never been to another Kingdom. She is married to Naphtali's Prince Jalil who, like Auntie Bana, is a second child.

I wonder how long we will have to stay there if we are forced into leaving. Mother said she did not know but she looked funny when she said it.

Parisa put down her pencil, closed the journal, and stared into space for a minute contemplating this new development. Had it even been a week since Parisa Zirhaan's birthday? She was beginning to understand how the journal might have easily been left behind. She opened the journal again and flipped through the pages and shook her head. It looked as if the next entry was the final entry.

She was dying to read it, but she needed to get down to breakfast and she didn't want to be caught with the journal when Niloufar knocked on her door. Parisa quickly replaced the diary and notebook in the window seat and placed the dictionary carefully on her desk before returning to her sofa. She also wanted to talk to Körbl about the journal. Maybe they could meet down on the beach later that day after she'd had a chance to read what the Princess had written before she had to flee the Kingdom of Pelf.

Niloufar's emphatic knock stirred her from her reverie, and she jumped up and hurried out of the room. Maybe she'd get lucky and be able to get a seat next to Körbl this morning.

But it was not to be. Körbl and his family, along with her mother, were already seated when she arrived. Parisa hurriedly fixed her plate and seated herself next to her mother as Körbl was flanked by his sisters on the opposite side of the table. When she was seated, Prince Raynor pushed back his chair and stood up, mug of coffee in hand.

"Our astrologers have informed us," he told them, pushing in his chair, and standing behind it at the head of the table, "that the most auspicious date for the coronation will be on the Vernal Equinox at 10:51 in the morning."

"Exactly?" Parisa blurted.

Leleua chuckled. "Yes, the astrologers are very precise."

"Is that when the crown is placed upon my head," Chokhmah asked, "or when the ceremony begins?"

Prince Raynor stared at her blankly. "That is a very good question. I will have your answer at lunch although I suspect the latter."

"That makes sense," Leleua agreed. "It would be difficult to time the ceremony so that the time of the crowning lands on the exact minute."

"Things can happen," Chokhmah agreed.

"Chaos theory," Parisa and Körbl said together.

"Curses," shouted Parisa and flashed the sign to ward off the evil eye as Körbl shouted, "Jinx".

"Jinx?" Parisa asked.

"It means you can't talk until someone says your name, Parisa," Hauata giggled.

"It's amazing how things differ from Kingdom to Kingdom," Parisa said. "Do they say something different in Favonia or Simoon?" she asked her aunt and uncle.

"Jinx is Pelfan but in Favonia we always just say, 'Omni Bless' just to ward off any potential bad luck," Leleua said.

"I believe my aunt must have started that," Chokhmah said, "because the Roma do the same thing."

Leleua nodded. "I can remember Grandma saying that. I believe Favonians said something similar but in Favonian."

"And we always said, 'Curses' and flashed the sign to ward off evil," Raynor said. "I believe that is the most common response."

"Interesting that they made it into a kind of game in Pelf," Parisa said, taking a bite of her bacon.

"So," Leleua changed the subject, nudging Chokhmah with her elbow, "it looks as if we have a lot to accomplish in the next 11 days. The most important thing will be having a gown fit for a queen made for you. We can work on that today. Then we can see about what Parisa and the rest of us will wear."

"That is fine," Chokhmah said.

"Are you going to pick something like the gown in our dreams?" Parisa asked, quietly.

Chokhmah nuzzled her daughter's ear, whispering, "Absolutely."

Parisa saw Körbl watching them, and she mouthed, 'I'll tell you later.' Out loud, she said, "Lessons then, this morning, like usual?"

"Yes," Raynor, Leleua, and Chokhmah said.

'Curses', 'Omni Bless', and 'Jinx' rang out from the three children, and the table erupted in laughter.

Prince Raynor downed the remainder of his coffee and stood. "Well," he said, "there's a lot to be done. I have a meeting with Zartusht to discuss the ceremony. I will see you at lunch."

Leleua stood, as well. "And Golpari is waiting for us in the sitting room so that you can look at some dress patterns."

Chokhmah raised an eyebrow, and Leleua chuckled, "Yes, Auntie, I already knew about the coronation date."

Chokhmah chuckled and took a final sip of her tea as Parisa hurriedly ate the last of her hardboiled egg and washed it down with the glass of juice she had yet to touch.

"Mmmm," she said, before setting the glass down. "What was that? I thought it was cranberry juice."

"Pomegranate," Foehn informed her.

"I like it," Parisa said, and stood.

Körbl was already standing and Foehn and Hauata groaned and pushed back their chairs.

Parisa glanced over her shoulder. Her mother and Leleua were already out the door. She, Körbl, and the twins followed them, and as they turned into the sitting room, they continued down the hallway. When they reached the schoolroom, she tapped on Körbl's shoulder and indicated that he should let his sisters go ahead.

"I need to talk to you, privately," she whispered. "Do you think we can meet at the beach this afternoon?"

"Does three o'clock work?" he asked after a moment's thought.

"Yes," Parisa said.

He nodded, and indicated she should enter before him, closing the door behind them when they had passed through.

"I heard that your mother's coronation date has been set," Roozbeh said to Parisa, handing her a textbook. "I thought this was as good a time as any to discuss the stars and planets as they are what determined the date and time."

Parisa's eyes lit up. She'd never really thought about it before but suddenly she found the subject very interesting.

PARISA WAS GLAD when lessons were ended, lunch finally over (it turned out the ceremony was to begin precisely at 10:51 the morning of the Vernal Equinox as that was the point when the sun would cross the planet's equator), and she could retreat to her tower room.

As it was only her second full day there, she easily begged off afternoon activities, promising that she would begin the following week once she felt fully settled in.

Once in her room, she quickly retrieved Parisa Zirhaan's journal and her transcription notebook from the window seat and grabbed the dictionary and a pencil from her desk. Just one more entry. She was both excited and scared. Unless Queen Njima could find out more, this might be the last she would know of her namesake.

With trembling fingers, Parisa opened the journal:

4TH ESFAND, 4611. Now I know why we have to leave. According to Leily, the Mobeds have managed to find an ancient weapon of mass destruction. I do not understand how it is possible that it still works. How we can still be threatened by it. Whether it is a nuclear, radiological, chemical, or biological weapon, Leily does not know,

I do not understand how it has not broken down by now. It has been millennia since the Thirteen Kingdoms were formed following the sixth extinction. I guess the question that Father and his advisors now have to answer is whether or not the threatened use of whatever weapon they have found is an actual threat to the Kingdom of Pelf.

Anyway, supposedly if Father does not meet their demands,

*they say they will destroy Buta on the Vernal Equinox, which is
their most holy day of the year. I guess then they will force whoever is still alive to worship their god and follow their rules. How
will the other twelve Kingdoms react to that? More war?*

PARISA CLOSED THE JOURNAL, mind racing. Well, she thought,
that explained the why and the when of the Devastation of
Pelf. It had happened on the Vernal Equinox on purpose. And
now, 700 years later, the Kingdom of Pelf would finally have
someone from the royal family sitting on the throne again.

But Buta had not been destroyed so the weapon had not
been in the city. The explosion had occurred practically on the
border with Naphtali and had sealed off the Djed Sea so that
now, 700 years later, it was mostly salt although there were still
a few freshwater rivers that flowed into it.

So, what had happened? Had the weapon been too
unstable to bring to Buta? Had it detonated when they tried
to move it? She guessed that whatever happened would always
be supposition. Although Parisa did find it somewhat ironic
that in trying to force the Kingdom of Pelf to worship their
deity, the Mobeds had wiped themselves off the planet. To her
knowledge, they had never been heard from again.

Those who had worshipped the Sacred Three, including
Prince Raynor's parents, had also come to a bad end. Those
things alone were enough to make you believe in the power of
Omni, Parisa thought.

Parisa looked down at the journal now resting in her lap.
Now she could put into action the plan that had occurred to
her this morning—she would find out just how trustworthy
Prince Körbl could be.

After entrusting him with the secret of the journal, she
would wait a couple of days to see if his sisters, his parents, or

even her mother approached her about it. She had planned to tell her mother anyway, so waiting a couple of days wouldn't hurt.

If Körbl kept the secret, then maybe he could be confided in about her actual secret. She would eventually shift, probably sooner rather than later, and Parisa really needed someone other than her mother to help her in case things went awry.

She also thought that the next 11 days, less now that it was after noon, were her best chance of evading anyone who might be keeping an eye out for her. At this point, it was only Niloufar looking out for her, at least to the best of her knowledge. Once her mother was crowned, there would be a greater need to keep them safe. It was possible they would assign a guard to the tower, as well, despite what Ghodsi had said. That meant, if she wanted to explore it, she would have to do so soon. If she could trust Körbl, then he could help her with that, as well.

She glanced at the wind-up clock on her bedside table. The hands pointed to two-thirty-six. She walked over to the window overlooking the beach and glanced down. The beach seemed empty, and it didn't look as if Körbl was walking down the steps yet. Actually, she wouldn't mind getting there first.

Parisa slid the journal and notebook into her leather book satchel along with a wool shawl because it was probably cold on the beach. If Niloufar spotted her, she could say she was meeting Körbl in the library to study. But when she left the room, the landing was empty.

Probably not surprising, she thought as she hurried down the stairs to the next landing and ducked into the changing room. She imagined the entire palace staff was busy with preparations for the upcoming coronation.

Parisa's hand was twisting the handle to the door that led out of the tower when two simultaneous thoughts stopped her in her tracks. If she could get in and out of the palace this easily, she thought, wouldn't it be just as easy for someone to get to the palace from the beach if they approached it by boat? What did they do when King Alborz and his family lived in the tower? She would ask after the coronation. For the time being, she preferred the access and extra privacy.

As she opened the door and descended to the beach, she considered the other thought. Wasn't it normal for the rulers of the other kingdoms to be in attendance at the coronation if possible? Even if they sent out pigeons today, there wouldn't be enough time for most of the kings and queens to travel to Pelf. She thought Eluned and Uriel could make it in time, maybe even King Cian and Queen Chelli because they could travel by sea. But it was just too far for everyone else.

Of course, Raynor and Leleua had known for a while that Chokhmah and Parisa would be traveling to Buta as soon as the winter storms abated. If they had let the other Kingdoms know ahead of time, it was possible that some of the rulers could have made plans to travel here, as well. Njima and Yona would want to be here, she thought. She'd ask at dinner tonight. It would be interesting to see who made the effort to show up. Would King Irirangi show up? Her mother was his great aunt.

Parisa stepped onto the beach and lay her satchel against the wall. She could look for shells while waiting for Körbl to arrive. Walking down the beach to where the last line of shells had been deposited, Parisa mused on the fact that Parisa Zirhaan has once wandered this same little beach searching for her beloved seashells. She wondered what type of shell her favorite had been. She leaned over and picked up a cone shell admiring the delicate spirals as it came to a point. The Princess had never had a chance to study shells with Leily nor had she been able to write about them in her journal.

If she had had a collection, it was long gone. I wonder if she took one or two of her favorites with her to Kamea, Parisa thought. She would never know, she sighed, watching the waves crash against the rocks sending sprays of foam and water into the air. She heard Körbl shout her name. Pocketing the shell, she turned to greet him.

Like Parisa, Körbl was silent when he finished reading through her transcription of the journal. He stared out at the waves, lost in thought.

Parisa shivered and pulled the shawl from her satchel. The breeze had picked up, which made the beach colder.

"I wonder how they found the weapon," Körbl finally spoke. "We're talking millennia later. Were the Mobeds searching for some ancient religious site, maybe?"

"That makes sense," Parisa agreed. "Maybe there used to be a town on the shores of the Djed Sea where they had a temple or something."

"In which case it would have been obliterated immediately," Körbl said.

"So, if other people managed to escape from the fallout both in Buta and elsewhere in Pelf," Parisa wondered aloud, "then why didn't King Alborz survive?"

"I think he was making sure that as many people as possible evacuated until it was safe again," Körbl said. "I think he was among the last to leave and died not long after he arrived in Dziron."

Parisa nodded. Maybe knowing that his children had escaped was sufficient for his peace of mind, but she was surprised that his son had chosen to resettle in Sheba rather than return to Buta. Was he afraid that the Mobeds had taken over and that he would be executed if he returned to claim the throne?

"If you could do me a favor and keep this to yourself a

couple of days, I'd really appreciate it," Parisa said. "I am going to tell my mother, of course, but I'd like to have the journal to myself for a little while longer."

"Any particular reason?" he asked.

"No, not really," Parisa said. "It just makes me feel more connected to her, somehow. But I know it's a valuable piece of history and needs to be taken care of properly so I will make sure my mother knows about it before the coronation."

Körbl nodded. "No offense, but I can't wait until that is over with."

Parisa laughed. "One big event a month is enough for you?"

"I imagine it's going to start getting really crazy next week when guests start arriving, and the Palace is hosting anyone royal that shows up. They're already hiring more staff to help with all the extra work that will need to be done."

"I hadn't thought of that," Parisa said. "There will be more mouths to feed, more rooms to get ready and clean."

"Not to mention all the preparations needed for the coronation, itself—flowers, banquets, music . . ."

"And the clothes being made for us."

"And," Körbl added, "Buta will fill up with guests from other parts of Pelf and maybe other Kingdoms, too, if families that were originally from here return or visit just for the coronation."

"So what you're telling me is that for the next ten days," Parisa said, "things are going to be so crazy here that we'd better take advantage of it?"

"Do you have something in mind?"

"I'm hoping I can get up to the guard room at the top of our tower before they assign someone to it again."

"Is it locked?" he asked.

"I haven't had a chance to check yet," Parisa said. "I need to find a time when Ghodsi is not around because I can't risk getting caught. I'll see if I can keep an eye out the next couple of days and see if she has a routine." Then she groaned.

"What is it?"

"Tomorrow I have to pick out a pattern and fabric for a dress."

"Do you not have any idea what you'd like?"

"Actually, I do have some idea. My mother will be wearing a gown of gold brocade, so I was thinking of finding a similar pattern and using white brocade."

"Did she show you the pattern at lunch?" Körbl looked confused.

"Actually, my mother and I sometimes have prophetic dreams, and I dreamed of her wearing a gold brocade dress and wearing the Crown of Pelf while sitting in the tower throne room."

"Wow," he said, "that's impressive. Does it happen often?"

Parisa shook her head. "Almost never. And now that I think about it, I never described to her what the dress looked like other than the fact it was gold brocade with long sleeves so who knows what she'll actually pick."

"But if it's prophetic, won't she just naturally pick what you saw?"

"Well, my," and Parisa stopped herself. She had almost said that her mother had seen her as a white wolf with copper wings flying with a raven, and there was little likelihood of that happening. "Hmm," she continued. "I never thought of it that way. I guess we'll see." She shivered again. "It's getting chilly. Maybe it's time to head back inside."

Spring

"Behold, my friends, the spring is come;
the earth has gladly received the embraces of the sun,
and we shall soon see the results of their love!"
                                                    -Sitting Bull

"The day the Lord created hope was probably the same day he
created Spring."

                                                    -Bernard Williams

Chokhmah & Parisa

The landing was blessedly empty when a couple of days after they'd met on the beach Parisa and Körbl arrived there ready both to talk to her mother and explore the guard room. Parisa asked Körbl to go check if the door to the tower was unlocked while she waited with hand raised to knock on her mother's door if a distraction was necessary.

He tried the handle and the door swung open. Parisa was about to step in that direction when she heard another handle turning. She motioned Körbl to her side, simultaneously knocking on the door with her other hand.

He was kneeling between Parisa and the tower door, pretending to tie his shoe, when Ghodsi stepped out of her room.

"If you are looking for your mother, she is having her dress fit . . ." she was saying just as Chokhmah opened her door.
"That looks exactly like the dress from my dream," Parisa said, staring at her mother opened-mouthed.
"Does it?" Her mother looked surprised. "I had forgotten to ask you to describe it and hoped this was close."
"How did you do that? I only told you it was gold brocade

and had long sleeves. That's barely a description," Parisa said.

"The dream becomes more and more real," Chokhmah smiled. The square-collared dress had form-fitting sleeves and hugged her body tightly to the hips where it then fell in an A-line to the floor. "I hear you opted for a similar style?"

"Yes," agreed Parisa. "But instead of a square collar, it's round, and they talked me into having the brocade studded with pearls."

"And sapphire velvet ribbons around the collar and the ends of the sleeves," Körbl added.

Parisa nodded. He'd been listening when she told Foehn and Hauata about her dress. "I think they want it to match the crown."

"Or, at least," Chokhmah agreed, "not clash with it."

"I am sorry your Majesty," Ghodsi said, "I had assumed your fitting was downstairs."

"That is quite all right, my dear," she said to Ghodsi. "We were just finishing up. Did you two want to see me?" she asked Parisa.

"We'd like to talk to you privately, if possible," Parisa said.

"Certainly," Chokhmah ushered them in. "I think they intend to do something with rubies and black velvet with mine, but we had to make sure the fit was right, first.

"Good afternoon, Golpari," Parisa said. "Mama's dress is beautiful."

"Thank you, Princess," the head seamstress bowed. "I am sure your dress will be just as lovely."

"Have a seat you two," Chokhmah indicated the sofa, "while I change."

Within ten minutes, Golpari had left the room with Chokmah's pinned dress and Körbl was carrying her desk chair over to the sitting area in front of the fireplace so that Parisa could sit with her mother.

"What is it you want to speak with me about?" Chokhmah

asked once they were all settled and Ghodsi had arrived with a tea tray, unasked for but welcome, and departed.

Parisa opened her leather satchel and pulled out the journal and notebook with her transcription.

"I found the journal in the window seat in my room," she told her mother the half-truth. She and Körbl had agreed that having a secret hiding place was worthwhile though it would probably eventually be discovered because Niloufar would know she had cleaned the inside thoroughly. She would now have to find another place to hide her journal. She needed to explore her armoire and desk more thoroughly. Or maybe there was some place in the bathroom. "It belonged to the Princess Parisa that fled the Palace seven centuries ago."

Her mother had opened the journal and was looking at the frontispiece tears blurring her vision. "Zirhaan," she murmured. "That is a lovely name."

"I really like it," Parisa agreed. "I was thinking when you are crowned, and are Queen Parisa, that I can start going by that name."

Körbl grunted and then coughed.

"What?" Parisa asked.

"Nothing," he said. "I like it. I just swallowed wrong."

Parisa handed her mother the notebook. "Because the Pelfan was so old, I tried writing it down in the Common Tongue so it would be easier to read."

Chokhmah opened the notebook and while she read the scant entries, Parisa and Körbl sipped their tea, the latter nibbling on a cookie, as well. Parisa needed to do something about the lack of protein snacks. Jerky, hard-boiled eggs, hard cheese, pumpkin seeds, peanuts, almonds—were all things she could easily keep stashed in a desk drawer and satchel in case she was feeling faint, which, honestly, she was feeling more and more these days.

When she asked for a steak to go with her eggs that

morning at breakfast, her mother had looked horrified. She had blushed and explained it had been one of her favorite breakfasts at Bogaine and that she had been craving it. Then, when no one was looking, she glared at her mother. She had been the one who told her to keep her true nature a secret.

"How terribly sad," her mother sniffed and brushed away a tear when she had finished reading. The truth was that she had always focused more on the Pelfans at Kuna and not on her family. The journal had made them come to life for her—the brave but distracted father, the worried mother, young Alborz already trying to step into his father's shoes, the wise but still 11-year-old princess, and the already fragile Gaspar.

Chokhmah wondered what had become of Leily. Did she get to travel with them to Kamea or did Souri have that honor?

"I wonder what happened to Leily," she mused aloud.

"I hope she made it to Dziron or Kamartha," Parisa said. "I liked the fact she didn't think Princess Parisa was too young to understand what was going on."

Körbl nodded. "It's very annoying when grownups won't tell you things. What I can imagine is far worse than what it probably actually is."

Parisa laughed, "I know, right? So, what are you going to do with the journal, Mama?"

Chokhmah handed it and the notebook back to her daughter. "Bring it with you to dinner tonight. Do you know if there is some sort of museum or archives here, Körbl?"

"There is definitely a Royal Archives, but I think they've been keeping everything related to the royal family in safe-keeping for so long that a museum hadn't occurred to the Councilors."

"Well, there's something else you can do, Mama," Parisa said. "There should be a history museum here."

Chokhmah nodded. That was an excellent idea. "We can discuss that at dinner, as well."

Parisa stood. "Körbl and I have some homework," she said, and he stood also.

"We were going to go to Parisa's room to study if that's okay?" he said.

"Of course, my dears. What are you studying?"

"Roozbeh has been teaching us astronomy," Parisa said. "I meant to tell you, but we've been so busy."

"Astronomy. That sounds interesting. Are you enjoying it?"

"Yes," Parisa and Körbl exclaimed simultaneously and a beat later, "Omni Bless!"

Chokhmah could not help but laugh with them. "When did you both decide on 'Omni Bless'?"

"We were telling Roozbeh about it the other day, and we all agreed it made the most sense of the three," Körbl explained. "Enjoy studying, my dears," Chokhmah said as she walked them to the door. "I will see you at dinner. I need to freshen up before I meet your father to discuss coronation plans," she said to Körbl, ushering them out the door and shutting it behind them.

"It's now or possibly never," Parisa whispered, feinting toward the stairs in case her mother was looking. When the door clicked shut, they rushed over to the door to the guard-room and Körbl hurriedly opened it, shutting it quietly behind them as soon as they stepped inside.

They let their hearts return to a normal rate while their eyes adjusted to the gloom.

"Should've brought a candle," Parisa grumbled.

"Just put your hand against the wall until we get closer to the top," Körbl suggested. "I imagine the windows will start letting some light sift down the further up the stairs we get."

"That makes sense," Parisa agreed as they started up what had become a winding staircase.

After a couple of turns, occasional slit windows cast some

light into the gloom and by the time they reached the door to the guardroom, itself, their eyes had fully adjusted to the light. "By Omni, I hope that door is unlocked," Parisa said as she watched Körbl stretch out his hand to turn the handle.

It was. Parisa guessed there was no need to lock a door to a mostly empty room. A couple of wooden chairs and a small, dust-filmed table were all that remained, or perhaps, all that had ever been there.

They walked over to the window that overlooked the Bay of Besu leaving a trail of footprints in the dust on the floor.

"If anyone were approaching from the ocean, they would be seen," Körbl remarked. Parisa had told him about how easy access in and out of the palace had seemed from the beach door.

"Good point, and there'd be plenty of time to warn someone," she said. They stood in silence for a minute enjoying the view.

Parisa chuckled. "I feel like a raven perched high in a pine tree. An eagle in its aerie."

It was Körbl's turn to laugh.

"Why are you laughing?"

"Two things," he said. "First, my name, Korbinian, means raven."

"What? Really?"

He nodded. "So, I actually am a 'raven' perched high above the ground. Speaking of which, do you miss Pallas?"

"That's funny about your name," Parisa smiled thinking that maybe the dream had been right about the wolf and the raven. "And yes, I do. He was a pal. But now I have a different raven pal. Who could've known?"

Körbl laughed again. "That also reminds me," Körbl said, "of what you said earlier about going by the name Zirhaan."

"What about it?" she asked, turning and walking toward another window that faced westward.

"It's an old Pelfan name that means 'someone who resembles a wolf'. Seems even more appropriate now, doesn't it?"

Parisa stopped in her tracks, heart suddenly pumping wildly, sending a flood of color to her cheeks. She turned to face Körbl, mouth open and eyes wide. "I d-don't understand," she stuttered.

Körbl shook his head. "Parisa, I've known since before we started writing each other."

"Why didn't you say anything?"

"I figured you'd tell me when you were ready."

Parisa lowered herself into one of the chairs ignoring the layer of dust. "But Mama told me I should keep it a secret."

"And my mother told me she met your father when she was a teenager, and that he had even shifted for her and Talei once while they were still on Favonia because they had been so curious about him."

"She saw my father as a wolf?" Parisa was stunned. Her mother had never said anything.

"She said he was a beautiful wolf," he looked pained at having to bring up her father.

"He was," Parisa said, eyes filling with tears. "Sometimes, I miss him so much. I haven't shifted yet and I'm terrified of doing it without him."

Körbl brushed the dust from the other chair and sat, taking Parisa's hands in his. "If you want me to be there when it happens, I will do that for you," he said.

"You're not afraid or," Parisa paused for a second, "or disgusted or something?"

Körbl laughed. "No! Should I be? I did some research after my mother told me, and the shifters of Dyfed aren't dangerous unless you threaten their lives or the lives of their loved ones."

Parisa nodded. "That's true. Even actual wolves rarely attack. But that would be true of most animals, humans too."

"I have been noticing that you are eating more protein

lately," he said. "Do you think it's going to happen soon?"

Parisa's lip trembled, and she caught it in her teeth. "Yes, something feels different within me. I can't explain it. I just know that Papa and my uncle and my cousins told me that I would know when, so not yet. But it's definitely coming. All I know is that I want to be alone the first time it happens."

Körbl looked hurt but hid it quickly.

"I mean alone with you," Parisa assured him. "I don't want anyone other than us around. Did your mother tell you that I have to remove my clothes to shift?" She found herself blushing again.

"She did say that Faolan went into a room by himself and then gave three short barks when he was ready for them to open the door."

"I'll have to have some kind of plan like that," Parisa stood up. She didn't want to talk about it anymore. Brushing the dust from her behind, she walked over to the window. She pointed northwest. "Those woods don't look that far away. Do you ever get to go there?"

"We go horseback riding there once a week," he said.

Parisa's eyes lit up and she grinned. "I'd love to do that." She had imagined they'd been walking the horses around some indoor or outdoor ring.

"Maybe we can do that tomorrow," Körbl said, "get a last ride in before the insanity ensues."

"Insanity?"

"Get ready for a crazy week," he said. "People will begin arriving next week, and there will be banquets every night that we'll be expected to attend not to mention all the people we'll be expected to meet."

"Or people we have to reacquaint ourselves with," Parisa said, thinking of Njima and Yona. And who would come from Dyfed? Cian had been a friend briefly. Would Eluned bring Fuchsia and Gavreel? Parisa groaned, thinking about all the people about to descend on Zhaleh Palace. "In that case, I really could use to get out of here even if only for a little while."

"It makes the day after the Vernal Equinox seem like a long time from now, doesn't it?"

"It may end up being the longest week of our lives," Parisa chuckled, walking over to the final window, which looked eastward over the palace walls. Parisa could see the rooftops of the city of Buta, and the Bay of Buta dotted with sailing ships.

The views were lovely, but Parisa wondered if a permanent guard was needed in the tower anymore. Maybe only at night when they were all asleep and it would be easier for someone to sneak up on the palace. And a crossbar on the door downstairs could remain open only when someone was on the beach.

She told Körbl her ideas, and he agreed that they sounded significantly better than full time guards. Of course, he, like her, liked time to himself.

He returned to the window overlooking the beach and looked westward. Parisa joined him. The sun was getting low in the sky.

"I guess we've been up here longer than I thought," she said.

"And we were with your mother a while, too," he agreed. "I guess we better go before we've been missed."

"I'm sure we have been," Parisa said. "Our only advantage is that we told my mother that we'd be in my room. If they are looking for us and don't find us there, they might look in the library or schoolroom before getting worried."

They hurried to the door and made their way back to the landing outside out Chokhmah's room. Fortunately, it was empty, and they hurried down to the next landing.

Parisa's hand was on the door handle to her room, and Körbl was starting down the stairs when Niloufar stepped out of her room.

"Oh, good," Niloufar said when she saw her, "I was just

coming to warn you that it is time to get ready for dinner. Also, your dress fitting will be tomorrow morning after breakfast in your room, if that meets with your approval, Princess Parisa."

Körbl turned to address Niloufar. "Princess Parisa would like to be addressed as Princess Zirhaan after the coronation."

Niloufar nodded. "Princess Zirhaan," she repeated.

"Thank you, Prince Korbinian," Parisa smiled. "I had forgotten to tell her. And thank you, Niloufar. I felt it would be a lot less confusing to have only one Parisa around."

Niloufar bowed, smiling, "Yes, Princess Zirhaan."

"See you at dinner, Zirhaan," Körbl said, winking at Parisa, and continued his descent down the stairs.

Niloufar opened the door to Parisa's room, and followed her in. "Is there something you would prefer to wear tonight, Princess Zirhaan?"

"Is it true that next week is going to be night after night of banquets?"

"Yes, Princess."

"In that case, something simple. I'm going to have to double-wear some of my best gowns, as it is."

"As you wish, your highness," Niloufar said, moving toward the armoire, but Parisa caught the pleased look on her face. It appeared the Kingdom of Pelf was truly happy that the royal family had returned.

CHOKHMAH WAS OVERWHELMED by the influx of people arriving at the palace and in Buta for her coronation. Eluned and Uriel and their children were the first to arrive. Fatemeh had begged them to come along as nanny to Gavreel and Fuchsia so that she could be present for the historic event.

Parisa and her mother got to spend one glorious day with

them before the next guests arrived, which meant that for one day they filled up the table in the private dining room and relaxed in the sitting room after meals catching up on what had happened since they had left the Kingdom of Aden.

"It hasn't even been two weeks," Parisa said at one point, "but I feel like it's been an eternity."

Fuchsia quickly made friends with Foehn and Hauata and it wasn't long before the three were inseparable leaving Fatemeh with only Gavreel to keep an eye on.

King Cian and Queen Chelli were the next to arrive, bringing their grandson, Cian, with them. Parisa was happy to introduce Cian to Körbl and they took him horseback riding in the Máámin Forest, the woods Parisa had seen from the tower.

Njima and Yona arrived not long after the King and Queen of Dyfed. They were accompanied by Dev and Prince Uwem of Sheba who now resided in Naphtali with his husband, Talib. Chokhmah was delighted to see Uwem again, and they spent an entire afternoon entertaining Talib and the others with tales of their trip to Mjipya and Mifugo when searching for Pelf's lost treasure.

"Another one of your prophetic dreams," Eluned reminded her, not that she needed reminding. She did not have so many prophetic dreams that she could not keep track of them. The only dream she had never shared, though, that she still held close to her heart, was the dream she had the night Yitzak gave her his scarf.

The dream had quickly fast forwarded through time to the beginning of his illness only ten years into their marriage. She had known because in the dream he was giving her a tin heart that he had painted with tones of blue and silver to hang over their bed. That was the traditional gift. Faolan's tenth anniversary gift had not been quite so romantic—a small sun dial for her herb garden—though she had treasured it just as much. The dream had continued with Chokhmah watching helplessly as her husband's health continued to spiral downward for the next 15 years. She hadn't known from the dream exactly how long it would be, but in the dream, she was looking in a mirror, head covered in a black scarf, and her face had aged even more.

And yet. And yet, she had walked out of the vardo she shared with her parents that morning wearing Yitzak's scarf determined to make the next ten years the happiest of her life. And now, once again, her life was changing. Omni only knew how many years she had left, but she was once again determined to live them as fully as possible.

Chokhmah returned her attention to the story Uwem was telling, and it made her secretly happy to see Talib hanging on his every word. She liked his husband a lot; he was about five years older, quiet, and distinguished looking, which seemed to harmonize well with Uwem's youthful exuberance. Although, she thought, he was hardly that awkward 16-year-old boy anymore. At 28, he had grown into his manhood.

The following day they found themselves inundated by the arrival of three more royal families. Eluned's parents, King Seraphim and Queen Ceridwen of Zion arrived almost simultaneously with Uwem's parents, King Adeyemi and Queen Yobachi of Sheba.

They were just sitting down to lunch in the great room where Queen Parisa's and her daughter's welcoming banquet had been held, when King Irirangi and Queen Bala of Favonia arrived with Princess Talei. Leleua let out a high-pitched squeal before jumping from her seat and throwing herself into her twin sister's arms. Irirangi stood behind them rolling his eyes at his wife.

"You see what I had to put up with growing up?" he asked her.

Bala laughed and pointed at Dev, who was already

coming around the end of the table. "That is just one of my seven siblings. Believe me, I know."

Dev hugged his older sister. "Amit and Amala were never quite that physical, were they?" he laughed.

"Oh Div, I mean Dev," she hugged him back. "It is so wonderful to see you looking so well."

"Thank you, Bala," he replied. "The years have been good to you, as well."

The next afternoon Raynor's brother, King Kaiser of Simoon, arrived with queen, Luise, along with Prince Bemot and Princess Lioba and their 14-year-old son, Grini.

Overcome by her feelings, Chokhmah choked back a sob. The Kingdom of Simoon had spawned some of the best and worst moments in her life. In Castle Rodolph, she had stolen one of the Hallowed Treasures, the Whetstone of Tudwal Tudglyd; conceived her child; and saved the life of the infant Prince Grini. But that Kingdom was also where Faolan had broken his leg so badly that he nearly had not made it back to Sheba alive. How ironic that it was also the place he later lost his life. How different life would have been had he died there the first time. She could not even begin to imagine what that would have meant. Would she have rejoined her Roma family? Depended on the kindness of Eluned or maybe, Olcan? She could not even begin to contemplate those thoughts. That is not what happened.

She brushed back a tear and smiled at Grini. "And now here you are," Chokhmah's voice hitched, "a healthy young man. I was so terrified you were going to die. And you," she turned to Bemot and Lioba, "I cannot believe you have chosen to forgive me for stealing Simoon's Treasure."

"Honestly," Bemot said quietly, "I was already embarrassed back then by my father's actions. If stealing the Whetstone meant we avoided war, then it was worth it."

"Yes, and besides," Kaiser said. "It is now back where it belongs."

"With a lock on the drawer, no doubt," Chokhmah raised an eyebrow.

Kaiser laughed. "We now have it properly displayed, but yes. I have to admit that at that time my father had convinced me that war was necessary, but in hindsight I would much rather have my son grow up in a peaceful world. Who's to say how long a war amongst the Kingdoms would have lasted— a month, a year, decades? And not only would I have had to fight, but my brothers, as well."

"And our children," Raynor said, having joined them, "when they came of age."

They stood in silence for a moment before their solemnity was broken by the arrival of King Janak and Queen Lakshmi of Kamartha who were delighted to see their children, Bala and Dev. Janak seemed to have come to terms with the life choices of his youngest child who had started life as his daughter, Divya.

By this point in the week, the dining room had been set up as a buffet for breakfast and lunch as the arrivals were so sporadic. As more people arrived, more tables and seats were added. And, because there were only eight children all between five and fourteen, they had their own table.

King Zhang and Queen Ling of Dziron arrived that evening in time for the dinner banquet. Their daughter, Princess Xiang, had traveled with them and was excited to introduce her husband, Lord Jian, to Eluned who had saved her from an arranged marriage to a man who was 22 years her senior. Like Eluned, she had wanted to marry for love. Fortunately for her, Prince Aahil had been happy to remain with Merieme, his consort and the mother of his children.

There were only three days left until the coronation, and Chokhmah was just wondering if the Kingdoms of Annewven, Adamah, and Tarshish intended to send representatives, when the arrival of King Boutros and Queen Elamia of Tarshish was announced.

Good, Chokhmah thought as she rose to meet them. Despite the fact that Tarshish had acted as the neutral meeting ground after the Treasures had been gathered, they had always remained at arm's length from the other Kingdoms. And Chokhmah still suspected that it was Fatimah's husband, a Lord of Tarshish and the Kingdom's Ambassador to Simoon, that had killed Faolan. King Kaiser insisted that they had not discovered who had done it, and while it was entirely possible for some random hunter to have killed what he thought was a wolf only to find his arrow in a human, her gut instinct was that it was Fatimah's husband. She did not even know his name and had never asked Uriel to find out because somehow, she just did not want to know.

But Boutros and his wife, whom she remembered from her brief visit to Iqbal Palace in Tartessos all those years ago, Parisa a babe in arms at the time, had been gracious enough to make the trip to Buta and she would treat them without suspicion. Although, she chuckled to herself, after greeting them and having a servant take them to the dining room for a late breakfast while their room was prepared, she suspected a number of people were showing up out of sheer curiosity. It had been centuries since Buta had been open to the other Kingdoms, after all. She could not blame them if they were interested in the infamous Kingdom.

During the day, while Raynor entertained those who were interested in the outdoors—sailing, hunting, horseback riding and that type of thing—Chokhmah and Leleua were kept busy entertaining the others, at least those who wanted to be occupied with something more strenuous than reading a book in the library. Numerous sitting rooms were engaged so that folks could gather to play games of tarok, chess, and other board games. They could also just sit and talk and get to know each other better or catch up if they had not seen each other in a while.

Parisa and Körbl helped keep Grini and Cian occupied while Fatemeh tried to keep up with Gavreel who just wanted to annoy the twins and Fuchsia. Mahasti, the nanny who cared for Foehn and Hauata, easily kept an eye on Fuchsia as well.

They were all at lunch, a couple of days before the coronation ceremony, when some unexpected guests were announced. Chokhmah pushed back her chair so quickly that it fell over with a loud crash when she stood up. It took a second longer for Uwem to recognize who had just arrived.

They rushed to the door calling out their greetings, grins splitting their faces.

"Daniel," Chokhmah exclaimed, hugging her nephew tight, before turning to Avigail for another hug while Uwem hugged his fellow traveler.

"Talib," Uwem called over his shoulder. "This is Daniel and his wife, Avigail." He turned back to Daniel. "We were just talking about our trip to the coast of Sheba."

"This is such an unexpected pleasure," Chokhmah interrupted. "I cannot tell you how happy I am to see you two again. And who is this?" A teenage boy stood quietly to the side, eyes downcast, and clearly uncomfortable.

"This is our son, Yuda," Daniel said, slinging his arm around his son's shoulders. "He was born the same year as Parisa, but in the Autumn."

"It is so good to meet you, Yuda," Chokhmah said. "Come, I am sure Parisa, and the others, want to meet you." She nodded at a servant who hurried to place another chair at the children's table. "Daniel and Avigail, come, I'll join you at the end of the table," she said, spying a few empty seats. "I have so many questions." She turned to face the table and did a quick scan. Other than Seraphim and Ceridwen, and Uwem, of course, none of the others had met her nephew.

"Let me introduce you all to my nephew, Daniel, his wife, Avigail, and their son, Yuda," she said. "Daniel and Avigail traveled with Uwem and me when we sought Pelf's lost treasure. Some of you have heard the stories. I will let you introduce yourselves privately, as you see fit." Then she led them to the end of the table while Yuda joined the children's table.

Parisa stood up with her plate and moved to the newly placed seat at the head of the table, a seat away, "You can take my seat, Yuda," she said. "It's probably more appropriate for me to sit at the head."

"The next Queen of Pelf," Cian said, "that makes sense. I'm Prince Cian of Dyfed," the boy with curly black hair and brown eyes introduced himself. He was sitting directly across the table from Yuda.

"And I'm Prince Grini of Simoon," the boy with fair hair and dark eyes said. "I'm his cousin." He pointed to the boy sitting across the table from him.

"Körbl," he said, sticking out his hand, "nice to meet you."

Parisa smiled, inwardly, amused. Cian and Grini seemed determined to show off, but Körbl, though younger, always held his tongue and seemed more approachable. "I'm Parisa, by the way," she told Yuda, "but once my mother is crowned Queen Parisa, the day after tomorrow, I'm going to start going by Zirhaan so it will be less confusing. Parisa Zirhaan was the name of the Princess who fled to Naphtali 700 years ago."

Yuda nodded.

"Because they're so many people, we're eating more casually for breakfast and lunch," Körbl told him. He pointed to the buffet on the far wall. "You can take your plate and go get what you want there."

"Thanks," Yuda stood with his plate and walked over to the buffet where his parents were in the process of filling their own plates.

"He is kind of lucky he arrived so late," Parisa observed. "I'm getting tired of having so many things to choose from on the buffet.

The three boys grunted their agreement. The four of them had made the mistake the first couple of days of loading too much food on their plates, and they had barely been able to touch their food at the banquet those nights.

Yuda returned with a modest amount of food on his plate, and they looked at him in disbelief.

"There were so many choices I got overwhelmed," he explained. "I can go back for more if I need to, right?"

Parisa nodded. "Of course you can." Whether he was overwhelmed or not, she was impressed. It would have been much easier to pile more things on his plate. But, by the time Cian, Grini, and Yuda departed Buta for their respective homes, Parisa would find herself hard-pressed to choose which of the three had worked the hardest to impress her. From boasting to stupid feats of strength and prowess, only Körbl seemed immune from the antics. She could blame that on the fact he was the youngest, but she thought, perhaps it was because he was the most mature. It was probably also the fact he knew he'd still be there when they were gone. She would know for sure in the next few years when, doubtless, these young princes might be her future suitors.

On the final morning before the huge event, the last two royal guests arrived having traveled by ship from Seagirt together—Prince Simeon of Adamah, the nephew of King Hevel, and Queen Morrighan of Annewven, the illegitimate daughter of that Kingdom's former King, Arawn.

Arawn, who had killed Jabberwock when he lost the chess match in Tartessos that had determined the fate of the Hallowed Treasures, was now imprisoned in the dungeons of Iqbal Palace. Arawn's co-conspirators, the former King Hamartia and Queen Foehn of Simoon were now exiled on the island of Paliaina in Favonia. King Hevel, who had barely been involved had served his prison sentence and was in charge of the Kingdom of Adamah again. Apparently, he was still too embarrassed to make the trip himself.

"Lady Yona," Prince Simeon greeted her. "I was just a child when you disappeared with our treasure. Have you been back?"

"Not on my list," Yona told him. "And once my parents died, I didn't see any need to return." Both her parents had died when their yacht was caught in a storm in the Anoon Ocean, killing everyone aboard.

"I understand you grew up in Seagirt," Simeon said.

"Yes, but I spent time in Stonehelm, as well. And you?"

"Mostly Stonehelm, but we spend our summers in Yanshoof."

"Oh, that's a beautiful place. It's a resort in mountains northwest of Stonehelm," she told Njima who was standing next to her. "And how is Hevel doing?"

"Actually," Simeon said, "not bad. Working in the vineyards helped him to refocus his priorities, or so he said to me."

"And that changed . . .?"

"He has a boyfriend now who lives with him at Castle Lavieven. He seems very content."

Yona smiled. "You know, it makes me really happy to hear that. Good for him. I hope he can make it to the Year XV meeting."

Queen Morrighan who had been standing there listening added her thoughts. "I agree, Yona. I didn't know my father well. At all, honestly. But I did appreciate that he tried to do his best for me even if he never really intended for me to become Queen of Annewven," she chuckled. "But I was glad to have the opportunity, and I was so lucky to meet Prince Huang and fall in love with him. That wouldn't have happened if he had not sent me to Dziron."

"And, I have two beautiful grandchildren," Queen Ling, who was standing nearby, said. "I only wish Huang and the children could have come."

"Don't worry, mother-in-law," Morrighan said, "We will

all be back in three years when Pelf hosts the Year XV meeting of the Thirteen Kingdoms."

"What?" Chokhmah said walking over to join them, looking panicky, "I have only three years to prepare for that?"

Njima chuckled. "How long did you have to prepare for this?" she indicated the dining room and the breakfast spread on the buffet table.

"Less than a year, it is true. I believe that Leleua, Raynor, the Councilors and the palace staff began working toward this as soon as they heard we planned to return."

"So, you're worrying for nothing," Yona said.

"Well," Chokhmah corrected her, "not for nothing. This is a truly impressive gathering of people. I would like things to be even better for them the next time we gather."

"Oh it will be, Queen Parisa," Morrighan said. "I am sure of it if this," she indicated the dining room, "is any indication." "Are you hungry?" Chokhmah pointed to the buffet. "There is still plenty of food."

"Ravenous," Prince Simeon said. "It was too choppy to eat on the ship this morning."

Morrighan nodded agreement. "And I finally feel like I am starting to get my land legs back," she said, and followed Simeon to the buffet.

DAWN ON THE DAY OF THE VERNAL EQUINOX revealed a cloudless day, the sun's warmth bringing a hint of the spring to come. Chokhmah took a moment to still her frayed nerves by opening her window and breathing deeply of the salt-scented air. The rising sun sparkled on the waves and cast a rosy glow on the beach below. She had noticed Parisa and the Princes playing on the beach several times during the past week. They had probably taken Yuda down there yesterday; she was pleased with the way they had taken to her great nephew considering he had been raised in a gypsy camp. Royalty could be snobby, but Parisa and Körbl, at the least, had seemed to avoid that. She remembered that Cian had seemed pretty down to earth, as well. Grini's parents were probably a little overprotective, but she could hardly blame them for that, particularly as Lioba had not been able to conceive again.

Chokmah shook her head and laughed at herself. There was so much more to worry about today than Grini. She needed to eat a little breakfast before dressing for the day. The plan was to leave for the Cathedral early so that they could begin the Procession at 10:51 on the dot.

A knock at her door alerted her to the fact Ghodsi had arrived with her breakfast tray. She had decided the previous night that facing the 40 odd people who might be in the dining room this morning was more than she could take first thing. She tried to ignore the fact that there were probably already people lining the streets in order to get a good view as the royal parties made their way to the Cathedral in open-air horse-drawn carriages. She and Parisa would be in the first carriage followed by Raynor, Leleua and their children, and then alphabetically by Kingdom, which they had all agreed seemed the most fair. That meant that Prince Simeon would be behind them, and the cortege would end with King Seraphim and Queen Ceridwen.

She called for Ghodsi to enter and walked over to the sofa as her tray was being placed on the table in front of it. Ghodsi poured her a cup of tea while Chokhmah buttered a roll. There would be enough rich food later on that day. Right now, she just needed something that would sit well in her belly.

"How are you feeling today, Your Majesty," Ghodsi asked.

"Trying not to allow my nerves to have the best of me," Chokhmah said. "If it were just the Coronation, it would be easier."

"But the Banquet afterwards and the Ball this evening?"

"I am going to be so relieved to be laying my head on my pillow tonight; at least, I hope it will be tonight and not in the wee hours of the morning."

"You are the Queen, you can choose when you wish to leave," Ghodsi said.

"I will not be the last, I promise you, but neither will I be the first. That would be rude."

"We have several older Royal couples in attendance," Ghodsi said. "I imagine amongst them, a couple or two will do you the favor of leaving first."

"It is kind of remarkable, really," Chokhmah said. "I believe King Zhang and I are the oldest monarchs here. For some reason, that makes me feel really old."

"If I may say so, Ma'am, he seems a lot older than you."

"Thank you, Ghodsi," Chokhmah smiled. "And he would probably not look as good in my gold brocade dress."

Ghodsi snorted and covered her mouth with her hand. "I am sorry, but the image was too much."

Chokhmah chuckled. "It is difficult to imagine, is it not?" She picked up her tea and took a tentative sip, then smiled. "Perfect."

"Shall I return in 15 minutes, Ma'am?"

"That will be fine, Ghodsi, thank you."

An hour later, Chokhmah was fully dressed in her brocade dress, her braided hair sparkling with the golden ribbons entwined in it. She and Ghodsi stopped at Parisa's room where she was waiting with Niloufar.

"Oh my darling, you look breathtaking," Chokhmah said when Parisa stepped out of the room. "And your hair."

"Niloufar and I thought it would be fun to braid mine like yours but with blue ribbons," Parisa explained. "Is that okay?"

"Of course, my dear," her mother said, "and the crown matches everything perfectly."

"Niloufar told me the Coronation Crown is incredibly beautiful," Parisa said. "I can't wait to see it."

Chokhmah took a deep breath. "That will be happening sooner than my nerves are prepared for."

Parisa hugged her mother. "Mama, you always get nervous, but no one ever knows that you are. You always seem to know exactly what you are doing."

"Thank you, darling. Are you ready?"

"You know what? Körbl and I thought this past week was going to be really tedious, but we've had a lot of fun with Cian and Grini and now, Yuda. I'm actually excited about today. I've never been to a Coronation and now I will be a part of one."

"And someday be participating in your own," Chokhmah said.

"True! I'd better pay attention, huh?"

"Before we head downstairs, let us pray," Chokhmah said taking Parisa's and Ghodsi's hands in hers. Parisa took Niloufar's who took her mother's, and they formed a small circle.

"Almighty God, Omniscient, Omnipotent, Omnipresent, we your unworthy servants do give You our most humble and hearty thanks for all Your goodness and loving-kindness to all creatures. We bless You for our creation, preservation, and all the blessings of this life; but above all, for Your inestimable love in the redemption of our world by our Lord Jesus Christ; for the means of grace, and for the hope of glory. And, we beseech You, give us that due sense of all Your mercies, that our hearts may be unfeignedly thankful, and that we show forth Your praise, not only with our lips but in our lives; by giving up ourselves to Your service, and by walking before You in holiness and righteousness all our days; through Jesus Christ our Lord, to whom with You and the Holy Ghost, be all honor and glory, world without end. Amen."

"Amen," the other three women said.

"And now," Chokhmah said. "I am ready."

The Cathedral of Christ the Savior in Buta was the largest church Chokhmah had ever seen. She had been attending the daily morning Mass in the chapel in Zhaleh Palace, which she had considered the size of a church, but the Cathedral made the Chapel of Saint Isho'sabran appear the size of Saint Colmán's Chapel at Bogaine, which held a dozen people if they squeezed together on the pews. And while the structure was noticeable from the outside with its soaring arches and domes and other ornamentation, once they crossed through the doors of the temple, the Cathedral really opened up.

The interior of the building was truly luxurious: the walls decorated with gilded carvings and frescoes depicting the life of Jesus Christ. The cathedral also had a large dome decorated with frames from the Old Testament beginning with the history of the creation of the world, Adam and Eve and the expulsion from Eden to the flight from Egypt and the glory of King Solomon.

After Chokhmah was shown how they would be processing from the west end of the church through the nave and choir and to the chancel where the Coronation Crown, Scepter, and Rod were displayed, they returned to the end of the church and began lining up. Chokhmah, when told she would lead the procession, balked, insisting that a cross-bearer, torchbearers, and a deacon holding high a book of Scripture go first. She and Parisa, she insisted, would be the last to process in, side by side.

"I am here for the people," she explained. "I will not put myself above everyone else."

So, the Archbishop of Pelf, Navid of Betnicator, lined up behind the deacon followed by the Lord High Chancellor and Councilors, the Kings and Queens of the Thirteen Kingdoms, and, finally, Queen Parisa now with a heavy crimson cloak over her shoulders, and her daughter, Princess Parisa Zirhaan.

Looking ahead, Chokhmah was nearly overwhelmed by the number of crowned heads in front of her. She touched the top of her head as if assuring herself it was crown free. Even her daughter was wearing a crown.

As they processed, verses from Psalm 122 were sung by the choir and those occupying the pews. "I was glad when they said to me: Let us go to the House of Omni…Peace be within your walls and quietness within your palaces…Because of the house of Omni our God, I will seek to do you good."

Perfect, Chokhmah thought, as they brought up the rear of the Procession. I am right where I should be.

At the end of the song, everyone cried, "Long live the Queen!" three times.

When everyone was seated except Chokhmah and Parisa, the Archbishop of Pelf stood and presented their new queen to the people.

"Omni save the Queen," they shouted.

Queen Parisa then proceeded to take the Oath of Sovereignty, swearing to govern faithfully with justice and mercy, to uphold the Gospel, and to maintain the doctrine and worship of the Church of Omni.

She was then presented with a leather-bound book of Scripture.

"To keep your Majesty ever mindful of the Law and Gospel of Omni as the rule for the whole life and government of the Kingdom of Pelf," Archbishop Navid said before proceeding with the Eucharistic service.

Following the hymn, the choir sang an ancient hymn invoking the Holy Ghost and Chokhmah's crimson cloak was removed as she was led to the Coronation Chair, an intricately carved seat of ebony wood upholstered in gold velvet, which faced the altar. Four of the Councilors stepped forward and held a black satin canopy over the throne, and concealed from view, the Archbishop anointed the new Queen with holy oil on the hands, in the air over her chest, and on the forehead, consecrating her as monarch for the duties of a Sovereign. Meanwhile the choir sang the anthem of Zadok the Priest:

Zadok the priest
And Nathan the prophet
Anointed Solomon king
And all the people
Rejoiced, rejoiced, rejoiced, and said:

Omni save the queen
Long live the queen
Omni save the queen
May the queen live forever
Amen, amen, alleluia, alleluia, amen, amen
Amen, amen, alleluia, amen

Queen Parisa then stood in front of all present, and a cloak of cloth of gold was placed around her shoulders. Then, with the Coronation Chair now facing the congregation, she was seated once again, and presentation of the regalia began.

First, Archbishop Navid presented her with the Scepter of Pelf, symbolizing royal power. The scepter was gold with a black kraken sitting atop a large black pearl. She then received the Rod of Pelf in her left hand, which was also gold with a golden griffin, front right leg raised, and wings spread, adorning the top of the rod, which symbolized Christ and His justice and mercy, and therefore, the new queen's.

Finally, the Archbishop retrieved the Coronation Crown from the High Altar and placed it on Chokhmah's head.

The Coronation Crown of the Kingdom of Pelf was constructed of two gold and silver half spheres, representing the land and water, as both were inseparable to the Pelfans. The crown was divided by a foliate garland and fastened with a low hoop that contained 80 pearls and 5,000 diamonds forming oak leaves and lotuses, land and water, and the symbols of strength and nobility, purity and wisdom. The crown was surmounted by a ruby spinel, that belonged to a Mobed emperor long before the Kingdom of Pelf existed, and a diamond cross symbolizing the dominion of Omni over humanity. A layer of red velvet padded the bottom of the crown.

Now fully regaled, trumpet fanfares sounded, and the congregation acclaimed their new Sovereign with loud and repeated shouts of "Omni save the Queen!" and "Long Live the Queen!"

Queen Parisa was then led from the Coronation Chair to the Coronation Throne located between the sacrarium and the quire. Then supported by the Archbishop, the Lord High Chancellor, and the Councilors, Chokhmah was placed on the Throne, a large chair of heavy, dark wood. The back of the throne was oval like the sigil and featured the black kraken on crimson. The seat itself was a tapestry embroidered with krakens, sailing ships, and flying dragons.

As she officially took possession of the Kingdom of Pelf, enthroned before the people, Queen Parisa began to receive the homage of the people beginning with the Lords Spiritual—the Archbishop and the few other Bishops of the scattered Pelfan dioceses. And then by the Lords Temporal—the Lord High Chancellor, the Councilors, Prince Raynor and Princess Leleua, and the Governors and Ambassadors from the Provinces of Pelf.

During this time anthems were sung followed by more fanfares and acclamations but by this point Chokhmah was beginning to feel the weight of the day and was beginning to tune out the noise.

After this, the Eucharist resumed with the Offertory and Chokhmah felt herself begin to return to a place of common ground. After receiving the Holy Communion, the Gloria was sung, and the Archbishop gave the Blessing.

While the choir sang a final hymn of praise to Omni, Chokhmah was led to the side chapel of Saint Yazdoi, the Patron Saint of Buta, where she exchanged her gold cloak for one of purple velvet and the Coronation Crown for the Royal Crown, the crown she was wearing in Parisa's dream—a lighter crown of gold with pearls and diamonds and a black kraken carved into a large ruby.

Finally, carrying the Scepter and the Rod, Queen Parisa processed through the Cathedral back to the west end where she was lifted into the open carriage where Princess Zirhaan sat waiting for her. Then they began a sinuous route back to the palace so the people of Pelf could hail their new Queen.

PARISA LEANED OVER AND WHISPERED something in Körbl's ear when the other three boys were distracted by a silly argument over whether Queen Morrighan with her copper locks or Princess Xiang with her exotic eyes and glossy black hair was the prettier of the two.

Körbl nodded and lifted his glass of water, nonchalantly taking another sip. Then he excused himself.

"I'll see you all at the Ball tonight?" he asked. "My mother said I needed some down time this afternoon if I want to stay up that late." Leleua had said no such thing, but they didn't know that.

A few minutes later, after she'd finished the last of her chicken, Parisa stood and also excused herself.

"I'm sorry, guys," she said. "I am exhausted after this morning. I think I am going to see if I can nap for a while so that I won't be too tired tonight."

"Actually, my parents said I need to rest this afternoon too," Grini said.

Cian and Yuda nodded.

"Probably not a bad idea," Cian admitted.

Parisa fled the hall, waving her goodbyes over her shoulder. She needed to get down to the beach as soon as she could, but first she had to run to her room and change out of her gown and crown.

Chokhmah saw her leaving and wondered how soon she could disappear herself.

Eluned saw her face and quickly stood. "I don't know about you all, but I am about to fall asleep in my plate," she told the people around her. The church bells had just rung out the hour of four. Chokhmah stood and she was amused to see the entire dining room rise with her.

"I need to rest before tonight. I will see you all at the Ball," she said.

She and Eluned left the dining room, and Uriel, Njima, and Yona quickly caught up with them.

"Grandmom and Granddad have offered to take the kids for an hour," Uriel said.

"Why do we not go to my informal throne room and begin to wind down," Chokhmah suggested. "That way we can be sure no one will interrupt us. It would be nice to spend some time alone with my old friends."

Ghodsi was seated next to the staircase when they arrived.

"Niloufar just went up to help Princess Pari, I mean Zirhaan, out of her gown, Your Majesty," she said, "and I thought it possible that you would not be far behind."

"We are going to spend a little time in the throne room first," Queen Parisa said. "Could bring us a bottle of that light wine? The sparkly one? You know the one I mean? I think it would help settle us so that we can nap more easily."

"Yes, Ma'am. I will be there directly."

"Thank you, Ghodsi"

They climbed the stairs to the first landing and Chokhmah ushered them into the room, collapsing onto her throne as the others pulled a sofa and a couple of armchairs closer.

"I have been this tired before," Chokhmah said, eyes closed, "but not in a very long time."

"I was definitely this tired a number of times on the Quest," Eluned agreed.

"Did I eat at the banquet?" Chokhmah asked. "I feel like I spent the whole time greeting and thanking people."

Njima and Uriel chuckled.

"I have to admit that my Coronation was pretty much a blur," Njima said.

"It was indeed," Uriel agreed.

They made small talk until Ghodsi arrived with a tray bearing a couple of bottles of wine and five glasses.

"Thank you, Ghodsi," Chokhmah said. "I'll let you know when I return to my room."

"Very well, Ma'am," she said, leaving them to unwind.

As Ghodsi was closing the door behind her, Chokhmah thought she saw the door across the landing closing, as well. She shook her head. It had been an exhausting week. She was probably just seeing things.

KÖRBL WAS WAITING DOWN ON THE BEACH for her, blanket in his arms. "What do you need me to do?" he asked.

Parisa nearly burst into tears. Not 'are you sure?' or 'are you sure you don't want your mother here?' or some other stupid question. Just trust. She was glad that her mother asked Prince Raynor to stay on as her Viceroy. Parisa would hate to lose Körbl before they'd really gotten to know each other.

"I need you to hold up the blanket like a screen so that anyone who might be looking down from the Palace can't see anything."

Körbl obligingly held up the blanket and Parisa stepped behind it, already pulling off her boots.

"Okay, I'm taking off my clothes now."

"Don't worry, I won't look," he said.

Oddly, his looking had never occurred to her. It seemed out of character for him. She took off her skirt and folded it, placing it on top of her boots. Then she pulled off her sweater and folded it, as well. All that remained were her under garments. She removed her camisole without a thought as her chest was still more flat than not, and then her knickers a little more self-consciously. She shivered in the nearly constant beach breeze and crouched down.

"Are you okay?" Körbl asked.

"So far," she said. "A little chilly but that should change as soon as I'm covered with fur, right?"

Körbl laughed in response.

What next, she wondered. She felt strongly that the ability to shift was now there; felt it like she'd always been told she would. But how did she make that transformation. I know I'm a wolf, she thought, I feel it in my bones. She felt a wave of dizziness and the next thing she knew she was crouched over her paws.

"Körbl," she barked.

He dropped the blanket and stared at the form behind it.

"Parisa," he said, eyes wide with awe. "You did it!" He hooted. "You are so amazing. You don't even look like a normal wolf. Look at yourself, you're whiter than the sand. Only your eyes are the same."

Parisa turned her wolf head to survey her side. He was right. Her fur was entirely white just like in her mother's dream, and hers.

"Can I touch you?" Körbl asked.

She nodded, and as he reached out his hand to stroke her back, the sun flashed off his hair like she had often seen it do off the feathers of Pallas, a glint of midnight blue and royal purple. So Körbl really was the raven of her dream.

"Want to try out running on four legs?" he asked. "We could run down the beach and back."

Parisa let out of yip of assent and took off down the beach, sand flying from beneath her paws.

CHOKHMAH HAD FINISHED HER WINE and set it down on the table beside her. She was getting drowsy. She let her head fall backwards against the throne, dislodging her crown. As she straightened it, she had a sudden flash of memory.

This was it. This is where she was and what she was wearing in her dream when she saw Parisa as a wolf with copper wings flying with a raven outside that window to her right.

She bolted out of her chair and hurried to the window.

"What is it?" Eluned asked and hurried to her side, the others following.

"My dream," she said. "Remember my dream?"

"Is that Parisa and Körbl down there?" Uriel asked, peering over his wife's head.

"Yes," Chokhmah whispered.

"What are they doing?" Njima asked, looking over Chokhmah's shoulder.

Parisa was stepping behind the blanket.

"Is she putting on swim clothes?" Yona wondered.

"I think . . ." Chokhmah began.

"She's finally shifting," Eluned sighed.

They watched avidly as Körbl patiently held the blanket arms spread but back turned.

A few minutes later, without warning, he dropped the blanket. And instead of seeing Parisa standing behind it, a white wolf crouched there.

"My white wolf," Chokhmah said, eyes filling with tears.

They watched as Körbl stroked the fur on her back, then, seemingly as suddenly as he had dropped the blanket, Parisa took off running down the beach, Körbl not far behind her.

"So, the wings really were about freedom," Eluned said.

"What a beautiful wolf," Uriel said. "She looks nothing like her father."

"Nor her uncle or cousins," Chokhmah added. "I wonder where that came from?"

"A genetic mutation?" suggested Njima.

"Something Pelfans seem prone to," agreed Chokhmah thinking of the Kuna Community in Naphtali.

They watched as Parisa and Körbl ran back and forth down the beach several times before the boy collapsed next to the blanket and Parisa lay down next to him, tongue lolling.

"A boy and his dog," Uriel laughed.

Down on the beach Körbl turned his head and glanced up at the tower. Clearly seeing them, he waved and said something to Parisa, who looked up at them as well.

She pawed the blanket and Körbl picked it up, and the wolf stepped behind it. A few minutes later, Körbl dropped the blanket again and Parisa picked up the other end and helped him fold it. Together they began making their way back up the steps to the palace.

Chokhmah and the others returned to their seats and poured another round of wine awaiting the arrival of the Princess and Prince.

When the door opened, Chokhmah stood and rushed over to pull Parisa into her arms.

"You saw," Parisa stated.

"I suddenly remembered the dream and I had to look out the window," her mother explained.

"It looks like the dream is finally complete," Parisa said. Her mother was Queen of Pelf, she was a white wolf, and her best friend was a raven-haired boy.

"Oh, no, my darling," Chokhmah said, kissing the top of her daughter's head. "I believe the dream has only just begun."

THE THIRTEEN KINGDOMS

In Year XII of the Accord

I. The Kingdom of Adamah

Ruled by Princess Huda, 52, of Tarshish, and Chancellor Chazak of Adamah from Year 0 to Year V.

King Hevel, 54, is allowed to rule again beginning in Year VI.

Children: King Hevel is unmarried and has no children. His sister's son, Simeon, 26, will be his heir. Simeon is also not yet married.

II. The Kingdom of Aden

Ruled by: King Uriel (35) and Queen Eluned (32)

Children: A daughter, Fuchsia, b. Year V (7); and a son, Gavreel, b. Year VII (5)

In addition to Ponike, Queen Eluned founded schools in Himyar on the Caumeda River, Qataba on the Sandcana River, Yahirr at Lake Baxcour, and Awsan, a port town on the Anoon Ocean west of Ponike.

III. The Kingdom of Annewven

Ruled by Prince Aahil (50) and Princess Merieme (47) of Tarshish from Year 0 to Year X. They have 2 children, a son, Hichan, 22, and a daughter, Shatha, 18.

From Year X on, Queen Morrighan (29), the illegitimate daughter of King Arawn, and her husband, Prince Huang of Dziron (30), rule Annewven. Children: They have two children: a daughter, Morrighan, 8 born in Year IV; and a son, Ling, 5, born in Year VII.

IV. The Kingdom of Dyfed

Ruled by: King Cian (59) and Queen Chelli (55)
Children: A daughter, Gittan, 37, m. Cadfael, 40. They have 3 children: Two sons, Cadfael (Cadoc), 15, and Cian, 13; and one daughter, Arianell, 11. And a son, Bryan, 35, m. Gwendolyn, 35. They have 2 sons: Madoc, 10, and Rhodri, 8.

V. The Kingdom of Dziron

Ruled by: King Zhang (58) and Queen Ling (53)

The Kingdom will pass to their eldest son, Qiang, 36, who is married to Nuan, 33.

Other Children: Sons, Chao, 34, m. Ai, 30, and Huang, 31, m. Queen Morrighan of Annewven, 29. One daughter, Xiang, 29, m. Jian, 30.

VI. The Kingdom of Favonia
Ruled by: King Irirangi (32) and
Queen Bala (32)
Children: One son, Rangatira, 10;
and one daughter, Lakshmi, 7.

When Irirangi was 30, his grandmother,
Queen Miryam, was 80 and she turned
the throne over to him. His mother,
Princess Elili, is still alive.

Irirangi has twin sisters, Leleua, 30, who is married to Prince
Raynor of Simoon (see The Kingdom of Pelf) and Talei,
30, who is married to Kaika, 32. Talei and Kaika have three
children—2 boys, Kekoa, 8, and Ikaika, 6; and one daughter,
Hōkūlani, 3.

VII. The Kingdom of Kamartha
Ruled by: King Janak (57) and
Queen Lakshmi (54)

The Kingdom will pass to their eldest
son, Amit.

Children: Amit and Amala, twins, 35.
Amala is married to Jarvis of Simoon,
32, and resides in that Kingdom.
Baldev, 33; Bala, 31, is married to King Irirangi of Favonia.
Chandra, 29, is married to the singer, Vollmar, and resides
in Simoon. Chetan, 27, once the youngest son, still resides in
Kamartha. Divya, now Dev, 25, resides in Naphtali.

VIII. The Kingdom of Naphtali

Ruled by: Queen Njima (42) and her partner, Yona (34).

Children: Njima and Yona do not have any children. But their adopted son, Dev of Karmartha, 25, is being trained to take over the rule of the Kingdom,

IX. The Kingdom of Pelf

Ruled by: Prince Raynor (36) of Simoon and Princess Leleua (30) of Favonia.
Children: One son, Korbinian (Körbl), 10, b. Year II; and twin daughters, Foehn and Hauata, 7, b. Year V.

The only remaining heir to the throne of the Kingdom of Pelf is Chokhmah (Queen Parisa), 58, who lives at Bogaine in the Kingdom of Dyfed with her husband, Faolan, 49, and their daughter, Parisa, 12, born in Year 0.

X. The Kingdom of Sheba

Ruled by: King Adeyemi (57) and Queen Yobachi (53)
Children: Three sons—Daud, 34, m. Afia, 33; Paul, 30, m. Nkiru, 28; and Uwem, 28, and partner, Talib, 37.

Uwem and Talib reside in the Kamea in the Kingdom of Naphtali.
Two daughters—Nala, 32, m. Jabari, 39; and Prisce, 26, m. Wekesa, 25.

XI. The Kingdom of Simoon

Ruled by: King Adeyemi and Prince Daud of Sheba from Year 0 to Year V.

In Year VI, King Kaiser, 46, of Simoon became ruler of the Kingdom along with his wife, Queen Luise, 41. They have one son, Kaiser, 16.

Kaiser's brothers are: Jarvis, 44, m. Amala of Kamartha, 35. Bemot, 41, m. Lioba, 38. Chokhmah saved their infant son, Grini, now 14, when she was in Simoon to steal their Treasure. Raynor, 36, m. Leleua of Favonia, 30.

XII. The Kingdom of Tarshish

Ruled by: King Boutros (54) and Queen Elamia (52). King Dodi, 78, and Queen Chahindra, 73, retired when King Dodi was 72.

Children: One daughter, Fadia, 32, and one son, Bulus, 30.

Boutros' siblings are: a sister, Huda, 52, m. Ghazal, 53. They have two boys, Fouad and Nasr, and two girls, Arwa and Zahra. His brother, Aahil, 50, m. his consort and the mother of his children, Merieme, in Year 0. Their children are a son, Hichan, and a daughter, Shatha.

XIII. The Kingdom of Zion

Ruled by: King Seraphim (54) and
Queen Ceridwen (56)
Children: Queen Eluned (32)
m. King Uriel of Aden (35)

Upon their deaths/inability to rule, Zion
will be ruled by Eluned or one of her
children.

In Year V of the Accord, Zion hosted the meeting of the XIII
Kingdoms.

OTHER CHARACTERS

Dyfed: Bogaine and Castle Abbert
Faolan: Chokhmah's husband and the father of Parisa. Faolan joined the Quest in the second book of the trilogy.

Olcan: Faolan's older brother
Beibhinn: Olcan's wife
Fianna: The daughter of Olcan and Beibhinn
Gruffyd: Fianna's husband
Dylan: The infant son of Fianna and Gruffyd
Conall: The son of Olcan and Beibhinn
Bledwen: Conall's wife
Bryn: Bledwen's brother
Gwen: Bryn's wife
Enfys: Bryn's and Gwen's oldest daughter
Eiriol: Bryn's and Gwen's youngest daughter
Mistress Chani: the tutor of Princess Arianell

Aden: Ponike
Faltuel: Gavreel's nanny and
Zimbra: Fuchsia's tutor
Haniel: The Adenese woman who paints Parisa's room
Columba: Haniel's wife
Folade: Ambassador from Naphtali
Abayomrunkoje (Abayo): Folade's husband
Yantine: wife of Ambassador from Adamah

Pelf: Buta

Mahbod: The servant who leads Chokhmah and Parisa to Ghodsi

Ghodsi: Chokhmah's First Lady of the Bedchamber (Assistant)

Niloufar: Ghodsi's daughter, and Parisa's First Lady of the Bedchamber

Parisa Zirhaan: The Pelfan Princess who fled the Kingdom of Pelf with her mother and brothers seven centuries previous.

Alborz: Parisa Zirhaan's older brother

Gaspar: Parisa Zirhaan's younger brother

Leily: Parisa Zirhaan's tutor

Souri: Parisa Zirhaan's First Lady of the Bedchamber

Roozbeh: Tutor for Körbl, Hauata, Foehn, and Parisa

Avizen: Körbl's Nanny when he first arrived at Zhaleh Palace

Amir: Head servant of the Queen's private dining room

Banafsheh: also, Bana, the sister of Parisa Zirhaan's mother

Jalil: Bana's husband, a prince of Naphtali

Mahasti: Foehn's and Hauata's nanny

Daniel: Chokhmah's nephew

Avigail: Daniel's wife

Yuda: The son of Daniel and Avigail

Navid of Betnicator: Archbishop of Pelf

Acknowledgements

I'd like to thank my mother, Laura Campbell, and my husband, Frank Logue, for all their help with this book. Because of some pandemic-related mishaps, it took longer coming to fruition than I might have liked. I am currently working on two other Thirteen Kingdom books—one stand alone and another that will feature Princess Zirhaan and Prince Korbinian traveling into the Devastation of Pelf in search of dragons. Hopefully, those won't take as long to be finished.